Just Like the Classics

First published by Amelia Critchley 2023

Copyright © 2023 by Amelia Critchley

All rights reserved. No part of this publication may be reproduced, stored, or transmitted in any form or by any means, electronic, mechanical, photocopying, recording, scanning, or other wise without written permission from the publisher. It is illegal to copy this book, post it to a website, or distribute it by any other means without permission.

Amelia Critchley asserts the moral right to be identified as the author of this work.

This is for all the people who feel like they don't belong anywhere.

TW:

Some characters within this book have past traumas including death of relatives, implied attempted SA, alcohol abuse, homophobia, and transphobia.

Book Playlist
──── ★·☆·★ ────

The Very First Night - Taylor Swift

Paris - Taylor Swift

Scott Street – Phoebe Bridgers

Glitch - Taylor Swift

Mess It Up - Gracie Abrams

Two Slow Dancers - Mitski

Team - Lorde

Me and My Husband - Mitski

Young and Beautiful - Lana Del Rey

Cardigan - Taylor Swift

New Romantics - Taylor Swift

Seven - Taylor Swift

Block Me Out - Gracie Abrams

August - Taylor Swift

Little League - Conan Gray

Not Strong Enough - boygenius

Would That I - Hozier

Going Going Gone - Lucy Dacus

It Can't Get Worse - Chloe Ament

Cool About It - boygenius

We Fell in Love in October - Girl in Red

ICU - Phoebe Bridgers

Yellow - Coldplay

I Know the End - Phoebe Bridgers

Sparks - Coldplay

Your Best American Girl – Mitski

Say yes to heaven – Lana Del Rey

Radio – Lana Del Rey

Summertime Sadness – Lana Del Rey

Video Games – Lana Del Rey

Mirrorball - Taylor Swift

Invisible String - Taylor Swift

Perfect Places - Lorde

The Louvre - Lorde

Ribs- Lorde

Cinnamon Girl - Lana Del Rey

400 Lux – Lorde

Punisher – Phoebe Bridgers

Rivals

Chapter 1 – Vivienne

°•. ❀ .•°°•. ❀ .•°°•. ❀ .•°

The final dust covered box drops to the floor, its contents spilling out. Books, notepads, textbooks, all onto the freshly polished floor of the college dorm room. Bending to pick them up, Vivienne silently curses under her breath, quiet enough that her lingering little brother doesn't hear.

"I heard that," he says, jumping onto her back and wrapping his arms around her neck, "and I'm going to tell dad."

"Oh really?" She teases. "And what makes you think I'll let you?"

"What-" he starts, but she spins and picks him up, holding him upside down by the waist. Him being only nine years old and half her height makes it easy. "Hey! Put me down!" he squeals, waving his arms around in a frantic motion.

"Promise you won't tell dad then?" She smiles, lifting him higher in order to see his face. Trying to frown, but failing massively, he crosses his arms and shakes his head. "Fine then, you'll just have to stay like this forever, then."

"Noooo…" he squeals as she spins him round. After a long, long time, she pauses and holds him to face her again.

"Rethinking my offer?" She smirks and he sticks out his tongue.

"Fine. I won't tell dad."

"Won't tell dad what?" A voice says from within the doorway behind them. Her brother runs and begins to pull at her father's burgundy blazer, a bold statement for her first day, the beginnings of a smile pulling at his lips. Her brother is always like this, no matter the situation, he was always cheerful and excitable. It's something she envies about him, though she'll never admit it, she wishes she can be as relaxed as he always is. Part of it is because of his age, but even back then, Vivienne still hadn't been able to be as much of a kid as him. When she was Ollie's age, so much was going on that there wasn't really time to be a kid.

"Vivi swore! She said a bad word, then she made me say I wouldn't tell you by holding me upside down!" Ollie jumps up at her dad, then stands beside him, smiling at Vivienne before sticking his tongue out.

Her Dad looks to her brother, then to her, a smile playing on his lips. "Oh, and what did she say, Ollie?"

"She-she said-" Ollie jumps up and down as he desperately tries to stutter out his answer, but Vivienne gets there first.

"Sugar. I said sugar." she interrupts, smiling at her Dad, then her brother.

"What? No you didn't!" He protests, pulling harder on her father's clothes. Her Dad sighs and shakes his head, but Vivienne can see the smile spreading across his face. Vivienne loves when he smiles, he didn't used to smile this often, but now it's all she sees him do. Whenever her and her brother fight, he smiles and shake his head, whenever he breaks a plate while washing or drops files all over the floor, he just smiles. Vivienne remembers when that wasn't what happened, she remembers when things like that were so hard for him that Vivienne ended up doing it, before he'd get back from work or when he'd fall asleep at his desk.

"Oh yes I did, you must've misheard me." Vivienne taunts her brother, raising one eyebrow at him and tilting her head to the side. Sitting on the corner of her bed, legs folded underneath her, Vivienne watches as her brother dramatically turns to their Dad and starts pulling at his jacket again.

"What? Dad-"

"It doesn't matter who said what." Her father lifts his hand up in the way he always does when settling an argument between her and Ollie, "This is Vivienne's final day with us before we have to go home, and she starts school, stop bickering."

"What, but-"

"Ollie, you start with her books, and I'll do the clothes."

Vivienne smiles and begins to pick the textbooks off the floor, then the notepads, and places them on the desk in the corner, where her laptop rests open on a document of already completed coursework. Closing it, she moves to another box and begins to unload it, placing most of its contents into the drawers of the desk, the rare item staying on display. A sudden noise of boxes falling comes from behind her, quickly followed by an 'oof'. Turning to see what the cause of the chaos is, she finds her brother sitting on the floor, covered from foot to waist in books.

"How is it possible for someone to own this many books?" he asks, pushing them off his legs and standing on his tiptoes to reach the top shelf, but missing anyway.

"It's not *that* many." Vivienne insists, moving to help him. She picks up as many as she can carry and starts lining them onto the higher shelves.

"It's enough to bury a person," her brother sighs.

"No, it's enough to *half* bury a nine-year-old."

"A nine-year-old *person.*"

"You are by far the sassiest nine-year-old I know," Vivienne teases, putting the last of what is in her hands onto the shelf and starting on the desk again.

"Sass is wit that people just don't acknowledge. You had quite the mouth when you were his age and look where it got you." Her Dad sits on the bed, lifting a box onto his lap and routing through it. Every now and again he passes something to her, which she places in a draw or up on a shelf.

"Into college with no friends?" Vivienne asks, laughing quietly to herself.

"Into *college*, the no friends bit you can sort while you're here. I mean you're literally sharing a dorm with someone, tell me that isn't friend making material right there."

Vivienne sighs and sits on her bed, the sheets freshly washed and carefully laid with no creases, and stares at the door to the main room of the dorm. The dorm she is sharing is fairly big, for college standards anyway, which is unlucky in her case. More space means she and whoever she is sharing with won't be forced to talk to one another, it means they will barely see each other if their schedules are different.

Although, the one positive aspect of her situation is that her roommate is a boy. When the dorm applications came through, she was asked if she would be willing to share with the opposite sex and had gladly ticked 'yes'. Talking to boys was easier than talking to girls, they didn't notice the small things that Vivienne often forgot, like how blush isn't supposed to cover your nose or how it's 'rude' to sit with one leg on the furniture. Especially at this age, when they're all looking for girlfriends and, after getting the 'I'm just not into that' talk, will hopefully leave her alone, hopefully. Weeks after the application, she was emailed confirming that her roommate was a boy, but it told her nothing else.

Her dad is, of course, unaware of the arrangements as he would never approve. It's been like this for a while, no matter what she tells him, whenever a boy comes within ten feet of her, he fixes them a deadpan look that sends them to the other side of the room, or in some cases, the other side of the train station. That is one of the reasons she's gotten here so early, so her dad can help her unpack then get out before her roommate arrives. If he is still here, then she will soon find herself in a two-bedroom dorm on her own because of her Dad's pure will to keep her 'safe from boys', in his words. Why she needs to be kept safe, she doesn't know.

He thinks boys are dangerous and will take any opportunity to steal and exploit her which, in his defence, was true where she grew up. However, they haven't lived there since she was fourteen, after that they moved to a nicer district nearer to her high school. He had scrimped and saved to move them there after her mother died, he worked extra shifts and was practically never home until the day they moved. Ollie, being only five at the time, doesn't remember any of it, but she does. She remembers having to wake her dad up at the ass crack of dawn if he slept through his alarm after only four hours of sleep. She remembers him falling asleep standing whilst he made dinner, burning his hand on the metal pot. That's one of the reasons she has tried so hard to get where she is, one of the top Ivy Leagues in her area. Why she had passed up an immeasurable number of parties and sleepovers to study for exams, why she nearly screamed when she got declined from her *backup*. She'd gotten into her dream school, but was outraged at being rejected by her *backup,* which her dad had found amusing, especially when she came out of her room an alarming shade of red.

"Well, that's all of it, Pumpkin," her Dad says, interrupting her thoughts and sighing slightly. Pumpkin, a nickname her Dad had coined and started using when the kids in her kindergarten started using it to insult her ginger hair. At the time, it had really upset her, but her Dad said they were only mean because they envied her. He'd said her Mum was bullied the same way, but he still loved her hair, and that she would find someone who would too.

"*Dad.* Please don't call me 'Pumpkin' in college, it could catch on. I thought you wanted me to make friends." She mocks a glare at him.

"Well what do you want me to call you then, Vivienne Anna Carter?"

Comically cringing at the sound of her full name, she sighs and says, "Just call me Vi, like a normal person."

"Well unfortunately for you, *Pumpkin,* I'm not a normal person."

"I'm aware." She smiles and turns to the clock on the wall. It is quickly approaching three o'clock, the recommended time of arrival, the time at which Vivienne expects her roommate is going to appear for the first time, the time her dad *needs* to leave.

"Thanks for the help, Dad, but now I need to go scout out the campus and my classes."

"Look at you, kicking out your poor old dad just to go and look at a campus. You can do that later, let's go get takeout and eat your first official meal in your dorm."

"Dad, it's 2:45 in the afternoon, it's far too early for takeout."

"It can be a late lunch." He leans against the doorway and crosses his arms.

"We've already had lunch, Dad, and I need to find my classes and prepare a route."

"Prepare a route? My goodness where do you get that sense of organisation from? It certainly isn't me. My first year of college I lost two pounds running around trying to get to my classes on time." He beams at her and sticks his chest out in pride.

"You're making that sound like a brag."

"Did I or did I not say I lost two pounds?"

With that, he leaves the room and makes his way into the main area, pulling out his phone. Vivienne sighs and leans back on her bed. Ollie runs towards her and sits on her lap, tilting his head up, "Want me to get him out of here?" he offers, dropping his chin into his hands.

"That would be much obliged, Ollie." She smiles at him and ruffles his hair, earning her a small whack on the arm.

"Obliged?" His brow furrows and Vivienne smiles at him, sometimes she forgets he's only nine.

"I would appreciate it."

"Appreciate?" His head tilts to the side, confusion clear on his face.

"I would like for you to get our father out of here."

"Okay." He smiles and bounds out of the room. It's mere seconds before his whining is heard through the walls, begging her father to let them get ice cream from the store nearby. Standing from the bed, she walks from her now furnished bedroom and joins the rest of her family in the room, her brother now pleading with his hands clasped together.

"Daaadddd, I want ice cream! You promised we would go to the shop near here, it looks so goooood!"

Her dad has one hand on his forehead and the other in his trouser pocket, putting back the phone he was just using to no doubt call a takeout. Seeing her enter, he begins towards her, bending his head down and whispering low, "As much as I would like to stay here, despite your eagerness for my leave, this one," he gestures behind him, "is about to throw a top-level tantrum if we don't go to the ice cream place we saw on the way here."

"It's okay Dad, how about dinner tonight? Not in my dorm, off campus, pizza maybe?"

"Perfect, you have time for your schedules, and I have time to wait on your brother hand and foot." He laughs and turns to Ollie, "Come on then, we'll see your sister tonight and then we're off for good."

"Yay!" Ollie jumps into the air and runs from the dorm completely.

"See you tonight, Dad," Vivienne says, smiling at him. He tries to return it, but it's weak and shaking. He turns to leave, discreetly bringing a hand to his eye and makes towards the door.

"Dad, wait," she breaks into a light jog and waits for him to turn around, finding tears in his eyes when he does. Without saying anything, she wraps her arms around his shoulders and pulls him into a tight embrace. "Thank you."

When she pulls away, he's smiling, enough that she can see his teeth, "I am so unbelievably proud of you, you've done me *and* your mother proud." This time it's her tearing up. "Oh come on Pumpkin, don't cry, you can't start crying on your first day of school."

"You say that like I'm starting Kindergarten, not college."

"What's the difference, in a place like this you could step on someone's foot and they will be in fits of tears within minutes." He smirks and steps backwards towards the door. "Now I must be off, if I don't follow him soon he might pull me out by my ears."

She laughs and he walks from the room, waving once more before disappearing completely.

Looking around the room, she takes in the half-decorated main room of the dorm, the place she is about to spend a year of her life in. The walls are a drab, peeling white wallpaper that is covered partially by the occasional Taylor Swift poster she has hung up on the wall to her bedroom, and the wall adjacent to that has one of the three bookcases she brought with her from home, the other two being in her bedroom. Apart from that, nothing of hers is in the main room, the rest of the furniture - a large cream couch and two smaller matching armchairs - was complimentary of the college. This place really is fancy, they literally provide furniture. Pulling one of the many novels off her bookshelf, she sits on the couch and immerses herself in it, relaxing completely and forgetting the impending stress that is to begin the next day.

*

Vivienne soon realises she could have had takeout with her family *and* created her class schedule in time for her roommate to arrive, which isn't at all at the time she expected. She had gotten back from her walk around campus, after stopping a little longer at one of the many on-campus coffee shops, at six o'clock to find piles of boxes scattered around the room, all of which blocking the door to her room.

"Hello?" No one is in the main room, but the door to the second bedroom was is and looks the way it was when she left. "Is anyone here?"

No reply. Searching the room and looking behind the boxes, she finds nothing but piles of clothes separate to the already large boxes. Whoever this is, they have a lot of stuff, and she isn't sure how half of it is going to fit in their dorm. Honestly, she doubts even a quarter can. Why they need so much stuff is a mystery, most of it doesn't even look essential. One box is full of hoodies and jerseys, another has an ice hockey stick and puck in, along with some ice skates, and the others mainly consist of sporting magazines and pictures of hockey games. Whoever this is clearly enjoys playing ice hockey, but they don't seem to be here on a sports course, because three boxes are labelled 'Medical Textbooks'. So, they are either a medical student, or some kind of weird creep who likes to read medical reports in their free time, and if it is the rare latter, she's definitely going to put in for a room swap. She doesn't feel like testing her ground with someone who could probably kill her without her even noticing by injecting some weird drug into her whilst she sleeps.

"Oh, hello."

Startled, Vivienne turns to the voice behind her, dropping the signed photo she'd been holding onto the floor. Panicking, she quickly picks it up and places it back into the box, muttering her apologies. When she finally stands up properly and looks at the source of the voice, she finds a tall, finely dressed boy standing in the doorway. His short, dirty-blonde hair waves forwards in a way that he hints he likes it that length to play with it, and his gold rimmed glasses are halfway down his freckled nose.

"And you are?" she instantly regrets her words, realising that's not how you would introduce yourself to a prospective friend, especially if it is one who read medical journals.

"Julian Patterson, and I'm assuming you're my roommate?" The boy says, his voice light and bouncy, not entirely what she expected if she's being honest.

"Er, um, yes I am. Vivienne Carter." Vivienne mutters, looking at the boy, taking in everything about him.

The boy, Julian, strides towards her and sticks out his hand, revealing one of those fancy fitness watches strapped to his wrist. She is now leaning towards sports student, but she knows she's probably wrong. Plenty of people work out and still study, although she isn't one of them.

"What are you doing?" She says, surveying the pale hand thrust in front of her.

"What does it look like? I'm introducing myself." The boy looks taken aback by the question, as if questioning a handshake is an absurd idea. Vivienne takes his hand regardless and shakes it, struggling to withhold her astounded smile.

"I don't know many people who still shake hands, you know. That is, of course, if you excuse business executives and old men making bets," she says, releasing his hand and making her way to the couch in the centre of the room, manoeuvring around the many boxes.

"Ah, well, you got me. Not only am I a business executive, but I'm also an old man." Julian jokes, following her. He doesn't find it anywhere near as hard to find his way through the mountains of boxes, as he merely steps over most of them. Vivienne watches as he sits across from her, perching on the table and running his hand through his hair. Closer up, Vivienne begins to notice more about him. His eyes, behind the thick glasses he wears, are two different colours. One is a light, olive like green, and the other is a deep, dark brown. He has more of a round face compared to other boys she knows, which she does admit aren't many, and his lips perk up at the sides, like he is permanently holding back a smile.

"How long have you been here?" Vivienne asks, sitting up in her seat and crossing her legs underneath her.

"About twenty minutes, long enough to get a feel of the place." He says, looking around the room. Trying not to snigger at his choice of phrase, which, up until recently, she has only heard in films, Vivienne smiles. "By the way, your room is pretty cool."

Vivienne starts at the comment, sitting up further and narrowing her eyes at him. Why has he been in her room, what was he doing in there? Maybe she's right, maybe he is a creepy sports major, and he's just gone into her room to scope out the ways he can sneak a sedative into her.

"Why were you in my *room*?" She asks, looking at him, then her door, then back to him again.

"I wasn't being a creep, relax," he says, sighing and shaking his head. Did he really think saying he wasn't a creep was going to change her mind? How does going into someone's dorm room whilst the owner isn't there not creepy? "The door was shut so I assumed it was empty, then I walked in to find a very stylishly decorated room." he says, looking at her expectantly. When she doesn't respond, he laughs, "Listen, if I were some creep, why would I tell you I went in your room? Surely a creep would keep that fact to himself?"

After a short, speculative silence, Vivienne smiles again, "Fair enough," she says, relaxing. Instead of thinking further into the matter, like she knows she shouldn't, she thinks about the comment Julian made about her room, about how he complimented it. She thinks about the amount of thought she put into that room. The weeks she spent planning what to bring and what to leave at home, what she was going to spend the money in her 'college furniture' jar on that was in her room at home, something her dad has told her countless times would be safer in her bank account. She'd even saved for a record player, something she has wanted for a while but her room at home can't accommodate, so when it was delivered, she had to store it under her bed gathering dust.

"Thank you," is all she can manage over the pride rising inside her. Maybe she's wrong about the large quarters cutting off communication between her and this boy, Julian, and she is definitely wrong about thinking he's any kind of creep. Her Dad has always told her she is far too cautious of people, that she sees things that aren't there, purely because she wants to convince herself of a reason to not talk to them. The longer she is sitting with Julian, the more she is starting to realise that he's right. That is something she needs to stop doing in college. If she wants to make friends, she needs to stop being so anxious, and she needs to stop speculating in her head.

"I like your flag as well, the one over your bed."

Vivienne freezes, looks at him, then back to her room, she'd forgotten about that. Completely forgotten. As if he can tell she is partially panicking at the discovery of the flag she usually hangs with pride, quite literally, he gestures to one of his many boxes.

"I have one too, although it doesn't match my room in the way yours does. I mean, you've literally got your sexuality colour schemed to your room." He's right, although it hadn't been purposeful, she just likes muted oranges and beiges, and off whites too. Pink and purple she isn't too fond of, but she does have a couple of blush pillows and blankets strewn somewhere.

"Oh, and you don't?" She jokes, the knot in her chest releasing as she relaxes back into the couch, "you're the first person I've met who doesn't do that."

"Well as much as I would love too, bright turquoise carpets are hard to come by, and embarrassing to carry around." He laughs and stands up, moving to sit next to her.

"You're funny," she says, a smile now spread across her face. He lies down on the couch, propping himself up against the armrest, and stretches his legs out. They stick out far enough that his feet land in Vivienne's lap, despite her being sat on the other end.

"Excuse me?" Vivienne says, her tone light. She raises an eyebrow at him, but he just smiles, ignoring the fact that he is covering her lap with his feet. While she would normally be offended, as most people are if someone's shoes are dirtying their clothes, Vivienne isn't. She is glad he's comfortable, because it makes her comfortable, and while he does express it in an odd way, they seem to be getting along better than she'd ever hoped.

"Well, I'm glad someone thinks so," Julian carries on, "I made a similar joke with a girl in the other building and she gave me the coldest look, I genuinely felt the temperature around us drop."

"What were you doing in the other building?" Vivienne asks, looking at her watch.

"I got lost, went to the wrong building," Julian starts, but Vivienne is already out of her seat, bolting for the door. Frantically grabbing her coat and draping it over her arm. Julian shifts to look at her, confusion clear on his face. "Have I scared you off already?" He asks, standing and making his way over to where Vivienne is desperately looking for her key. How has she let time run over this much? She made sure she set a reminder on her phone, in case she was reading. It must've gone off, or she'd just ignored it whilst she was talking with Julian.

"No," she says, finding the keys and shoving them into her coat pocket, "it's just that I have dinner with my Dad and brother in two minutes, and the restaurant is ten minutes away."

She opens the door and bolts through it, closing it quickly behind her, not stopping to catch Julian's reply.

Chapter 2 – Jinx
—— · ₀° ☆ : *.☽ .* :☆° . ——

    This is single handedly one of the most disastrous ways college could've started for Jinx, and while she'd seen issues coming up, she hadn't predicted half of what she's had to experience. She hasn't even reached her dorm yet, but all she can expect is the worse, if it's anything like the rest of today.
    The ride up here was a pain, the bus she'd scheduled to catch was late, it was pouring down, and on top of that, the bus driver had refused to let her bring her suitcase on. He said it 'wasn't that kind of bus', except she knew it was, because she'd been bringing stuff onto it for the last week. She couldn't fit all her belongings in one case, for obvious reasons, she's moving to college, not going on holiday, so for the last week, she's been transferring it all to a footlocker near the college. When she told the driver this, he claimed that he didn't believe her, and Jinx ended up caving and giving him a twenty dollar note, which persuaded him to let her bring the suitcase on. That twenty was all she had for food tonight, she had more in her account, but she doesn't want to risk taking it out in case she needs it. After she gets a job, which she intends to look for the minute she is in her dorm, she will start to withdraw money for stuff, but until then, she's running on scraps. It's not as if she can use the money for herself anyway, and she knows why she can't, it's the same reason she has to get the bus to college, like she is in high school.
    After the painstakingly long bus ride, which nearly missed her stop altogether, she had to drag her luggage through town — where it was also heavily raining — and it was starting to get dark. The walk to the college was brisk, but with her case, it nearly doubled the effort required, and by the time she reached

her building, she was cold, wet, tired, hungry, and fed up. None of this was helped by the obnoxious boy she then ran into in the corridor, who claimed to be lost, although she highly doubted that fact. 'I'm lost' is one of the most frequent pick-up lines she's heard from men, women not so much, but it's all men seem to be able to think up. Geniuses in the making they are.

The boy asked her for directions to another dorm room, directions she had but didn't want to give, purely because it might have led to further conversation, so she denied him, trying to walk past. Clearly having no grasp of social cues, the boy carried on talking to her, making terrible jokes and pointless small talk, all of which she ignored and he eventually just walked off. She doesn't have energy for people like him, she never does, but especially not tonight.

Finally reaching her dorm, Jinx lies against the wall, replenishing her energy and waiting for her head to stop spinning. With all the time wasted with the bus and the case, she hasn't had time to eat or drink since early this morning, and even then, all she had was a breakfast bar and some coffee.

Walking into her dorm, she finds a single person, two room dorm, one room as her bedroom and the other as general living space. She knows she should be happy about this, it's bigger than her room back home, but she can't be. Through the walls, she can hear the makings of a party starting, and it's only 6:30 in the evening. The small thump of the music will no doubt grow louder the later it gets, and there is no questioning the fact that by 7:30 the whole floor will probably be cramming themselves into that dorm to experience their first 'college party', something she is determined to avoid entirely.

Dropping her case in the middle of the room, she makes her way towards the door, not bothering to fix her still damp hair, or change out of her wet clothes. She doesn't care about changing, not right now. All she needs now is to get away from that dorm and to avoid it as much as possible. The whole point of her going to college was to get away from people like that, places like that. She'd grown up in between two apartments exactly like that, hers occasionally was one, and she'd vowed that the minute she could, she would get away, as far and as fast as possible, but here she is. Again.

Before she leaves, she grabs her laptop from her satchel, which she'd dumped near the door. She needs something to do whilst she's out, and she isn't about to leave her most valued possession in her dorm with a load of drunk teenagers around, whether the door is locked or not.

The walk through the corridor is quick this time, now she doesn't have her case with her, she is back to her regular pace, which is so fast she might as well be running. She's walked like this ever since she can remember, and while most people find it irritating, she doesn't mind it, mainly because it keeps her ahead of the people who do find it irritating. The stairs, which she had nearly fallen down countless times moments ago, are easy. She glides down quickly, turning sharply at the corners by holding onto the handrails. The people she passes don't pay her much mind, thank god, and she doesn't see the obnoxious talkative boy again as she crosses the bottom floor of dorms and leaves, pushing the door with her foot whilst pulling out her phone.

As the cold autumn air meets her, she pulls out her headphones and plugs them into her phone, hitting play on her playlist and carrying on down the path. She has no idea where she's going, but when a coffee cart comes into view, she stops to browse the options. They don't have much for food, and she doesn't have much to pay for it, but the coffee looks good, and the boy serving won't stop staring at her. Perfect.

She isn't wearing anything particularly garish, and she is surprised he hasn't noticed the dampness of her hair, but she still watches as he stutters and stumbles over his words as he asks her what she wants. Giving him her nicest smile, which is hard considering he's making a simple job look unbelievably hard, she slowly starts to flirt with him. She does this quite a lot, men make it easy in all fairness, and while she doesn't enjoy it, it almost always pays off. Like now, the boy has given her a free pastry along with her coffee, which he has also lousily scribbled his number on the side of. While she has no intention of reading it, she is glad to be able to finally eat. She isn't proud of what she does, but she knows that she needs to, and she knows it works, so on the rare occasions she can't provide for herself, she lets dumbfounded men do it for her.

"H-have a nice d-day," the boy stutters as Jinx walks away, coffee in hand. She barely hears him through the music blasting from her earphones, and carries on, sipping her coffee lightly. Her phone vibrates in her pocket and, after tucking her laptop under her arm, she pulls it out and swipes up the screen. It isn't anything important, just the generic News notification, pretty much the only notification she gets, but whilst she is on her phone, she swaps to *Spotify* to change her music.

Preoccupied with changing the music, and not being able to hear due to the already playing song, Jinx doesn't notice the girl running in front of her, also frantically tapping on her phone. She also doesn't notice that she is running straight towards her, and when the girl collides with her, she is knocked onto the floor, her drink and laptop still in hand. She falls backwards and hits the floor *hard*. Pain bursts through her arm where she'd hit the floor, and the laptop flies to the side, scattering along the floor, the cover no doubt scratching in the process. The lid of the coffee comes off and the liquid flies out, drenching Jinx's top and burning her chest.

"*Fuck!*" She yells, flinching from the burn. The pain spreads as the coffee seeps down her shirt, dripping down towards her trousers. Her glasses falling off the edge of her nose, she shakes her chestnut hair out of her face, trying to figure out what just happened.

"Shit, shit, sorry." The girl murmurs, crouching down and facing her, pushing her hair out of her face. She holds her hand out to help, but it freezes mid gesture, retracting slightly. "You..." she mutters, and Jinx looks up from where she's been pulling at her shirt. She knows this girl, she can't possibly forget her, not after the last four years she's spent fighting her, competing with her, *beating* her.

Brushing her wavy red hair from her face, she surveys Jinx again. The freckles that dance across her nose and cheeks are still obvious, despite the fact that summer has long since passed, and her usually full lips are now pursed in a tight line, her frustration clear. Long lashes cover ocean-like eyes that are glaring at her, their lids slightly closed, revealing a small line of eyeliner flicking up at the sides. Jinx knows that expression far too well, she's seen nothing but it for years, and no one wears it better than Vivienne Carter, the girl she's spent the summer trying to forget.

"Carter." Jinx says, smirking at her and sitting up slightly. Vivienne glares at her and stands up, straightening her back and putting her hands on her hips.

"My name is Vivienne." She insists, looking down her nose at the state Jinx is in. The coffee has ceased to burn, but the stain on her shirt is still very clear, and her laptop is halfway across the wide pavement. The pastry she put in her pocket was no doubt crushed by her fall, but is probably still edible. Her real concern is the laptop, if it has broken... Well, Vivienne better hope it hasn't. If she didn't hate her enough before, this would solidify it, make it even more permanent.

"Vivienne *Carter*," Jinx says, standing up slowly and walking past Vivienne, towards the laptop. "That is unless you've changed your last name over the summer?" She continues as she bends to reach it, cautious of the state it could be in.

"And what if I have?" Vivienne mumbles, crossing her arms over her chest. Walking back to where she fell, Jinx stands in front of Vivienne, raising her eyebrows.

"Then I would say you made a very petty decision," She smirks, bending her head slightly. She'd forgotten the great height difference between the two of them. Frankly, she hasn't seen her in so long, she underestimated it. Jinx is taller than most, and Vivienne shorter, so the difference is almost comical. In fact, it is, they just hate each other too much to see the comedy of it.

"It's hardly petty, especially considering I wouldn't have thought to ever see you again anyway." Vivienne glares at her again, then eyes the laptop. Something similar to concern crosses her face, and Jinx tries not to laugh. Sometimes Vivienne is too good of a person for her own good, even when it comes to Jinx. "Is it..." she trails off, gesturing to the laptop in Jinx's hand.

"Relax, Carter, it'll be fine. It's been through worse." She reassures her, but she's also reassuring herself. Surely it's fine? She doesn't know what she is going to do if it isn't, that laptop has all her work on it, her *life's* work on it. The draft she's been writing since she was sixteen, every little change, every edit, every small note, it's all on there.

"Okay, good." Vivienne says, her face dropping back into a careful mix of disgust and disapproval. She really hates Jinx, and no amount of kindness appears to be able to overpower that, apparently.

"You're being incredibly rude for someone who's just spilt hot coffee over someone, you know?" Jinx sighs, half expecting her not to respond and just walk off, but Vivienne merely rolls her eyes.

"You were the one with your headphones in."

"You were the one running."

"You were walking like a maniac."

"And *you* were running and somehow using your phone at the same time."

"How is that a bad thing?" Vivienne breaks the little pattern between their blame shifting and glances around, then to her watch, she clearly has to be somewhere.

"Carter, you can barely walk and stay upright, I highly doubt running *while* your attention is elsewhere could ever go down any differently than it just has." Jinx begins away, striding into her usual pace, but Vivienne doesn't seem to be finished. Great.

Jogging to catch up with her, Vivienne's breath is short as she tries to speak, "Still, you shouldn't have your headphones in while you're walking *and* staring at your phone." Is she ever going to give this up? She always has to win; it's so unbelievably annoying. Resisting a groan, Jinx turns to her, stopping completely and shaking her head.

"Yes, but I had my phone out for a moment, you, judging by your lack of breath, have been running for a while."

"Yes, but-"

"*And,*" Jinx carries on, cutting Vivienne off, "I shouldn't have to be wandering around campus on the lookout for clumsy, running girls with no spatial awareness." This is getting tiring now, Vivienne has a very annoying habit of draining her energy, no matter how much of it Jinx has. Now is not the time to be running into her, and it is definitely not the time to be having a verbal debate with her either.

"But-" Vivienne tries again, frustration clear on her face, her hands returning to her hips. She steps forwards, but Jinx merely steps backwards, her steps much larger.

"Don't you have somewhere to be, Carter?" Jinx says, tapping her own watch. Confusion clouds Vivienne's features, but it is quickly replaced with panic as she looks at her phone, which flashes with a name. Not saying anything else to Jinx, she answers the call and starts running down the path. Laughing to herself, Jinx begins walking away from the spot, her shoes catching on the lid of her coffee. Did that girl learn nothing from what just happened? Clearly multitasking isn't her strongpoint, but apparently, she doesn't care.

*

Last night was utter chaos. Even after the Vivienne incident, something that still makes her laugh but somehow mad at the same time, her evening got even worse. Her laptop was fine, thank god, but her shirt was humiliatingly stained, and the coffee doesn't appear to want to come out. Her coat covered most of it, but it made her boil when she finally reached the library, where she didn't stay long anyway because her laptop had died after a short while. Admitting defeat, she went back to her dorm, but the party was far from over, meaning she didn't sleep long, not with all the banging on the walls. So, groggy from lack of sleep, still annoyed about her shirt, and still overwhelmingly hungry, Jinx makes her way to her first class, *Introduction to Classical Literature*.

Finding the building isn't hard, all the literature-based classes are in the same building, the only one she will find herself using, aside from her dorm. It is the biggest building on campus, and most likely the oldest, dating back to the 1600's. Its white limestone pillars create a large entrance canopy dominating over the black and white polished floors, chequered like a large chess board. The double doors opening to the main hall, which are nearly double the size of regular doors, are deep mahogany, and the interior walls are decorated with intricate statues and old-style wooden bookshelves. A coffee shop hides in the corner, barely noticeable, and large tables border the room, each seating what looks like ten people.

Sitting on the armchair in one of the many seating areas, Jinx pulls out the assigned read for her first class, *Pride and Prejudice,* a book she personally can't stand. The whole point of how the main character can't go 200 pages without falling for a man is abysmal and outdated, and the idea that the female lead thinks she can change him, when, if he wanted to change so badly and become less prideful, he would do it himself. He shouldn't and wouldn't change just because he wants a woman to love him, that just isn't realistic. And what's to stop him reverting back to his ways once he has her bound in marriage? Of all the classics they could start on, of all the great literature of the past decades, the teacher picked *Pride and Prejudice,* not *Animal Farm* or *1984* or even *Jane Eyre,* but *Pride and Prejudice.* There was so much great literature out there, and yet they'd chosen *Pride and Prejudice.*

"Good book?"

Startled, Jinx turns around to see who asked her the question. While she isn't exactly thrilled about what she is reading, that doesn't mean she enjoys being interrupted. Standing behind her, bent down so their heads are level, is a girl, a dumbstruck smile plastered across her face. She is wearing a cropped white shirt, which sleeves are rolled up, dark flared jeans with smiling faces painted onto them, and coral converse. Her hair is the same colour as her shoes and is trapped under her satchel, which is covered in all kinds of pins supporting all kinds of causes. Eyeing the book in Jinx's hands, her smile somehow seems to grow, and she takes an eager step forward, hitting her knee on the back of Jinx's chair.

"Who are you?" Jinx asks, and the girl rounds the armchair, perching on the coffee table in front of her. What is she doing? Jinx isn't sure how 'Who are you?' sounds like an invitation to sit down, but the girl in front of her has anyway.

"Lilly Thomas, I'm in your Classical Literature class." The girl says, pulling out her own copy of *Pride and Prejudice* and waving it around like it's some sort of prize.

"Okay?" Jinx says, opening her own book further to hint to the girl that she isn't in the mood for talking. "And why did you feel the need to interrupt my reading?"

"Well, I wanted to know if you're enjoying the book." She smiles, putting her book back into the satchel, clearly oblivious to Jinx's intentional rudeness.

"Yes, that's obvious, but why?" Jinx is getting annoyed; she'd come here early so that *this* wouldn't happen. She planned to leave the minute it started filling up and get to class early.

"Well, because you're the only person here who's reading it, so I assumed you were in my class. I just wanted to make conversation, so that way I wouldn't go into class without knowing anyone."

"And talking to me was supposed to fix that?" Jinx questions, closing her book ever so slightly.

"In theory, yes, but I'm starting to think this was a bad idea and that you're not a very talkative person."

Jinx huffs a laugh, she has that right, then closes her book entirely, "Not usually, no, and especially not at seven in the morning," The girl, Lilly, looks a little disheartened and makes to leave. "However, I do find your courage very interesting. I could have easily been an ass to you when you came up *behind* me and asked about my book, but you did it anyway."

Lilly stops moving and looks at Jinx, "Well you can't make many friends by silently observing."

"And why the need for friends at all? Why not just wait for class to start and find some there?" Jinx sits up slightly, watching Lilly. This is an interesting interaction, especially considering how rude she'd been before. Most people tend to lose their shit with her by now and leave, yet Lilly is still here. It's fascinating.

Lilly smiles and crosses her arms, "Well, I figured everyone in class would either already have friends, or be too preoccupied with their studies to want to talk, so here I am."

Jinx smirks and leans back in her chair, "I'm not a big fan of this book to be honest, I find the plot abysmal and the characters pathetic." Surely talking to this girl can't be that bad, Jinx didn't expect it to turn into anything. After class they'll probably end up acting like they don't know each other, which is perfect. She doesn't need anyone, people cause distractions, and that is the last thing she needs during college, distractions.

Lilly beams and moves to sit on an actual chair, pulling out her copy of *Pride and Prejudice* once again, "I know! I'm so glad you think so, you have no idea how hard it's been to find someone who agrees with me. Everyone I know loves the book and I've never understood why."

Jinx resists a smile at Lilly's statement, reminding herself that she doesn't want to cement a friendship that won't last long enough to mean anything. Although, if this could go any other way, she would smile at the fact that she's finally found someone who shares her views, who sees this 'great piece of literature' for what it truly is, another pointless, predictable romance.

"Honestly, people are so basic," she sighs, leaning back into her chair and letting her legs fall to either side, resting her head on her propped-up arm. "There was a girl at my high school who practically worshipped Elizabeth Bennet."

Lilly mocks shock, "*Worshipped?* She must have had a very small reading range."

"That's the worst part, she didn't. She had what must have been two and a half bookshelves worth of books but couldn't see the issues with *Pride and Prejudice.*" Vivienne had always loved books like *Pride and Prejudice,* and when they did a speech in freshman English, she'd chosen her topic based on it. Technically there were no limits to what you could choose, you could do it on whatever you wanted, within reason, but Jinx hardly saw how a speech on her favourite book was appropriate. Jinx had chosen a much more reasonable topic, one that was sensible and simultaneously intriguing. In the end, despite her research and perfect delivery of an *appropriate* speech, they'd still tied for the highest grade, something they'd both tried to take up with the teacher, at the same time. The poor woman looked terrified by the end of it, and neither Jinx nor Vivienne had managed to negotiate themselves up any higher than the other.

"Wow. That's just disappointing. You should've shared your opinions with her, converted her to the Anti-Austen gang." Lilly shakes her head, then her gaze moves around the room, glancing at the large clock in the centre of the wall.

"If I could've, I would've, but she *hated* me."

Lilly tilts her head and pulls her hair from under her satchel strap, "Because of your *Pride and Prejudice* opinions or because of something else?"

"Oh no, we were rivals even before that. You know what she said to me once?"

"Ooo what?" Lilly leans forwards in her seat, putting her book on the seat beside her.

"'You ruin my chances of an Ivy League, and I will burn your world to the ground.'" Jinx says, making air quotes with her hands.

"Damn, intense."

"Right? We were *sixteen* at the time, most people didn't even know if they wanted to go to college or not yet."

Lilly and her chat like this for a good while before people start to fill up the hall, which is when they venture towards their class, narrowly dodging the more eager students. The walk there isn't a very long one, but Lilly keeps stopping to admire the architecture, which means they arrive later than Jinx had hoped, but the room is still practically empty. Lilly says she doesn't mind where they sit, so Jinx takes them to the front centre, where she wants and needs to be. This is one of her less important classes, and she's only really taken it to have a little break from her more intense ones, but she still needs it. Majoring in English means that she doesn't need to memorise facts anymore, like she had in high school for the more linear subjects, but it also means she has to write more essays, and in order to do that, she needs as much information from these classes as she can get, the more she knows, the less time she'll have to spend researching.

"What? You really want to sit here?" Lilly asks, surveying the seat and the proximity to the Professor, clearly nervous.

"You said you didn't mind, so don't start complaining." In all fairness, Jinx had thought that sitting this close to the Professor would've made Lilly move, sit near the back or in the middle, but she hadn't. It's getting harder and harder to stay separated from this girl, but if Jinx is being truthful, she isn't trying too hard to get rid of her. Normally she doesn't have to try to get rid of people, they tend to leave on their own, and when she does try it always worked, but Lilly seems to be intent on becoming friends. Why she is so determined is still unclear, but part of Jinx wants to find out.

"I wasn't going to complain, it's just…" She shrugs and sits in the aisle seat, Jinx sitting next to her.

"So, are you majoring in English?" Lilly asks and Jinx nods.

"Are you?" Jinx asks, letting her legs drop to the sides again.

"No, I'm an art major, I'm really only taking this because it seems fun, it's essentially talking about books." Lilly says, pulling her notepad and copy of the reading material out of her bag.

"And writing essays about them," Jinx reminds her, doing the same.

"I'll cross that bridge when I come to it," Lilly smiles, and Jinx smirks at her. She goes to respond, but the door opens behind her and grabs her attention. Two people walk in, one is a tall boy with glasses similar to hers and the other…

"You have got to be kidding me." Jinx murmurs, shaking her head as Vivienne begins down the stairs, her book tucked under her arm and coffee in hand.

"What?" Lilly asks, turning to see the two figures in the door.

"That's the girl," Jinx says, nodding towards where Vivienne is stood in the doorway, arms crossed across her chest. She scans the room, probably searching for the best seats, then her eyes land on Jinx. Only one word can describe the look that falls onto her face upon seeing her: utter, unbridled disappointment.

"Well, well, well," Jinx says as Vivienne walks down the stairs of the classroom and sits in the aisle seat opposite Lilly's, "I didn't expect to see you here, Carter."

"Vivienne." Is all she says, turning to face the front of the classroom.

"Knocked over any coffees lately, or is my shirt the only current victim?" Jinx teases, watching as Vivienne's friend looks confused, and Vivienne goes bright red. Composing herself, she scoffs and turns to face her and Lilly, "Is this a friend? I didn't know you were capable of having those, or at least most narcissists aren't anyway." She spits, any memory of last night cleared from her mind.

"Narcissist? That's rich coming from you, and it looks like you've managed to find someone too." Jinx smiles at the boy sitting behind Vivienne, "Jinx Keller, I imagine Carter has mentioned me considering the look on your face." He looks disgusted, as if Jinx is some disease, and she finds it amusing. Vivienne is very good at telling half stories, she's been doing it since they were in high school. Jinx had barely escaped detention the time she'd told their history teacher that Jinx had rewritten her report whilst they were in the library, and she'd only talked her way out of it because 'there was no proof of her messing with it'. What had actually happened was that Vivienne had deleted Jinx's *entire* report after she'd accidentally taken her coffee, so Jinx had messed with hers a little to get her back, of course Vivienne kept these details to herself, and only grassed Jinx up.

"Julian Patterson, and she has," the boy says, his eyes narrowing slightly. How much has Vivienne said, and how much has she not?

Vivienne elbows him and Jinx laughs, "Talking about me, are we? Gosh, and here's me thinking you'd get over the fact that I was Valedictorian, and you weren't."

Lilly pulls at Jinx's elbow, and she turns to look at her, a smirk still growing on her face. Lilly doesn't say anything, but her face is a mix of either confusion and shock, or fear and pride, either way, Jinx doesn't mind, what she is saying deserves both. She isn't like this with many people, she's been called cold before, obviously, because she is, but she isnt outright rude like she is with Vivienne. This has been the way they've been for years; they haven't yet had a conversation where they are remotely nice to one another, they only ever exchange insults. In fact, last night was probably the nicest interaction they've ever had, and Vivienne was only nice then because she thought she'd broken Jinx's laptop.

Vivienne scoffs, "You were only Valedictorian because I missed two weeks in senior year to go to my father's business thing in France."

"Excuses, Carter, excuses…" Jinx trails off, shaking her head and enjoying watching the four different shades of red Vivienne turns, her grip tightening on her armrest. She is so easy to annoy, maybe that's what makes it so fun.

"Excuses?" Vivienne furrows her brow, "How is that an-"

Before she can finish, she is cut off by the door at the front of the classroom opening and a tall, white-haired woman dressed in a mustard suit walking onto the platform before them, seemingly unaware of the four students sitting at the front. Taking off her blazer to reveal a long-sleeved shirt cuffed at the ends, she places a stack of books folders on the desk in the corner, humming to herself as she surveys the room, this time noticing Jinx, Lilly, Julian, and Vivienne.

"You're here early," she says, smiling, "or is this all there is for my class this year?" No one talks, so she just shrugs, "Not talkative, are we?"

This time Lilly speaks, "There are more people, we're just here early."

The Professor smiles, taking her glasses off and cleaning them with a cloth, "Ah, so are you friends or is this just chance?"

Jinx stifles a laugh, but Lilly doesn't manage to. "What's funny?" Asks the professor, placing her hands on her hips and raising an eyebrow.

"Nothing, Professor," Lilly mutters, eyeing Vivienne and Julian.

"It doesn't seem like nothing," the Professor looks towards Julian and Vivienne, then back to Jinx and Lilly.

After a while, Vivienne coughs and says, "It's just that this girl finds mine and Jinx's," she gestures to Jinx, "previous rivalry amusing."

Lilly scoffs at her words and Jinx shakes her head. 'This girl', is she serious? Considering she is such a 'nice person' she is being really rude to Lilly, and for no good reason, purely because she is associated with Jinx. This is why she doesn't want Lilly to follow her, this is why she should have ignored her when she'd asked her about her book, everyone who hangs around with Jinx is bad by association, they always have been, and she should've known better.

"A previous rivalry, interesting…" She looks between Jinx and Vivienne, "I hope this will push you both to the best of your ability, and *not* get in the way of your classwork."

"It wo-" Vivienne begins.

"Don't worry, Professor," Jinx turns to face Vivienne, smiling, "it won't get in the way."

"Good, now feel free to chat as you please until the other students arrive." With that, she turns to the desk behind her and starts to sort through some files. Jinx relaxes into her chair and turns towards Vivienne, who is now viciously glaring at her,

"Was that really necessary," she hisses through her teeth, bending low enough that the Professor can't hear her.

"Yes, it was." Jinx smiles, bending across Lilly's lap.

"*Why?*" Vivienne demands.

"Because it annoyed the hell out of you." With that, Jinx pulls away and begins a separate conversation with Lilly, who still looks partially shocked at what happened. After a long while, more students begin to fill into the classroom, taking seats everywhere but the front. Only Jinx and the other three end up occupying the front, much to the Professor's dismay. Once it seems like no one else is coming, the Professor takes up her place on the stage,

"Alright, listen everyone." The entire room turns to her, and all talking silences. "I am not going to take attendance, nor am I going to scold anyone who doesn't attend classes after this, all I am going to say before we start is that even if you don't attend this class, you will be taking the midterms and will be assessed on all assignments set. So, if you don't attend, you will fail, it's as simple as that." And with that, she begins teaching the class.

Chapter 3 – Vivienne
°•. ✿ .•°°•. ✿ .•°°•. ✿ .•°

    That was single handedly the *worst* lesson Vivienne has ever attended. Every time the professor would ask a question, Jinx would cut her off, every time Vivienne answered a question, Jinx would either correct her or follow it up with her own point. All of that was a pain, but that wasn't the worst thing, the worst thing happened when the Professor brought up Elizabeth Bennet in *Pride and Prejudice.* That was the one time Vivienne had beaten Jinx to a question, but then the professor, Miss Halloway, asked her to support her point. She had explained her evidence behind it and her opinions on the subject, then the professor had asked the class if anyone objected to her points, and Vivienne felt her stomach drop. No one throughout the entire class wanted to challenge her, everyone agreed with her opinions on Jane Austen's character building and choice, *everyone* but Jinx and the spineless girl beside her. They had both countered her point, objecting to her character choice and completely tearing her argument apart, making her look like an absolute idiot. It made her feel *so stupid.* After that, she kept silent, staring at her notebook and listening to everyone else's points, mainly Lilly and Jinx, and counting down the minutes on her watch. This class was supposed to be fun; it was supposed to be a break from her major, history, but now it is another competition, another constant fight with Jinx, and while she hates it, it is a fight she is going to win. She has to.

    The minute the Professor called an end to the discussions, she'd packed up her stuff faster than she ever had before, and bolted from the room, her pace as fast as possible, slowing only when she is a safe distance from the classroom. She hears Julian bounding up behind her in the corridor and relaxes a little, at least she has him. Throughout the class, every time Jinx and her friend had pushed her to the edge, he'd helped her, told her that they were trying to get a rise out of her, an outburst. He'd actually had to stop her getting out of her seat a couple of times and told her that cursing out Jinx in front of the entire class wasn't the best idea.

"My god, how did you deal with her for *four years?*" He pants, pulling her to a stop and walking at a normal pace. She must've been walking much faster than she'd thought, because he really is out of breath.

"It required *a lot* of venting; I literally took up Judo," Vivienne murmurs, checking behind her and feeling the knot in her chest loosen when she sees no one behind her.

"Wait, really?" Julian doesn't sound convinced at her statement, most people aren't, she doesn't exactly seem like the kind of person who did Judo.

Vivienne shrugs and slows her pace, heading for the coffee shop in the main hall, "Three years, you're looking at a black belt."

"*Black belt,*" he gapes, "you really are full of surprises."

"Aren't I just," she smiles, stopping in the cue for the store. They sell all sorts of things here, but she's only here for coffee, something to stimulate her and take her mind off the last lesson. She has a free period before her next class and was planning on spending it in the library with Julian, but she saw the girl and Jinx head that way and decided to find something else to do.

"Maybe you should make use of your skills on Jinx," Julian smirks as she approaches the counter, twisting her hands together. She never likes ordering from counters, she speaks too quietly most of the time and has to repeat her orders quite a lot. Not only that, but when she does order, she feels like everyone is looking at her, listening to her order, making their judgements about everything: what she is ordering, what she is wearing, how she is standing. Suddenly everything she does feels wrong, when she moves, she feels like she's inconveniencing people, when she breathes, she misses beats and ends up taking deeper breaths, and when she finally orders, she looks like she's trying to coach herself out of a panic attack.

"What can I get you?" the barista asks, smiling at Vivienne. She freezes for a second, just looking at the woman, who is smiling kindly at her.

"Oh, a takeaway mocha please." Vivienne practically whispers, looking at the counter and taking a step backwards.

"Coming right up," the woman chirps and walks off. Partially surprised she even heard her, Vivienne turns to Julian, trying to erase her doubts from her mind.

"Are you going to order, or shall we go and wait over there?" She gestures in the direction of the collection point, and he shakes his head. If Julian has noticed anything wrong, he doesn't say anything, carrying on with their conversation as normal.

"I'm not getting anything; I don't drink coffee."

"What? How can you not drink coffee and be this chipper, that's impossible." Vivienne says, mocking shock.

"Two words, sleep schedule." He waves his finger in her face and smirks, "something you clearly don't have." He has a point, but she isn't about to admit that to him.

"What do you mean? I have a sleep schedule."

"Vi, I went to the toilet at three in the morning last night and found you lying on the couch, reading. How is that a sleep schedule?"

"I don't normally do that," she lies, shrugging shyly in an attempt to feign innocence.

"The fact that you're full of energy now hints that it is a regular occurrence."

The woman calls her order, and she goes to collect it, talking to Julian as she does so, "It is not."

"Well even if that doesn't show it, your coffee habits sure do."

"What?"

"It's ten in the morning and you're already on your third cup of coffee."

Vivienne laughs and walks off, towards the doors leading to the campus.

"You're walking away because you know I'm right." Julian smiles, easily matching her pace. He's just so tall, it's not fair.

"So what if you are, you have your sleep schedule and I have my coffee, let's leave it at that."

"Fine, fine," he puts his hands up and ducks down, making her laugh. They leave the literature building and walk around campus aimlessly for a while before Julian practically forces her into the library, saying she 'shouldn't let Jinx dictate where she does and doesn't go'. It isn't that she is letting Jinx decide where she can be, it's just that Vivienne doesn't have the energy or patience to deal with her this morning. She had to stop herself from slapping Jinx in that class, and Julian had to stop her from getting out of her seat and leaving a few times too.

How can she be here? She must have gotten into tons of good schools, yet she picked this one? She could have gone all over the country, but she went hours away from her town, *their* town. It just doesn't make sense, at high school she had joined all kinds of extracurriculars and clubs after school because she wanted to be away from home so badly, why, Vivienne doesn't know, but she's heard things, and now here she is, at the closest possible Ivy League to there.

"You look worried," says Julian, pulling her from her thoughts. "We can leave if you really want to, there are smaller libraries on campus."

"No, I'm not worried, just thinking." She shrugs and surveys the enormous library. It's beautiful, truly beautiful. Stacks upon stacks of books line every dark oak shelf, each of which are tall enough to reach the looming ceiling, and two lit fireplaces stand at either end creating a warm glow within the room. In the space the bookshelves surround are four large tables, surrounded by ten chairs on each. In the corner there is a staircase leading to the upper levels, where the armchairs and quieter sections are.

"Thinking about what?" Julian asks, walking towards the stairs.

"Jinx." This always happens, she always lets Jinx play on her mind, ever since high school, and she has no idea why. She just can't erase her, after every encounter Vivienne finds herself playing through them, thinking about what she said, what she didn't say, what she could've said.

He sighs, "Jinx, why?"

"I'm just wondering why she's here, as in this college."

Following Julian up the stairs, she looks behind her and scans the room, Jinx is nowhere to be seen.

"What do you mean?" Julian asks, running his hands over the polished banister and craning his neck around the room, admiring the architecture.

"Well, she was always so desperate to get away from our town, in high school, and yet she's come to the Ivy League closest to there." Vivienne explains, trying to figure out what could've made her choose here.

"Maybe this is the only one that would take her?" Julian leans against the banister and crosses his arms.

"As if. As much as it pains me to say, she is one of the smartest people I know and-"

"Smartest person you know, eh?" No. Please, god no.. "That's quite a compliment coming from you, Carter."

That damn nickname catches her off guard *every time*, and she's not even sure why.

"It wasn't meant as a compliment." Vivienne says, turning to face Jinx behind her. Her short, chestnut hair is loose around her face, the layers flicking backwards, and her bangs are flicked outwards slightly. Her black turtleneck top, with sleeves rolled up to her elbows, is tucked into warm brown pants, which are being held up by a stylish black belt and she has her leather jacket slung over her shoulder.

"Like what you see?" Jinx teases and crosses her arms, "I imagine you've never seen me in anything but my uniform, and that wasn't the most flattering thing." She's right, but Vivienne isn't about to let this girl get to her. Their high school had been an elite school of the area, that's why Vivienne had to move to get into it, and those who couldn't afford the high tuition had to hope and apply for a scholarship. Both her and Jinx were scholarship students, they were both penalised for it, and yet they still made life hell for each other anyway.

Their uniform had been expensive too, especially considering you had to have *all* of it, otherwise you were punished, and for what it cost, it was unbelievably unflattering. Long kilts, baggy blouses with ruffled sleeves, everything was designed to make everyone blend in, until they were all a sea of sickening green. While she had loved the education she was getting at her school, she had wished they didn't have uniforms, like most normal high schools.

Tearing her eyes away from Jinx's clothes, Vivienne looks at the bag hanging on her shoulder. It's plain with a small black cat printed on it, and the top is hanging open, revealing multiple 'help wanted' posters.

Following her line of sight, Jinx quickly clicks the bag shut and pushes it behind her. "You didn't strike me as the staring type, Carter, but you do tend to be full of surprises."

"I wasn't staring; you were the one with your bag hanging open, its contents visible to everyone."

Jinx laughs and makes towards her, "I wasn't talking about my bag, Carter." She whispers as she walks past, having to bend down for Vivienne to hear. Confused, Vivienne turns to look at her as she walks up the stairs.

"You really do enjoy staring at me, don't you?" she shouts without turning around, and Vivienne is glad she didn't, god knows what she would have said about the blush creeping up her neck.

Beside her, Julian sighs and starts up the stairs again, having stopped when Jinx came up behind them, "She really does enjoy teasing you, doesn't she?"

"Yep," Vivienne shakes her head, "I'm fairly sure it's the *only* thing she enjoys."

"Probably," Julian mutters. "Although she does look like she'd enjoy dancing as well."

Having been sipping her coffee, Vivienne has to stop herself from spraying it over the stairwell as laughter tries desperately to escape. Julian smiles and looks to the top of the stairs, where the silence looms over them. "What's so funny? I genuinely think she'd love dancing, she seems like she's the person who throws her arms up in the air the minute music starts playing." Slowly he starts to laugh, clearly losing control of whatever serious air he's trying to emit, and they both burst into a fits of laughter. What he'd said wasn't even that funny, it's just so wrong that it's comical, Jinx would probably choose death over dancing if she was given the choice.

"You know, I'm not in the library mood anymore." Vivienne says, her laughter slowing and regaining her breath.

"Really? You've dragged me all the way here, halfway up a flight of stairs, and now you're not in the library mood?" Julian sighs, shaking his head. Vivienne would've thought he was being serious, but a large smile quickly spreads across his face, and she knows he's joking.

"Yes, because we've only known each other a day and I don't feel like sitting in silence studying instead of talking." She says, turning around and beginning down the stairs.

"Fair enough."

Vivienne smiles, watching as Julian follows her, taking the steps two at a time, "How are you doing that?" Vivienne asks.

"Doing what?" he asks, smiling and looking at his feet.

"You know what, taking the stairs two at a time." Vivienne tries to catch him up but ends up slipping and reaching for the railing.

"It's easy." Julian turns to face her and starts walking backwards, smirking at her. Now he's just showing off, and it is extremely annoying.

"*Easy?* For you maybe, but I trip over just walking around, never mind taking the steps two at a time."

"Come on, try it." He smirks and puts his hands on his hips.

"No."

"Come on, I'll race you down." He stops and waits for her, tapping his foot on the floor.

"A race? Julian, we're in a library." Vivienne walks past him, smiling.

"Oh yeah, what are they going to do?"

"Kick us out."

"On the first day, I highly doubt it." He is being so irresponsible, a race down the stairs of the library. It's so stupid, they could be kicked out, she could fall, they could cause chaos, so much could go wrong, *everything* could go wrong. But surely the whole point of college is to make more friends and to do things she didn't do in high school, like her Dad had said. If she were in a movie, this would probably be the point at which there would be a flashback of her Dad saying, 'just try it, have fun', something he's said a lot recently.

"Fine. But if I get kicked out, I'm going to kill you." Vivienne sighs, pushing her fears aside and ignoring the growing pit in her stomach. She needs this, she needs to be fun, she needs to show Julian that she isn't boring so he will stick around, she needs to try new things and this is where she is going to start.

All Julian does is shrug and say, "Fine by me," before pelting it down the stairs at top speed, still somehow taking the stairs two at a time.

"Hey! Cheat!" Vivienne shouts, running after him taking the steps two at a time. She's halfway down them when one of her laces becomes loose, untying beneath her, and she steps on it. Going too fast to stop, she's thrown forwards front first, her hands out in front of her in an attempt to break her fall.

Panicking, she doesn't hear the thud of a bag behind her or the frantic steps descending the stairs in her wake, all she feels is someone's hand catch the back of her collared shirt and another press hard against her chest, stopping her inches from the floor, their broad hand spread across her chest, holding her up.

"What the *hell* are you doing?" a voice hisses into her ear, "You could've hurt yourself."

Vivienne is pulled backwards and finds her footing on the stairs before turning to look at what she presumed was Julian. She nearly steps back in shock when a panting Jinx is stood in front of her, bag and jacket discarded on the steps behind her.

"You…" Vivienne murmurs, looking across the room at Julian, who is now running towards her, having reached the bottom of the stairs.

"Just saved your ass from getting a concussion, you're welcome by the way." Jinx spits, glaring at Julian, "What were you thinking? Have you *met* Carter, she can barely walk, never mind run down stairs." Vivienne doesn't speak, and neither does Julian, they just stare at her rival, noticing her heavy breaths.

"You ran from-" Vivienne starts, her voice soft and quiet.

"The top of the stairs, believe me I'm aware." Her voice is sour and rude, but something similar to concern clouds her eyes. She walks off, crouching to collect her bag from the floor, the papers scattered down the stairs.

Someone pulling at her arm takes her attention from Jinx, and she finds a panicked Julian standing next to her, "Vivienne, I-I'm so sorry. I-I didn't realise you were *that* uncoordinated."

"Oh believe me, she is, it's a miracle she got a black belt when running down stairs sends her flying." Jinx is beside her again, although she isn't stopping, merely walking straight past them.

"Jinx," Vivienne says, walking after her. Her speed is astonishing, "Wait,"

"I can't, I need to be somewhere."

Vivienne breaks into a jog in an attempt to catch her up, "Just wait, will you?"

"What?" Jinx demands, stopping and turning to face Vivienne.

"Thank you," she says, staring her straight in the eye.

"Try anything like that again, Carter, and I won't be the one running down the stairs to save your *sorry ass*." She snaps, any and all concern free from her features, then she's walking again, her bag clutched tightly in her hands.

Chapter 4 – Jinx

─ · ₀° ☆: *.☽ .* :☆° . ─

Jinx doesn't know why, but when she'd seen Vivienne running down those stairs, she knew something was bound to go wrong. You don't spend four years in high school together and not pick up the obvious things, like how unbelievably clumsy Vivienne is. She once doused their English teacher in water when she tripped up the stairs with her bottle in hand. Then it was funny, but now, she could really hurt herself. Then her shoelace untied underneath her, then she stood on it, Jinx panicked.

She started down the stairs, discarding her bag on the steps behind her, trying to reach Vivienne before she hit the floor. Vivienne's hands shot out in front of her, but they would just increase damage when she met the solid marble floor fast approaching. Jinx was running down the stairs, taking them two at the time, and reaching for Vivienne's collar, thank god she was wearing a collared shirt, if she wasn't, Jinx didn't know what she would've caught. Why Jinx was doing this wasn't clear, she should just let her fall and feel the consequences of her actions, and as a bonus she would miss a few days of classes which would set Jinx ahead in *Introduction to Classical Literature.* But she couldn't, that kind of flooring could break bones, she didn't want to see her in hospital because of that stupid boy's stupid ideas.

That idiot of a boy that had talked her into this, the next time she and him were alone she was going to give him a piece of her mind. What part of him thought getting a clumsy girl to run down stairs two at a time was a good idea? What part of him didn't stop to think about what could happen if she fell? What part of *her* didn't stop to think about whether or not this was a good idea? Vivienne is usually so cautious, she usually thinks everything through, sometimes too much, but now? Now she was falling down a flight of carpeted stairs, well on route to collide with the rock-hard floor.

When her hand hook on the back of Vivienne's collar, she moves her other to push against her chest, she doesn't want to strangle her by holding only her collar, that would defeat the purpose of her running down the stairs to begin with. Only once Vivienne is up did does realise that she is panting, that she has exhausted herself trying to save this girl, and that Vivienne is about to turn around and notice.

"You…" Vivienne murmurs, and Jinx snaps something petty back, looking up the stairs to the splayed contents of her bag on the stairs, looking anywhere but at Vivienne. She doesn't want her to know what she'd done to stop her from falling, how she'd quite literally dropped everything to help her.

"You ran from-"

"The top of the stairs, believe me I'm aware." She had run from the top of the stairs, to save this spoiled know-it-all. What had gotten into her? Turning from the startled girl and walking up the stairs, she hears the fool of a boy run towards Vivienne, stuttering to the end of a pathetic apology. As if an apology would've cut it if she'd fractured her wrist or dislocated her shoulder. What would an apology have done to fix that? Jinx's anger is slowly boiling over, but she keeps reminding herself that this is Vivienne, and that she shouldn't be protecting her. God knows she has enough people doing that anyway. If she wants to make stupid decisions and put herself at risk, then let her, let her fracture collar bones and break ribs running down stairs, and Jinx will just watch next time. She'll watch as someone else no doubt saves her, catches her as she falls, she'll watch as the world bends over backwards to accommodate that girl, she will watch from the side, looking after herself, saving herself, watching her get saved, and she won't care. She will make sure she doesn't care.

Collecting her bag and coat from the floor, along with the scattered flyers for jobs, Jinx pushes back her thoughts, or at least the ones that are worried for Vivienne. She doesn't need thoughts like that clouding her judgement. No matter how many times she falls down stairs, Vivienne will still be the spoiled brat from high school, the one determined to make Jinx's accomplishments worthless.

"Vivienne, I-I'm so sorry. I-I didn't realise you were *that* uncoordinated." the boy beside her mutters, his face pale, regret twisting his features. Pathetic. He's apologising as if he isn't the one who started it?

"Oh believe me, she is, it's a miracle how she got a black belt when running down stairs sends her flying." Jinx walks straight past them, making sure to avoid looking at Vivienne.

She is almost clear of the stairs before Vivienne tries to walk beside her, failing miserably. If Jinx wants to get away from somewhere fast, there isn't a human on earth that can match her walking pace. Not running, running is obvious. Walking is subtle and effective.

"Jinx," she pants, now practically jogging. You clearly don't need to be sporty to learn Judo, because Vivienne is anything but. Even Judo is an astonishing accomplishment. "Wait." Vivienne pleads, trying her hardest to catch up with her without breaking into a full-on sprint.

"I can't, I need to be somewhere," that isn't entirely a lie, she does have to go and scout out how many of these jobs will take her.

"Just wait, will you?" Now Vivienne is jogging. Reluctantly, Jinx turns around, a glare fixed on her face.

"What?"

"Thank you," she pants, staring Jinx dead in the eye. She'd thanked her, *thanked her.* Not once in their history has she ever thanked Jinx before, *ever*. And Jinx has no idea how to respond, so she just says what she imagines Vivienne would say if the roles were reversed, with some alterations of course.

"Try anything like that again, Carter, and I won't be the one running down the stairs to save your *sorry ass*." Then she is off, her hands clasped tight enough around her bag that she can hear the papers inside crumpling together.

*

This place is perfect, well as perfect as you can get for a coffee shop, but considering the way the last five interviews went, Jinx isn't getting her hopes up. Throughout the past hour she has been going to anywhere that is looking for employees and offering herself up, but none of them would take her. For some she was 'too young' and for others she was 'just perfect', that was until they looked at her bank statements. After that it was, 'we're actually not looking for anything yet, but if anything comes up, we'll contact you', three out of the five had said *exactly* that, the other ones were toeing the line of it.

This is the last place, the only place within a sane distance from her college, and the only one that is willing to pay her what she needs.

Opening the door, she is met with a wave of fresh hazelnut and coffee, the combination of which smells like heaven. Looking around the room, she takes in as many details as she can before she is inevitably told they're no longer in need of help. It's an average size, eight small tables with two chairs to each, decorations up on the walls – fake plants, framed pictures of pencilled drawings and shelves – and a small counter, which is conveniently placed to the side of the entrance door. It is there she sees a man with dark skin frustratingly trying to fix a coffee machine, the owner, she presumes.

He is a man of average height and build, with short cut hair and a trimmed moustache occupying his upper lip. He's wearing a white t-shirt with what looks like a band name printed on the front, from the red lips in the top corner, she guesses *The Rolling Stones.*

Jinx coughs and the man merely says, "We're closed today, technical difficulties as you can see." without looking up.

"I'm not a customer," Jinx musters, slowly approaching the counter, "I saw the help wanted sign in the window."

This time the man looks up from the coffee machine, surveying Jinx. After a long moment of silence, he turns back to the machine, "Do you think you could fix this? I've been closed for two days now because the repair man is on holiday, and I can't, for the life of me, figure out what's going on."

A little confused, but keen to make a good impression, Jinx walks behind the counter and observes the machine. She can't see anything obviously wrong with it, so decides to give it further inspection.

"Can I?" she asks the man, gesturing to the back of the machine.

"Go ahead, it's not as if you can break it any more."

Turning the machine around and removing the back, Jinx instantly notices the problem. She's seen it a million times before with the one they had in the shop in her town. She had worked there pretty much every day after school when she was a kid, and on the weekends when she was in high school.

Pushing wires and tubes out of the way, she pulls out the bit of clumped coffee powder from down the coffee chute.

Turning around and handing it to the man, she explains what happened, "This happened a lot at the coffee shop in my town, all you need to do to stop it from happening again is to regularly clean the chute. If you don't, clumps of powder can get stuck like they have there."

The man looks from her to the machine, and then back again. "You're hired."

"What?" How can he just hire her like that, on the spot, surely he needs to check her deposits and things first? Surely he has security to go through, a form to fill, surely. This doesn't make any sense otherwise, it's too easy, and nothing easy is ever good, not in Jinx's experience anyway.

"I said you're hired; I've been having that problem for the last two months and have never known how to fix it. You're here two minutes and you've fixed it, along with giving me tips on how to stop it." He looks impressed and smiles at her, laughing at her clear confusion.

"What about bank statements and recommendations?" Jinx is so confused, for all he knows she is some law-breaking thief who wants a layout of the shop before ransacking it. There is no way he's okay with just hiring her like that, he can't be, he has to have some ulterior motive or something, he must.

"I'll check your bank statements tonight, and do you even have recommendations? I mean you look about eighteen." He has a point there, she doesn't exactly have any recommendations, but he still should've checked.

"I am eighteen, and I don't have recommendations, but surely you should've asked? I mean, how do you even know I can be trusted?"

His brow furrows, "Do you want the job or not? Because you're fighting me on it in a way that would suggest you don't." He has a point, considering how desperate she is, she doesn't exactly know why she is fighting this so much. Maybe because it is too good to be true, after what happened at all the other stores, she was sure this one would reject her too, but it hasn't. She has a job, she actually has a job, well, for now, anyway. The minute he checks her employment and credit history, there is a good chance she will be fired, no one wants someone with a record like hers working for them. That is one of the reasons the last store she'd gone to had turned her down, because of habits that cover her record.

The record isn't hers, of course, but it always looks that way. Every time she stops at a store or picks up an order, it is for her mum. Every time she swipes her card or puts in her pin, she isn't buying anything for her, but they never look that far into it. Unfortunately, for a long while now, Jinx has looked older than she is, and the way she dresses doesn't help, so whenever she goes up to a desk or checkout, she never gets checked for an ID, no matter how much she wants to be, they just ask her for her card and that is it.

Now, those moments stain her bank statements, and all stores see is an eighteen-year-old girl who has unnecessary amounts of transactions with liquor stores miles away. They don't think to actually look at her, see her, see that she very clearly isn't an alcoholic. She never drinks, ever, and she never intends to. She's seen what alcohol can do to someone, how it can destroy them, and she vows that she won't touch it. It isn't worth the destruction it can cause, destruction she knows all too well.

"Oh, no, I want the job." She insists, a little more eager than she likes. She really is desperate, and it is painfully clear.

"Good. You start tomorrow. I assume you attend a college nearby?" The man doesn't seem to notice her embarrassing eagerness, or just doesn't care, and turns back to the coffee machine. "Do you have experience?"

"Yes, I worked at a store in my old town, three years." She says, trying to control her own eagerness, and partial surprise at getting the job.

"You can be paid hourly then, considering you'll need to attend classes and study. I'll just need the times and days you'll be in at the start of the week."

"Yes, okay, I can start whenever you want me too." She says, walking back to the right side of the counter.

"You free now?" he asks, grabbing a green apron from under the counter and tying it around his waist. The small silver name tag has 'Tony' written on it in printed cursive writing, and underneath in a blockier font is 'Owner and Manager'. Jinx watches as he walks towards the door and turns over the sign hanging on it, so *Closed* is now facing them, and *Open* can be seen through the glass.

"Yeah," she says, walking behind the counter again and hanging her jacket up on a nearby hook. "Although I doubt you'll get many people in here at this time of day." It has just turned four in the afternoon, most of the college students will have a class or be studying, the only reason Jinx isn't is because she'd gotten everything done in the early hours of the morning, when the partying near her dorm got loud enough to wake her up.

"You'd be surprised." Tony mutters, standing behind the counter, "College kids don't tend to come here, so locals do, y'know, to avoid you lot."

Jinx sighs and smirks, shaking her head to herself, he has a point. She goes to the college, and even she finds the people there pretentious, especially some of the boys in her classes. Earlier today, four of them interrupted a lecture, and an interesting one too. In the middle of the Professor's discussion, one of them ran in, clumsy to the point where he seemed drunk, and stood on the desk, his hand on his heart. Clearly used to this, the Professor stood to the side, muttering something about making it quick, and the boy had started some long-winded ballad to a random girl on the back row, who was loving every second of it. It was all pathetic, and to make it even worse, after about thirty seconds of the miserable speech, another boy burst through the door. He began apologising to the class, sticking his nose in the air, then winking at another girl in the front row. He then grabbed ballad boy and hauled him out of the room. He was shouting the name of the girl on the back row as he was being pulled away, Brooke, or something along those lines, and when they were finally at the door, they stood up straight and bowed, while the rest of the class burst into applause. Jinx had ignored it all and carried on with her notes, focusing on getting all the points scribbled on the chalkboard into her book and not the childish theatrics that were unfolding before her. Honestly, how old did they think they were? The hall isn't a playground for children or a stage to act on, it's a lecture hall, where people go to listen to *lecturers*, not stupid boys fulfilling dares.

When they left, the Professor sighed and carried on teaching, looking equally annoyed as Jinx felt, but nothing was done with the boys, why would anything happen? Where she goes isn't a normal college, it's a college full of people who can pay the high price of attending, and very few who have been given financial aid. Those with aid keep quiet, silently grateful to be there, and those who can pay are obnoxious, rule bending, pretentious idiots who get away with everything because they can afford the price, or don't have to pay at all. In places like this, privilege gets you further than most knowledge does.

"Hello?" Tony taps her on the shoulder and Jinx steps backwards, being pulled from her thoughts.

"Sorry," she mutters, stepping towards the counter again and taking the apron he put there for her. "Lost in my thoughts."

"Yes, I noticed." He smiles at her, then gestures to the door. "Now I am going to go and sort out the back, while you watch for customers, and if they come in," he stops and surveys her, putting his hands on his hips, "Give them your most pleasant smile." Jinx breathes a laugh and watches as he smirks, raising an eyebrow at her, "What? Too hard?"

"People are quite irritating; can I not just tolerate them instead?" Jinx jokes, her gaze falling back to the door.

"Try and tolerate them pleasantly then," he smirks, "That's what I have to do." He begins into the storeroom, his back to her, and Jinx lets herself smile slightly. This is going to work, for once she feels certain, this is going to work.

Chapter 5 – Vivienne

°•. ✿ .•°°•. ✿ .•°°•. ✿ .•°

Two months. It has been two months since the first *Introduction to Classical Literature* class. Two months of dealing with Jinx's teasing and cockiness. Vivienne has started to think that she'd only saved her on the stairs so she could hold it above her and use it for even more mocking. It's all she seems to do, at every spare moment, every free word she gets she will use to mock her.

However, putting that aside, she's had a good start to college, one her dad would be very proud of. Her and Julian have done all the things they assumed roommates did together, including ordering far too much takeout and having to eat the leftovers the next day. Her dad dropped by a few times, Ollie sometimes with him, and whenever he does, Vivienne makes sure they don't meet up in her dorm room. She knows he'd probably like Julian if he got to know him, but her Dad won't give him the time. He will see Julian, and instead of seeing an amazing, caring, stupidly funny boy, he sees danger. Someone who can and will exploit Vivienne in every way, and he won't change his mind no matter how much she tells him, how much she shows him that Julian really is nice, and definitely doesn't have any interest in her. If what Julian is doing is some elaborate ploy, he's a pretty good actor, and extremely dedicated.

Now is a perfect example of Vivienne's keen avoidance of her dorm. Last night, her dad had text her, telling her he was going to drop by, so she suggested meeting him at a coffee shop in town. She's never been in it before, but what she sees through the windows makes it look like a nice place, cute pictures on the walls, tables with two chairs on each, and fake plants on the metallic shelves bolted into the walls. Not only that, but there are books piled all along the walls, ranging from new releases to old classics, and the sign near the shelves says, 'Take what you like, just don't ruin it.'. Maybe she'll have to come here on her own some day, to sit with a coffee and borrow a book, let her mind at ease away from the chaos of the campus.

Reaching the store, Vivienne stands outside, wrapping her arms around herself and shivering. It's early winter, but for some strange reason, she'd managed to leave the dorm without a coat. If she hadn't left it so late to leave, she might've had time to go back and get it, but she doesn't want to risk her Dad coming and looking for her.

Deciding it's getting too cold to stand outside, she decides to wait inside, her dad will be able to find the place without her, she's sure. The place smells amazing, a blend of hazelnut and coffee that makes her breath deeper, taking in every smell around her. The inside is beautiful, now that she has a full view of the place, she notices that everything is laid out perfectly. The tables are placed out of the way but still in perfect areas where they aren't too far from everything, and the small barrier separating the seating area and walkway leads straight to the counter. Whoever arranged them knew what they were doing. There is a small counter on the side wall near the back, but no one is there. People are sitting at the tables, fresh coffee and pastries in front of them, but the counter is empty.

Walking up to it, Vivienne begins to search for any sign of employees, or the manager, but no one is there. She stands there for a good while, teetering along the side, running her hand over the marble counter, before a deep voice shouts from the storeroom leading off from the counter, "There is someone at the counter! I'm not paying you to hide in the storeroom and read." Who they are shouting too is unclear, but they get a quick reply,

"Oh, but it would be so much better if you did."

That voice is familiar, so familiar, she can't not recognise it, not after she's heard it for the last two months, not after it has been teasing her for the last two months. Not here, please not here, not now. This is supposed to be relaxing, fun, a break from the stress, but with her here, it will be anything but.

Jinx walks out from the storeroom, her hair messily scraped back with a clip, a waist apron tied around her.

"Well, we don't live in a perfect world, get over yourself and socialise." The voice from the storeroom says, something playful in his voice.

"You know that's not my strong point," Jinx murmurs, not taking any notice of Vivienne and walking towards a coffee machine in the corner. "I'll be with you in a second, I just need to…" She hits the machine with the side of her hand, and it stutters to life. With what Vivienne assumes was a broken machine now working, Jinx finally looks forwards, still unaware of who is waiting for her.

Stopping dead, Jinx freezes and they both stare at each other, neither knowing what to say. After what feels like far too long, Jinx looks down at Vivienne's hands and says, "What are you doing here?" Vivienne has gotten new rings recently, they have little spinning daisies and buttercups on them, and at the time she thought they were cute. Now she doesn't, now they feel too cutesy, to bright.

"What does it look like?" Vivienne shoots back. 'What does it look like?' What does that even mean? Top grades for four years in high school, and yet the minute she's around Jinx, her entire grasp of knowledge slips from her. Of all the things she could have said, all the things that would have made sense and not sounded like a pathetic attempt at sarcasm, she said that.

"Do you really want me to answer that? Because it's a stupid question and therefore deserves a stupid answer." Jinx says, smirking and leaning forwards on the counter, her hands spread either side of her.

"No, no I don't." Vivienne sighs, trying to think of something to order, but every thought flees her mind when Jinx's eyes move up and down, lingering on her top. Vivienne blushes and takes a step back, suddenly aware of how tight her green polo top is, and how her jeans flare a little too much, revealing dirty converse with fraying laces. She loved this outfit this morning, why does she hate it now?

"Are you getting a drink or what?" Jinx's question brings her back to where she is, away from her embarrassment. Why should she be embarrassed, she looked nice, just because Jinx doesn't like it doesn't mean she can't, and Jinx clearly doesn't like it. Why would she have looked at it for so long if she wasn't judging it? Jinx's main goal in life is to be as judgemental as possible with as little effort as possible.

"I-um-well," Vivienne starts, her thoughts taking over her again. Her shoes feel too tight, her top is tucked at the back, her jeans are caught on her shoes, everyone can see it, she should've sorted it before she came here, she looks so stupid, everyone can see it, everyone is looking at her, everyone is whispering about her, everyone can see everything that is wrong, everyone…

"Jesus, don't hurt yourself, relax," Jinx says, beginning away from the counter. When Vivienne doesn't respond, she comes back, tapping her on the shoulder, "Carter? You alright?" Worry clouds her voice, but Vivienne steps back on instinct, pulling away from her and shaking her head.

"I'm fine, I'm fine." She mutters, more to herself than Jinx. Without questioning anything, Jinx walks away and starts making a drink in a tall cardboard cup. "I didn't order?" She didn't, did she? Maybe she'd mumbled something whilst she was trying to regain her thoughts, maybe she'd said something in the middle of it all.

"No, you didn't," Jinx says, as if there isn't anything unusual about what was going on. "Meeting someone?" she says, apparently eager to change the subject.

Not too eager to ask any more questions either, Vivienne follows her change of subject, looking towards the door. "What?" She looks at Jinx, then back to the door, then back to Jinx, a little confused. Why is everything so confusing with her?

"You're looking at that door like Jane Austen's about to walk through it, and while that would be interesting, it's highly unlikely, so, who is it? Someone from Classics? Your roommate maybe…?" Okay, this is teasing.

"You know for a fact that it isn't my roommate, and no, it's not someone from Classics."

"Then who is it?"

Vivienne starts to respond, but the door opens, and Ollie runs into the store, sprinting at his top speed down the narrow aisle.

"Vivi!" he squeals, wrapping his arms around her legs.

Jinx laughs behind the counter, pouring the drink she'd made into a cup, "Bit young for my taste, but…" She shrugs, eyeing Ollie. As if sensing her gaze, her brother turns to Jinx.

"You know my sister?" He says to her, and Jinx smiles at him.

"Yes, we go to college together."

Ollie giggles and looks between the two girls, "Are you her roommate?" He asks and Jinx crosses her arms, leaning on the counter,

"N-"

"Yes." Vivienne cuts her off, looking at her brother. "She's my roommate." Vivienne lies, turning to Jinx and nodding her head. Jinx sighs and returns to making Vivienne's drink, muttering something to herself as she does.

"But she just said no?" Ollie asks. Where the hell is her father, she needs to change the subject. She doesn't want Jinx to tell Ollie about Julian, it's going so well, she doesn't need her dad finding out and demanding to meet him, and no doubt, scare him off.

"What, no she didn't Ollie she said-"

"I was going to say," Jinx is beside her again, coffee in hand, "that she isn't *just* my roommate," What the hell is she doing, where was she going with this?

"Oooo?"

Jinx smirks, pulling a pen from her pocket and writing Vivienne's name on the cup. She places the cup on the counter, then bends down to Ollie's height, "She's my *girlfriend* as well." Vivienne glares at Jinx, not bothering to hide any of the anger she feels. What was that?! Why had she done that? What the *hell* is she doing? Ollie giggles and Vivienne just stares at Jinx. What the *hell* is she saying, and *why*?

Jinx is smirking, her eyes narrowed slightly, and Vivienne's fists clench at her sides. "Ollie, can you go get a table for us and Dad please." Vivienne smiles, hiding the anger in her voice. Her brother smiles, then nods and runs off to search the café. The minute he's out of earshot, she turns to Jinx.

"What the *hell* was that?" She demands, snatching her drink off the counter, her voice a whispered shout.

"Oh, just a little fun. I'm going to enjoy watching you explain to your brother and parents how we aren't dating."

"*Why?*"

"I'm bored, and you're incredibly amusing when you're angry." She smirks at her and leans against the counter, arms crossed.

"Oh you-" Vivienne starts, putting her cup down on the counter hard enough that some of her drink spills out of it.

"And you know what's going to make this even better?" Jinx interrupts her. What has Vivienne done to deserve this? She hasn't been rude to her, last time she checked they were just being normal, well, their normal.

"*What?*" Vivienne seethes.

"Watching you explain this to them." She points at the cup and Vivienne turns it towards her. On the side of the cup is her name, written in beautiful cursive, with hearts where the dots on both I's should've been.

"Oh you little-"

"Your father's here," she smiles, nodding her head towards him. Vivienne turns to see her dad standing in the doorway, snow sprinkles on the shoulders of his coat.

"How do you know-"

"Lucky guess." God, this girl is such a pain in the ass.

Her father makes his way towards her and Jinx smiles at him, not in her cocky way either, but in a genuine way Vivienne has never seen before. She is surprised she even knows how to smile, it's certainly out of character for her.

"Pumpkin," her Dad says, then sees Jinx. "Sorry, *Vivienne.*"

Jinx looks at her and raises her eyebrows, seemingly saying *So, which d'you think is worse, Pumpkin or Carter?*

"Pumpkin, cute." Jinx smiles, softening her gaze in an unnerving way as she turns to Vivienne. "I might start using it."

"What?" Her dad asks, raising his eyebrows and turning to Jinx. She smirks and turns back to her workstation, beginning a coffee that no one ordered. Fine, if she wants to play this game, Vivienne is about to show her who she's playing with.

"Yes, Dad, me and Jinx are dating."

Jinx drops a glass on the floor behind the counter and it shatters into tiny pieces, scattering across the floor in every direction.

"Jinx? As in…" he trails off, but nods his head towards the now crouched Jinx, who is picking up the larger pieces of glass with her hands.

"Yes, I'll explain it all at the table. You go find Ollie and I'll come join you in a second."

When her father walks away, Vivienne turns to Jinx. The larger pieces of the glass she'd dropped are now in the trash, but the smallest ones are still scattered on the floor. Jinx isn't moving to clean them up, instead, she is wrapping her hand in tissue paper from under the counter. Had she cut herself? Vivienne had wanted to say something cocky and leave, but instead the better part of her takes over.

"Do you not have a vacuum or something?"

Jinx murmurs something about how it had broken yesterday, and the brush is being used in the storeroom. Vivienne has half a mind to offer to help, but she is still pissed at what had happened with her dad and brother, so instead she says:

"Two can play at your little game, you know, and I am definitely *not* going to be the one who tells them we hate each other."

"Well, neither am I."

Jinx is back at the counter, the tissue still wrapped around her hand, covering the large slice down the middle. Vivienne is glad she can't see the blood, she doesn't need anything else going wrong today, and her reaction to blood isn't pleasant.

"Well, I guess you'll just have to pretend to like me for the next hour." Vivienne smirks, crossing her arms over her chest.

"You make it sound so easy," Jinx sighs, then turns away and walks into the storeroom.

*

That was...interesting. After the incident with Jinx, Vivienne had walked to her table, where her Dad and brother were sitting chatting together, and her Dad had sprung what felt like hundreds of questions on her, but the odd thing was, she didn't find it hard to answer them, it came almost naturally. He asked when they met, she told him in Classic's, he'd asked why she'd stopped hating her, Vivienne had told him it was because their high school rivalry was behind them, and when he'd asked how long they'd been seeing each other, Vivienne said it was just over a month. She knew she should've felt worse about lying to her Dad, but the whole time she couldn't bring herself to tell him the truth, he looked so happy. Every detail he got, every time she told him something new, his face lit up. He smiled like it was the best news in the world, like the reassurance that Vivienne wasn't alone let him feel at peace. He hadn't met Julian, and Vivienne wasn't sure she'd even told him she had friends, but now he knew she had Jinx, or at least pretended to. When she left with her Dad and brother, she'd waved to Jinx without thinking twice, and Jinx had waved *back*. She'd smiled and waved back, sitting up on the counter as she did so.

Once she'd walked her dad to his car, Vivienne began back to her college, refusing his offer for a lift because it was out of the way, and the roads were too icy the closer you got to the college.

Rummaging through her pockets, she pulls out her headphones and puts them on, searching for her phone. Not finding it in the pocket of her jeans, she starts frantically checking all the pockets in her bag, but it isn't anywhere. Panic rising within her, she crouches on the floor and begins to empty the contents of her bag onto the ground. Once the bag is empty and there is still no sign of it, she racks her memory, trying to remember when she'd last used it. She'd looked for directions to town this morning, used it to show her Dad pictures of the college, then she'd…

"Looking for this?" Worried out of her mind, Vivienne spins around, falling into the snow as she does so. "Good god, you really are clumsy." Jinx says, looking at Vivienne lying in the snow.

Much to Vivienne's surprise, Jinx bends down and reaches a hand out to her. Vivienne stares at her for a long while before Jinx pushes her hand out further.

"Are you going to take it or just sit in the snow getting your clothes wet?" She has a point; water is quickly seeping through her clothes. Extremely reluctantly, she grasps Jinx's hand and is hoisted up. When she is set back on her feet, Jinx waves Vivienne's phone in front of her.

"How did you get that?" Vivienne asks, grabbing for the phone.

"How do you think? You left it on the table at the shop." She pulls the phone further away and turns the screen to her. "You have a really guessable password, by the way."

"What? How did you-"

"You're lucky I found it, actually, I mean birthdays are everyone's first guess."

"What do you mean?" She's such a pain in the ass.

"For your password, obviously." Jinx steps away and types a code onto the screen, then shows it to her. She is on her phone; she has used her password to get into her phone.

"I'm surprised you know my birthday," Vivienne teases.

"It's hard to forget, you had an absurd party every year."

"I would hardly say they were absurd."

"You invited the *entire* class *every year.*" Jinx says, throwing the phone to Vivienne, who barely manages to catch it. She'd hated those parties, no one came, and even if they did, they talked to everyone but Vivienne. They always ended with her sitting up in her room, door shut against the noise, a book in hand.

"Not the *entire* class."

"Right, not the entire class, everyone *but* me." Jinx says, beginning the way she was going. She has a point, but it's not as if Jinx had ever wanted to come anyway, she'd hated Vivienne from the start, even if she'd never said so, she'd made it clear. If Vivienne had invited her, it would have given Jinx more reasons to make fun of her, she would use it to tease her every year, then not show up anyway.

Wanting to change the subject as she catches Jinx up and walks back, she asks "Are you going back to the college?"

"Yes, I assume you are as well," Jinx says, now staring at her own phone. Vivienne nods and looks around them. The town is nearly deserted because of the weather, and most shops are closed early.

They walked in silence for a long while, Vivienne's cold, shivering breath being the only thing heard. It's freezing enough in this ridiculous top, which isn't anywhere near thick enough, but now she is soaking wet too, cold water seeping through her jeans.

"Will you stop shivering so loudly?" Jinx mumbles, not taking her eyes off her phone. Seriously. Vivienne's *shivering* is disturbing her.

"Are you seriously *that* self-centred, the fact that I'm freezing is disturbing you?" Vivienne says, glaring at her and crossing her arms across her chest.

"It's not that it's disturbing me, it's-"

"It's what? What could possibly justify you finding my freezing annoying?"

"Nothing. Nothing justifies it, happy?" Jinx spits, her voice short, as if something has gotten to her. Vivienne goes silent and wraps her arms around herself tighter, not wanting to press any further, what she'd said had really gotten to Jinx, she doesn't normally snap like that. She gets annoyed, she i short and snarky, but she never snaps like that.

"Are you really that cold?" Jinx murmurs, barely audible.

"No, I'm just wrapping my arms around myself tightly for visual effect. Of course I'm *that* cold, I literally fell into snow."

Jinx sighs and takes off her coat, then her jumper, pulling it over her head and passing it to Vivienne. It is far too long for Vivienne, it's meant to be a long jumper anyway, but it looks more like a dress compared to what she usually wears.

"Put this on and stop shivering,"

"What? Why?" Why is she giving Vivienne her jumper, that's not something Vivienne has ever seen her do for anyone, never mind her.

"Well because your shivering is *extremely* annoying, and who am I going to compete with in Classic's if you get the flu or something?"

So that's why; she doesn't want to lose her competition in class.

"Well, if that's why, then I won't take it." Vivienne turns away from Jinx and crosses her arms tighter against her chest, it really is getting cold. They walk in silence again, but Jinx doesn't put her jumper back on, only her coat. After a long time of shivering, Vivienne reluctantly puts her hand out to Jinx and she gives her the jumper.

"Thanks," Vivienne murmurs, pushing it over her head and pulling the sleeves over her hands. It is far too long for her, it fits her shape fine, but Jinx is much taller than her, so the knitted jumper covers most of her upper body. It's soft, comfortable and smells like cinnamon, so Vivienne soon finds herself wrapping it tighter around her, the deep olive sleeves pulling against her arms.

"Plus, what kind of a *girlfriend* would I be if I didn't give you my jumper?" Jinx smirks, looking at Vivienne.

"You're insufferable." Vivienne sighs.

"I know." She smiles.

*

When they arrived back at the dorms Vivienne begins to take it off to give back, but when it's over her head and out the way, Jinx is gone. Her clothes still not fully dry, she puts the jumper back on, slowly making her way towards her dorm.

Chapter 6 – Jinx

─ · ˳° ☆: *.☽ .* :☆° . ─

    Returning to her room, Jinx wraps her coat tighter around her to block out the cold. She shouldn't have given Vivienne that jumper, she should have let her shiver, but it was *so* annoying. Not only that, but she also knows exactly how that cold feels, she knows how not being able to stop it feels like you are losing control. There have been countless times when she's felt that exact feeling. When her mum had gambled away the money for bills or used the last of their savings at clubs and bars. Countless winters when Jinx had slept wrapped in blankets and coats just to keep from freezing, encased in layer after layer in a desperate attempt to keep warm. Every time Vivienne had shivered, every time she'd wrapped her arms around herself, just reminded Jinx of the cold, of memories she'd tried her hardest to push far into the back of her mind, to erase from her thoughts, to leave behind and never return too.

    The snow is coming down with incredible force, making it impossible to see anything as she blindly makes her way towards her dorm. It is halfway across campus; she doesn't even know why she'd bothered walking with Vivienne when walking on her own would have been quicker.

    Giving up with walking and breaking into a run, she tries to avoid benches and trash cans that appear out of nowhere as the snow thickens. How are classes still on in this kind of weather? It is hardly safe. Ice has frozen over the paths, the wind is picking up, and the snow just keeps getting heavier, coming down with such intensity that it is practically blocking Jinx's ability to see.

    Deciding running isn't the best idea, she slows into a fast walk, flicking the collar of her coat up against the wind. Despite her speed, neither running nor walking would've stopped her from catching her ankle on the side of a bench she didn't see, slipping in the ice nearby and losing all balance, crashing onto the ground with enough strength that her wrist cracks on impact with the concrete, pain bursting in her arm, searing through up to her elbow and making her head spin, her breath cutting short.

"Are you okay?" Someone shouts through the storm around her, but anything else that's said is lost to the wind. She couldn't see who was talking to her, and she had half a mind to tells them to leave her alone, she really doesn't need someone chatting to her right now, but when the tall boy from Classics appears in front of her, crouched down, she can't think of anything to say. This is the one that Vivienne hangs around with, the one who practically held her back in lessons when Vivienne looked ready to slap Jinx, the one who brought her coffee, this is her roommate. This is the boy Vivienne didn't want her dad to meet, the boy she'd lied about to the point where it was barely believable, the reason Vivienne's little brother thought Jinx and Vivienne were roommates. This is the worst boy she could have run into in this situation.

"Jinx?" he shouts, tilting his head to the side. Even shouting, it is hard to hear him, but that doesn't make him any less annoying.

"Surprisingly no," Jinx shouts back, sitting back onto her legs and holding her wrist in her hand on instinct.

"What?" he says, leaning forward. The wind is making this worse than it already is, she doesn't feel like talking to him, never mind repeating it.

"Nothing." Jinx sighs, shaking her head.

"Are you okay?" He gestures to her wrist, which is slowly beginning to swell, a large bruise forming.

"I'm fine." Jinx stands up, but drops back to her knees, her head spinning. Had she hit that on her way down?

"You don't look fine." The boy looks at her, taking in every detail about her. "Your forehead is bleeding, and your wrist is swollen." Her forehead is bleeding? When had that happened, surely, she would've noticed it, felt it? Apparently not.

Noticing her confusion, the boy's face draws with concern. "Can you not feel your head?"

Jinx shakes her head, admitting defeat. She knows he's a medical major, and his help is better than none, especially considering she doesn't plan on going to the hospital, she can't afford it, not for something as small as this.

"That's not good," he mutters, "it must mean your wrist is pretty bad." Jinx stands up, and he follows, still shouting over the snow. "You need to get that checked out at the hospital."

Jinx shakes her head again, not letting go of her wrist. Now he's mentioned it, Jinx can feel the trickle of something warm down the side of her head, dipping into her temple before running down her cheek. She can't afford to go to the hospital, not right now, and even if she can, there is no way she is getting there in this weather.

"Jinx, you have to…" The boy starts, but he drifts off when she shakes her head again.

"I'm fine, it's just a bruise."

"If it was just a bruise you would be able to feel your head." He steps closer to her, gesturing to her wrist, which has swollen more during their conversation. "The pain in your wrist is distracting you from the damage to your head, which means it must be bad, otherwise you would be able to feel both. It's a distraction wound, and if it hurts that much you have done something pretty severe to it."

Why isn't he dropping this? He doesn't even like her, she is pretty sure he hates her as much as Vivienne does, and yet here he is insisting she go to the hospital for a bruise on her wrist. She would've said he seems worried about her, but that can't be true, they know nothing about each other, they've never talked, and Vivienne has spent the last month feeding him lies about her, no doubt.

"It's not that bad, really, it's just a bruise." Jinx insists again, stepping away from him and looking around, trying to find which way her dorm is.

"Why are you so stubborn?" He shouts, "If you won't go to the hospital, at least let me check it out. If it's broken, it could heal weirdly and permanently ruin your wrist if you don't wrap it."

Her wrist is throbbing in her hand, nausea pulling at her, this couldn't be the worst idea, besides, it's either go with him or try and fix this on her own. Reluctantly, Jinx sighs and nods. "Fine. But only if you shut up."

He laughs and shakes his head. "Do you even try to make yourself liked?" He says, smiling as if it is a joke.

"Why bother, if people don't like me as I am, I'm not going to lie to them and pretend I'm something I'm not." Jinx says, following as he gestures for him to follow her.

"What?" he says, looking over his shoulder.

"Nothing."

*

Forcing the door open with his shoulder, the boy holds it for Jinx, expecting her to walk through. She doesn't, instead she waits and nods for him to go first, which he does, after a long moment of confusion. His dorm building is warmer than Jinx's, the main room is, anyway, and all the chairs surrounding them are empty. Everyone has no doubt cleared out, retreating to their dorms to avoid the weather, so there is no one around to see her follow him up the stairs, her wrist resting lightly in her hand, the throbbing still prominent. Even the stairs seem nicer than the ones in her building, these are carpeted and have a polished wooden banister, meanwhile hers is rusty metal that no one dares touch out of fear of getting tetanus.

He begins down the corridor of the third floor and towards a door in the far end, which is shut, its wooden frame facing them. Some of the doors on the corridor hang slightly ajar, people moving in and out of one another's, trading textbooks and notes, headphones and books, cups and plates full of food. It seems like a community up here, as if the corridor is just a corridor in a big family house, not a dorm building full of teenagers.

The boy, however sociable he is, walks past all this. He doesn't say hello or smile at any of them, he doesn't even return the waves that half of them send his way, he just keeps on track towards the dorm, his head bowed slightly. When they reach the door, Jinx leans against the doorframe and tilts her head to the side,

"For a seemingly friendly guy, you blatantly ignored them." She observes, kicking her foot behind her leg and watching as the boy fiddles with the key in the door.

"Those particular people aren't the best," he mutters, smirking to himself, "although you'd probably like them."

Confused, Jinx stands up straighter, "Why?"

"Well, you have something in common," he pulls the key out of the door and turns the knob until it clicks, "You all love to make fun of Vivienne." He rolls his eyes as Jinx looks behind her, glaring at the now empty corridor.

"What do you mean? What do they do?" She asks, stepping forwards, her wrist fading into the back of her mind.

"Nothing," he sighs, opening the door and walking in.

His and Vivienne's room is warmer than the corridor, and Jinx finds herself shaking off her coat, careful as it travels over her wrist. Even the light weight of the fabric on the injury makes her inhale sharply, though the boy doesn't seem to notice; he is too preoccupied routing through his own cupboards, cursing under his breath.

"Are you sure this is your dorm? You don't seem to know your way around it." Jinx smirks, sitting on the edge of the small counter, where plates are lying wet in a rack.

"Vivienne likes to rearrange it when she's bored, it's very annoying." He opens another door, sticking his head in, then closes it loudly behind him. "Give me a sec, I just need to…" He trails off, walking into his own room, leaving Jinx alone on the counter of the kitchen. She presumes Vivienne isn't here, her bedroom door is open, and no one is in there, and their main room is empty, with the exception of Jinx. It is a nice little dorm, every part of it looks lived in, decorated. The far wall has two bookshelves on it, books piled disorderly on the shelves, collapsing against one another, and in between them is a tall plant, the leaves of which are steadily growing brown. Lilly would have a fit over that, she loves plants with all her heart, when she isn't painting or begrudgingly studying, she is caring for the absurd amount of plants in her room.

A small couch takes up the centre of the room, blankets strewn on it, a half open book left on the arm. Nearby is a small coffee table and an armchair, where even more blankets are folded, slightly neater. The crackling of a candle draws her attention to the nearest corner to Jinx, where a small cabinet sits, a candle burning away in its glass casing on top of yet another pile of books. Ignoring the fire hazard aspect of it, Jinx smiles slightly, it's cute, homely.

This dorm is nothing like hers. Her room, of course, is decorated to her own taste, but her actual dorm room is barren. She stuck up a few posters when she moved in, but the walls are practically bare aside from those, and she doesn't have much furniture. The couch she does have is always littered with papers, coated in inky scribbles of notes, novel ideas, and the books that aren't in her room are simply piled on the floor, forming tall stacks in the corners that nearly reach her hips. Furniture isn't at the top of her priority list, and definitely isn't in her budget, so she manages with what she has.

"Julian, I-" Vivienne's voice draws Jinx's attention from the room and her head spins to the door, where Vivienne is standing, snow coating her hair, cheeks red from the cold. "You've got to be kidding me," she mutters, stepping fully into the room and shutting the door behind her. She is wearing *Jinx's* jumper, still.

"Relax, Carter, I'm not here for you." Jinx mutters, her injured wrist shuffling back behind her, out of sight but hardly out of mind, the pain sharpens with every movement.

"Then who are you here for?" Vivienne sighs, dropping the bag she'd been holding on the counter and pulling out two cardboard boxes. The smell of Chinese wafts towards Jinx, hunger pulling at her.

"Found it!" The boy, Julian as Vivienne says, shouts from his dorm, and both Vivienne and Jinx turn to look at him. He walks out of the door, but freezes when he sees Vivienne, a first aid kit in his hand.

"What do you need a first aid kit for?" Vivienne says, turning back to Jinx. This time she actually looks at her, and something similar to fear covers her face when she sees the blood on her forehead, something she clearly hadn't noticed before.

"What happened?" she asks, stepping forwards slightly, her hands cast to her sides.

Jinx shrugs as she uses her hand to pull her wrist forward, it has gone limp enough that it isn't moving on its own without immense pain. Vivienne inhales sharply through her teeth as she lays eyes on the now blackening bruise on Jinx's wrist, which has swelled to twice the size it usually is.

"What happened?" she repeats, stepping closer again and looking at her wrist with scrutinising intensity.

Jinx laughs as Vivienne looks up at her again, concern written across her face. "Careful, Carter, you're bordering caring about me."

She doesn't know why she said that, it wasn't called for, but it's the only thing she can think to say. The way Vivienne looks at her feels unnatural, and part of Jinx likes it, part of her likes the concern, but the other part of her is scared of it, or more importantly, scared of how nice it feels. So all she can do is be herself. Be sarcastic, be cold, keep everyone at a distance, keep feelings to a minimum, the less she feels, the less she'll miss when it ends.

"Oh, shut up, now is not the time to be sarcastic." She says, bending down and running her fingers over the bruise, casting a glance to Julian. "What are you going to do?" she asks, and Jinx ignores the sensation of Vivienne's skin on hers, the warmth it brings, the pain it doesn't summon.

"She refuses to go to a hospital," Julian sighs, shaking his head, "so I'm going to use some numbing cream and painkillers to lower the pain, wrap it, and put a support in there. It looks broken, but it could just be a bad sprain."

Vivienne looks back at Jinx's wrist, lifting it slightly and looking underneath it. Jinx pulls back slightly, pain rushing through her, and Vivienne hesitates, but doesn't stop.

"Sorry," she mutters, examining Jinx's wrist further. Is she aware that she isn't the medicine major, because Jinx doesn't think she is.

"Carter, what are you doing?" Jinx asks, looking at Julian with raised eyebrows. When Vivienne doesn't answer, Julian looks at her, then Jinx.

"When she gets really bored, and she has nothing to read, she steals my medical journals. Only the fun ones," he smiles, "about stuff like this. Then she likes to brag about how she knows how to identify breakpoints and fractures, despite me telling her that it takes years of practice to properly-"

"There." Vivienne states, holding Jinx's wrist up vertically. The motion sends white hot pain through Jinx, and she moves backwards, hitting her head on the cabinet, cursing under her breath. She is still sitting on the counter, and the cabinet door had a sharp corner, but Vivienne doesn't seem to notice, she is simply triumphantly pointing to Jinx's wrist.

"Oh you've got to be kidding me," Julian mutters, bending to look at Jinx's wrist. At this point, Jinx feels more like an experiment than a person, but that doesn't stop her from being curious at what Vivienne is pointing at. Leaning forwards, she cranes her neck to look at the inside of her own wrist.

"What is it?" she asks, not sure what is so interesting. Her wrist is purplish black around the centre, and the swelling only subsides at one point, revealing a jutting point of her skin, where something seems to be pushing outwards.

"It's a deformity, which would hint to a break, not a sprain." Vivienne says, letting go of Jinx's wrist and stepping back triumphantly. "Am I right?" she asks Julian, whose eyebrows are raised.

"You know," he says, returning to the first aid kit and pulling out a packet of bandages and a similarly coloured wrist splint. "Your talents are wasted on history."

Vivienne laughs and shakes her head, "I could never go into medicine, blood freaks me out too much." That explains her initial fear when she'd seen Jinx then, it wasn't worry after all. For some reason, while it should reassure Jinx, instead it leaves her feeling a little empty, the thought of someone being worried for her is something she dearly misses, no matter how much she tries to deny it.

"Why do you just have a wrist splint?" Jinx asks, as Julian pulls a vial out of the bag, taking the lid off it and handing it to Vivienne. She looks at it for a while, but Julian doesn't instruct her on what to do, so she merely stands there, clearly confused.

"I've wanted to be a doctor since I was a kid, and like any kid with similar aspirations, I went through a phase of bandaging my stuffed animals. My parents got me the splint so I'd stop tearing through the bandage so fast, and I kept it just in case."

"It's come in pretty handy, then." Jinx mutters, looking at her wrist again, then to the small tub in Vivienne's hand. Noticing her gaze, Vivienne blushes slightly, any of the former cockiness she'd experienced from being right gone. "What's that?" Jinx gestures with her good hand to the tub.

"That's numbing cream." He says it as if it's a normal thing to have, clearly not aware that Jinx has never met anyone who's owned it before. "And Vivienne is supposed to be putting it on you, while I find the pins." He bends down to look at the kit closer, and Jinx turns to Vivienne, smirking slightly.

"Come now, Carter, you were just poking and prodding me like an experiment, is relieving my pain too big of a task?" Jinx teases, but she's moved too much and the pain in her wrist makes her flinch. Vivienne sighs and takes her hand again, gentler than before.

"Why are you always so cocky?" She asks, looking at the instructions on the cream, still holding Jinx's hand aloft. Her hands are warm, warmer than Jinx's, but Jinx tries not to pay attention, tries not to notice the creeping heat along her neck.

"Why do you blush so much?" Jinx retorts, twitching her head forwards and smirking as Vivienne's face flushes pink, colouring her ears and decorating her cheekbones.

"Why do you think so highly of yourself?" Vivienne says, her eyes focused on Jinx, the blush fading ever so slightly.

"Why don't you?" Jinx leans closer, watching the red trailing up Vivienne's neck, but she doesn't move away. Instead, she leans in too, close enough that Jinx can see the flecks of snow on her eyelashes, and the water making the end of her nose shine.

"I have no reason to." she breathes, smirking slightly. Jinx ignores the flush on the back of her neck, the feeling of Vivienne's breath so close, focusing on her reply.

"And neither do I."

"I find that hard to believe, you walk around like you think you're better than everyone else, the way you talk is automatically belittling, you clearly see yourself as better than others." Vivienne mutters.

"Or maybe that's merely your judgement, your idea, *your* insecurity playing with *your* mind."

"Ahem," Julian coughs, and they both turn to him, not moving apart. He looks between the two of them, confusion written across his features, before shaking his head and carrying on, "Have you put the cream on?"

"Yes," Vivienne says, letting go of Jinx's hand and removing her other hand, which Jinx hadn't noticed had been applying the cream.

"Good. I'll put the splint on, then you can go."

Chapter 7 – Vivienne

°•. ✿ .•°°•. ✿ .•°°•. ✿ .•°

    Classics has become a class Vivienne dreads, despite the fact that it is supposed to be relaxing, fun, an excuse to talk about books. Now, when she thinks about it, all she can think about is Jinx, and the multitude of ways she is bound to humiliate Vivienne that day.
    Trudging through her room and pulling on her clothes, she sighs as she grabs her phone, bag, and copy of *Pride and Prejudice*. Last night keeps playing on her mind, images plaguing Vivienne's thoughts, the bruise on Jinx's wrist, the blood on her forehead, the way she flinched when Vivienne pressed on her wrist, how she kept sighing, her breath restricted. When Julian put the splint on her wrist, Jinx had shuffled back on the counter, her fist balled at her side, knuckles whitening, and Vivienne worried for her. For a short, dangerous second she'd stopped hating her, stopped seeing the worst, stopped reminding herself of what Jinx had said, what she'd done, and for a second, Vivienne wanted to help her, to comfort her. But she didn't. She didn't, and part of her felt selfish that she hadn't. No matter how calm Jinx looks, how cold her expression is, no matter how much she pretends to not feel it, Vivienne can still see her fist, hidden behind her back, tension steadily growing, pulling at her skin.
    The door to her room is already open, she hadn't shut it last night, and Julian hadn't appeared too either. When she enters the living area, she finds that Julian has already left. He must've had a class earlier, but there isn't any sign of him having left at all, his bag is still here, books toppling out. Deciding not to

overthink it, Vivienne grabs her coat from behind the door and leaves, not bothering to lock her door. No one comes near her room anyway, nothing valuable is ever left in there, her laptop is always on her, as is Julian's, and neither are ever without their phones, so all that is left in there are books, which she can guarantee no one on the floor will be eager to steal. The corridor, thank god, is empty, most people have left for classes, and those who haven't are studying or sleeping. Her building is never busy at this time in the morning, the other students clearly aren't morning people, and she doesn't expect them to be. From what she hears, they stay up till early hours of the morning, swapping dorms, having movie nights, or just hanging around in each other's company, and when they do sleep, it's never all at once, some will come and go at all hours, it really is peculiar.

  The campus is just as empty as her building. Her class is set at an unusual time, it starts later than most but lasts two hours, meaning a large portion of students are in class while she is walking, and she is in class while they swap over. She doesn't mind it much, less people mean it will be easier to get to the literature building, as people won't be queuing for coffee or running past her with their arms full of books, blocking the paths.

  Reaching the literature building with time to spare, Vivienne slows her previously fast pace to a relaxed one, stopping occasionally to look at the amazing architecture that surrounds her. She's been in this building countless times over the last few months, but no matter how many times she looks at it, the overwhelming beauty still astounds her. It is by far the oldest building on campus, and the most glamorous, with subtle carved statues of marble and wooden bookcases that look older than her, long, wooden stars with a carpet running down the middle, polished bannisters and delicate fireplaces. It truly is her favourite place to be, and she wishes she had more than one here.

While Vivienne could've admired the architecture for hours, a quick glance at her phone tells her that she needs to get to class, it is nearly 9:00, and she doesn't want to be late, not when it will give Jinx another excuse to tease her.

*

The classroom is empty when Vivienne arrives, but she takes her seat anyway, wondering why no one else is here. She is always early, but even then, people are normally still here, although it is mainly Jinx and her friend, Lilly or something. She can't think of any reason why anyone would be late, it is now 9:10 and class should've started ten minutes ago, even Professor Halloway isn't here.

Opening her copy of *Pride and Prejudice*, Vivienne sits back into her seat and starts to read, relaxing a little. She is tempted to put in her headphones, but she decides not to, if the Professor comes in and starts talking, Vivienne doubts that she will be happy about a student sitting at the front not listening, and Vivienne doubts she will notice.

Without her headphones in, she can hear the door behind her opening and shutting, followed by two muffled voices. Assuming it is some students she doesn't know, Vivienne doesn't pay them much mind, but as they get closer, pieces of their conversation become more audible.

"I still don't understand why you won't tell me what happened?" That's Lilly, Jinx's friend, which means-

"Because it's not important," Jinx sighs, and Vivienne turns slightly to see them both walking down the aisle, towards the front row.

"You broke your wrist! Explain to me how that isn't important." Lilly says, her voice raising slightly. She seems so enthusiastic about everything, even in class she seems excited and wild about the smallest of things, it makes Vivienne wonder why she is hanging out with Jinx of all people, someone who definitely does not match her enthusiasm. Vivienne has never seen Jinx enthusiastic about anything, in fact, she's never seen her show anything other than cool calm around everyone.

"Knowing how it happened isn't important, and you can clearly see it's sorted, and that's all you need to know." Jinx says, clearly wanting to change the subject.

"But-" Lilly doesn't drop it, and without thinking, Vivienne sits up, clearing her throat and closing her book slightly. Lilly stops her question and turns to Vivienne, who is sitting alone on the aisle of the front row, her stuff on the chair next to her. Julian still isn't here. Lilly doesn't speak, but smiles at Vivienne before sitting down, Jinx sitting beside her, also on the aisle seat.

"I see your little puppy isn't following you around?" Jinx says, letting her legs fall to either side and relaxing into her chair. "Or is he getting you a coffee like a good boy?"

Lilly shakes her head, hiding her smile behind her hand and turning her attention to her satchel.

"He's…" Vivienne tries to think of where he could be, but her mind empties, "I don't know where he is." She sighs, looking at the door.

"I saw him going into my building earlier," Lilly pipes up, offering Vivienne a smile. Jinx doesn't react, she merely pulls out her phone and starts scrolling, seemingly disinterested in the conversation.

"Really? Did you see what he was doing?" Vivienne sits up straighter, what was he doing in Lilly's building? All his friends from hockey live on the bottom floor of their building, and he always complains that he doesn't have any friends in his classes. Who was he seeing?

"He was dropping some books off, I think, to a boy on the bottom floor. He's really sweet, quiet though. I'm surprised he is friends with someone like Julian." Lilly says, looking to the door, then back to Vivienne.

"Why?" Vivienne asks.

"Well, I know he's into guys more than he is girls, and he always gets quiet around them. During the building mixer, he sat at the back of the room and only started talking to me because... well, I don't actually know, but he did." Lilly sits forwards, so Vivienne can see most of her. She is wearing cute jeans with patches of material sewn into them, and rips on the thighs and knees, with a green, long-sleeved top, that covers just past her wrists.

Vivienne smirks slightly, then it grows steadily into a full smile. Julian never lends anyone his books, he says he doesn't want them ruined and doesn't trust anyone with them, even Vivienne, but if he is giving this boy his books...

"Why are you smirking?" Lilly asks, raising her eyebrows and smiling slightly. "Are he and Julian...?" she drifts off and Vivienne outright laughs, shaking her head and thinking through it.

"Julian *never* lends anyone his books, not even me, so this boy really must be something." Is all she says, leaning back in her chair again, smiling to herself. This is really cute; no wonder Julian had left so early this morning and forgotten his bag. Vivienne is looking forward to interrogating him about this later and teasing him for the foreseeable future.

The rest of the class passes pretty smoothly after that, Professor Halloway comes in shortly after Vivienne and Lilly's chat, explaining that she had sent out an email to reschedule for later, as the traffic was horrific on the way in because of the weather. Lilly, Vivienne, and Jinx clearly hadn't gotten said email, which explains why they were sitting in the empty room for so long, but Julian had, and showed up at the recommended time. By the time he sits down, Professor Halloway has already begun to speak, so Vivienne doesn't get the chance to tease him, but she will, nothing can make her forget, it is far too fun.

"For the next few months, we will be doing a group project," The Professor says from her stance in the middle of the room. The empty space where she stands looks smaller today, and it is only when she mentions the group projects that Vivienne notices why. There are tables around the edge, waiting for people to swarm around them. "It's a debate-based exam and will make up a large portion of your performance in my class. Before you complain and start saying 'but we didn't take debate', it won't be on anything proper, just some literature. The board is bored of essay after essay, and while I find them perfectly effective, they've decided that they are going to give you an essay question as a debate topic instead." She sighs and shakes her head, looking through some papers on her desk, "You will each be required to pick a piece of literature and answer the question 'How are women perceived in this piece, and why do you think that is?'" She reads off a piece of paper, before folding it up and putting it back on her desk.

"What d'you reckon the teams will be?" Julian whispers, leaning in so his voice is quiet.

"It's a debate, so it will have to be more than two, maybe she'll let us pick." Vivienne says hopefully, trying not to think about the catastrophic combinations Professor Halloway could force on her. She could split her and Julian, or merge her and Jinx, or do both. Either would be horrible.

"Your teams will be your rows," The Professor carries on, looking around the room. Her eyes linger on the front row, where Julian, Vivienne, Lilly and Jinx all sit, each as worried as the next. "The teams are a minimum of four, you guys will have to join each other."

Vivienne freezes where she is, her heart sinking into her stomach.

"Professor-" Jinx starts, sitting up abruptly, Lilly looking shocked beside her.

"Remember when you promised me your rivalry wouldn't get in the way of your work, Miss Keller?" Professor Halloway says, without turning from her desk.

Vivienne sighs and shrinks into her seat.

This is a nightmare; this is a genuine nightmare. Her, work on a project *with* Jinx? She must stop it. She's grown use to having her in this class and has tolerated running into her on random occasions. Even what happened at the coffee shop was tolerable, as she doesn't see her dad much anyway, but this. This is weeks and weeks of working together, meeting up and structuring debates until the *end of the semester.* This is going to be hell.

Neither of them move; they both sit deathly still in their seats, leaving the civility to their friends. Julian moves from next to her and walks towards Lilly. They turn away from the pair on the chairs and begin a hushed conversation with one another, while Jinx and Vivienne just sit there in silence. After their discussion, Julian and Lilly turn back to them and Julian speaks,

"Are you two going to be civil or are me and Lilly going to have to do all the work?"

"What book are we doing?" Jinx says, not answering Julian's question. No one speaks, but Vivienne can tell Julian and the girl, Lilly, are racking their brains for a book that both Vivienne and Jinx will agree on.

"What about a Shakespeare? There are tons of female characters we could choose from with him, and I doubt many people will do his pieces because he's an English writer." Julian suggests, looking mainly at Jinx.

"Shakespeare wrote plays, not books." She states, sighing. "There are book versions of his plays, and the idea is the same." Lilly says.

"Let's ask the Professor if it counts, Miss Halloway!" Julian calls and the Professor begins towards them. Once she has stopped at the edge of her platform, Julian looks up at her, "Can we do Shakespeare for this assignment, or is it strictly book-based literature?"

Miss Halloway laughs and looks at the group, "Shakespeare is fine, as long as you read the script properly in book form. I have a few spares if you need them."

"That would be much appreciated," Lilly chirps in.

"Hang on, have we decided on Shakespeare then?" Vivienne asks, glancing towards Jinx.

"I don't mind what we do, but if it's something romance based like *Romeo and Juliet,* I want to take the Con debate," Jinx sighs, standing and joining the others near Miss Halloway.

"How surprising," Vivienne scoffs, looking towards Jinx, "I guess we're good to go, then, I like Shakespeare anyway."

"Great, I'll get you the copies of *Romeo and Juliet* now, and you can keep them."

When the Professor leaves to get the copies of the book, Jinx jumps up and sits on the platform. Lilly joins her, but Julian comes to sit next to Vivienne again. It is quickly back to silence until Professor arrives with the books, saying she hopes the debate goes well and that she has particular hope in them. Once they all have a copy, they sit in their silence until Lilly finally asks, "So, if Jinx is doing the Con debate, who wants to take the Pro?"

Vivienne sticks her hand up and says, "I'll do it, then you two can choose which side you want to take as backups."

Lilly nods and looks at Julian, "Do you have a preferred opinion on *Romeo and Juliet,* or can I pick first?"

Julian looks around at the three of them, then looks directly at Lilly, "I'd like to be on the Con side in all honesty, but if you want to…" That shocks Vivienne if she is entirely honest, Julian has chosen to work with *Jinx,* not her. Although, in his defence, he is always complaining about the Romance Genre in general. Vivienne, being a fan of cheesy rom coms, is always watching something romance centred, and whenever Julian walks in, he makes a gagging noise that is closely followed by an 'ouch', a product of Vivienne's retaliation pillow.

"That's fine, actually, because I want to take the Pro." Lilly smiles, looking at Vivienne. *That* is surprising, Vivienne thought she was as anti-romance as Jinx, but clearly not.

"Well, that was sorted easy enough, now what about meet up times?" Vivienne says, smiling slightly, maybe this won't be as bad as she thought.

"I can do any day, if you exclude classes, apart from Thursday nights, I have dinner with my brother then." Lilly says, pulling out her phone and typing something in.

"That's convenient, I have hockey practice on Thursday nights." Julian chimes in, "Should we make a group chat or something to arrange times?"

"Good idea, do you all have Instagram?" Lilly says, looking at Vivienne, then Jinx.

"Yes." Vivienne nods, and Julian joins her,

"Yes." He mumbles, already opening his phone.

"No." Jinx says, and everyone turns to her, "I don't have WhatsApp either." They all stare at her in disbelief until Julian asks,

"What *do* you have that can be used for communication?"

"Just the normal message that comes with iPhones." she states, holding up her phone to the group. Wow, she has next to no apps, just Spotify, Pinterest, and her messaging app – along with the basics as well.

"Well, I have a different phone to you, so that won't work." Julian says, looking at his phone, "Can you not set up an Instagram account?"

"W-" Jinx starts, but she is cut off.

"She can, I'll help her later and add her to the group. You add Vivienne and me, then I'll add Jinx." Lilly says, giving Jinx a 'stop talking' look as she does so. This girl has nerves, Vivienne has never seen someone look at Jinx like that and get away with it, but apparently this girl is different, because all Jinx does is shrug.

Once Julian adds them all to a group, Jinx claiming she'll join later, class ends, and they begin to leave. Jinx and Lilly go first, Lilly taking Jinx's phone as she does so, no doubt to catch Jinx up on modern communication.

As they're leaving, Julian stops by Miss Halloway's desk to ask her some questions about the debate times and statements, all the stuff they'd forgotten to ask her as a group earlier, and when he comes back he's beaming. "Considering you're the one who needs this class the least out of all of us," Vivienne starts, pushing the class door open for Julian, "you're the one who seems to care the most about it."

Julian sighs and turns behind him, checking The Professor is out of ear shot, "I don't really care about the class, I just love Shakespeare *so much*, even if we are doing one of his sappy romances. If we were doing something like *Wuthering Heights* or *Of Mice and Men*, I wouldn't be anywhere near as interested, and…" He trails off and tilts his head down.

"And what?" Vivienne pushes.

"Well, you and Jinx were a bit preoccupied glaring at each other to sort any of it out, so me and Lilly figured we'd take charge." That is fair enough.

"That girl, Lilly, have you met her before, or talked to her about something that wasn't Shakespeare today?" Vivienne asks, and Julian shakes his head, wrapping his coat around him tighter as they walk through the doors, out into the cold,

"Why?" he asks.

"It's just that she's not like Jinx, not at all. The only thing they have in common is this class, so I don't really understand why they're friends…" she shrugs and pulls her phone from her pocket. The Instagram group already has five notifications, so Vivienne opens it to see what is going on.

> Lilly: 11:27am
> *Hi guys I have added Jinx! She has no idea how this works though so be patient…*

> Jinx: 11:28am
> *Lilly, you're making it sound like I'm a five-year-old girl who's playing with plastic pots. I think I can figure out how texting works, I'm not that socially lacking.*

> Lilly: 11:28am
> *You do realise your use of proper punctuation isn't helping your case right?*

> Jinx: 11:29am
> *Just because we're texting doesn't mean we should drop grammar, it's what gives texts' tone.*

Lilly: 11:29am
You sound like the professor.

Julian peers over her shoulder and laughs, pulling his phone out and opening the thread. He types something up and shows it to Vivienne, who laughs and clicks send for him.

Julian: 11:29am
Can you too take this bickering to a private thread, your making my phone vibrate like crazy

He turns his phone off and puts it in his coat pocket, breathing deeply as he does so. It's slowly getting colder as they approach Christmas, and Vivienne's closet is lacking the clothes to facilitate the weather. While her clothes are mainly pants, which are perfect, she doesn't have many jumpers or coats. Well, she has two jumpers, the one she is wearing now and Jinx's jumper, which she still hasn't given back yet, and doesn't feel like doing so anytime soon. If she ignores the fact that it's Jinx's, it is the best jumper she's ever worn. It is so comfortable, and smells amazing, like sweet cinnamon. In fact, she'd accidentally fallen asleep in it last night, nearly going to class with it on this morning. But it's Jinx's, and she will have to give it back at some point, she knows that. Just, not now.

"Do you have a class?" Vivienne asks Julian as they walk down an ice-covered path.

"Yes, but not until 11:30."

"And where is your class?" Vivienne asks, trying to subtly make him realise that he'll be late if he doesn't leave now.

"In the main building, it's only a five-minute walk so I can walk with you for a bit."

"Julian, as much as I do enjoy your company, Classics was rescheduled for later, remember? Which makes it…" he really is slow sometimes, no matter how smart he is.

"Oh, I have to go!" He shouts, running down the path towards a building in front of them.

Vivienne chuckles to herself and turns back, beginning towards the library. This is the day she only has three classes – one in the morning, *Classical Literature,* and two others in the afternoon, both history based – so she is extremely lacking in something to do. Half tempted to go back to her dorm, she stands still and looks out onto the campus. This is a nice-looking college any day, but when it is coated in snow it just looks magical. Almost all the buildings are old and brick, making the whole area seem like it is better placed centuries ago, and tall, elegant trees line the pathways, beautiful even without their leaves. Closing her eyes, Vivienne breathes in the crisp air around her, letting the chill seep through her jumper and dance on her skin, it felt amazing.

"Watch out!"

Completely absorbed in her own thoughts, Vivienne doesn't get a chance to react before a football hits her in the middle of her face, sending bursts of pain through her nose. She's knocked backwards and onto the floor, pain spurring through her legs and wrists as well. Despite the shock, her eyes still haven't opened, the pain in her nose is preoccupying her. She hears distant apologies and footsteps running towards her from multiple directions, but that does nothing to comfort her, instead, it further raises her panic. She has to get out of here, she can't have a scene, she can't handle people crowding around her, it only makes things worse.

"A-are you ok?" She opens her eyes and finds a short, well built, boy standing in front of her. Trying to nod, she brings her hand to her nose, only to have sharp, white hot bursts of pain greet her. Pulling her hand away, she stares at it in horror. Crimson blood covered her fingers, trickling down to her palm and pooling at the dip before her wrists.

"Oh-oh my…" the boy in front of her steps back, his face pale. He doesn't help, neither does anyone else, they all just stare as she tries and fails to get up, falling once again onto her backside.

"What the hell are you doing? Don't just stand there…" a voice carries through the now crowd of people, but it is quickly drowned out by a ringing in her ears and a pounding in her head. This is so bad, everyone is looking at her, they are all staring at her. No, no, no, no…. Her vision begins to blur, either in panic or loss of blood, but she feels someone grasp her arm, "Get up." They demand, *she* demands, it's a girl's voice.

"Is she…" another voice begins.

"Come any closer, I dare you." The girl hisses at them, shifting Vivienne onto her feet and balancing her out. That voice, she *knows* that voice. The familiar hiss that is normally directed at her, or in her direction anyway. It can't be, not *again*. Please not again.

"Come on," Jinx says into her ear, pulling Vivienne away.

Chapter 8 – Jinx

─ · ₀° ☆: *.☽ .* :☆° ˛ ─

Vivienne is quickly becoming dead weight on Jinx's shoulder as she hauls her to Jinx's building. Jinx had watched that entire event, including when the football hit the fool in the nose. What was she thinking, closing her eyes and *breathing* in the busiest bit of campus, and, not to mention, in the freezing cold. Then, once she'd been hit, all those pathetic excuses for students had just stood around her gawking instead of helping, she was sitting there *bleeding* on the floor and all they could think to do was record her. They'd *recorded* her.

Pushing the door to her building aside, she helps Vivienne up the stairs, to her dorm. Vivienne really is faint, she lost a lot of blood, but she could at least try to stand. Carrying her is making Jinx's wrist throb again, but she doesn't have any other choice, if she moves her arm even a little, there is a good chance she'll drop Vivienne on the floor.

"Can you stand on your own?" Jinx asks, trying to find her room key in her pockets. Vivienne doesn't speak, but she nods, and Jinx lets go, only for the girl to collapse onto the floor. "That isn't standing, you know."

Vivienne glares, despite her pale face and quivering lip, and Jinx unlocks the door. After opening it wide enough, she bends to help Vivienne again and she stands, barely. Jinx attempts to take her to the couch, but Vivienne pulls back, shaking her head.

"Do you really think you're in the position to be picky about where you sit?"

But Vivienne doesn't stop pulling, and points towards the bathroom. *The bathroom,* oh god no. Frantically picking up the pace, Jinx helps the probably nauseous girl to the bathroom and opens the door. Vivienne doesn't wait before falling inside and slamming the door behind her. She sits on the couch, putting her headphones in as she does so, hearing someone vomit is the last thing she needs right now, especially when it makes her do the same.

It's a good five minutes before Vivienne opens the door, her face paler than the walls of Jinx's small main room. Neither of them say anything, they stay in silence as Vivienne cautiously walks towards the couch. Her nose bleed has stopped, but fresh blood still covers her upper lip. Jinx hates it, and she hates the boy who did it to her, accident or not. Without saying anything, she throws a packet of tissues at Vivienne, and she takes them in her hand.

"Are you okay?" Jinx asks, nervously eyeing the toilet. Following her gaze, Vivienne sighs,

"Relax, I cleaned up. If I remember correctly, vomit makes you feel ill?"

Jinx fights back a smile and nods, "How do you know that?"

"Well, twice in freshman year you were sent home because that boy, Thomas, had either gagged or thrown up in homeroom, then you'd done the same."

"I think he did it just to torment me," Jinx says, partially shocked at Vivienne's memory, "and surely, you'd want to do the same? Leave your delightful vomit in my bathroom and make me ill for the next two days?" Vivienne frowns and sits on the edge of the armchair across from Jinx. She is still *so* pale, "Are you sure you're okay? You're whiter than the walls." Jinx says, gesturing around them. She still hasn't decorated properly, she doesn't have the time, or the energy. Besides, she is only here for a year, then she'll be getting an apartment off campus.

"I'm fine, it's just the sight of blood makes me..." Vivienne trails off and wrings her hands in front of her, clearly still shaken.

"Nauseous? Well, it's a good job neither of us took any interest in medicine." A smile tugs at Vivienne's lips, and Jinx carries on, "Although, you were pretty good with this." She lifts her wrist into the air and gestures to it. The throbbing has subsided, but even moving it like this is a little painful.

"Is that a compliment? My, my, I must've been hit really hard." Vivienne raises an eyebrow, smiling slightly.

"Don't get too excited, I'm only humouring you, give it a couple of days and I'll be back to my usual arrogant self." This is kind of nice, for once they are having a conversation that doesn't involve directly insulting each other.

Vivienne is quiet for a long while, and Jinx begins to wonder if she's pushed it too far, although how, she isn't sure. All she did is joke about herself, how would that stir Vivienne?

"Thank you," she mutters and Jinx watches as Vivienne looks out her small window. "Why did you help me, again? I mean, I'm fairly sure you hate me and I'm definitely sure I hate you, so why?" She turns back to Jinx and waits, her deep ocean eyes pinned on Jinx in an unnerving way.

"What makes you think I hate you?" Jinx's voice is quieter than she would like, but Vivienne doesn't seem to notice.

"You don't?" Vivienne looks confused and crosses her arms. Of course she doesn't, Jinx wants to say, how can she? Vivienne is one of the smartest, bravest people she knows, she could never hate her. Why Vivienne begun to think that she did always confused Jinx, and she'd wanted to tell her that for years, but she never did. She never did, and she never will. Besides, what is the point? Vivienne hates her anyway, so there is no point in Jinx admitting that she feels otherwise, not when it will only end in humiliation.

Jinx shrugs and answers Vivienne's previous question, "I was just going to walk past, if I'm brutally honest, but then I saw your face when you looked at your hand. You looked like you were going to have a panic attack, and those are a bitch, *especially* in front of a crowd of people." Jinx sits further back in her chair, her legs falling to either side, "Besides, I owe you one from when you helped fix my wrist."

Vivienne sighs, "Thank you, again. I don't think I've ever thanked you so much in my life as I have in the last two months."

Jinx breathes a laugh and lies back on the couch, "Feel free to carry on, it inflates my ego a little bit every time."

Vivienne puts a hand to her head, "God, you are such a pain in the ass."

"I could say the same to you, Carter."

"Oh for-"

Her phone goes off in her pocket, her ringtone being the standard 'ding', and she pulls it out to check. Moments later, Jinx's phone does the same,

Lilly: 11:54am
Lunchtime study session? Its never to early to start!

Julian: 11:54am
Hell yeah! Vivienne? Jinx?

Vivienne: 11:55am
I'm doun

Vivienne: 11:55am
***down**

Jinx: 11:55am
Sure. 12:30?

Lilly: 11:56 am
Yes!

Julian: 11:56am
See you there

Lilly: 11:56am
WOOHOO!

Jinx: 11:57am
Lilly, serious question, how much coffee have you had today?

Vivienne laughs from across the room, startling, and amusing, Jinx. She quickly stops herself, but Jinx is already looking at her with amusement, tilting her head to the side for effect, "Something funny, Carter?"

She doesn't respond, instead she turns off her phone and begins to head for the door. She gets to the handle before Jinx stops her, saying from the couch, "You still have blood on your lip."

Jinx hears her mutter a curse, then gets up and joins her at the door, "Need these?" she asks, holding out another packet of tissues for Vivienne. She takes them without thanks and pulls one out, nervously touching it to her face. After an excruciatingly long time, the blood on her lip is still there, and Jinx sighs.

"Pass it here," she mutters, holding her hand out for the tissue. Vivienne gives it to her reluctantly, and Jinx shakes her head as she brings it to Vivienne's lips, "Honestly, being around you is like babysitting a toddler."

Vivienne smiles slightly, and Jinx does the same, pulling away, tissue still in hand. "Pass me the bloody ones as well, I'll put them in the trash." Vivienne hesitates, then passes Jinx her bloody tissues.

"I'll see you in the English hall at 12:30?" she asks, her back to Jinx and her room.

"Yep, prepare for literary warfare." Jinx jokes, shutting the door behind Vivienne.

*

The English hall is quiet as Jinx wanders through the doorway, the bag on her shoulder heavy with the weight of her laptop. Searching the room, she doesn't see any signs of the others so decides to choose a table for them, one of the smaller ones in the corner of the grand hall. Placing her bag on the table, she pulls one of the comfier chairs towards her and sits down, pulling her laptop out of her bag as she does so. Being there early and having nothing better to do, she clicks open one of the many documents on her screen. Most of them are assignments, some are articles from her favourite online papers, but this, this is her most prized possession. It is the only thing on the laptop that is actually worth anything. If she had to wipe the hard drive clean and only keep one thing, this would be it. Her manuscript. Not the manuscript of some already published book, not extracts from classics, no, this is *hers*. Something she's been working on since she was sixteen.

The document is massive, it includes planning, plots, characters and most of the novel itself. This is what she came to college for, so she could publish *this*. So she could get a literary degree and write more like *this*. It is nearly finished, but she hasn't had the nerve to show anyone, to get feedback from anyone who would actually care. Not even her mum has read it, not that Jinx wants her too. Her mum isn't smart, but she isn't stupid either. Far too much of her plot has come from moments in her life, none of them good, and if her mum saw that, Jinx fears what will happen if she doesn't get the laptop away fast enough. No one she knows is shed in a very positive light in this book, but not many people she knows are in it. Lilly, Julian, and Vivienne are safe, most of her classmates, her professor, all safe, in fact, it is just her Mum. Well, her Mum, and anyone centred around her, boyfriends, one-night stands, anyone.

Scrolling through the pages of endless words, Jinx stops at where she left off last time, where she is editing. Not much of the book itself is happy, it is all very melancholy, but this is one of the happier moments. Jinx has never enjoyed romance, she *hates* the genre and the whole idea of it, but this book is centred around it. Not in the conventional way, boy meets girl and all that nonsense, no. This is a story of loss and grief, struggles and guilt, an internal battle that ends with the main character giving up. The love aspect only comes across in the flashes of a time before, when the character was blind to the world and its effects, blind to any feelings that weren't bliss or happiness.

Putting on her headphones, the old-looking noise cancelling ones she uses when writing, she begins typing away, the music a stimulant for her never-ending thoughts.

Absorbed in the world of her making, she doesn't see Vivienne approach, and with her headphones on, doesn't hear her sit in front of her and pull out her own laptop. Because of this, Jinx doesn't think twice about letting her head fall to the table in annoyance and stress, or about the frustrated curse she mutters to herself as she stares hopelessly at the screen in front of her. Putting her head on the table again, she feels a pencil tap her shoulder and bolts up, causing her glasses to fall off her face and crash onto the table.

"What the hell-" She picks up her glasses and places them on her face again, finding Vivienne watching her from the other side of the table. Her hair is messily tied back into a bun behind her head, and she has a small plaster to the side of her nose. Jinx can't see her legs, but she presumes she is wearing the same jeans as this morning, but she is wearing a different jumper. *Jinx's* jumper. Ignoring the feeling deep in her chest, she rolls her eyes and turns back to her laptop, making a mental note to tease her about the jumper later.

"What are you doing?" Vivienne asks, bending her head round to see the laptop.

"Assignments," Jinx says, pulling the laptop away and facing it towards her.

"It doesn't look like assignments to me," she teases, opening her own laptop and typing in her code.

"Why would you care, anyway." Jinx sighs, pulling on one side of her headphones. Vivienne looks at her headphones, then at her phone,

"What music are you listening to?"

Why is she asking all this? It is getting extremely annoying, "You're asking a lot of questions, Carter, dare I say you're trying to get to know me?" Jinx's attempt at cold only seems to make Vivienne more intrigued. She sits up and sighs, shaking her head,

"In your dreams. I'm merely being nosy and trying to make conversation until the others arrive." She states, watching Jinx carefully, occasionally glancing at her wrist. Neither seem too keen to bring up each other's injuries, both of which have been humiliating for everyone involved. Well, everyone but Julian.

"You've never tried to make conversation before, why now?" Jinx looks away from her laptop and back to Vivienne, who is looking at her laptop.
"I'm trying to be friendly." As if. Vivienne is never friendly to Jinx; she's never even tried.
"We both know it's not that, try again." Jinx sighs, leaning back in her chair and putting her hands on either arm.
Vivienne looks away from her laptop and pulls out her phone, showing Jinx the screen, "Julian's making me." On the screen is a thread of messages between Julian and Vivienne. None of them are very interesting, all they seem to talk about is classes, but at the bottom are three short messages.

Julian: 12:25pm
We actually have to get stuff done today, please try not to go on any tangents of bickering with Jinx

Vivienne: 12:26pm
You make that sound easy

Jinx: 12:26pm
Just be nice, that can't be hard, you're a nice person

Jinx breathes an airy laugh, "I knew it, and I pity you, at least I'm not being told to 'be nice' by someone I've just met."
Vivienne looks offended and turns back to her laptop, "Me and Julian haven't just met, we've been roommates for months now."
"Fair enough, but you can't deny that he *is* telling you to be nice."
She shrugs and begins to type something on her laptop, Jinx trying to do the same. After trying again and again to write the same sentence correctly, she gives up and just stares blankly

at the screen, she can't stop thinking about that jumper. *Her* jumper, and how comfortable she looks in it. Some part of her is telling her to ask for it back, but she doesn't want to listen to it. For some insane reason she likes seeing Vivienne so cosy in it, she likes the way it absolutely drowns her, covering her hands completely, and how when she slouches in her chair it almost looks like she is covered in a dark green blanket.

"You're staring," a voice says from behind her, and Jinx spins to find Lilly smiling at her.

"Yes, because I can't figure out what to do about this chapter," Jinx sighs, turning back to her laptop.

"I wasn't on about the laptop, Jinx," Lilly says, looking at Vivienne across the table, who has abandoned her laptop and is now fully submerged in a book, clasping it with an adorable intensity. Jinx goes to reply, but Lilly is already moving to sit in between her and Vivienne.

"Good book?" she asks Vivienne, startling her a bit as she does.

"Oh um…" Vivienne puts down the book and turns to Lilly, her hair somehow scruffier, "Not really, if I'm honest, well not at the moment anyway."

"Why?" Lilly asks. Jinx takes off her headphones and turns to her laptop, not wanting to be excluded from the conversation, but not wanting to talk either.

"Do you read?" Vivienne asks, and Lilly nods her head,

"Obviously."

"Well, I can describe the problem with this book in one word," Vivienne sighs, looking at Lilly who is now leaning on the table with her elbows, "Miscommunication."

"No," Lilly says, dragging out every syllable of the word and putting her head on the table. They both have a point, Jinx agrees that the miscommunication aspect of books can ruin them, but she doesn't feel like telling them that, not when it means agreeing with Vivienne.

"What have I missed?" Julian asks, approaching the table and nervously eyeing Lilly. Vivienne looks at Julian and holds up the book in her hands, to which he just laughs, "Did I or did I not tell you it's the most frustrating book in human history."

Vivienne sighs and puts the book back into her bag. Julian sits down across from Lilly and takes out his copy *Romeo and Juliet,* the others following suit. After two minutes, all their materials are on the table in front of them.

"So…" Julian starts, opening his book to a page marked by a long leather strip. "I've read up to around halfway, and have a good idea of the characters and scene, has anyone else read any?"

"I've read about twenty pages, how have you read half the thing?" Lilly says, clearly impressed with Julian.

"My medics class was really boring and wasn't anything relevant, the Professor just put on an hour of doctors and surgeons getting Nobel Prizes for 'fun', as he called it, so I thought I'd read ahead."

"You're telling me you bolted to that class, nearly breaking your ankles on the ice as you did so, just to sit there and read." Vivienne says, looking across the table at Julian.

"Yes."

"Fair enough." She shrugs and opens her book. "Me and Jinx did some of this in high school, but I might have to re-read it, we didn't do much."

"*We?* Who's this 'we' you're on about? I did, as the teacher suggested to the *class,* extra reading and finished it. Did you not, Carter?" Jinx teases, relaxing back into her chair and raising her eyebrows.

"No, I didn't, because I was too busy revising for a debate against *you*, which *I* won."

Jinx rolls her eyes, "Are you really about to throw that *one* debate at me, compared to the amount *I* beat *you* in. What was the ratio again, 10 to 1?"

Vivienne scowls and turns back to her book, muttering something under her breath as she does so. Julian coughs and Lilly carries on with the original conversation, "Anyway, considering we are all at different points in the text, we could start planning the structure of the debate instead of its contents, so everyone knows what they're doing?"

"Good idea," Julian agrees, opening a large notepad and writing something in it.

They plan the debate, Jinx and Julian taking the Con approach and Lilly and Vivienne doing the Pro, and then assign parts. They decide that Lilly and Julian will do the introductions at the beginning and the questions at the end, leaving the arguments and summaries to Jinx and Vivienne. After sorting that out, they work in silence for the next hour, only Julian and Lilly speaking at random intervals to ask for one another's notes. Jinx wonders if Vivienne and her should do the same, but she doesn't ask, mainly because if Vivienne says no, it will be embarrassing.

The hour passes and when they are packing away, Julian asks if anyone has any classes next. None of them do, but Vivienne says she has one in an hour, history or something like that. Seizing the opportunity, Lilly asks everyone if they want to get lunch together in the main canteen.

"That sounds fun," Julian smiles, turning to Vivienne and Jinx. Jinx is stood behind her chair, her stuff fully packed away, but Vivienne is still sitting down, laptop on the table. Julian and Lilly nervously await their answers, but neither of them do. Jinx pulls her bag higher on her shoulder and makes to leave,

"I can't, I have more subjects to study for." She mutters, walking past Lilly and Julian. She doesn't care if they think she is rude for blowing them off so abruptly, she had checked her watch while packing away and realised the session had run over. If she doesn't leave now, she'll be late for her shift at the coffee store.

"I'll come." She hears Vivienne say before she's entirely out of earshot. Quickening her pace, she is practically running when she reaches the college gates and makes for the town, pulling her deep green apron out of her bag as she does so.

Chapter 9 – Vivienne

Lunch was fun, they went to one of the quieter shops on campus and sat down, talking about anything but *Introduction to Classical Literature*. Turns out, Lilly is *nothing* like Jinx, in fact, she is more like Vivienne. She loves reading, especially romance, and even likes the same shows as her. The only thing they disagree on is *Pride and Prejudice,* but Vivienne found that easy to forget whilst they talked. Julian and her kept making jokes that made Vivienne choke on whatever she was eating. They seemed to time the best ones for when she had a mouth full of water, which Vivienne then had to try her hardest to keep in her mouth.

Some horrible, twisted part of Vivienne wishes she'd met Lilly first, wishes that Lilly would come to her senses and see that Jinx isn't the right friend for her. Lilly doesn't know what Jinx is really like, she may be putting up an act now to lock in their friendship, but after a few more months that act will stop, and Lilly will see the true Jinx. The horrible, success centred brat who fails to acknowledge other people's feelings. Even when she'd saved Vivienne on the stairs months ago, she only did it so Vivienne could still come to class and be humiliated by Jinx. And today, when she'd saved her from throwing up in front of half the college, she'd only done that because…. Well, Vivienne doesn't know why she did that, but she probably has some selfish reason, it was probably to even the score after she broke her wrist.

"You really need to get a better thinking face; you look like you're plotting to kill everyone." Julian brings her from her thoughts, and she smirks at him.

"Maybe I am."

He smirks and holds a hand up to her head, "With your height? I don't think so, you have to be at least 5'5 to commit mass murder, sorry."

Vivienne clicks her fingers and sighs, "Damn it, now I have nothing to do after class."

"Sorry, I can't change the rules." He shrugs.

Lilly left them a while ago, saying she had a class to get to in the Art block, so now it's just them two again. Vivienne has a class in ten minutes, so they are walking towards the building.

"I've got a question," Julian says, putting his hands in his pockets.

"Go on." Vivienne says, wrapping her jumper tight around her.

"Why are you wearing *Jinx's* jumper, what happened to your yellow one?"

"I'm not..." Looking down at herself, the words stop in her mouth. She hadn't realised she was wearing Jinx's jumper. Damn it, she'd just picked up what was on her bed, why did it *have* to be this one. She'd worn it in front of Jinx as well, although she hadn't said anything, maybe she hadn't noticed. Oh who is she kidding, of course Jinx will have noticed, she doesn't miss anything. If she noticed, why hadn't she brought it up? Maybe she wanted to, but that would've meant her needing to say something that wasn't an insult, and Jinx is completely incapable of that. Maybe she thought Vivienne looked stupid in it, it is nearly drowning her now she is looking at it. Most clothes did that, she isn't very tall, but maybe this is so big it makes her look shorter, *that's* why Jinx hadn't mentioned it, so Vivienne would walk around looking like an idiot. Surely. There can't be another reason, not one that isn't spiteful or cruel, anyway. Those options, however, are entirely impossible, Jinx only acts out of spite when it comes to Vivienne, it has always been that way. Why would things start changing now?

Julian coughs and raises his eyebrows high enough that they nearly disappear beneath his hair entirely, "You haven't answered my question." He states, smirking at the unwelcome heat creeping up Vivienne's neck.

"Who says it needs answering?" she says, looking away from him and willing the cold to cover the distinct pink in her cheeks. She doesn't know why the pigment of her face is quickly changing, there is nothing to make her blush the way she is, nothing. Julian laughs and nudges her with his elbow,

"I can still see your neck." He teases, pulling her to face him. Vivienne pulls back and crosses her arms, the jumper covering her hands. "I'm going to ignore your suspicious, and quite odd facial expressions and ask an easier question," Julian says, and Vivienne grunts, pushing her entire body into his in an attempt to knock him over. "What happened to your yellow jumper?"

This, she can answer, "I got blood on it and can't get it out."

Julian stops dead in the path and stares at her, "*What?! How the hell did you get blood on it?!*" He exclaims, loud enough for the whole campus to hear. Vivienne laughs quietly and ushers him to keep moving.

"Calm down, it was only a nosebleed, nothing serious."

"Nothing serious?! You were bleeding, that's *serious!*" He says, concern written across his features, making his eyes wide and restless.

"You say it as if I was bleeding from an important organ or something, but it was *just a nosebleed.*"

He sighs and puts his hand on his forehead, "How did you get this *nosebleed*? You don't seem like the type to get them under pressure, mainly because I've seen you under pressure and you have a habit of colourfully swearing instead."

Vivienne laughs, mainly because he's right. That's why she always tries to keep her cool around her Dad, because if he heard what she says when she's stressed, he would throw a fit. Throughout her childhood, whenever he'd hear a swear on the TV or in a song, he'd give her the big 'You don't ever say those words, understood? It's not cool and not smart' lecture. He'd only begun to loosen up when she turned seventeen, and even then, all he permitted was the odd murmured 'shit' when she'd do something clumsy like drop a pan on her foot. Something she's regrettably done countless times.

"Well, I was standing in the middle of campus after you'd run off to your class and this guy threw a football that hit me square in the face." She points at the near invisible plaster on her nose, "I'm surprised you didn't notice." He looks at her nose and squints. Stepping closer, he takes her face in his hands and brings his eyes, so close they're almost touching her nose itself. "Do those glasses do *anything*?" She asks once he steps away, having found the plaster after a large amount of searching.

"They're supposed to, but I need to get my prescription updated." He states, crossing his arms and looking around the campus, "Now tell me which jerk threw the ball so I can break every bone within his body, whilst naming them."

Vivienne laughs and Julian pounds his fist into his hand, "I'll teach him to throw a ball at my friend."

"You're so overprotective, and look, I'm fine. Jinx-" she stops herself and Julian turns around to face her, stopping once again. At this rate, she's going to be late for class.

"Did you just say Jinx-"

"Nope." She says, quickening her pace towards the building in front of them. Julian easily catches her up, crossing his arms and smirking.

"What did *Jinx* do?" he asks, stepping in front of her.

"Nothing." Vivienne insists, moving around him. "I'm going to be late." She tells him, her walk now becoming a borderline run. Julian doesn't stop following her, now laughing as he catches her up.

"There's no point running away, I can just ask you when you come back to the dorm tonight."

"Well, if you're that eager to know, you can wait till then, can't you?" She pants, taking the steps to the building two at a time, tripping multiple times in the process. Julian laughs a final time before stopping completely and letting her walk off, bidding her goodbye as he does so.

When she clears the doors of the building, she stops and leans against a nearby wall, catching her breath as quickly as possible before she *has* to get to her class. While she is doing so, she tries to clear the previous conversation from her mind, along with the countless thoughts about Jinx. In all the commotion and pain, Vivienne hadn't had time to think about the fact that Jinx had saved her *again*, at least not properly. Jinx hates her, and yet she keeps coming from nowhere when Vivienne needs someone, like on the campus earlier today, or when she was shivering whilst walking back from the coffee shop. *The coffee shop,* she hadn't had time to properly think about that either, or how Jinx had spun that lie to Vivienne's father, the lie that Vivienne had gone along with just so Jinx had to be the one to tell him that they weren't dating. Except she didn't, and now her father is sitting at home thinking that her and *Jinx* are *dating*. **Dating**. As in making out behind bleachers, calling each other cute nicknames, and *cuddling* dating. He thinks they are doing *that*. What a ridiculous idea. Ridiculous and preposterous. They hate each other, they aren't even willing to be nice to one another, never mind do all *that*. Vivienne can't even think about it, can't even begin to entertain the possibility of showing affection to Jinx. Doing things like helping her tie back her short, untamed hair, or forcing her to watch the live action *Pride and Prejudice* and then scolding her when she would no doubt turn to her phone within the first twenty minutes. She can't imagine them snuggling down when the cold becomes too much and watching *Gilmore Girls* together – something Vivienne usually does alone – eating all kinds of junk foods and then falling asleep on one another. She just can't see it, and she wonders why Julian clearly does by the way he raises his eyebrows at her countless accidental comments.

She is almost past all her thoughts, pushing them all to the back of her mind as she walks to class, when her phone buzzes in her back pocket. Pulling it out, she is prepared to see a text from Julian pestering her about Jinx, but she nearly drops her phone when she sees Jinx name light up the screen.

>   **Jinx: 2:14pm**
>   *Nice sweater, Carter.*

Shit. She noticed.

Chapter 10 – Jinx

— · ₀° ☆ : * . ☽ . * : ☆ ° . —

The coffee house is rammed this afternoon, every table is occupied by boys in their mid-twenties with laptops, denim jackets and half beards that they are trying desperately to pass as goatees. Walking through the long queue and behind the counter, Jinx looks around for Tony. Someone leans over the counter, insisting that they ordered ten minutes ago, but she ignores them, walking into the storeroom.

"Tony?" Jinx shouts, looking around the storeroom for her ominous boss. "Tony, where are you?" she asks a final time, walking far enough into the storeroom that she reaches the last row of shelves.

"Hello?" a voice shouts from behind her, but it isn't Tony. This person sounds younger, and the voice has a higher touch to it. "Is anyone there?" the voice calls again and Jinx begins towards it. Rounding the row of shelves nearest the door, she finds a tall kid, around her age, half buried under cans of condensed milk. Their bronze skin is slick with sweat and their short cut ebony hair has fallen flat around their face due to the heat of the storeroom. They, too, have the company apron on and underneath they are wearing a subtle pink jumper and ripped jeans.

"Who are you?" Jinx asks, eyeing the stranger sitting on the floor in front of her.

"Kit." They state, lifting their hand out from under the cans and sticking it out to her.

"Well-"

"They/them." Kit says, blushing slightly and almost cringing backwards into the tins. Jinx looks at them, a coolness spreading over her face as she leans against the shelf next to her.

"I'm assuming you don't usually get a nice response to that part," she asks, "considering you look like you're trying to turn *into* the cans around you."

They shrug and try to shift out of the cans again, "Most of the time I get this." They imitate a look, creasing their eyebrows and pursing their lips. Jinx laughs and offers them a hand to get out of the cans. They grasp it and she pulls them up.

Once Kit is on their feet, Jinx begins back to the door, "Do you mind explaining why you were just buried in milk, when you're supposed to be dealing with this." She opens the door and gestures out into the shop, the queue having now grown a few more people.

"Well, when I ran out of cream, I went to look for some more. Then the entire shelf fell on me." They sigh, looking at the counter in front of them. Jinx bends down and opens one of the many doors attached to it, revealing four cans of cream and other long-term dairy products.

"Did you not think to check here?" she asks, standing up and kicking the door shut with her foot.

Kit just stares at her in shock, mouth open and everything, "I didn't know that was there?!" they exclaim, bending down to look at the cabinet. Jinx almost laughs at their utter shock about a cabinet, but she thinks better of it and waits, ready to serve the never-ending line of customers.

"You new then?" she asks, starting on the first man's drink, an oat milk latte.

"I started yesterday, but this is my first day without Tony." Kit says, taking the next person's order, a sweet, smiling old woman, one of the few people here not in denim today. What is going on with these people, is there some kind of convention or something? Practically all of them have laptops open on the tables and stacks of paper scattered to the point where some of it coats the floor.

"Where is he, Tony, we could really use him. The place is rammed." Jinx places the order on the counter and moves onto the next person, two months of this making her work like a well-oiled machine. Kit does the same with their order and moves onto the next one, not as quickly as Jinx and knocking over a good number of things while they do so.

"He went out to see what's going on, you know, with all these people." Jinx supposed that was a good idea, considering that she has *never* seen the place so full. In fact, it has never come close to this. Every table is occupied, and the line is *still* going out the door.

Her and Kit carry on making drinks for the next hour, Kit slowly falling to a similar rhythm as Jinx. They knock over a few drinks every so often, but everyone does that their first time, when Jinx first went to work for the one in her town, she spilled drinks over *two* customers. Thankfully, she'd know them personally and all they did was laugh, but she'd still gotten a scolding from her boss.

When the hour is done, most of the customers are served and the queue is gone. This is when Tony waltzes through the door, arms swinging lazily at his sides and a proud smirk written across his face. He rounds the counter and approaches Jinx and Kit, who are leaning against the counter and sipping drinks of their own.

"Where have you been?" Jinx asks, raising her eyebrows at the cocky calmness Tony is projecting. He is normally sweet and friendly, the kind of guy who would hug a random person on the street if they asked for it, but now he is a completely different person, or at least he is trying to be.

"Guess what?" he says.

"What?" Kit asks, standing up properly and taking their arm off the counter. Tony turns to Jinx and smirks.

"Do you remember when I told you about that unbelievably expensive coffee that went on the market two weeks ago?"

Jinx nods, "Yes, you were really annoyed at the pricing and were grumpy the whole day because you couldn't afford it."

Tony cocks his head to the side, "I wasn't *that* grumpy."

"You sat in the storeroom for half an hour sulking like a five-year-old. I would call that grumpy."

Tony sighs, "Moving on. So the stuff was dead expensive and both the stores down the street bought bulks of it." His smile grows and his eyes widen, "and guess what was in it!" He's at the point where he's shouting. Ah, here is the Tony she knows.

"What?" Kit asks, leaning forward with intrigue while Jinx stays leaning on the side.

"Turns out that there was a shipping problem, and it mixed with some other, less appropriate, products," he whispers, and Jinx stands up straighter, her drink still in hand.

"Wait, so those stores…" Kit drifts off and looks at Tony.

"They were giving their customers the coffee, and when one of the customers reported it, the police went to investigate. Both places have been shut down!" Tony exclaims, throwing his hands in the air. *That* explains all the guys with laptops, one of those shops had been massive with the technology department at her college (mainly because almost every table had a charging port), so when that shut down, they must have all come here. Although, that doesn't explain why they all dress the same, but nothing can explain that. She will never understand tech majors.

Jinx lets the smile pulling at her lips win and Kit jumps up, "That means we're the only operating one around here then, right?" they ask and Tony nods. This means *a lot* more business, which means *a lot* more profit.

"That's why I took you on, Kit, Jinx here is going to need the help." Tony pats her on the back, something she normally hates him doing, but right now she doesn't care. She can't believe it, with those two shops gone it won't just be locals coming in for their regular coffee, but students from her college will be coming here as well. Most of them wouldn't normally come near a place like this, they are all rich brats who stick their noses up at places like this, but without any other options they have no choice (unless they felt like paying the absurd prices at the on-campus stores which, even for them, are a lot).

"Look who's smiling for once," says Tony, eyeing her with amusement, "never thought I'd live to see the day."

Jinx feels like she should be offended, however she's been told by multiple people that she has a 'resting bitch face' as most call it. "I smile." She protests, crossing her arms under her chest.

"No, you *smirk*, there's a difference." Tony teases, and Jinx smirks, "See, you're doing it now."

"I know, I'm doing it on purpose." Jinx says and Tony breathes a laugh, turning to Kit.

"Good luck working with this," he gestures to Jinx, and she sighs.

"I'm looking forward to it, actually." Kit says and smiles broadly at Jinx, showing off two rows of perfectly white teeth. This kid is looking forward to working with *her*, that's new. Tony laughs and walks into the storeroom, where the pile of cans is still on the floor. She'd forgotten about that.

"Kit, get in here." Tony says, coming out the door again and raising his eyebrows. "Did I not tell you that we have spare supplies already in here, the storeroom is the last resort."

"I showed them," Jinx says as Kit nervously walks into the storeroom, Tony following in after them. Once they're in the storeroom and the door is closed, Jinx laughs and jumps away from the counter, the news about the coffee stores still fresh in her mind. She can't believe her luck, and theirs, that she had been turned down by those very stores months ago and now they are shut down. It's exhilarating. Jinx's celebration is short lived, though, as the doors behind her opened and she has to make herself presentable again. Turning around the ordering desk, she stops completely when she finds Professor Halloway, her Classics Professor, standing, waiting to order.

Hoping she won't recognize her, Jinx walks up to the counter, "What would you like?"

Professor Halloway looks away from the phone she was staring at and looks directly at Jinx. "Oh, Jinx, I didn't know you worked here."

Jinx suppresses a sigh as the Professor looks her over, apron and all. Jinx hasn't felt this embarrassed since she was a kid and her mother *had* to pick her up from school, when she was almost always intoxicated and in something ridiculously inappropriate. Of course, the minute Jinx could get the public bus on her own without it looking *too* suspicious, she took the chance and ran with it. It was what she had to do. That started in fifth grade.

"Do you work here often?" Miss Halloway asks, looking behind Jinx, "Are you alone?"

"I'm not alone, two of my colleagues are in the back; and I work here quite often, Professor." Jinx says and the Professor merely smiles.

"There aren't many students in your class that do this on top of clubs and classes, this is very impressive." Jinx knows she's only flattering her, a lot of people in their college don't need to work on top of classes, they don't even have to worry about money for the future, it is all set up for them.

"Thank you, Professor, can I get you anything?" Jinx asks, looking back to the door to check if anyone else has come in.

"Could I have a latte, and please, don't call me Professor, it's not as if we're in class."

Jinx half smiles at her, then turns to begin on the drink. She's never seen Professor Halloway outside of class, although she doesn't dress much differently when she is. The only things that have changed between now and this morning is that she's swapped her burgundy blazer for a white jumper, her short white hair (that is obviously dyed that way, as she only looks around forty) is waved back behind her ears and her lips are darker than they'd been this morning, a telltale sign that she has applied lipstick as well. The polished leather satchel she usually carries around like a lifeline has now been abandoned and replaced with a small clutch that is a similar shade of red as her silk pants. That's when it clicks. Miss Halloway is meeting someone here, and from what Jinx assumes, it is more than just a casual meet up.

"Do you mind if I ask you a question?" Jinx says, pouring steamed milk into the cup in front of her. She doesn't entirely know why she is asking this, she isn't usually nosey, but something about Professor Halloway knowing she works here makes Jinx want to know something in return.

"Not at all, fire away," Miss Halloway says, pushing her glasses further up her nose.

"Are you meeting someone here? You're dressed differently than this morning."

The Professor doesn't answer, and Jinx fears she has crossed a line without thinking about it, but after a short silence Miss Halloway turns to Jinx over the counter and says, "Yes, I am." Jinx smiles a little and bends her head further over the cup to hide it. "Now can I ask *you* a question?" She carries on, and Jinx turns to Miss Halloway, who now has her hands resting on the counter.

Jinx shrugs and says, "Sure." despite the doubt creeping up within her. She could ask why she's working here, which Jinx doesn't want to tell her, or she could ask why she and Vivienne hate each other, which she can't tell her, because she doesn't know why Vivienne hates her. There are so many questions the Professor could ask, why had she said yes?

"How do I look?"

The question takes Jinx by surprise, and she lets loose the breath she was holding deep in her chest. With the drink finished, she turns back to Miss Halloway and surveys her. She looks nice, although there are a few things that could make her look just that bit better.

"You look nice, but do you want some suggestions?" Jinx asks and Mrs Halloway smiles, nodding as she steps away from the counter so Jinx can see her whole outfit. "Maybe try tucking your jumper into the pants," The Professor does as she says, and it's a good improvement. "That looks good, how bad is your eyesight?"

"Not that bad, I only really need these for reading." The Professor gestures to the glasses on her face. "I was going to take them off, but I forgot until I was on the walk here, and they don't fit in the purse." She sighs and looks at the door, a frown pulled across her face.

"If you want, I could keep them behind the counter for you until you're done." What. What had she just offered to do, what possessed her to say *that* of all things, not 'you look nice anyway' or 'relax you'll be fine', but what is the equivalent of, 'why don't you give me, your student who could easily steal these and abandon your class, your personal belongings for me to store behind the counter of this store you've never been to before that could easily be some cover for a mafia operation'. Instantly regretting her decision and worried that she has stepped over *another* line, Jinx begins to turn away with an empty cup in hand and makes a drink for no one in particular.

"You'd really do that?" Professor Halloway says from behind the counter and Jinx turns around. Nodding, she begins back to the counter and stops an arms length away from her Professor. This is so odd and confusing, Professor Halloway has no reason to trust her, and Jinx has no reason to offer to help, and yet here they are. "You're a lifesaver, Jinx." She smiles, taking her glasses off and handing them out for Jinx. Jinx doesn't speak as she takes her Professor's glasses and puts them on the counter.

"I wouldn't call me that, I don't think your date would mind if you're wearing your glasses anyway." Jinx reassures, leaning against the counter and looking at the door.

"In all fairness, he does see me in them all the time, but I'd still like to impress him."

Jinx goes to make a reply, but the door opens behind her and Miss Halloway blushes, stepping back from the counter. Turning to see who it is, Jinx nearly drops the half-finished drink in her hand when she sees another Professor from her college standing in the doorway. He is tall, pale skinned and has deep ebony hair that is neatly parted and gelled until it's practically flat. Unlike Professor Halloway, he hasn't changed from what she'd seen him in early this morning, so he is still in his drab grey suit. As he walks towards Professor Halloway, and they take a table at the far end of the café, she tries to remember who he is.

He doesn't teach in the English department, she knows that for sure, but aside from that she knows nothing about him. She only recognised him because she had walked past him shouting at a group of boys yesterday. The boys in question had merely been kicking a ball around on the pathway, but he'd given them an earful of 'soccer balls are for soccer *fields,* not sidewalks'.

Picking her phone up off the counter, her finger hovers over the *Instagram* icon. She could just text Lilly, informing her of the whole situation and asking if she knows who the ominous Professor is, but she can't help but consider sending it out to the study chat. She doesn't have anything against Julian, the boy Vivienne hangs out with constantly, and it would increase her chances of finding the name of the man sat with Professor Halloway, but she doesn't know if it would be too assuming of what she is sure is a temporary bond between the four of them. After a long while of staring at her screen, Jinx decides and clicks on the icon, what's the worst that could happen? Even if they found her annoying and overstepping, why should she care, she doesn't need them anyway.

Jinx: 3:34pm
Really long story, but the short version is that Professor Halloway is on a date at the coffee store with another Professor, however I don't know who he is. If I describe him, do you reckon one of you could identify him?

Jinx shuts off her phone and places it back on the counter, only to pick it up moments later when the screen flashes with Lilly's name.

Lilly: 3:35pm
Hold on, back up, Professor Halloway is on a date?!

Lilly: 3:36pm
What's the address of your coffee store? I must know. Immediately.

Julian: 3:37pm
Calm down, let's not become stalkers. How do you know that he's a Professor if you don't know who he is?

Jinx: 3:37pm
Because I saw him shouting at a group of boys yesterday for kicking a ball around. That's a pretty Professor-like thing to do, don't you think?

Julian: 3:38 pm
You never know, he could just be a very crazy man who likes wandering into colleges and shouting at students for no reason.

Lilly: 3:38pm
Julian. Have you walked around campus? I don't think movie sets have as many cameras as our college does, how would a man like that even get in?

Jinx: 3:39pm
Sorry to interrupt this tangent conversation, but can I get to describing him? That way we can determine if he's a Professor or a lunatic, and I can get back to work.

Lilly: 3:40pm
Anyone else kinda hoping he's a lunatic, just for the sake of interest?

Julian: 3:40pm
No Lilly. No one else is hoping that.

Lilly: 3:41pm
You guys are boring. What does he look like?

Jinx begins to describe the Professor to the chat, looking over every so often to make sure she gets the details right whilst trying to not look as nosy as she was being.

Jinx: 3:43pm
Tall (taller than me), black hair, small rectangle glasses, has a brown briefcase and an unbelievably bland grey suit.

Lilly: 3:45pm
No clue.

Julian: 3:45pm
Never seen him before.

Lilly: 3:46pm
You know what that means...

Lilly: 3:46pm
Professor Halloway has a date with a lunatic! How interesting...

Jinx: 3:46pm
Why is this the only time you're using ellipsis properly?

Vivienne: 3:47pm
What kind of weird ass conversation have I joined?

Julian: 3:48pm
Vi, good, can you please identify this teacher so we can stop Lilly from thinking Professor Halloway has a date with a lunatic.

Vivienne: 3:48pm
Umm ok. Just let me read the chat first so I can convince myself Lilly is still sane.

Lilly: 3:49pm
I am perfectly sane.

Jinx: 3:49pm
Lilly, what have I told you about lying?

Lilly: 3:50pm
Fine. I'm sane most of the time...

Jinx closes her phone and places it back down on the counter when she sees someone open the door to the store and make towards the counter. She takes the man's order, and he places a ten dollar note on the counter. Confused, Jinx puts the ten into the register and pulls out eight dollars to give back to the man in front of her. This time it's him looking confused.

"Two dollars for a coffee? I need to come here more often," he murmurs as he places the five in the tip jar beside Jinx. As she starts on the man's drink, she hears her phone go off in the background and tenses when Tony pokes his head through the storeroom door. He raises his eyebrows at her, and his gaze moves to her phone. She knows what he is suspecting, he thinks she has broken his one rule which prohibits using phones whilst behind the counter, which she has, but he doesn't need to know that. Shrugging at him, she pours the drink into a cardboard cup and places it in front of the man and he murmurs his thanks. Tony approaches her with Kit in tow and looks between her and the phone, which buzzes twice more. Deciding it's for the best, she picks up her phone, silences it, and places it into the pocket of her apron.

Apparently satisfied, Tony goes back to the storeroom and Kit stands next to her. They cross their arms and huff, glaring at the door Tony just walked through.

"What did he say about the pile of tins?" Jinx asks, craning her neck to make sure Tony isn't looking through the small window in the storeroom door before pulling out her phone again.

"Not much, just how it can't happen again because I might burst one, which makes the storeroom stink, apparently."

"It does, trust me." Jinx clicks on Instagram again and reads her missed messages.

Vivienne: 3:54pm
I know him, he teaches one of my history classes, his name's Mr Lau.

Julian: 3:55pm
See Lilly, a perfectly normal history Professor. Not a lunatic.

Lilly: 3:56pm
Damn it. Why does life have to be so boring, why can't it be like in books?

Vivienne: 3:57pm
As much as I do agree with you, I don't like the idea of being taught daily by a lunatic who shouts at students, so I'm thankful in this situation.

"Jinx." Tony is in the doorway again, staring at her with surprising intensity. "What is my only rule?" He crosses his arms and leans against the doorway.

"Sorry." Jinx mutters, placing her phone back into her pocket again and returning to work.

Chapter 11 – Vivienne

Vivienne is met with a bustle of noise as she pushes open the doors to *Dave's Pizzeria*, where she meets her dad and brother every other week for dinner. She still doesn't understand why they do this; the drive from her Dad's house is two hours, without any traffic, and the fuel costs a lot, but for some reason her dad insists on seeing her in person instead of using his perfectly functional phone to call her. Some parents don't even bother with that when their kids go off to college, but of course her dad has to go all out and travel miles for what is usually a one-hour conversation in an overwhelmingly loud family restaurant.

Reaching the desk nearing the front, she stands idly next to the 'Wait here to be seated sign' and pulls out her phone. Her dad had said they were two minutes away ten minutes ago, but a second ago she'd gotten a text from him saying the traffic is piled up, so she should just get a table and wait for them there. She doesn't know what is causing the traffic, but she'd seen it on the walk over and can understand why her dad is late. The queue was so long that she couldn't see the end even when she stood on her tiptoes, and the cars that were queued were all honking at one another, a thing her dad has always despised. He always says 'It doesn't get you anywhere any quicker, so why bother annoying the neighbouring cars with your nonsense' when they are driving anywhere, making both her and Ollie laugh every time.

A short woman wearing a red top and a black skirt stands at the desk with her hands folded in front of one another, "Table for one?" she asks, her voice cracking as she plasters on a smile that shows all her teeth but doesn't reach her eyes.

"Um, no," Vivienne says, looking back to the door. "My family is coming soon; can I have a table for three?" She asks, looking back to the waitress. Her name tag has 'Dianne' written on it in printed cursive writing, and it stands out stark against her shirt. Her dirty blonde hair is tied back in a messy bun and has a clip through it that is holding the loose strands in place. She doesn't seem much older than Vivienne, although the creases forming above her brows make her appear older.

"Sure." She smiles again and takes three menus from the box to her left. "Follow me."

Dianne leads Vivienne through the restaurant, taking a path so complicated that Vivienne struggles to keep up with her whilst trying to avoid the countless chairs flying out into the walkway as children stand up without warning. They walk for a while and Vivienne begins to wonder if Dianne is just walking her around in circles, until they finally stop at a booth on the left wall, closer to the window than Vivienne expected.

"Thank you," Vivienne smiles and slides into the booth.

"I'll be back in a couple minutes to get your drink, and I assume you're going to wait for the rest of your party before ordering?" Dianne says, her tone flat.

"Yes." Vivienne nods, and Dianne walks away, adjusting her hair as she does so. Ignoring the menu, Vivienne pulls out her phone and opens one of the many books she has loaded up on there. Most of them are romances, obviously, but some of them are different. It's one of these other ones she opens and begins to read. The plot isn't very interesting, a basic murder that is easily solvable within the first ten pages, however the characters themselves are peculiar, so she forces herself to carry on, having never started a book and not finished it.

Ten minutes passes whilst Vivienne is immersed in the world of ink on paper, or in this case, font on screen, until Dianne returns with a small notepad and a pencil in hand. "What can I get you to drink?" she asks, looking expectantly at the unopened menu in front of Vivienne. Vivienne orders an iced tea, as she always does, and Dianne leaves again. Returning to her reading, Vivienne tries her hardest to block out the cries of children all around her. She hates this place. She hates how loud it is, she hates how many children scream for no reason, crying for their mothers when they are right beside them, and she hates how the fathers sit absent minded while children haul food at one another until they are sticky and stink of whatever meal they have.

Her parents had never taken her places like this when she was younger, they couldn't afford to go out much, but when they could, they didn't go places like this. In fact, not many places like this existed where she used to live. Family restaurants were scarce and if you could find one, the food was limited. Instead, when her parents scraped enough together for something that wasn't made at home, she, her Dad, and her Mum would drive through the nearest drive through, a Burger King two miles from her house and use the rest of the money to buy tickets to whatever was showing at the drive-in cinema on the outskirts of town. The films were never any good, mainly old black-and-white films about cowboys in the west or cheating businessmen in big cities, but it was fun, nonetheless. Her Dad would always tease her Mum about her food combos, how she would coat her burger in ketchup but wouldn't put a drop of it near her fries saying they 'made her fries soggy', and her Mum would always chastise her Dad for getting mustard over his shirt when he took a too-big bite of his burger.

She misses times like that, something she knows she should be over by now, but whenever she thinks about those times, something in her chest twinges and tears prick at her eyes. Ollie only came with them a few times, but he was still a baby, so he doesn't remember too much, but Vivienne remembers it all. Including when it all stopped, the day her Mum was diagnosed.

At first it wasn't too noticeable, her Mum would carry on as normal and only disappear for an hour a week for an appointment, but after a while it was something none of them could ignore. Her mum's hair began to fall out, so much so that she was forced to shave it, and she became weaker, sometimes staying overnight at the hospital when things got really bad. She stopped being able to work, so her Dad took up a second job and was barely around. Then she had to move to the hospital permanently, constantly hooked up to one machine or another. Vivienne hated that bit, because Vivienne hated hospitals. It was the only way she could see her mum, the *only* time she could talk to her, but whenever she did, some far-off thought plagued her mind. An anxiety that pulled at whatever her mum was saying, so Vivienne was never fully focused, and she *hated* it. She *hated* that she could barely remember those last precious moments with her mum, all because of some stupid feeling that sprung from nowhere. Her last memories of her Mum were blurry because of *her*.

"You okay, Pumpkin?" Her Dad's voice cuts through her thoughts, and she looks up at him. He places a hand on her shoulder and shakes her a bit. "Vivienne?" Coming to her senses, she looks away from him again and mutters,

"Yes, I'm fine, just daydreaming."

Her Dad smiles at her and slides into the booth beside her, Ollie quick to follow. She hadn't noticed them come in, or walk up to her, how immersed in her thoughts was she? Ollie climbs over her Dad's legs and reaches for her arm, while her Dad tells him that isn't appropriate in a restaurant. Ollie responds by sticking out his tongue and wrapping himself around Vivienne,

"But she's my sister, and I haven't seen her in aaggggeeess." He whines, pulling on her arm and signalling for her to back him up. She shrugs and looks back to her Dad, still partially fazed by her thought spiral. She hasn't thought like that for years now, maybe it's because she hasn't been around her family for so long, she doesn't know. But, whatever is causing this is bound to stop, so she smiles broader and messes with her brother's hair.

"Have you had a haircut, little man?" She asks, rubbing it with her hand and pulling it down to measure against his face. He has, she knows because she'd seen it on her father's Instagram, however she likes to tease him with the nickname 'little man' because it annoys him.

"Don't call me that. I'm not little." He states, crossing his arms over one another and pouting in a childish manner. Vivienne laughs and turns to her father,

"He's still in denial, isn't he?" Vivienne asks, and her father nods his head, smiling at Ollie. "Oh, poor kid, you're not going to get much taller, so unfortunately, you are little." She's right, and Ollie knows it. There's a slim to none chance that he is going to grow more than three feet the rest of his lifetime. Their entire family is on the shorter side, even the far back relatives, and Vivienne herself is only 5'3, possibly bordering 5'4. It's one of the many things Jinx takes advantage of, or used to in high school, anyway. Neither of them were very sporty, both too consumed in studies to be too interested in anything that took time and wasn't beneficial in an academic way, however they were forced to do mandatory gym classes until they graduated. As they were mandatory, the high school weren't too picky about what was actually *done* during these sessions, and most of the time it resulted in some lazily played team game that the sporty kids put together. It was in one of these games, one of the first in her high school life actually, that Jinx acknowledged their height difference. Vivienne could remember every detail about the situation, including the game and the team balance. It was basketball, because what else would it be to further exaggerate Vivienne's disadvantage, and her team was made up mostly of the kids who didn't want to be there, like her. Jinx, however, had the team full of the try-hard sporty kids who were barking orders throughout the group, so of course she won. However, it wasn't when they won that Jinx noticed, it was during the game and Vivienne had somehow ended up with the ball. Halfway across the court someone had thrown it to her, so she froze, looking for someone to pass to instead of having to dribble (something she has always been terrible at). For some unbelievably inconvenient and annoying reason, her team were all behind her, so she had to dribble, only for Jinx to sweep up behind her and snatch the ball from her on the second bounce. Vivienne can remember what she was wearing, not that it was anything special, just the school mandatory sports kit. Although Jinx had made alterations throughout the game, taking off the thick, loose shirt to reveal a sports bra that stretched down to the bottom of her ribs. She shouldn't have been surprised, all the other girls had done the same and the boys were shirtless, but Jinx had caught her off guard, she was so close and towered over her. Vivienne remembers exactly how the conversation between them went.

    Vivienne had sworn under her breath, though apparently not as quietly as she'd hoped.

    "Wow, quite a mouth on you, isn't there Carter?" Jinx had teased, bouncing the ball just out of Vivienne's reach.

    "Surprised?" Vivienne panted, trying to reach for the ball.

"Oh, not at all, although your height has thrown me off a bit. I don't think we've ever been close enough for me to acknowledge how short you truly are." Jinx had smirked and Vivienne swore again, directing it at her instead.

"Ooo, colourful. Now if you don't mind…" she trailed off, stood up straight and threw the ball straight over Vivienne's head. "You make it too easy, Carter." She'd whispered into her ear before jogging back down the court to join her teammates. Vivienne had stood in that spot of the court for a good while, her temper rising so much she clenched her fist, so much so, her knuckles were white. She was only brought away from her thoughts and back to the game when the ball had hit the back of her head when one of her teammates had tried to shoot.

"Vivi?" Her brother pulls on her hair and, again, she is pulled from her thoughts. What is with her today? First, she'd started spiralling into thoughts about her mum, and now she's thinking about Jinx. *Jinx* of all people. Numerous people had pointed out her height throughout the years, but the first person she thinks of is *Jinx*. Maybe Julian's right, she might have to alter her reading times and get more sleep, she's losing control of her thoughts.

"We lost you again, sweetheart, are you sure you're okay?" Her Dad asks again, putting his hand on Vivienne's shoulder, "You're not overworking yourself, are you? And you're definitely getting enough…sleep?" The prolonged pause before 'sleep' has Vivienne raising her eyebrows at her father.

"What do you mean, sleep? Why did you say it like that?" she asks, bringing her iced tea to her lips. She doesn't remember having that brought to her, either. Her mind really is somewhere else tonight.

"Well, you and Jinx-"

He is cut off when Vivienne chokes on the liquid in her mouth, spraying iced tea everywhere. Her brother bursts into laughter, but her Dad just stares at her.

"Ollie, go get napkins for the table, please." He says, smiling at her brother.

"But-"

"Please, Ollie."

Her brother reluctantly does as he's told and wanders through the restaurant, which has calmed down enough that she can see where he's going. Vivienne has no idea what her Dad is on about, in fact she can't even remember him meeting Jinx, so how did he get the idea he is very clearly portraying with his facial expressions.

"Dad, what the hell are you suggesting?" she asks, nervously looking around them to see if anyone she might remotely know is around. If someone heard this extremely confusing and embarrassing conversation, it could get back to Jinx. Oh, she would have a field day with this.

Her father crosses his arms over his chest and sighs, "You know perfectly well what I'm suggesting, young lady. She is your girlfriend, after all."

What. The. *Hell. Girlfriend?* Has he lost his mind, Jinx isn't her girlfriend, and he must know that. Vivienne has spent hours shouting to him about how much of an asshole Jinx is, and here he is suggesting *this*. What could have possibly made him think about this? They aren't even friends, they never even meet up outside of college if they aren't working as a group. The *one* exception is when Vivienne runs into her at the…

The coffee shop. *The coffee shop.* Where Jinx had been the biggest asshole yet and told Vivienne's Dad that they were dating, just so Vivienne would be awkward and have to let him down by telling him that they weren't. But she hadn't, she'd gone along with it. It was a good idea at the time, and it threw Jinx off, but she still hasn't told him. She was going to make Jinx do it when they undoubtedly ran into one another again, as her father has grown quite fond of the store she worked at, but they still haven't had the chance.

"Oh, yes, well..." Vivienne trails off and looks around the restaurant. "Can we talk about this later? And yes, I am getting enough sleep." Five hours is enough, right? It's not like she's going out partying or anything, just sitting on the couch and reading.

"Okay, as long as it isn't affecting your schoolwork." Vivienne nearly cringes at the thought, and desperately looks around for her little brother in the restaurant. She strains her neck to look over by the cutlery stand, but he isn't there. Next, she checks the door to the bathrooms and the desk at the front where there are multiple different kinds of colourful pens, but he isn't there.

"Dad, where's Ollie?" she asks, turning back to her father. Fear is starting to creep up within her, fear that he may have left the shop and gone out into the night. No, he won't have done that, her brother isn't stupid. He probably went to the bathroom or something, or maybe he's doing that thing where servers pretend he's an adult and ask him funny questions about the wine menu.

"I don't know, is he not where the napkins are?" Her Dad asks, leaning over the table to look out into the restaurant. Vivienne shakes her head and gestures to the bathroom.

"Can you go check the bathroom, I obviously can't."

"Okay," her Dad nods and slides across the booth. He stands and makes his way towards the bathroom, stopping and turning to her again before he is too far away, "Don't go anywhere, in case he is just wandering around the restaurant."

"Okay, if he comes back whilst you're gone, I'll give him a good scolding." She smiles at him, and he tries his hardest to return it, but she can tell he's worried. As he disappears behind the bathroom door, Vivienne stands up in the booth and cranes her neck so she can see as much of the restaurant as possible, but there is still no sign of him.

Sitting down again, her hands fold together and she squeezes them tight. She knows that she's worrying for nothing, not much can happen to him, they are in a family restaurant full of kids and parents, what's the worst that could happen? Maybe he's spilt something, and people are helping him clean it up? Maybe he's made friends with one of the other little kids? She doesn't know, but he's probably fine. He is fine.

She finds herself repeating that to herself over and over whilst she waits for her Dad to come out of the bathroom with Ollie, but he doesn't. He comes out alone.

Getting out of the booth and walking towards him, she pulls her hands apart and uses one to pull out her phone. Her Dad shakes his head, "What are you doing? He's probably somewhere in here," But Vivienne isn't convinced, and she doesn't think her Dad is either.

While her Dad ventures into the restaurant, Vivienne's phone begins to vibrate in her hand. Checking the time on her watch, she wonders who's calling her. It's 7:30 on a Thursday, so Julian is at practice, Lilly will be at her brother's house and apart from them, she can't think of anyone else who would be calling her. Without checking the name, she ignores the call and silences her phone, she doesn't need distractions right now. Leaving her post at the table, she also starts to look through the restaurant, but before she can get far, the phone vibrates in her hand again, just silently this time.

Instead of ignoring it, Vivienne checks the call ID, but there isn't one. Well, there is, but it's just numbers. Assuming it is a scam call, Vivienne again ignores it and turns her attention back to the restaurant, only for the phone to ring a third time. Figuring this isn't going to stop until she answers, she finds a quieter spot in the restaurant and answers her phone.

"Hello?" Vivienne says, holding her phone close to her ear.

"You need to get better at answering your phone, Carter." Jinx's voice is muffled when it comes through the phone, and Vivienne is fairly sure she can hear traffic in the background. Why is she calling, and what does she want? This is an extremely bad time, Vivienne has other things to be focusing on.

"What do you want?" she asks her, ready to hang up the phone, if Jinx is doing this just to annoy her, Vivienne is going to lose it.

"No pleasantries? How rude." Vivienne knows that Jinx is smirking on the other end of the phone, and it makes her want to scream.

"I'm hanging up now, asshole." Vivienne says, pulling the phone from her ear and getting ready to end the call. Before she can, she hears something even more muffled through the speakers and then a loud,

"Wait!"

Vivienne reluctantly brings the phone back to her ear and sighs into the microphone, "What. What is so important-"

"Aren't you missing a sibling?" Jinx asks, and Vivienne nearly drops her phone. That's when she hears the familiar whining of her little brother in the background.

"Where are you?" Vivienne asks, trying not to sound as scared as she is.

"Relax, Carter, I'm walking back to the Pizza place now, you don't need to be so worried. What am I going to do, kidnap him? I'm not *that* horrible." Vivienne bites back a laugh but doesn't manage to stop the smile spreading across her face. "And if I were to kidnap anyone, it wouldn't be him. He's far too much like you."

This time Vivienne does laugh, though not loudly like she does around Julian, just a quiet chuckle. Jinx seems not to notice and goes quiet. Beginning to look around the restaurant, she finds her Dad talking to one of the servers and makes her way towards him. Her Dad has clearly grown even more worried since they split up, because his brow is furrowed, and his eyes are feverishly dotting around the restaurant.

"Dad, I've found him." She says, beaming and gesturing to the phone in her hand. His face lights up and he thanks the server before following Vivienne outside.

"I'm on the corner," Jinx says, and Vivienne cranes her neck to try and see her brother. When she doesn't see anything, she begins to panic, maybe they are going to the wrong place, or maybe Jinx is lying, or maybe they've both been intercepted by someone dangerous... "Other corner," Jinx sighs through the phone, somehow projecting the same cool calmness as she does in person.

Vivienne spins to find her brother standing next to an extremely tired, fed-up looking Jinx. Her brother is grasping Jinx's arm and pulling on the sleeve of her coat, childishly complaining about something Vivienne can't hear, but when her Dad shouts his name, he freezes. Ollie turns to look at them, then runs towards Vivienne, colliding straight into her stomach and wrapping his arms around her waist.

"Vivi, it was so scary. I got lost in the restaurant and there were loads of people and..." he murmurs into her top and

Vivienne glances towards her father. He looks ready to scream all kinds of warnings at Ollie, but Vivienne shakes her head, she can tell by her brother's disposition that getting lost is punishment enough. He seems terrified.

Her Dad sighs and pulls Ollie away from Vivienne, lifting him into his arms and carrying him back to the restaurant. Ollie squeals and tries to squirm out of her father's grip, claiming it is embarrassing to be carried around, but her dad smiles and tells him that losing a child is embarrassing, too. Making to walk back to the restaurant, Vivienne forgets about Jinx stood behind her until her Dad turns around and shouts,

"Thank you,"

At first Vivienne is confused, then she turns around and finds Jinx smiling back at her Dad. When he is through the door, it instantly drops and is replaced with the same, straight-faced calm she saunters around campus with. It's a shame, because when she smiles, she looks...nice, even if the smile is forced and fake. Vivienne has never seen Jinx *actually* smile, she's only ever seen the false ones she plasters on when getting awards or the cocky smirk that arises when she is doing something that particularly annoys Vivienne. She's been smirking like that a lot lately.

Vivienne knows she has to thank her, again, but she can't bear to do it. She hates thanking her, because she shouldn't have too, it's not as if Jinx ever thanks Vivienne. She's done countless things to help her through the years, tons of stuff Jinx either didn't notice or just chose to blatantly ignore, and she's never once even come close to saying thank you. In fact, Vivienne has never heard Jinx say thank you to anyone, ever. She never thanks people in award speeches, something Vivienne does a lot, not even her *parents*. Surely she should thank her parents? Whenever Vivienne got an award in the big assemblies at the end of the year, which parents regularly attend, she always thanked her Dad. She never said why, but he knew.

"Your thanks are much appreciated." Jinx smirks, mocking an exaggerated bow.

"I never thanked you." Vivienne murmurs, crossing her arms over her chest.

"Yes, but you ought to, if it weren't for me your brother would be miles from here in some back-alley."

Vivienne's stomach sinks at the thought and she finds herself playing with the ends of her jumper. Jinx stops smirking and her arm jerks at her side, "Relax I was only joking."

Vivienne glares at her, "It wasn't funny."

"Noted." Jinx nods and crosses her arms, her coat folding under her arms. She is wearing the one she always wears when she's out, a long black-leather trench coat that is tied tightly around her waist. It matches perfectly with the brown checked pants Vivienne can see sticking out from underneath.

"If you carry on staring at me like that, I'm going to start thinking you actually like me," Jinx is smirking again, and Vivienne tries desperately to stop the red creeping up her neck at the thought. She doesn't want Jinx to think she is blushing at that, she isn't, she just blushes whenever Jinx teases her. She didn't used to, but something must have changed over the summer because now whenever Jinx says anything that remotely teases her, she blushes all over. It's embarrassing and humiliating, although Jinx hasn't appeared to notice yet.

"Don't get your hopes up." Vivienne shoots at her, only to watch Jinx raise her eyebrows. Annoyed and cold, Vivienne asks, "What are you still doing here, don't you have somewhere to be?"

Jinx pulls a hand out of her pocket, her phone in it, and checks the time, "No, I've got time to kill."

Vivienne sighs and puts a hand on her forehead. "Try not to look so annoyed, your Dad's watching, and by the look on his face, you clearly haven't broken the devastating news to him that we aren't dating."

Vivienne curses under her breath and looks back at her Dad, smiling for him. "Why did you have to tell him that? How did it benefit you?" she says when she's facing Jinx again.

"It didn't, I just enjoy annoying you, and at the time that was the most annoying thing I could do."

"Seriously? You couldn't think of *anything* else? This is lasting weeks and you're telling me you couldn't have done anything else."

"Nope." Jinx shrugs and puts her hand back in her pocket, spinning in a circle as she does so.

"Has anyone ever told you that you have a very slappable face?"

"On multiple occasions, why? Are you feeling the need to slap me?" Jinx teases, taking a step closer to Vivienne and bending down so their faces are level. "Go on, slap me." Jinx is still smirking when Vivienne brings her hand inches from Jinx's face.

"Do you think I'm seriously *that* stupid?" she whispers, taking Jinx's cheek in her hand. "That would lead to me having to explain the slap, and that would be very complicated," Vivienne steps close enough that she can feel the heat from Jinx's face radiating from her. She brings her face to the side of Jinx's, so close that her lips are almost touching the tip of Jinx's ear, "But this, this doesn't even need explaining, he can assume what he wants about what I'm saying to you."

Jinx doesn't speak for a long while, and Vivienne doesn't miss the tips of her ears turning red for a slight moment, until she eventually whispers into Vivienne's ear. "You want to play this game? Good luck." Then Jinx's hand is sliding around Vivienne's waist before she can object, and Jinx pulls her to the side. Completely flustered and desperately trying not to blush, Vivienne doesn't think to stop as Jinx pulls her towards the restaurant again, her fingers resting lightly on the top of Vivienne's hip. Trying to ignore the warm sensation creeping from the spot, she focuses on getting her, and hopefully Jinx, out of this dinner, but her mind empties of solutions when Jinx's hand slides into hers and she holds the door open for Vivienne to walk through.

"Thank you," Vivienne mumbles, then scowls at her own incompetence.

"You're very welcome, after all, what's a girlfriend for?" Jinx smirks at Vivienne.

"I hate you." She whispers, plastering on a smile as she approaches her father, who is now back at his table.

"I know."

That's all Jinx says before yet again plastering on a false smile and quickening her pace towards the table. She is alarmingly good at that, the smile thing, and Vivienne wonders why. Vivienne herself is good with smiling when she doesn't win awards she'd hoped for, but apart from that she can't do anything of the sort. She's terrible at hiding her emotions, especially if she is annoyed or upset. That's why she tries not to be annoyed or upset in front of anyone, except Jinx. She can't help but be annoyed in front of Jinx.

When they arrive at the table, Jinx smiles at her father and he smiles back, glancing over to Vivienne and smiling at her too. This is the worst thing about the entire situation, her dad is very clearly so happy to see she's found someone she likes who likes her back. There had been countless times in the early moments of high school where she'd come home in tears over a crush on one of the countless straight girls in her class. It's not as if she had control over it, there weren't any other lesbians in her class and Jinx was the only bi girl, so there weren't many options. Whenever this happened, her Dad did the thing friends were supposed to do, which is trash-talk them, watch romantic movies, cry over them with her, and eat unhealthy amounts of ice cream until they both felt ill. Her Dad is the best heartbreak fixer, and she means the *best*. If he hadn't gone into tutoring and business, he would've made a brilliant teenage therapist, especially for heartbroken girls.

As they slide into the booth, Vivienne makes sure to knock into Jinx with particular force when she sits down. Much to her disappointment, Jinx does the same to her in a playful way and her Dad beams at them. Trying not to focus on how close she and Jinx are in the small booth, or on how Jinx's legs keeps knocking against hers because they won't fit under the table properly, she turns her attention to Ollie.

"How's school, Ollie?" she asks, watching as her brother turns bright pink at the words. "Are you…blushing?" she looks to her Dad, "You're seeing this too, right? He's totally blushing."

Her Dad laughs and looks at Ollie, "Are you going to tell Vivi or should I?"

The boy blushes even deeper and her Dad pats him on the shoulder, "He's got a crush," he says, and Vivienne smirks.

"A crush, eh? On who?" she teases, nudging his legs under the table, "Is it someone in your class? Ooo who could it be…" Vivienne brings her hand to her chin and purses her lips, mocking a serious face. She taps her chin and smiles, then Jinx shifts beside her. She'd forgotten about Jinx, and she's just made a fool of herself. Dammit.

"Well…there's this girl in Mrs Taylor's class…" he trails off and Vivienne turns to look at Jinx. To her surprise, Jinx isn't smirking or frowning, she is still smiling, except now it looks more realistic. Deciding to ignore the awkward presence beside her, she begins to tease her brother again. After all, it is her family dinner, she doesn't need Jinx ruining it.

"Hmmm...who could it be?" Vivienne lifts one eyebrow and the corner of her lip twitches up.

"You look like Sherlock Holmes," Her brother laughs, smiling so wide it shows his teeth.

"No," Jinx says, and Vivienne turns to her. She is shaking her head and squinting at Vivienne. "To look like Sherlock Holmes, she needs a stupid hat..." Jinx trails off and shifts in her seat. She pulls up her coat from where it had fallen on the floor beside her and takes one of the sleeves. Lifting it past her and over Vivienne, she places it on the back of Vivienne's head, "There we go, *now* she looks like Sherlock Holmes. You can't have a Sherlock Holmes without a silly hat."

Ollie bursts into laughter, curling over with his hands on his stomach, and her Dad joins him, though not as enthusiastically. Vivienne smiles and covers her mouth with her hand, hiding the quiet giggles that are escaping from her. Jinx lies back in her chair and her smile broadens, although there is something about it that Vivienne can only see when they are this close, her smile isn't reaching her eyes. They are still dull beneath her lashes, and there is something else there, something Vivienne can't quite place.

"So, tell us who she is," Vivienne's Dad chuckles, relaxing into his chair and crossing his arms.

"Just this girl...Sofia..." Ollie mutters, the pink once again returning to his cheeks.

"Ooo, Sofia..." Her Dad trails off.

"Oh Sofia!" Vivienne shouts, pushing her hand to her heart, "Oh, I love you Phoebe! I want to marry you!" she theatrically falls, but at the same time loses her balance, causing her fall into Jinx's lap. With her head behind the table, all she can see is Jinx's face, which looks partially startled and confused. She smirks and Vivienne finds herself blushing uncontrollably, for what reason, she doesn't know, but it's embarrassing. There's something different about Jinx when she's smirking at Vivienne, instead of it looking fake and dull like her smile does, it looks real and closer to happiness then any smile ever has. Did teasing her really bring her that much joy, how can it? Surely Jinx has better, happier, things to do.

"Can I get you anything?" a server appears out of nowhere and Vivienne shoots up again, only to stop halfway when Jinx grabs her elbow. Vivienne turns to see what Jinx is doing and notices where her elbow is. She clearly hadn't thought about it when she shot up, but her elbow is moments from colliding with the underside of the table. It would have, as well, if Jinx's hand hadn't grasped the bottom of her elbow and stopped her.

"You're so clumsy, how do you cope when you're on your own?" she whispers and raises her eyebrows, "Is this why Julian is always by your side, to make sure you get back to your dorm intact?"

Vivienne angles her head away from her family and rolls her eyes, "I can handle myself just fine, thanks."

"Really? Because the last time I saw you on campus without Julian, you had been hit square in the face with a football."

Vivienne glares at her and turns back to her family, the new server waiting in front of them.

"Dianne's shift finished a while ago, so I'll be taking over." He smiles, more genuinely than Dianne had. His nametag says *William* in the same fancy cursive, but it looks newer than hers.

"Have we been here that long? Shall we order?" her Dad says, looking around and stopping at Vivienne and Jinx, who is smiling again.

"Yes, yes, um..." Vivienne trails off and picks up the menu, scanning it quickly before picking what she always orders. Her Dad and brother do the same, then they all turn to Jinx expectantly.

"Oh, no, I've already eaten, thanks." She holds her hand up and her Dad shrugs. As the server walks off, he asks Vivienne about school, mainly about her history classes, and Vivienne feels herself relaxing. Not entirely, it's hard to relax with Jinx's hand still wrapped around Vivienne's waist, but slightly. She soon finds it isn't hard not to instinctively shift away whenever Jinx moves, and eventually finds herself lying back in her seat, trapping Jinx's hand where it is. Maybe pretending to date her isn't that bad. *Pretending* of course, and only when her Dad is around. Not anywhere else, at any other time. Yes, she can handle this, she just needs to outlast Jinx, and that can't be hard. She knows, after a lot of watching her behaviour in high school, that Jinx can't grow close to anyone without pushing them away the minute it gets too serious, even with friends, so all she needs to do is wait. Wait, and pretend to enjoy it. *Pretend*. It can't be that hard.

Chapter 12 – Jinx
─ · ₀° ☆: *.) .* :☆° . ─

"Get home safe, girls!" Vivienne's Dad shouts as her and Jinx walk back towards the college, still hand in hand like they were when they left the restaurant. That dinner was…something, something Jinx isn't entirely sure she hated. She didn't like it, of course, in fact the first little bit of it made her want to scream and walk out of the restaurant, but she'd stayed and eventually it became bearable.

Vivienne and Jinx walk in silence for a long while until they round a corner leading down a street, where Vivienne finally let's go of Jinx's hand. Jinx tries not to think about the surprising cold that appears in the absence of her hand, focusing instead on the street around them. It isn't too late in the evening, so it's still bustling with people. Every shop, café and restaurant have their lights on with people meandering in and out, the streetlights let off a warm glow that casts shadows down the far ends of the road, and groups of kids around their age are clumped together tightly to keep out the cold while they sip on hot chocolates. It's early November, so some bold stores already have Christmas lights up, but not most. It's still too early for Jinx to see a point in them, but they do add to the winterly feel around her and Vivienne as they begin down the sidewalk.

A cold breeze wraps around them, and Jinx feels Vivienne shiver beside her, "I've never seen someone get as cold as you do so quickly, Carter, you need to start dressing appropriately." Vivienne doesn't reply, instead she wraps her arms around herself and pulls the tops of her shirt over her mouth and nose. "Okay, this is getting annoying, come with me."

Jinx grabs Vivienne's wrist and leads her across the street, towards a small stall in an alcove. Jinx has been here multiple times over the last few weeks, with the weather progressively getting colder and her only good jumper with Vivienne, she's needed something that keeps her warm during the journey from the coffee store back to the college. She spotted this place on one of her journeys back, the hot chocolate is amazing, and the prices are even better, so this soon became her regular stop after work.

"What do you mean annoying? It's only shivering. You said this last time I was cold, after I'd fallen in the snow."

Jinx shrugs and approaches the woman behind the stall. She's short, with long brown hair that curls at the ends and big roses in her wrinkled cheeks. Jinx knows her name, Ashleigh, as she is always here serving the drinks. She runs the small stall every day and Jinx quickly became her favourite customer with her regular hot chocolate stops.

"Ahh Jinx, lovely to see you again, the usual?" Miranda smiles, pulling a cardboard cup from the stack next to her and grabbing a steaming metal jug. She looks beside Jinx, at Vivienne, and raises her eyebrows. Jinx ignores the accusatory glance and tries to shift the conversation to what is usually is,

"Two of the usual, please."

Miranda smiles and begins to make the drinks as Vivienne pulls Jinx to the side and whispers, "What the hell are you doing?"

"For someone who's so smart, you act quite dumb. I'm obviously buying hot chocolates-"

"But why? My Dad's gone you don't have to be nice to me, it's not as if I'm returning the favour."

"I'm not being nice to you; I'm stopping you from shivering because it is annoying *me*. You'll be happy to know that I'm doing this for my own completely selfish reasons, relax."

"Why-"

"Here you go girls," Miranda smiles and places two tall cardboard cups on the counter. Jinx pays her and they begin off again, Vivienne now quietly holding her hot chocolate tightly between her hands. They walk in silence until Vivienne finally sips her hot chocolate, something she hasn't done since Jinx bought it, and her eyes widen. At first, Jinx thinks it might have been too hot and burnt her tongue, but Vivienne sips it again and again.

"Good drink?" Jinx teases, taking a sip of hers, which is already half empty. Vivienne doesn't respond, staring ahead of them. Jinx doesn't say anything after that, letting them walk and enjoy the soft rumble of noise around them. Not many cars come down this street in the day, and in the evening even fewer, so more lively sounds can be heard over the usual rush of traffic. Music flows out of the stores around them and warm glowing light bleeds through the polished glass windows. Jinx notices Vivienne sip her drink again, tilting it far enough back to indicate it is empty. Her hair is tied up in a high bun, which is rare, but waved strands are hanging by her cheeks. She is wearing an oversized green and white checked cardigan, which she's wrapped tightly around her waist against the cold, and what looks like a new pair of flared jeans. They look different to the ones she usually wore, and they looked nicer too, the material clung nicely to her but not so much it looked like they were restricting.

"Something amusing?" Vivienne asks, turning to Jinx.

"No, what gave you that idea?" Jinx says, looking ahead again, she hadn't realised she was staring. She *wasn't* staring, merely observing, something she did with most people.

"You were staring, have I got something in my hair?" she lifts a hand up to her hair and nervously feels around for whatever she thinks Jinx was staring at.

"No, no, your hair's fine." Jinx murmurs and Vivienne lets her hand drop to her side again. "Although," Jinx steps in front of Vivienne and bends down to look at her face, "you do have chocolate on your face."

Vivienne blushes, something Jinx is trying *not* to do, and drags the side of her hand across her lips.

"Is it gone?" she asks, doing it again but missing the spot completely.

"No, you keep missing it."

Vivienne tries again and again, missing the corner of her lip every time, and appearing to get increasingly frustrated every time she misses. "Oh, I give up, let's just go." She pushes past Jinx, pulling at the sleeves of her cardigan. Jinx begins to walk next to her again but stops moments later when Vivienne tries to remove the chocolate from her face, again.

"Here," Jinx says, holding out a packet of tissues for Vivienne, who takes them and pulls one out. This time she manages to get the stain off her lip and throws the tissue in a passing bin. "It's gone." Jinx sees Vivienne turn her head towards the opposite sidewalk and she does the same. It looks practically the same as the side they are on, but something seems to have caught Vivienne's eye.

"Tonight doesn't go beyond us, okay?" Vivienne murmurs, her eyes still on the other side of the street.

"Okay? Who am I going to tell anyway? Do I have to remind you that I have all of *one* friend?" That is true, her only friend being Lilly, and Jinx is pretty sure she's Lilly's only friend too. Although she does seem to be getting closer to that Julian boy Vivienne always walks around with.

"Yes, and even that's surprising, but it doesn't stop you from spreading it through our literature class. And the last thing I need is Julian hearing and hounding me with questions like last time we-" she stops and shakes her head, but Jinx is intrigued.

"Last time you what?" she teases, although she has a good idea of what she's talking about.

"Nothing."

"Nothing, eh? Then I suppose you won't mind me telling Julian, after all, if it's nothing, then nothing can arise from it."

Vivienne sighs, "Are you capable of speaking like a normal person or do all your sentences have to sound like they came from a nineteenth century novel."

"A nineteenth century novel, why thank you." Jinx smirks and Vivienne turns back to the main path, only to freeze when she does. Confused, Jinx looks up the sidewalk, which she had not been paying attention to before, and smirks.

Julian and Lilly are stood three stores away, both of them admiring something in the display. Lilly is in a green raincoat which opens to reveal a cropped white top that has *Chill Out* printed on it in brown bubble letters, and straight denim jeans. Julian is in similarly styled attire, except instead of a duffle coat and *Chill Out* top, he's wearing a navy-blue varsity jacket on top of a plain white t-shirt. Jinx begins towards them, her hands back in the pockets of her coat, but Vivienne grabs her arm and pulls her backwards, hard enough that Jinx nearly falls. Vivienne pulls her away from their friends and into the small alley between two shops. It's tight and compact, meaning Vivienne is closer to her than Jinx finds comfortable.

"Carter, as much as I enjoyed *pretending* to be your girlfriend in front of your father, this is a bit far, don't you think?"

Vivienne sighs and rolls her eyes, "How have you gotten this far in life without someone punching you in the face?"

"People don't want to ruin a face this pretty." Jinx smirks, gesturing to her face. Vivienne puts her hand on her head, nearly elbowing Jinx in the nose, and curses under her breath. She doesn't speak, instead she sticks her head out into the street.

"Do you mind explaining to me why you pulled me into an alleyway, or is it top secret?" Jinx asks, amusement clear in her voice.

"Why do you think, genius?" Vivienne retorts, shifting to let Jinx look out from the alley. Julian and Lilly have moved from the third shop down to the second and are now laughing at whatever they've seen in there.

"Lilly and Julian are there, what's the big deal?" Jinx asks, making to leave the alley before Vivienne grabs her arm again.

"If they see us, they'll ask what we were doing, and then we'll have to explain, I do not have the energy to explain how this entire situation started right now." Vivienne crosses her arms over her chest and shakes her head, as if that is a simple conclusion to come too.

"Well, you can stay in this delightful alley, but I'm going to go and hang out with them."

"And what happens when they ask you why you were out here?"

"I'll lie. It's easy, watch." Jinx strides out the alley, brushing the dirt off her coat as she does so, and approaches Julian and Lilly. They are still staring into the shop she'd just seen them at, and they are both oblivious to her coming towards them.

"Anything catching your fancy?" Jinx says when she nears them, rubbing her hands together against the cold. Lilly spins round and runs up to Jinx, Julian in tow. Her cheeks are pink because of the cold, and she is beaming from ear to ear.

"Jinx! I didn't know you were here, you should have called and joined us!"

Julian smiles at her from behind Lilly, although Jinx isn't entirely convinced he isn't smiling just to be nice, "Didn't expect to see you here." He says, looking from her to Lilly, then back again.

"Why not? Do I not seem like the 'going into town for fun' type?" Jinx smirks and puts her hands on her hips.

"I took you for the 'sitting in a library with a laptop and notepad no matter the weather' type of person if I'm honest." Julian responds, smiling a little more genuinely.

"You're not entirely wrong, I am here to buy *more* notebooks. My last one ran out last night, otherwise I would be sitting in the library, as you suggested."

Julian breathes a laugh and rolls his eyes, "You know, as much as you'd hate to hear this, you and Vivienne are quite alike. I haven't seen her much today, but most of the time she is either in our dorm reading, or in the library reading."

"We're such social butterflies, aren't we." Jinx puts her hands in her pockets. Lilly laughs and looks between her and Julian, her smile growing. "What?" Jinx asks, eyeing Lilly suspiciously.

"Oh nothing, it's just that you two have actually managed to have a civil conversation, and I orchestrated it."

"We've had plenty of civil conversations," Julian protests, walking towards the door of the stationary store. Lilly follows him in, and Jinx follows her, looking around for Vivienne before closing the door behind her. Where has she gone? Has she gone back to the dorms or is she still in the alley? Surely she won't still be in the alley, she isn't stupid, it's dangerous down there and she knows that. No, she will have gone back to the dorms.

The store is a typical stationary store you'd find in most places, the far wall has assortments of coloured pencils and art supplies, the right wall is entirely pens and pencils, and the aisles in between that and the register have notebooks, newspapers, and books stacked on them. Julian walks straight past these and towards the right wall, where at the bottom there are sticky notes and other study materials. He crouches and scans the bottom, while Lilly and Jinx stand idly next to him.

"Remind me why I have to be here for this, and why I can't be looking at the books instead." Lilly says, playing with a loose pen she'd picked up from a pile on a shelf.

"Two reasons. One, I need your opinion, and two, you're on a book-buying ban. If I let you look at books, you'll get excited and end up buying one, defeating the purpose of the ban." Julian mutters, leaning in further to examine the sticky notes.

Lilly groans and puts the pen back. "But this is boring, why do you need new sticky notes anyway? You bought some last week, a massive pack of them."

"And I've run out." Julian states, and Jinx is partially surprised.

"How?" Jinx asks, bending down to look at the sticky notes he is so focused on. How does someone go through a packet of sticky notes, and a big one according to Lilly, in one week.

"I'm studying medicine, I use sticky notes more than I use pencils." Wow. Jinx is grateful her inability to witness vomit steered her away from that career path. It sounds like *a lot* of studying, even for her.

"Damn. Most of my classes just require a book." She sighs, putting her hands in her pockets and leaning against the shelf.

"Lucky. I haven't slept for more than five hours a night in the last week, the only person I know who sleeps *that* little is Vivienne."

Jinx finds herself sighing and smirking. She may not have known Vivienne well in high school, but there wasn't a person in their homeroom class that didn't know about her sleep schedule. At least once a week she would send out emails in the middle of the night, and then when no one replied she'd come to her senses and realise that, unlike her, most people were asleep at 3 AM. Jinx wasn't, but she never replied for obvious reasons.

"What does she do to get that little sleep, is she taking the medical courses as well?" Lilly asks, perking up and leaning over Julian's side.

"No, she's majoring in History, and gets most of her assignments and studying done within reasonable hours," Julian sighs and reaches for a packet of sticky notes. It has quite a lot of variety, including the small thin ones Jinx uses for annotations in her books, and the large square ones that she personally hates because they are a pain to stick into books as they cover half the text. The colours are also very varied, Jinx counts six different ones in total, what did he need to annotate that required *that* many colours?

"I reckon I can guess what she was doing." She smirks, wandering past them and towards the notebook section. She wasn't lying when she said she was running out of notebooks, most of them are full and in a pile on her desk, full to the brim with ideas, notes, and sketches centred around her novel. Thinking about it, that's what most of her room looks like, a mess of papers, notebooks, regular books, with all kinds of half sane scrambles pinned onto the cork board in the corner, and the odd band poster. It's an absolute mess, but it's an organised mess, and it's not as if Jinx needs to clean it up. No one ever goes in there, and whenever Lilly is in her dorm room, she stays in the main room. Unless, of course, Jinx puts on a film about something history related, which makes her stand from wherever she is sitting, and trudge over to the bathroom, claiming she won't come out until the movie was over. Thankfully for Lilly, Jinx would rather sit through some boring comedy with a friend than watch historical films on her own. She normally did *that* during the early hours of the morning when her brain refused to function but also wouldn't let her sleep. Despite Lilly's desperate evasion of historical films, Jinx had gotten her to watch *one* the whole way through with her, on the condition Jinx kept quiet (she had a habit of correcting the films misconceptions or pausing it entirely to give Lilly unwanted background information and facts). It wasn't even a *proper* war film, it was a black comedy based off of the second world war, but it was enjoyable. Even if Lilly kept asking questions, then told Jinx to 'Shhhh' when she began answering them.

"Oh yeah, what then?" Julian asks, walking in front of her and putting his hands on his hips.

"What?" Jinx asks, she had *not* been listening.

"You said you could guess what Vivienne was up till the early hours doing. What was she doing?"

Jinx smirks and picks up a notebook off the shelf. It's stiff but bendable and is a walnut colour that makes it look like leather from far off. This is perfect, it has a thin piece of elastic holding it shut and is thick enough to last her at least a month.

"Reading. I can guarantee she was reading, and it was probably a romance book that was 'just getting good', in her words."

Julian raises his eyebrows and smirks, "For someone who hates her, you sure know a lot about her habits."

Of course she does, it's hard to miss when Jinx has spent years purposely watching out for them. Not in a creepy way, of course, or in a way someone would watch a crush, Jinx did it so she could see what *she* needed to do in order to be better than her. Like when she found out Vivienne studied for three hours a night, Jinx studied for four. Or when she'd seen Vivienne volunteering at the local nursing home, Jinx had asked the local newspaper if she could volunteer there, which she had, on top of her job (she'd even written a few pieces that were published).

The only thing Jinx noticed and purposely avoided was the girl's obsession with romance books. She had a new one almost every day in high school, each one more pathetic than the last. All of them ending perfectly, of course, because she couldn't possibly read anything that had realistic expectations. The love interest always had a perfect family, and if they didn't, they found family in someone else's, and they all had loads of friends, one of which they would have a massive fight with but remarkably make up when they both apologised for a random list of things neither had done. It was all pathetic and completely unrealistic, *especially* the family bit.

"When you learn the habits of your enemies, you learn how to be better than them." Jinx says, checking the price of the notebook, which she is relieved to find is on sale and not an unreasonable price. "Have you never heard that quote from King Henry VIII, 'Keep your friends close, and your enemies closer.'"

"I don't think King Henry VIII knew his enemy's late-night habits," Julian murmurs, picking up a plain A4 notepad from the shelf. He looks around and sighs, putting his hand to his head, "When did Lilly leave?" he murmurs, more to himself than her.

"I don't know, but I can hazard a guess as to where we'll find her." Jinx smirks, watching Julian shake his head slowly.

Julian sighs and begins towards the centre aisle of the store, where all the books are kept. "Why does she say she'll stop buying books, and then do this." He says loudly, rounding the aisle and stopping almost immediately.

"Why does anyone do anything they're not supposed to? For fun, I assume." Jinx tells him, rounding the corner as well.

There are numerous things she'd expected when she rounded the shelf, finding Vivienne standing there was not one of them. In fact, she thought she'd sooner see Lilly buried to her waist in books before she saw Vivienne here, considering how desperate she was to not be seen twenty minutes prior.

"Vivienne," Julian says, approaching her and Lilly, who are standing in the romance section of the long lines of books on either side of them. Typical. "What are you doing here?" he asks, looking around at Jinx, then back to Vivienne.

"Carter." Jinx nods, then walks past them, her eye on the historical fiction section of the shelves. Contrary to Vivienne's beliefs, Jinx reads a lot, she just doesn't read *romance*. That's a lie, actually, she occasionally reads a romance, but only when it's thrown in with another of her favourite genres (classical literature and historical fiction, obviously), and even then, she tries to avoid it, and never enjoys it.

"Jinx." Vivienne sighs, returning to her romance books. They stand in silence, Lilly, Julian, and Vivienne in the romance section and Jinx on the opposite side. After what feels like at least ten minutes of awkward silence, Jinx picks a book off the shelf and walks towards the group. What she's picked is a book she's been meaning to read for a while, but instead of following the list of books she wants to read like she intended too, she has a tendency to see a book, read it, and ignore the list completely. It is, unsurprisingly, a mystery that is set in the 1980's, and the matte black cover makes it seem very intriguing. She's heard of the author before, *M.L Rio*, but hasn't actually read the book yet.

"What did you get?" Julian asks, nervously eyeing Vivienne in front of him like she was going to shout at him.

"A murder mystery sort of thing, are you picking anything?" Jinx asks, stacking the notebook and the other book on top of one another.

"You think I have time to read for leisure? The only things I read are medical textbooks and specifications." He laughs, gesturing to the packet of sticky notes in his hand.

"Riveting." Jinx says, giving him a pitiful look. "Lilly, I'm assuming you're going to ignore your ban and get a book, so what is it?"

"I'm not getting a book..." Lilly lies, moving her hands behind her back and looking at the ceiling. Jinx can't tell if she is pretending, or if she is really *that* bad at lying. Without saying anything, Jinx holds her hand out and gestures for Lilly to pass her what is inevitably hidden behind her back. After a bit of hesitation, Lilly sighs and hands her the book. The cover depicts a dimly lit street with multiple neon signs and a lamp in the bottom corner.

"You should be proud of me, its historical!" Lilly exclaims and points to the back. Jinx scans the blurb to find that Lilly isn't lying, it is historical, but it's also a romance. Jinx looks up at Lilly and nods,

"Yes, it is historical. Although, I doubt you'll learn much about history from it." She hands it back to Lilly, who laughs and tucks the book under her arm.

"And what do you learn from those historical films you force me to watch, except new curse words." She says, looking back at the shelves and picking up a random book.

"I think you'll find I learn plenty from those films." Jinx crosses her arms and begins down the aisle, towards the register. Lilly follows her, mumbling something petty under her breath and putting her hands on her hips. Jinx doesn't look behind her, but she hears someone else footsteps on top of Lilly's. Assuming it is Julian, Jinx approaches the register, the self-serve sort as no one is at the normal register. She scans her things and takes her purse from her pocket, but before she can bring it to the card machine, she hears someone shout from behind her.

"Hey!"

Jinx turns to see what's going on, knocking her notebook onto the floor as she does so. Julian and Lilly are nowhere to be seen, but Jinx spots Vivienne still near the romance section, except she isn't looking at the books anymore. Instead, she has her back to the stand and is being blocked by a large boy. He looks twice their age, well built and he is stepping dangerously close to Vivienne. Where had Lilly and Julian gone? Why had they left her over there? Without thinking it through, Jinx abandons her shopping at the register and begins towards the boy and Vivienne.

"Come on, relax, it was only a pinch..." the man drawls, his words slurring into one another.

"Hey, asshole," Jinx says, walking down the aisle as fast as she can without breaking into a run. "What do you think you're doing?" She asks as she reaches him and Vivienne. The entirety of Vivienne's weight is completely against the shelf, so much so that it is tilting back.

"Who are you?" The man asks, stepping backwards. Taking that as an opportunity, Jinx steps in between him and Vivienne, blocking him completely.

"Why does it matter who I am? Now answer the question, what do you think you're doing?"

He laughs and glances towards the register, where there is still no one. "Why should I, and what does it matter to you? Move." He tries to shove Jinx out of the way, but she catches his arm and pushes him backwards, into a shelf of books. He stinks of beer and is clearly drunk, but even so, he regains his balance surprisingly quickly. Standing, he makes towards Vivienne and Jinx again, and Jinx steps backwards, a hand moving behind her back.

"You bitch, who do you think you are pushing me-" Jinx doesn't let him finish before she punches him hard, right in the nose. He stumbles backwards and hits the shelf again, knocking books onto the floor, and Jinx walks up to him. She grabs his shoulders and holds him against the shelf, trapping him against it. He's shorter than her, and his drunkenness makes it easy for her to use his own weight against him.

"Try to touch her again, I *dare* you." She whispers, tightening her grip on his shoulders. "You don't go near her again, do I make myself clear?" Jinx says, trying not to flinch at the strong stench of alcohol that clings to him. Her clothes are probably going to smell like that for a while now too, damn. "*Understood?*" she repeats, throwing his shoulders into the shelf again.

"Y-yes," he stutters, fear now painted across his features. Jinx lets go of him and walks backwards towards Vivienne.

"Okay, now get the *fuck* away from her." Jinx spits, but the man doesn't move. Instead of telling him again, Jinx lifts her hands up and silently counts down with her fingers. Without another word, the man frantically begins towards the exit, dropping what he'd been holding on the floor. Unsurprisingly, it is a large candy bar and some dirty magazine that Jinx quickly kicks under the aisle before turning to Vivienne.

"Are you okay?" she asks, her hand resting on Vivienne's arm. Vivienne doesn't say anything, she just looks at the door and wraps her arms around herself. "Carter?" Jinx presses, she has to know if she's okay, what that man was about to do to her...

"I-I-" she trails off and looks at the stuff in her hands. Following her gaze, Jinx notices that she isn't just holding her stuff, but Lilly and Julian's as well.

"Where did they go? Why did they leave you?"

"L-Lilly left her p-phone so t-they..." she trails off and points at the door. Jinx was going to kill them, why did they leave her alone? They left her alone in that aisle, they left her, and that man had taken advantage. They are *so* dead. "Y-you..." Jinx returns her gaze to Vivienne, and finds she is staring at her arm. Where Jinx's hand is. Pulling her arm away, Jinx takes several steps back, so many that she nearly walks into the shelf behind her, the one she'd just *pinned* a man to. "W-why did..."

"Why do you think? That man was assaulting you, or about to, anyway, so I stopped him."

Vivienne looks Jinx up and down, then shakes her head and stands up straighter. "You *pinned* him to the *shelf*, you *punched* him; you could have just told him to leave." She says, walking away from Jinx and towards the register, where there is now an old man who's reading a newspaper, clearly unaware of what just happened.

"And you think that would've worked? I pushed him backwards and he still tried to come after you."

"Maybe if you had just talked to him, he would've let us be and carried on with his evening."

Vivienne places her stuff on the register and the old man begins scanning them. Is she serious? Jinx just helped her, stopped her from whatever that man planned on doing to her, and she's acting like this. What's wrong with her?

"Fine. Next time you're in a situation like that, I'll let you be and you can talk yourself out of it." Jinx says, crossing her arms over her chest and standing to the side of Vivienne. She scans her things, along with Julian and Lilly's and pays, asking for a bag as she does so. Jinx isn't sure why she's waiting with her, she has every right to walk out of that shop and leave Vivienne on her own after what she just said, but some part of her won't leave. That man can't have gone far in the short time they've been paying, and for all she knows he could be waiting for Jinx to leave so he could take another shot at Vivienne.

Vivienne thanks the cashier and walks towards the exit, so Jinx follows. They walk down the street, towards where Julian said he and Lilly had gone, neither of them talking. Jinx gets halfway there before she realises, she left her notebook and book at the till in the stationary store. She needs to go back and get them, but Vivienne won't stop walking, her pace gradually quickening as they draw closer to Julian and Lilly, so Jinx carries on, she can get her things another time. The wind had picked up whilst they were in the stationary store and Jinx wraps her coat tighter around her, pulling up her collar against the bitter wind that bites at her from behind. Vivienne has done the same, except her cardigan doesn't seem to be having the same effect, as her neck is still exposed to the bitter wind. She shivers and wraps the cardigan tighter around her; she really doesn't know how to dress for the weather, and it makes Jinx wonder if she even has the appropriate clothes too. Without a word, Jinx drops back and stands behind Vivienne, hoping she can stop some of the vicious wind that is causing goosebumps to crawl under Vivienne's neck. They are only small, but Jinx can't stop looking at them. Shivering is one thing, but goosebumps, they mean someone is genuinely freezing. Or really scared. Jinx doubts it's the latter, and if it is, she still wants to stop the cold. Tonight really isn't Vivienne's night. Jinx had clearly ruined her night with her father, she nearly lost her brother, she had some man corner her in a store, and she's now freezing.

Julian and Lilly appear through a window moments later, arm in arm and in fits of laughter. If Jinx didn't know better, she'd have thought they were a couple. They aren't, of course, Lilly isn't interested in any of that, she made that very clear when they first met. She said she didn't feel 'that way' about anyone, and that when people assumed she did because of her reading habits it really got on her nerves.

When they notice Vivienne and Jinx, they wave at them and gesture for them to come in, and Jinx begins to, but Vivienne stops dead on the spot. Reaching the door, Jinx makes to hold it open for her in a mocking way, but Vivienne is still standing in the middle of the sidewalk. Confused, Jinx walks back to her and looks through the window. Vivienne's eyes are fixed on something, but Jinx can't tell what it was. She isn't looking at Julian and Lilly, who have turned their backs to the window and are now browsing the shelves behind them, and she isn't looking at anything in the display in front of them. Jinx stares inside the shop for a while before she spots it, before she spots *him*. The man from the shop. Jinx knew he wouldn't have gone far.

"Lets go," Jinx murmurs, pulling Vivienne away from the shop and pulling out her phone.

Jinx: 7:54pm
We're going to head back; I have everything I need, and Vivienne has soaked herself in ice water by falling into a puddle like an actual moron. You guys stay and finish your shopping, I have your stuff from the stationary store, and I'll give it to you tomorrow in Classics'.

She starts to walk away, but Vivienne stops again and checks her phone. Her eyes move across the illuminated screen before she puts her phone back in her pocket and catches up to Jinx. Jinx's phone vibrates in her hand and she checks it as she turns left, Vivienne in front of her.

Julian: 7:57pm
What?! Vi are you ok? Do you want me to come back with you, I don't really need anything else, I can walk back with you

Lilly: 7:57pm
Relax Julian. She only fell over, and Jinx said she will walk her back. You stay with me and have fun, this is the only time your not studying

Julian: 7:58pm
You could've said that to me in person

Lilly: 7:58pm
I know but talking requires so much effort

Jinx sighs and puts her phone in her pocket, catching Vivienne up and walking beside her. They walk in silence, again, but it isn't the usual silence. The usual silence has an 'I can't stand you, so I don't talk to you' feeling to it, but this is really more of an uncomfortable silence. Not for Jinx, Jinx feels fine, but Vivienne looks really uncomfortable. Every few seconds she glances backwards and wraps her cardigan tighter around her. Whenever she does, Jinx follows her gaze, checking for what she knows Vivienne is worried about.

When they've walked like this for a while, Jinx stops to cross the street, and Vivienne follows suit. Jinx cranes her neck around the corner and checks either way for cars, then begins across the street. Vivienne follows her but is a good few feet behind, so when Jinx reaches the sidewalk, she waits.

"I don't need a bodyguard; you don't have to wait." Vivienne sighs, walking ahead of Jinx, her arms wrapped tight around her.

"I'm not being your bodyguard. I'm merely walking back with you, I know you don't hang around with many, but that is something people do." Why did she say that? Vivienne is clearly having a hard time and all Jinx is doing is making it worse. Vivienne shrugs and carries on walking, checking behind her again. Jinx starts to walk, having stopped and given Vivienne time to get ahead, checking behind her when Vivienne isn't looking.

"Why are you walking behind me?" Vivienne asks, stopping and turning around, her arms now crossed lightly over her chest. "It's a very bodyguard-like thing to do."

"I'm walking behind you because you won't stop looking over your shoulder."

"Why does that make you want to walk behind me?" Vivienne asks, and Jinx walks towards her, pulling her phone out of her pocket as she does so.

"Well, I know why you're doing it, so I figure if you see me instead, you'll realise that I'm the only person following you." Jinx shrugs, pulling her headphones out of her pocket and plugging them into her phone. "Plus, whenever you look at me you pull a face that makes you look annoyed out of your mind, and I'm hoping that your pure hatred of my presence takes your mind off what just happened, even if it's only for a small bit. Never underestimate the power of pure annoyance." Jinx waves a finger in Vivienne's face and puts one of her headphones in her ear, offering the other to Vivienne, "Music works better, though."

Vivienne looks taken aback by the offer, raising one eyebrow at Jinx. That is something Jinx has always wanted to do, she'd even spent hours as a kid trying to do it in front of the mirror, which resulted in a lot of headaches, but she never managed it. Of course Vivienne can do it.

"Why are you being nice to me? It's unnerving." She asks, nervously eyeing the headphone like it has some kind of disease.

"Tonight has *not* been your night, so I'm being nice. Don't expect this kindness to extend any further than the next twenty minutes." Jinx smirks, holding the headphones out again and gesturing for her to take it, "I mean I can be a bitch if you want…" She trails off and Vivienne hastily takes the headphone and puts it in her ear, shaking her head and sighing as she does so. Jinx presses play on her phone and hears Vivienne laugh beside her. Something in the pit of Jinx's stomach flutters at the sound, but she ignores it and raises both eyebrows at Vivienne. She shakes her head,

"Are you capable of listening to happy music?"

"Yep. Completely incapable. If it isn't remotely sad, it isn't music." Jinx states, smirking and putting her hands in her pockets once again. "Do you not like *Phoebe Bridgers?*"

Vivienne looks ahead and Jinx follows her gaze, trying not to think about how Vivienne has picked up on Jinx's music habits, when they've never talked about music before, or ever referenced it.

Chapter 13 – Vivienne

°•. ✿ .•°°•. ✿ .•°°•. ✿ .•°

Flicking the lights on in her dorm, Vivienne walks through the room and flops onto the couch, her shoes leaving wet marks on the clean wood floor. Pulling one of the cushions from behind her head, she covers her face and screams into it. She screams for so long that when she finally stops, the back of her throat aches and her head is spinning. Fine. Everything had been fine, Jinx didn't seem to care about the dinner with her Dad and hadn't mentioned it to anyone, but then in the store.... Vivienne could've easily defended herself against that man, he was drunk and clumsy, but she hadn't moved. She wanted to, she wanted to push him against the shelf as Jinx had and then ran, but instead she'd frozen. She stood there, no doubt looking dumbfounded, until Jinx helped her. *Jinx,* of all people. Some part of her knows she should be mad at Julian for leaving her, for going with Lilly to get her phone, but she can't find it in herself. If Julian hadn't gone with Lilly, she might have suffered the same fate, except on her own. It wasn't as if she was completely on her own, either, technically she was with Jinx. Vivienne also knows she should be grateful Jinx was there, and that she'd done what she did, and she is, but it's what came after that threw her off.

Vivienne is used to Jinx. She is used to the Jinx who teases her at every opportunity and beats her at everything, she likes being used to *that* Jinx. Not the Jinx she just walked back with. Not the Jinx who walks behind her to make her feel safe, not the Jinx who waits for her across the street, and definitely *not* the Jinx who shares her headphones with Vivienne to take her mind off things. This Jinx is new, and Vivienne isn't sure how to act around her. It's awkward, uncomfortable, and Vivienne much prefers it when Jinx is being an asshole, because then Vivienne can be an asshole back. But when Jinx is like this, Vivienne doesn't know how to act around her. When Jinx is being nice, Vivienne's automatic reaction is to be suspicious, Jinx is never nice, but then Vivienne feels bad for being standoffish when she is. It's confusing. Very confusing.

Although, it did feel nice not having to waste energy on finding ways to counter her constant sarcasm and cockiness. It wasn't *relaxing,* but it wasn't tiring either. If Vivienne could keep it like this, she probably would. She doesn't enjoy the awkwardness, but that will pass, and having Jinx as a mutual acquaintance will definitely be better than having her as a constant rival. Having a rival takes up so much energy and it's the last thing Vivienne needs on top of her ever-growing schoolwork. Of course, Jinx will probably laugh at the idea and use it to tease her further, she seems to thrive off their rivalry, which isn't surprising, but Vivienne can't help but play the idea in her head.

Thankfully, years of being co-captain of the school debate team has helped her prepare for issues like this. Jinx was the captain, but she tended to work off illegible notes that only she could read and a 'gut feeling' as she put it, which left most of the planning, which went to the moderators to be assessed, to Vivienne. As they were never told what position they were taking until the day, teams always had to make balanced Pro and Con lists for their debates, like her group are at the moment, so her ability to see equal sides of an issue is extremely strong.

Rolling off the couch and leaving the pillow on the floor, Vivienne reaches for the notepad and pen that is on the small table next to her. She really should be sitting at a table, her writing is horrendous when she writes without a solid surface underneath her, but she can't find the energy to get up and walk to her room, which isn't a great distance away, but it has been a long night.

There are many things she could be doing instead of this, including two assignments that are due within the next week, but again, her laptop is halfway across the room, and she doesn't feel like routing through over two hundred years of history to write a four-page essay. Surprisingly, writing a list to justify a friendship between her and Jinx is more appealing, despite the fact it will probably lead to no outcome, and waste paper in her favourite notepad. It isn't special in any way, it looks like the usual pads you find in every college student's dorm, but it has notes on her favourite historical moments throughout history, along with *a lot* of practice for questions that she hopes will appear on her finals, and if they don't, she will be very disappointed. Pulling a pen from her back pocket, she writes the words pro and con on the top of the page. Like she assumed, it is slanted and practically scribbles, but she can read it.

Racking her brain, she begins to write down as much as she can think of for both sides and after at least half an hour, the page is full. Not full in the usual way, which means completely covered in unbelievably detailed notes, instead the page is filled with no more than nine short sentences that are stretched so they somehow take up two lines each. It looks like Ollie's Christmas list.

The right side, containing the con points, has four bullet points,

> Con:
> 1. Jinx is a pain in the ass.
> 2. If she says no, she won't hesitate to tease me about it.

> 3. She could steal Julian, using her nice-person façade.
> 4. She's mean.

Technically there are only two *valid* points, but Vivienne chooses to ignore logic and counts it as four. On the pro side, there are five points,

> Pro:
> 1. It would make classics easier.
> 2. Studying as a group wouldn't be as awkward.
> 3. Could become closer with Lilly, which would be <u>a-ma-zing.</u>
> 4. Jinx could possibly help out with the Pro side of the debate, as anti-romance as she is, she could probably find better points than the ones already there.
> 5. It would make going to that little coffee shop so much easier. The coffee there literally tastes like <u>liquid heaven.</u>

The pros clearly outweigh the cons, which is normally the decider for Vivienne. In most situations she would move straight onto the decision with the most points, but with her phone in hand she can't bring herself to open Jinx's DMs. Instead, she is staring at her Instagram account, which is completely empty aside from the one post that clearly wasn't taken by her. It's her and Lilly in a bookstore. Vivienne knows the place, she's been there countless times, but she didn't know Jinx went there too. Jinx doesn't exactly strike her as the 'hanging out in a bookstore' type, but there she is, standing behind Lilly. She is facing away from the camera, seemingly very interested in the book she is reading. Lilly is holding the phone and beaming at the camera, her blue eyeliner in little wings at the corners of her eyes like usual. Underneath, the caption reads 'Trying to catch this one up with modern communication! She is extremely hesitant if you can't already tell.' Lilly has obviously written it, but Vivienne can't help but smile at the thought of Jinx reading the caption and glaring at Lilly in her usual way. Vivienne wonders why Jinx doesn't have social media in the first place. It isn't unusual for someone not to have Instagram, but Jinx isn't missing just that. She doesn't have anything that is media-based. Well, she has Pinterest, but that doesn't really count. People rarely use Pinterest as a platform for communication, it's just there to find inspiration for stuff, or, if you are Vivienne, it's where you can find couples doing things she's read about in her latest romance book (like kissing in the rain, something she is yet to experience, or when she's wearing a pretty dress, someone would compliment her and then just…).

    Sighing, Vivienne drops her phone to the floor and tears the list in half. This is pointless. She should just go back to being rivals with Jinx, it isn't *that* distracting. Plus, they only see each other a few times a week, what would be the point of forming some kind of friendship when it won't amount to anything anyway. If Jinx wants a friendship, or something like that, *Jinx* can ask. Vivienne isn't about to embarrass herself over twenty minutes of the *bare minimum* from this girl. That's all she's done. All she's done is the bare minimum in a friendship, and it isn't as if she's done it just to be nice. Jinx did it because she pitied her.

Because she pitied Vivienne after what happened in the store. That's all.

Vivienne lifts herself off the floor and picks up the torn pieces of the list. As she goes to throw them in a trash can, a large thump on the dorm door echoes throughout the room. Not thinking much of it, she walks from the can and towards her dorm door, getting her laptop off a nearby table as she does so. Because she wasted time doing the stupid list, she's going to have to spend longer on her assignments than she planned, meaning she won't be able to stop Julian from falling asleep at his desk, something he's made a habit of recently. She doesn't have to wake him up, he tends to wake himself up in the early hours of the morning, but Vivienne does it anyway. If he falls asleep at his desk, he doesn't sleep properly and will wake up with a strained neck. Considering he doesn't drink coffee, and he refuses to go near energy drinks, if he doesn't sleep properly, he'll feel half asleep all of the following day. Last week Vivienne forgot to wake him up and he ended up falling asleep in the middle of one of his lectures. Thankfully, college doesn't give out detentions and he was just told to go back to his dorm and sleep, how considerate of them.

Another large thud sounds from behind her door and Vivienne shakes her head. What's going on? Her building tends to be one of the quieter ones, and stuff like this rarely happens. She counts herself lucky, yesterday Lilly mentioned how her dorm is directly across from the rowdy sports boys. People like that must make *a lot* of noise, especially after campus games, and Vivienne feels bad for Lilly having to put up with it. She doesn't know what she'd do if she had neighbours like that. She has two rooms either side of her and she rarely hears anything from them. One is a single, and Vivienne is half convinced it's empty due to the astounding lack of noise coming from it, the walls aren't very thick and yet Vivienne hasn't heard anything, *ever*. The other room beside hers is a double, and she knows that it has people in it. She'd run into the students in there a couple of times, two boys. There is never much conversation between her and them, but she is fairly sure the taller of the two keeps trying to flirt with her, which is hilarious to watch considering he is unbelievably bad at it.

Curious about what is causing the unusual racket, Vivienne makes towards the dorm's main door. She is mere inches from it when it's flung inwards and Julian falls through, landing at her feet. He curses under his breath and Vivienne chuckles to herself as she watches him clumsily get up and brush himself off. He twists his body and grabs the bottom of his coat, craning his neck at something he clearly can't see.

"Have I torn my jacket?" he asks, his brow furrowing. Vivienne laughs out right and brings her hand to her head.

"Could you ask a stupider question? 'Have I torn my jacket?' I'd be more worried about how many of your bones survived that fall."

He looks up at her and sighs, "It didn't hurt that much, and bones don't break that easily, coats however…" he trails off and his attention is immediately back on the coat.

"Come here," she says, turning him around and crouching near the bottom of his coat. She can't see anything different; it looks the same as it always does, only wet. "It's fine, not a single thread is out of place." Vivienne smiles, waving her hands in an exaggerated way, "What would we have done if it was torn?! I left my emergency sewing kit at home, the paramedics would take forever and by then we'd have lost it…"

Julian rolls his eyes and shrugs off the coat, discarding it on the couch. He smiles and walks back outside, only to return seconds later, hauling a large, long box with him.

"What is that?" Vivienne asks, helping him as he places it on the floor.

Julian puts his hands on his hips, "A Christmas tree." He states proudly and Vivienne raises her eyebrows.

"Two things, one, where have you gotten the money for this Christmas tree from, you're broke, and two, it's November."

"I'm fully aware that it's November, which is why I bought it. It was on sale, perfect for college students like us who want to get into the Christmas spirit." He bends down and tears open the end of the box. Where has Julian found the money for this? It's obviously fake, but that doesn't stop it from costing a lot.

"How much was it?" Vivienne asks, sceptically, "and where do you propose we put it?"

"Like I said, it was on sale, and we're putting it over there." He points to the centre of the far wall, in between two small bookshelves. There is a small window a few feet off the ground, and Julian put up some plain curtains a while ago when it started getting really cold.

"*There*? How do you propose we fit a Christmas tree there?" It isn't a very large area; Vivienne can only just stand there without touching either bookshelf. "Are your glasses not working? We can't fit a tree there."

"Oh yeah? Want to bet?" Julian teases, sticking his hands into the narrow box.

"A bet? You really have let your twelve-year-old self take control today." Vivienne gets on her knees and pulls the end of the box and Julian pulls the tree from the other end. It's easier than she'd assumed, so Vivienne falls backwards as the box comes loose, banging her elbow on the corner of the coffee table. Cursing, she sits up again and removes the box entirely. Now she's seeing it, it does look like it will fit. It looks about three feet tall, and the branches are relatively short.

"I don't suppose you bought lights for this? Or are we just going to have a bare, plastic tree in our dorm for the next two months."

"Of course I bought lights," Julian smiles, pulling a long string of lights out of his pocket. He looks like one of those cheesy magicians you find at kids birthday parties, the type where if you look hard enough you can see how they do the tricks.

"If all else fails, it looks like you might have a career in magic." Vivienne laughs, looking at his pocket, where lights are still pouring out of. He looks confused for a second, then looks at his pocket and laughs, pulling the last of the lights out and dropping them on the floor. "Maybe not, actually, *real* magicians don't let the audience see the end of the string."

Julian crosses his arms, "Darn it, I really liked that idea. Plus, it sounds a lot easier than having to qualify as a paediatric surgeon."

"You've decided, then?" Vivienne asks, picking up the tree and bending out the arms. Julian has always said he wants to go into medicine, that's what he's majoring in after all, but he hasn't actually decided on what field he wants to go into. He's told Vivienne that he likes the idea of surgery, and how it seems less stressful than working in an ER, but he has no idea what kind of surgery. One week he says he's decided to become a Cardiovascular surgeon, and the next he will be overjoyed at his choice of General surgery. There are a few areas he knows he *isn't* going into, for example neurological surgery, which requires operating on the brain. He says he thinks it will be too much stress to go into an area like that, considering how particular the brain is. Apparently, there is more that can go wrong with the brain, and the after effects of mistakes will be a lot more drastic.

Vivienne has no idea why, she's never shown any interest in the medical field, she can't. She'd tried a few times back in Highschool, but she just couldn't. Every time she got an email from 'Medical News Weekly' or went onto a hospital website, she thought of her mum. Then she thought about how she'd let her mum down, how she'd failed her. Vivienne quickly shut down any hopes of becoming a doctor. It was kind of ironic, really. In films and books, when a parent dies early, it normally inspires the child to become a doctor or something, but it wasn't like that for her. Instead, her mum's death had made her terrified of hospitals, and all things associated with it. She can't even look at blood, even *that* freaks her out. It doesn't matter if it's her blood, or if someone on TV has cut their hand, it just *freaks* her out. She doesn't even know why. Her Mum's death hadn't been gory or covered in blood, if anything it had been toxically clean and sterile.

"Vi? Did you hear me?" Julian has moved closer and is crouched bedside her, bending the higher branches of the tree outwards. Vivienne's hand is still gripped to one of the lower branches, but she hasn't bent it out. Shaking her head, she looks up at Julian. It's surprising how he is still taller than her, even though they are both crouched. Julian is tall, but he's mostly legs, and yet here he is, taller than her, again. Why did she have to pick such a tall friend, it just makes her feel shorter than she already is.

"Sorry, I just…" she trails off and carries on bending down the branches. Most of them are already down, probably because of Julian, but she straightens some of them out anyway. Feeling Julian's hand on her shoulder, she looks back to him, trying to smile.

"Are you ok?" He asks, shuffling closer to her. "You look a bit fazed."

Vivienne shakes her head, "No, no, I'm fine." That's a lie, thinking about her mum *has* fazed her.

"Vi, you're clearly not fine, come here." He shuffles even closer and wraps his arm around her, forcing her to put her head on his shoulder. "What's up?" He asks, falling back from a crouch to a sit on the floor. Vivienne follows his motion, letting go of the half-assembled tree. Julian rests his head against hers and sits silently.

"I was thinking about my mum, that's all." Vivienne finally mutters, looking at the floor. Julian doesn't say anything, and they sit in silence. Julian never talks much when they talk about Vivienne's Mum, and Vivienne likes it. Whenever Vivienne brings up her Mum around other people, they always give her that pitied look and say something like 'Are you ok?' or 'It must've been so hard' and honestly, it makes her feel awful. When people give her that look it makes her feel like one of those sad dogs you see on YouTube, the ones on the street in a cardboard box whilst it's raining, and she hates it. When people pity her, it just makes the whole thing worse. Julian doesn't pity her, at least she doesn't think so, and she is so grateful for it.

Julian takes his arm from around her shoulder and stands up abruptly, causing Vivienne to fall backwards and hit her head on the wall. Julian doesn't seem to notice as he strides into his room, his arms crossed over his chest. Moments later, he comes out again, carrying two large, extremely fluffy blankets, and his laptop. Vivienne smiles and stands up to join him.

"I can't have you moping around like this, it just isn't right!" Julian sates, sticking his fist in the air like he's making a big announcement. "And what am I here for if not to cheer you up, hmm? If I can't do that, I'm utterly useless."

Vivienne hugs him, his hand still in the air. He stops talking and hugs her back, then pulls away to drop what he is carrying onto the couch beside them. "And, because you're feeling down, I am willing to sacrifice my sanity and watch one of your silly rom coms." He pulls a face, but Vivienne sees the smile tugging at his lips as she hugs him again. Julian always knows how to cheer Vivienne up, no matter the situation.

Once, in the library, she was so overwhelmed with schoolwork that she felt like she was going to scream, so he slammed all her books shut, which incurred the wrath of the librarian, and took her to one of the on-campus café's. At the time Vivienne was confused, especially when he ordered two coffees instead of one, considering he wouldn't touch the stuff, but then they sat down, and he just stared at her as he brought the cup to his lips. When he took a sip, he practically spat it back out again and sat there with his tongue hanging out of his mouth and making childish spitting noises. Vivienne was in fits of laughter, so much so that she had curled over in her seat, and her mind was completely wiped of all the mounting stress she'd felt moments before.

"A silly rom com? This is a golden opportunity, hmm…" Vivienne thinks through all the rom coms at her disposal, finally landing on one of the more Christmassy ones. "What about *Love Actually*?" Vivienne smirks as Julian, suppressing a comical eye roll, gestures to the couch.

"Fine. Now sit down and load up the film while I make us some 'Cheer up, it's nearly Christmas!' hot chocolates." Confused, Vivienne raises her eyebrows at Julian, who shrugs, "It's a regular hot chocolate with a candy cane in it."

"Where have you found candy canes *now?* We haven't had Thanksgiving yet; all the stores are still full of turkeys and autumn decorations." Vivienne asks, opening his laptop and typing in the code stuck on the inside. He really should get rid of that, but it does make it easier for Vivienne to look at his Classic's notes whilst he's out.

"My brother brought them back from England last week, over there the Christmas preparations are already in motion."

"What was your brother doing in England?" He'd said it as if it was no big deal. England is miles away, and the flights cost a fortune around the Holidays, what is he doing going over there? Vivienne has only met him once, Julian's brother, and it was only for a brief few minutes whilst he was dropping off some of Julian's textbooks he'd left at home. His name is Timothy, but Julian kept calling him Timmy, which annoys him because he's older and therefore 'too cool for that nickname now'. His words, not hers.

"He was visiting my parents." Julian hands her a hot chocolate and sits beside her, pulling one of the two blankets she has onto him.

"Wait *what*? Your parents live in *England*? As in the country that's over *2,500 miles* away?"

"Yes? Have I never told you that before?" He smirks and takes the laptop from her, placing it on the table in front of them and pressing play.

"You know you haven't, because you're doing that stupid 'I know something Vivienne doesn't' smirk."

Julian shrugs and lies back on the arm of the couch, stretching his legs out as he does so. His feet rest inches from Vivienne's face, and she immediately pushes them off, bringing her legs up to her chest. Julian gasps and brings his hand to his mouth in mock shock, but Vivienne just sticks her tongue at him, turning her attention to the laptop. She shushes Julian and points to the screen,

"You're missing the intro, and that's one of the best bits."

Julian groans in protest but doesn't say anything, crossing his arms over his chest and pouting like a petulant child instead. His aversion to these films reminds Vivienne of Jinx, although Julian seems to be more open about the ideas within them. Jinx just scoffs and says that it's all unrealistic and pathetic. She says people never go to these extremes for people they love; it just 'isn't how the world works'. Jinx always says that love and marriage are weak, idolised concepts created by those who can't cope with the world on their own. She says that love never lasts, that feelings always fade, and if they don't, people are inevitably torn apart by death anyway. What happened to Jinx to make her feel that way is something Vivienne has always wondered. She understands that people are allowed to not like romance and all that stuff, but Jinx doesn't just not like it, she attacks it at every opportunity, as if it has done her some kind of harm. What could have made her feel that strongly about it?

Chapter 14 – Jinx

⸺ · ₒ˚ ☆: *.☽ .* :☆˚ . ⸺

    Letting her head fall to her chest and running her fingers through her hair, Jinx sighs as she stares hopelessly at the pointless scramble of words in front of her. This is going nowhere. Her novel is going *nowhere*. She's been staring at the same damn page for the last half hour, and she can't think of *anything* to write. It isn't as if it is the climax of the story, or the heart-breaking ending she composed weeks ago. It's just a *memory*. A simple, romantic, happy memory. And yet her mind is blank, utterly empty, pointless, useless, worthless…

    A loud, dooming ping sounds from her phone, and she curses under her breath as she realises who it is. Only one person on her phone has the default 'ping', she changed the rest so she wouldn't have to hear it a while ago. Since she changed it, she hasn't heard it for a while, only once last week, and she ignored it then. Her phone goes off a second time, then a third, and a fourth, at which point she hesitantly picks it up and swipes up the messages. The screen is bright compared to the dusk-like darkness of her room, and the contrast makes her eyes sore. Her heart drops to her stomach as she scans the screen, reading the now seven messages consecutively sent.

    Her mother is a woman of few words, unless she wants something. Her entire childhood, all Jinx would get from her was scolding and drunken nonsense, unless she needed Jinx to do something. When she was little, her mother saw Jinx as completely useless and barely cast her a glance, but as she got older, there was more she could do. It slowly went from cold, resentful glances to 'do you mind, sweetie...' and 'I would but...'. Honestly, Jinx preferred when she was left alone, at least that way she wouldn't have been forcefully introduced to Kyle. After her Dad left, her Mum flitted around from man to man, each one worse than the next, but when Jinx was around fourteen, she found Kyle. Kyle stuck around all the way through high school and, as far as Jinx knows, is still there now.

As horrible as it sounds, Jinx hates when her Mum is with men, only because the men she dates are scum. If her Mum found a half-decent guy, Jinx might be less inclined to insult him at every opportunity and avoid him constantly, but that isn't her Mum. Her Mum doesn't use dating apps, or go to singles mixers, she doesn't even go to nice bars. Her mum goes to some of the shadiest clubs in town. Any self-respecting individual wouldn't be caught dead there, but her Mum had traded self respect in for a bottle of vodka a while ago. The places she goes are horrible, the men there have no restraint or control. They prey on women like her Mum, they called her 'doll' and say they are 'gorgeous', and her Mum falls for it *every time*.

Jinx has lost track of how many men have come in and out of their door, but a few stick in her mind. Every now and again her Mum will bring home someone who oversteps the boundary too much, someone who quickly takes their attention off her Mum and onto Jinx herself. There is no denying that Jinx is a pretty girl, she has some desirable features, but she doesn't give much thought to them, those men, however. It only happened rarely, and only when she was younger, but her Mum never did anything to stop them.

Every so often, normally when her Mum was passed out on the couch, Jinx would run into her 'boyfriends' as they were leaving. Most of the time they scoffed or rolled their eyes and carried on walking, but sometimes they would stop. Four of them had stopped. Four of them had given Jinx a second thought and followed her into the kitchen, or back into the living room. Their names are permanently etched into her memory, along with the memories of them. She can remember every detail of their faces, every look in their eye, every emotion she'd felt as she shouted for her Mum and tried to push them away. She remembered everything. *Everything.*

They always stopped at a point, whether it was because her Mum had stirred in the other room or Jinx had threatened to call the police. None of them got past a certain stage, she never let them. No matter how tired she was, no matter how scared she was, she never stopped fighting them. Once, on the final one she'd let get to her, she punched him between the eyes and slipped away. After the final one, Jonathan was his name, she taught herself how to fight. How to defend herself and how to use their strength against them. It only ever happened once after that, with Kyle, but even before that she avoided them, even if her Mum was fully conscious because, honestly, Jinx didn't know if she could rely on her to stop them. She didn't know what her Mum would do if she found them like that, she didn't know if her Mum would choose her boyfriend over Jinx. She has before.

Her phone vibrates in her hand and another message appears on the screen.

Mum: 8:10pm
Jinx please answer yur phonee. Im your mother and I neid you.

That is probably the longest text her mum has ever sent her, which is surprising. She must really need money, and it's probably to pay a tab at a bar. Sighing, Jinx types her response and clicks send, getting an instant reply.

Jinx: 8:12pm
What do you want?

Mum: 8:12pm
Why so rube?

Jinx: 8:13pm
Why so drunk?

As bold of an assumption it is, Jinx knows she's right. Her Mum only texts her when she's drunk, and only because she doesn't have enough money to pay her tab.

Mum: 8:14pm
Im not drbnk

Jinx: 8:15pm
You are. What do you want?

A stupid question, her mum wants money. She always does.

Mum: 8:16pm
Well me amd Kyle have gane oot for drimks, but my kard isnt working. Could you send me some money? Just a little bit. I love you, dont you luve me?

Jinx screams in frustration and throws her phone across the room, so hard that when it hits the pillows on her bed it bounces, landing on the floor. Love. *Love.* Her mother *loves* her? This isn't *love*. Jinx has waited her whole life for those words to sound genuine, she spent nights as a child wishing she had parents that *loved* her. Her mother doesn't *love* her, she loves the *money* that comes from her. *Love.* What a pathetic feeling. What a *weak* feeling. The word 'love' is meaningless, meaningless, and

193

tainted. Love isn't real, it's an idea, it's a word thrown around by the desperate, like her mother. Jinx's mother has never loved her, she's made that clear, but the minute she needs money to pay for whatever she's intoxicated herself with, all she feels towards Jinx is *love*.

The first time her Mum had said she loved her was the first time Jinx had gone on an 'errand' for her and come back with something she was far too young to understand. She ran straight to her room afterwards and literally jumped up and down with joy, that was how much it had meant to her then. The feeling lasted less than an hour. That's how long it took for her Mum to show her true colours again and become what Jinx had seen her as before. From that point on, every time she said it, it lost its meaning. A little bit at a time until, eventually, it just became another word, pointless, meaningless, common.

The main door of the dorm opens with a distinctive click, and Jinx stands from her desk. When Jinx enters the common room, Lilly is already sitting on an armchair, her shoes carelessly discarded in the middle of the floor. Her usual satchel is still hanging limp on her arm, and she is scrolling through her phone, apparently oblivious to Jinx. Since she'd last seen her, the amount of pins on her satchel has grown substantially, each one defending a different cause, or showing off another little bit of Lilly's personality.

"How did you get in here?" This isn't Lilly's dorm, and Jinx doesn't remember giving her a key.

"How do you think? You left your door unlocked," Lilly says, returning her phone to her pocket and turning to Jinx.

"What?" Jinx begins towards her now closed door and checks the locks. To her surprise, it opens with ease. She could have sworn she locked it when she came in, but apparently, she hadn't. Lilly laughs behind her and Jinx turns back, the door now locked. "What are you doing here?"

"I'm bored, and studying is making me want to scream, so now I'm here. Entertain me."

Jinx raises her eyebrows and sits opposite Lilly, her arms crossed against her chest. "You need to study, and don't expect me to tell you otherwise."

Lilly pouts and turns her head away in a dramatic fashion. She's like this, she loves the idea of being the overachieving person she reads about in books, but when it actually comes to studying, she procrastinates to the point of getting nothing done. It's not as if she isn't smart, she's very good at all the subjects she takes, she just puts too much pressure on herself and studies far too close to the deadlines. Thankfully, Jinx can push her to study without Lilly losing her temper or quitting, it's just something she can do. Maybe it's because of their friendship, but Lilly never snaps at Jinx, she never shouts or gets angry, she just has a constantly cheery demeanour about her, it's nice.

"I know, but I was hoping you could do something about my lack of motivation." Lilly says, uncrossing her arms and pulling notebooks out of her satchel. "I need to write an essay for one of my classes, it needs to be a minimum of twelve pages but I'm only on page four." She passes one of her notebooks to Jinx, who opens it. Withholding a laugh, she looks over the 'four pages' Lilly has written. Turns out it isn't four pages, it's two pages of planning, doodling and ideas, then two pages of spaced-out scribbles.

"Why have you handwritten it? Why not word-process it, it's so much easier."

Lilly sighs and tilts her head back, exposing the columns of her neck. Jinx always admires Lilly's choice in fashion, it's bold and creative. She always has the confidence to try combinations and colours others never dare to, for example, today she is wearing white and green checked, wide leg pants and a white lace corset top. How she isn't freezing, Jinx isn't sure.

"My laptop was dead and the short burst of energy I had was already beginning to fade, so I had to work with what I had."

Of course. It's typical of Lilly to always be unprepared for situations like this, she has a habit of letting her technology die and then forgetting to charge it. Knowing her, she probably used the last of her charge watching silly rom-coms.

"Do you have your laptop with you now?" Jinx asks, closing the hopeless notebook and handing it back to Lilly.

"No, it's still charging."

Sighing, Jinx gets up and begins towards her bedroom. As she grabs her laptop off her desk, she makes sure to close all of the documents regarding her novel. They are private, even Lilly isn't allowed to see them. When she enters the common room again, she passes it to Lilly who begrudgingly opens it.

"Ah, ah, not here." Jinx waves her finger in Lilly's face and grabs her own official-looking satchel from the small table in front of her. "There are far too many distractions and you won't concentrate, let's go to the library."

Lilly groans in protest but stands, Jinx's laptop still in her hand. Jinx fills her bag with some of her own study supplies and leaves, an extremely hesitant Lilly in tow.

*

The library is quiet and empty when they arrive, and most of the large tables in the centre are empty. Lilly begins towards it, but Jinx grabs her by her jacket and gestures to the grand stairs leading to the upper levels. Lilly protests, but Jinx reiterates the fact that there are too many distractions at the big table, too many people to talk to, and talking means she isn't studying. The upper levels are ridden with bookshelves, so much so that it is like a maze when you are trying to find a table. After a lot of searching, they come across a small, empty table in a far corner. It's surrounded by bookcases, and no one else is in sight. It's perfect.

"Sit." Jinx mockingly orders, pointing at one of the chairs. Lilly does as she is told and sits, opening Jinx's laptop in front of her as she does. Following suit, Jinx sits down opposite her and takes out her supplies, a notepad, her stationary, and a textbook.

"You're studying as well?" Lilly asks, leaning over the table and looking at the cover of the textbook. It isn't school mandatory, and she doesn't *need* it for any of her classes, but it helps. It's mostly full of writing tips, which she desperately needs at the moment. "*English Writers Manual*, what class is that for?" Lilly asks, completely ignoring the open laptop in front of her.

Jinx brings a finger to her lips and shakes her head, using her other hand to point at Lilly's essay. Rolling her eyes, Lilly sits back down and begins to type, seeming to completely forget about the mock draft she'd written up earlier.

Thirty minutes passes before Lilly puts her head in her hands and rocks back and forth. Jinx tries her hardest to ignore it, but after a little while she can't help but ask, "What now?" Her tone is soaked with irritation, but Lilly doesn't seem to notice.

"Nothing to do with my essay or anything, just a random question really, but how would you describe the feeling given off in this picture?" Lilly turns around the laptop and shows Jinx a picture of a café lit up in a small alleyway.

"That's Van Gogh, right?" Jinx asks, resting her elbows on the table and linking her hands together.

"Yes. It's *Café Terrace at Night,* what an original name, right?" Lilly says mockingly, but Jinx doesn't listen. Instead, she pulls the laptop closer to her and further examines the image. While Lilly anxiously awaits, Jinx tries to put her thoughts of this painting into words. She isn't too interested in art, but she does like Van Gogh, she always has. When she was twelve, her school went on a trip to one of the local art museums and there was a travelling exhibit on Van Gogh. She found his story heart-wrenchingly beautiful, and yet so sad, and that night had researched more of his work.

"I think this is quite an ironic piece, ironic beauty almost. Most of Van Gogh's paintings are of landscapes, and they rarely have people in, but this one is café. If you look into Van Gogh's history, he was seen as mad and shunned by everyone he was around, and yet he has chosen to paint a place he would most likely be thrown out of if he went near it. Don't you think that's sad? Despite the liveliness of the painting and the colours used, Van Gogh was probably never accepted there. Perhaps he painted it in such a way because that is how he wanted it to be, perhaps it looks so lively and welcoming because he was trying to see as everyone else did, how *he* wanted to be seen."

Lilly stares at her in silence, her hands resting lightly on the keyboard of the laptop in front of her. They sit like this for a while before Lilly finally speaks, her eyes wide, "Can you say that all again, just a bit slower."

Jinx sighs and shakes her head, "I can't do your homework for you, this isn't high school."

"It's not as if we're going to get caught, you don't take art. You should, but you don't." Lilly plays with the idea while Jinx turns back to her own studying, trying to ignore the constant annoyed muttering coming from halfway across the table.

"Please," Lilly asks again, dragging out every syllable of the word.

"No."

"Pretty Please."

"No."

"If you don't, I'll open this very interesting document labelled 'Private' that's hovering around on the screen."

Jinx freezes, her pen mid-word on the paper before her. She looks up at Lilly, who is smirking and toying with the touchpad.

"You wouldn't." Jinx asks, cautiously reaching for the laptop, careful not to knock Lilly's fingers that are ever so delicately messing on her keyboard. Seeing her move, Lilly lifts the laptop up and away from Jinx, waving it in the air just out of her reach. Jinx smiles and lunges for it, completely forgetting that they are in a library and that Lilly is supposed to be studying.

Excited squeals escape from Lilly, and she jumps away from Jinx's swiping hand, hoisting the laptop higher over her head. It's no longer about getting the laptop back, Jinx honestly doesn't mind if Lilly reads the first few opening chapters, this is now a matter of principal, who's going to give up first. And it isn't going to be Jinx. Diving again, she is barely inches from the corner of the laptop, but Lilly is fast and swerves around the table, putting it between them.

"Come on, Keller, I thought you'd be faster than this." Lilly teases. This is something they do often, usually over pettier things, but it's fun either way. Lilly will call Jinx by her last name, and Jinx will do the same to Lilly, it's their own way of messing with each other. Practically running around the table, Jinx lunges one final time for the laptop,

"You're screwed, Thomas." She smiles, but the expression is quickly wiped from her face as her foot catches on the leg of her chair, sending her tumbling down. Right into Lilly. Collapsed in a clumsy heap on the floor, Lilly bursts into fits of laughter and pushes Jinx to the side. Jinx smiles and shakes her head; Lilly is becoming a very silly influence. Highschool Jinx would be appalled at their behaviour.

"Lilly? Jinx?"

Both swivelling round, Jinx is surprised to find Julian and Vivienne staring at them. Vivienne looks confused and almost annoyed, which isn't surprising, but Julian is smirking down at the two, clearly amused.

"Care to explain?" his smirk grows into a full-fledged smile as he reaches a hand out to help them up. Jinx rolls her eyes and stands on her own, yanking the laptop out of Lilly's grasp as she does so. A little less reluctant to Julian's offer, Lilly takes his hand and uses him as support to hoist herself up. As she brushes herself off, Jinx sits back on her chair and suspiciously eyes Julian and Vivienne.

"What are you doing here?" She asks, her attention shifting to Vivienne.

"This library is free of use to the *entire* campus, so why wouldn't we be here?" Vivienne rolls her eyes as if it's a simple question, but Jinx isn't done.

"No, I mean what are you doing *here*, at this table. There are tons of other hidden tables in this labyrinth of a library, why not go and sit at one of them instead of coming to ours?" Jinx doesn't know why she is picking a fight, but she is going to anyway. It may be because she's embarrassed, or maybe it's just because picking fights with Vivienne is fun. She likes to watch her blush and get all flustered.

"Well, because this is our table." Vivienne states, and Jinx can tell she has already spotted her own mistake.

"But I thought this library was open to the *entire* campus, how can you reserve one table when there are others? A little selfish, no? And here I thought I was the selfish one." Jinx smirks as Lilly joins her at the table, Julian following her.

"Will you two *please* stop bickering. It's like I'm babysitting my brothers." He says as he pulls up a chair and wedges himself between Jinx and Lilly.

"I can't see why we can't all share one table, I'm quite fond of the lot of you, *and* it will help you two" Lilly waves her finger between Jinx and Vivienne, "get along better."

Vivienne sighs and rolls her eyes, but she grabs a chair and pulls it towards the table. Julian smiles at Lilly and leans over to look at Jinx's laptop screen, "Why were you too fighting over this, anyway, don't you have your own?" he points his question at Lilly who looks away, mocking innocence.

"Mine was dead, and I have to write this essay for art, but Jinx is refusing to help me." She crosses her arms like a spiteful child and Jinx has to refrain from rolling her eyes.

"Fine. Because you're finding it absolutely impossible to do this on your own without acting like you should be in kindergarten, I'll give you a *couple* of points, okay?"

Lilly smiles and claps her hand together, "Thank you." She says, her voice two pitches higher as she drags out the final 'u'. Admitting defeat, Jinx bullet points what she said to Lilly earlier along with some extra points she can think of. Lilly is lucky this is on Van Gogh, otherwise Jinx wouldn't have anything to say, at all.

Once she is finished, she hands the laptop to Lilly and packs her own study equipment away.

"Where are you going?" Lilly asks, eyeing her bag in suspicion.

"I'm not going anywhere, you can't be trusted on your own, but I have nothing to study for so instead," Jinx pulls her current read, *Crime and Punishment,* out of her bag and waves it in front of Lilly. She looks momentarily amused at the idea of Jinx reading, but Jinx doesn't pay the look much mind and continues to put one of her earbuds in. Lilly sits in silence and works on her essay whilst Vivienne and Julian begin to get their own supplies out. Julian takes out two large textbooks and opens them on top of each other, along with a notebook and some stationary. It takes up a great portion of the table, but no one else is really using it anyway. For some reason, Lilly has the laptop balanced on her legs instead of safely in front of her, but Jinx doesn't say anything, talking to Lilly will mean she won't stop talking and her essay will sit there not being done. Vivienne, too, has her laptop out, though hers is on the table, and she is frantically typing away at something.

Unlike Lilly, who's eyes keep wandering around the table out of boredom, Vivienne's attention is fixed on the screen in front of her, so much so that she almost looks panicked, worried. Why she would be, Jinx isn't sure, Vivienne is one of the smartest people she knows, not to mention the most organised, so whatever assignment she is clearly rushing, she will get it done. If Jinx knows Vivienne at all, Vivienne is probably going to get it done days before the deadline and still think she's handed it in late, because that's just how she is. It's her 'character flaw' as Lilly likes to put it, she will build up stress and bundle up her worries until she snaps, Jinx has seen it a few times in high school.

Once, in their Freshman year, Jinx had gotten to homeroom early to get some studying done but stopped when she saw Vivienne in there, on her own, silently crying with her head on her desk. Surrounding here were sheets of torn paper covered in illegible black scribbles and bleeding red ink, it looked like someone had massacred a stationary store. Jinx wasn't sure what was going on at the time, but later she would learn that Vivienne had lost some of her homework for her top class, it didn't matter anyway, the homework wasn't due until the following week.

Jinx waited for Vivienne to compose herself, then walked in, seemingly oblivious to what she'd just seen. She sat in her assigned seat, which was directly behind Vivienne's, and was silent. She didn't take out any of her study material, she didn't read or turn on her phone, she just sat there, watching Vivienne. For some selfish, regrettable reason, Jinx didn't help her either. She didn't know why, but she didn't, and she couldn't help but feel bad about it even now.

"Something amusing, Jinx?" Jinx's attention shifts to Lilly, but she is still typing away at her laptop, eyes glued to the screen. Julian is doing the same, so there is only one person left. Her heart drops to her stomach as she turns to Vivienne again, and finds her staring at Jinx, her head cocked to the side and her eyebrows raised. That's when Jinx realises, she must've been staring.

"Amusing? What makes you say that?" Jinx closes her book on her lap but keeps her one earbud in.

"Well, you were staring at me, so I'm assuming there is something amusing. Let me guess, I have something in my hair? I've made a mistake on my paper? My collar is sticking up? What is it?"

Jinx can't tell if she's joking or not, but she doesn't like it. There's nothing up with Vivienne which makes it harder to find an excuse, and she needs one, quickly.

"It's, um, nothing..." Jinx trails off and returns to her book, turning her face down and away from Vivienne. There aren't many times Vivienne catches her off guard, but when she does, it throws Jinx off. *She* likes being the one who teases Vivienne, not the other way around.

"Really, oh..." Vivienne says, but it's quiet and subtle, as if she is looking away as well. Not daring to look around, Jinx tries to be invested in the book once again. Instead, she stares at the page and focuses on the music blasting in from one ear. Music is her escape, something that never changes and is always there, when she can't rely on anyone else, she relies on music. Music understands her like no one else does, and it tells more of herself than she ever can.

Silence coats the four once again, but it's again broken when Julian stands up and begins to pack away his things.

"Where are you going?" Lilly asks, looking up from her laptop. Julian zips up his bag and swings it onto his back,

"Hockey practice, why?"

Lilly beams at him and slams the laptop on her legs shut. Jinx sighs and puts her head in her hands,

"If you keep putting it off, you're never going to finish it." she says as she takes the laptop from Lilly, who is eagerly picking up her own satchel.

"What are you doing?" Julian asks as Lilly puts her arm around his and smiles.

"I'm using you as my ticket out of here," She states and pulls him forwards, "because you can't possibly go the hockey practice alone, you need someone at the side cheering you on."

"I really don't-" Julian is cut off by Lilly's elbow digging into his side, "Ow!" He exclaims, but doesn't pull away from her. It is obvious what she is trying to do, and it would be futile for Jinx to try and intervene now. She did her best, now it's up to Lilly to decide whether she will do it in time or stay up to unseemly hours the night before and finish it. She probably will, and she'll probably wake Jinx up and call her in order to do so. That will be fun.

"Lilly, when you're frantically doing this," Jinx points to the laptop in her hand, "the night before it's due and you need my help, as usual, I will not be answering my phone."

"Then I'll come to your dorm, it's not as if you lock your door anyway." Lilly smiles and walks off, pulling Julian with her. He looks partially amused at the conversation he just witnessed, but also a little scared at the thought of being alone with Lilly. Most people are. Despite her positive demeanour, Lilly can be absolutely terrifying when she wants to be, and sometimes when she doesn't.

Glancing at Vivienne again, Jinx notices that she still has her eyes pinned on the screen in front of her, as if she is oblivious to the conversation going on around her. Julian and Lilly round the corner and disappear out of sight, leaving the two alone, which Jinx doesn't particularly mind. Knowing there isn't going to be any form of conversation between the two, she puts both her earbuds in and turns up the volume, loud enough that the world around her is completely tuned out. Instead of trying to pick up where she left off in the book she is reading, she opens her laptop and clicks on her 'Private' document, the one Lilly keeps threatening to open. Again, she scrolls through the pages until she hits the blank space in the middle of a paragraph. It isn't hard to miss, it takes up practically a whole page and is situated between two asterisks, like most of the memories are in her novel. Again, she stares at the blank space and racks her brain for anything, any ideas, absolutely *anything,* but her brain empties. It doesn't make sense, she has written an entire novel, beginning to end, planned it all out and created characters, settings, everything and yet when it comes to this simple memory, this one simple thing, her mind goes blank. Completely and utterly blank.

Scrolling up again, all the way to the top, to the start, she begins to read through it instead. Editing anything she can find and changing bits she doesn't think quite fit in, there isn't much left to edit though. She must've gone through it more than a dozen times whilst trying to think of how to fill the gaping hole in her work, and more than a dozen times before that. Now, all she can really do is read it. Read it and get increasingly frustrated every time her eyes wandered past the gap. The novel-destroying gap. As futile as it is, it being only a memory, without it, what comes later won't have the same effect. It won't pull at the heartstrings of the reader as it should, it takes the emotion away from the situation. Without this memory, what she has built up just reads like an accounting of events, void of emotion in every sense of the word.

Completely forgetting Vivienne is sitting inches from her, Jinx groans in frustration and hits her head on the table, giving up and putting her head in her hands. This is impossible, this is never going to work, she is never going to finish...

"You alright?"

Shit. *Shit.* Vivienne. Whipping her head around fast enough to give herself whiplash, Jinx finds Vivienne confusingly observing Jinx in her pitiful state. Why. Why. Why. Why. Why. Why. Why. Why...

"Jinx?"

Talk. Speak. Say something, *do* something. But she can't, Jinx is frozen on the spot, unable to say anything. This is embarrassing. In fact, this is worse than embarrassing, this is pathetic and stupid. Why can't she speak, and why is Vivienne looking at her in such an odd way. If Jinx didn't know better, she would say Vivienne looks concerned, but she can't be. There are very few things that girl feels towards her, but Jinx can guarantee *concern* isn't one.

"Jinx? What are you doing?" Now she just looks offended and annoyed, that makes it easier to finally talk to her.

"What?" Jinx says, turning back to her laptop and shutting it hard enough that she's surprised she hasn't smashed it.

"What do you mean 'What?', you just hit your head on the table *on purpose* then put your head in your hands like you were about to have a breakdown."

"There's a massive gap in this part of my novel and for some shitty reason I can't think of a single, remotely happy memory to fill it with. Over 130,00 words and I can't do this. Simple. Thing." What. *What.* Jinx froze. Actually froze. *Again.* What is she doing, *what* did she just say. Why is she even talking to Vivienne, she doesn't need to know any of this, and yet, for some reason Jinx is desperate to know, Jinx has just told her what she never tells *anyone.* No one knows she is writing a novel; no one knows how long it is, no one knows it *exists.* And yet she'd just told Vivienne. Vivienne of all people. This is why she doesn't speak to her, this and the fact that she can't be bothered with their petty arguments half the time.

"What?" Vivienne is watching her now, and Jinx rapidly starts packing her things away, including her laptop.

"Nothing." Jinx says, not looking at her and swinging her bag onto her back.

"Where are you going?" Vivienne asks, packing her own things away.

"Why do you need to know?" That's uncalled for, but Jinx needs to get away, fast. Thankfully, her phone begins to vibrate in her pocket, and she doesn't hesitate to answer it, not bothering to check the number. Vivienne stops talking and Jinx concentrates wholly on the conversation over the phone but is partially surprised when Lilly's voice comes through her speakers. She sounds like she's been crying and is talking too fast for Jinx to decipher, but it makes her panic.

"Lilly, slow down, tell me what's going on." Jinx has turned away from Vivienne to take the call, but she sees her freeze in the corner of her eye.

Jinx has to stop herself from dropping her phone as Lilly slows down to tell her what's going on. When she has finished, Jinx puts down the phone and grabs Vivienne wrist, pulling her into a run, leaving their stuff abandoned in the library.

"Jinx, what's going on?" Vivienne asks, trying to keep up with Jinx. She sounds as panicked as Jinx feels, but Jinx doesn't stop running.

"It's Julian," Jinx says, not slowing down, "he's collapsed."

Chapter 15 – Vivienne

°•. ✿ .•°°•. ✿ .•°°•. ✿ .•°

Beep.
Julian is in the hospital.
Beep.
He passed out.
Beep.
There is nothing she can do.
Beep.
They've taken him away.
Beep.
Through those doors.
Beep.
Through those doors.
"Carter? Are you all right?"
Beep.
He's gone.
Beep.
She can't talk to him.
Beep.
She doesn't know if he's ok.
Beep.
Those damn doors.
Beep.
"Carter?" Jinx shakes Vivienne's shoulder and her attention is momentarily shifted, but not entirely. "Are you ok?" She asks, taking her hand back and tilting her head to the side. Vivienne tries to focus, she really does, but all she can see is the

hospital behind her. The countless people sitting, waiting, all in a situation vastly different from the person beside them, all unaware of each other. Then, of course, there are the patients, the nurses, the doctors, all running around, wandering through, but never staying. The doctors are always called away, taking the nurses with them, and the patients are ushered out, called to appointments, or taken to be given treatment.

"I..." Vivienne trails off, flinching into her seat and clenching her hands into fists as someone is wheeled past on a bed. Swallowing hard, she tries to force herself to relax, but it's a futile attempt. There is nothing, *nothing,* that can relax her. Not now. Not here. The last two hours have been a blur, starting from when Jinx had pulled Vivienne out of the library with surprising rapidness. She hadn't realised that Julian mattered that much to her, Vivienne thought Jinx just put up with Julian because she had too.

When they reached Lilly, she was on the phone again, talking in rapid, panicked Spanish and pacing at the bottom of the steps. That was when Jinx let go of Vivienne's wrist and ran towards Lilly, who quickly ended her call and hugged her tight around the waist. Lilly explained what happened to the both of them, how Julian said he felt a little dizzy then just collapsed on the stairs, and she said she called an ambulance, which had just left. That's when her phone rang again, which she explained was her brother offering them all a ride to the hospital, which Vivienne accepted without thinking. It was only when she was in the car that she came to terms with where she was going.

Beep.

A heart monitor. Somewhere, there is a heart monitor.

Beep.

Somewhere, someone is hooked up to it.

Beep.

Somewhere, families are watching it slow.
Beep.
Watching the life drain from those they love.
Beep.
Like she had.
Beep.
No, like her father had.
Beep.
She hadn't.
Beep.
She's a coward.
Beep.

Jinx takes her by the wrist again, like she had in the library, but Vivienne doesn't take much note of it. She doesn't take much note of anything, and yet she thinks about everything. Her leg bounces, despite her efforts to calm down, and she tries to think of anything. *Anything* but what is slowly taking control of her mind. A thought she can't push away, as she normally can, and a thought only Julian can help distract her from.

"Come on."

Jinx pulls her up, and Vivienne doesn't protest as she is led away from their seats and into a quieter corridor. She doesn't care enough to protest; she can't spare enough thoughts to care.

Ping.

An elevator door opens, and Vivienne is ushered into it, Jinx following her. "Where…" she trails off when the elevator doors begin to shut, thinking she can finally be at peace from the bustling corridors. Even if only for a few seconds. Her hopes are shattered when a small, slipper covered foot sticks out and stops the doors in their path. Vivienne freezes, her nails digging into the palm of her hand. Her breathing becomes shallow and quick when a short woman steps into the elevator with them, draped in a hospital gown. Her features blur, everything blurs, all Vivienne can see is the tube trailing out of her arm and up into a bag hanging limp on a tall metal pole. A bag of...

"Bl..." Vivienne starts to feel faint as the doors close, trapping her inside the moving metal box. Falling back against the handrail, Vivienne feels bile rise in her throat and wills her eyes to close, but they don't, they stay fixed on the woman's stand.

"Look at me."

Jinx is in front of her. The bag shakes as the woman shifts to press a button.

"Don't look at her, look at me." Jinx places both hands on Vivienne's shoulder and steps closer. "Only look at me. Focus on me."

The woman sighs and leans against the handrail, pulling her stand closer to her. And Vivienne. She pushes herself hard against the wall, wishing she can disappear into it, become part of it, feel the cold metal wrap around her.

"*Vivienne.* Look at me."

Jinx is close to her now, standing between Vivienne and the woman. She is close enough that Vivienne can see her own reflection in Jinx's glasses. The frames are gold, or at least they look like gold, and circular. They aren't that dissimilar from the ones Julian wears; the only difference is the thickness. Vivienne has put on Julian's glasses before, they aren't that bad, but just by looking at them she can tell Jinx's are worse.

"How b-blind are y-you?" Vivienne says, still pressing against the wall.

Jinx smiles and breathes an airy laugh, "I am *very* blind." She murmurs something else Vivienne can't hear, but she doesn't care. She can't hear the woman anymore.

Very blind. She didn't know that. She also didn't know that Jinx has freckles. Not obvious ones, little ones on her nose. They are small and brown, unlike Vivienne's own, which are large and distinctive.

"You have freckles?"

Jinx nods and moves her arm down and off Vivienne's shoulder, holding her lower arm instead. "What else can you see?" she asks, and the elevator pings again, but Vivienne doesn't pay attention to who comes in. Instead, she looks at Jinx, she studies her, picking out every detail. She has a dimple when she smiles, and her eyes squint up into slits. Her eyelashes are long, and Vivienne can see where she has added mascara.

"A-are you wearing m-mascara?" This time, Vivienne lets herself relax and move away from the wall, resting on the handrail.

"Yes, I am. You have quite the eye, Carter." Jinx smirks and glances behind her. Following her gaze, Vivienne notices that the floor numbers are now in double digits. Where are they going? Vivienne doesn't care. There are more people in the elevator now, but she doesn't care, she doesn't notice any of them. Turning back to Jinx, Vivienne looks at her again, letting the whole elevator drain away, including the people standing with them.

"You have a s-scar. On y-your cheek." It's only small, and very light, but Vivienne can see it. She can't usually, but from this close it's obvious. Jinx looks a little taken aback by what Vivienne says, but she quickly regains herself and nods.

"I do." Her hand moves down Vivienne's arm and into her hand, sliding her fingers into her palm. She pulls Vivienne's fingers away, "And you'll end up with some if you don't stop this." Vivienne sighs and drops her head onto her chest. "I'm serious, Carter." She sounds so, as well. If Vivienne didn't know better, she'd say she sounds scared. After a short while, Jinx lifts her own palm up and reveals the inside of it, where little, crescent shaped lines are permanently carved into the smooth surface. Her wrist cast is gone now, discarded, and Vivienne can see the whole expanse of her hand.

"Oh.." Vivienne trails off and takes Jinx's hand without thinking, bringing it closer to examine. She spots Jinx blush slightly but ignores it, tracing the lines lightly. When had she done this? What had worried her so much to do so?

The woman with the bag sighs and rubs her arm, but it doesn't matter anymore, the movement barely registers in Vivienne's mind. All her thoughts are focused on Jinx, the scars on her hands, the dimple that shows when she smiles, how her eyelashes blend perfectly with the mascara, how she doesn't really need it, how her eyes are the perfect shade of green, a delicate jade that swirls deeply into emerald. All she can see is Jinx, all she can think about is Jinx, right now, she is all that seems to matter.

The elevator stops, and everyone gets off, except them. When the doors shut again, Jinx steps away, wrapping her coat tighter around her and leaning against the wall. Vivienne relaxes completely, and her breathing returns to normal. There is no one in the elevator. She is alone. She is fine. She is safe. Jinx had helped her. At least, that's what it looks like.

"Where are we g-going?" Vivienne asks, looking at the digital counter above the doors. This hospital only has around fifteen floors, and they are on floor thirteen.

"Patience, Carter."

Jinx had helped her, actually helped her, but why? Where are they going? Why are they going there? Why aren't they waiting for Julian to come out? They should be there, waiting.

"Stop worrying. Julian is fine, whilst you were zoned out the doctor came and said he's absolutely fine, they just need to keep him and run a few tests."

"I-I'm not worried." Vivienne states, watching as the floor number slowly goes up by one.

"Really? Because you've been pulling at the corner of that jumper for the last two minutes, you've literally pulled a thread loose."

She hasn't, has she? Looking down, Vivienne realises that Jinx is right, whether it was knowingly or not, she has pulled at least three threads loose on the sleeve of her jumper. How had Jinx noticed…

"We're here." Jinx says as the elevator doors slide open, revealing a nearly empty corridor. Jinx takes two large strides out and waits outside, gesturing for Vivienne to do the same. She is waiting. She isn't walking ahead or teasing her by quickening her pace whenever Vivienne catches up, she is *waiting*. Like she had after the stationary store. Unlike then, Vivienne isn't about to go wandering around a hospital on her own, so she walks beside Jinx.

Neither say anything, and they walk in silence for a long time, until they reach the end of a corridor, where there's a small door with a fluorescent green sign above it. Jinx opens it in a comically exaggerated way and holds it open for Vivienne. Why is she being this nice? And why did she do what she had in the elevator?

Confused, Vivienne wanders through the door and onto a staircase. She can see it twist down and around until the bottom floor, and the sight makes her swallow abruptly, Vivienne doesn't like heights. This makes it even more surprising when Jinx doesn't walk down, instead she begins up, taking the stairs two at a time.

"You coming?" she asks, dangling from the handrail ten steps ahead of Vivienne. Sighing, Vivienne follows her. It's the stairs or the hospital, and Vivienne would rather fall down fifteen flights of stairs then go back down there.

"Where are we going?" She asks, jogging to catch up to Jinx.

"Hazard a guess. We got off on the *top floor* of the hospital and are now climbing some stairs up," she points up with her finger, "where d'you reckon we're going? Narnia?"

"Very funny."

Jinx smirks and jumps up the final few steps, waiting at a small door for Vivienne.

"Carter, I present to you what is commonly found on top of buildings..." She opens the door and steps out, Vivienne follows, "a roof." Jinx gestures grandly to the flat expanse of concrete overlooking the city as if it is something interesting. Vivienne sighs and walks out, venturing as close to the edge as she dares. The minute she sees the sheer distance they are from the ground, she shoots backwards, back into the doorway.

"W-why are we here?" She says, turning to Jinx who is wandering along the edge as if there is nothing to fear. She doesn't answer, instead she waves one foot in the air and Vivienne clenches her hand into a fist. What is she doing, she could fall and seriously hurt herself. In fact, from this height, she would probably die, no matter how close they are to the hospital. "Jinx?" Again, no response, Jinx just puts her hands in her pockets and leans her neck over the side, unfazed by the sheer drop onto concrete. This is scaring her, why isn't Jinx talking? Vivienne is used to be ignored by her, but this is different, this isn't being ignored, Vivienne can tell. This is something else, and it's worrying. "What are you doing out there? You could fall."

Jinx isn't far, but Vivienne's voice feels strained in her throat, as if she is shouting, although she knows she isn't. Stepping out from the doorway, Vivienne begins to pull on the end of her jumper again, "Jinx, please, get down, you're scaring me." Her voice shakes as she takes another step towards the edge.

"Why is it scaring you? I'm the one on the ledge." Jinx says, looking out at the city and dangling a foot over the edge. It's scary watching her be so careless, it's scary seeing someone so smart do something so stupid, it's scary seeing Jinx act this way. In a way Vivienne has never seen before, in a way that makes Vivienne worry.

"Please, you could fall." If she fell, Vivienne would never see her again. Never hear her incessant mocking again, never be teased by her again, never be beaten by her again, never *talk* to her again, and that scares her. No matter what she feels towards Jinx, she doesn't want her to fall.

"Jinx, *please.*" Vivienne is close to the edge now, not on the ledge as Jinx is, but close enough that she can hear traffic below her.

"Ok." Jinx says, jumping off the ledge and sitting down with ease. It's uncanny, watching her go from dangling off a ledge to sitting smirking on the floor, and it makes Vivienne wonder. It makes her wonder how Jinx can swap so quickly, she goes from quiet and melancholy on a *ledge,* to mocking and sarcastically sitting on the floor, safe.

"Why are we up here?" Vivienne asks, sitting beside her, happy to be leant against something, to be able to feel the floor with more than just her feet. Jinx shrugs and looks at the door, tilting her head up and back.

"You looked like you were about to have a panic attack sitting down there, I've never seen you like that. You looked on the verge of passing out, crying, screaming, and giving up all at once, so I figured I'd take you somewhere that *didn't* make you feel like that."

Vivienne tries not to smile at the thought, not letting her guard down like she had in the elevator. What happened in the elevator would *never* happen again, and she only let it happen then because it was either to tolerate Jinx or pass out in a moving metal box full of hospital patients.

"Why do you care all of a sudden? Last time I checked, you hated me."

Jinx brings her head back down and shakes her head, "I don't hate you, Carter. I never did."

"Fine, strongly dislike me." Vivienne crosses her arms and pulls her knees up to her chest.

"Well, no matter how much I 'strongly dislike' you," she makes air quotes with her hands, "I didn't want you to sit and suffer in a place that made you so uncomfortable, especially after what happened with your Mum."

"I-" Vivienne stops, her words catching in her throat, choking her. Her Mum. Jinx knows about her Mum. She hasn't told anyone about her Mum, apart from Julian, no one from her old school knows, she kept it to herself. Completely to herself. "How?" Her voice breaks and she blinks back the tears threatening to spill out of her eyes. This is too much, the hospital, Jinx, all of it.

"I put it together a while ago. Your Mum used to pick you up all the time, she used to wait at the gates no matter how much you told her to wait in the car, it was cute. Then she stopped coming, and your Dad came instead, then he stopped too, and you started walking. At first I thought it was just because your parents were busy, then I saw you going into the hospital, eating meals out with your family and your Mum would be missing. Eventually you started being pulled out of class for different things, some days you wouldn't come in at all but I'd see you walking with your Dad, looking well enough for school, and I was confused. I didn't want it to be true, but I had some ideas. What confirmed it was when I sprained my wrist, I saw your Mum in the hospital cafeteria, hooked up to all these machines and wearing one of those caps..." She trails off and they sit in silence. Vivienne looks up and inhales deeply, exhaling as quietly as possible.

"Why didn't you say something?" She finally asks, gathering the courage to look at Jinx, but she isn't there.

"Up here." Vivienne looks behind her and finds Jinx sitting on the ledge she was just standing on, her legs hanging off the side and her hands propped up behind her back.

"What are you-"

"Just keep talking." Jinx says, not looking back. Confused, Vivienne faces forwards again and asks her original question.

"Why didn't you say anything? When you figured it out?"

Jinx is quiet, all Vivienne can hear is her steady breathing behind her. After a while, she says, "I figured you didn't tell anyone for a reason, and I knew the last person you would *want* to talk about it with," she pauses, "would be me."

Her voice is barely a whisper, but the words are enough to make Vivienne turn around and look at her again. She isn't staring out at the city anymore, instead she is staring at the ground, the ground miles beneath them. Unsure of what to say, Vivienne stands up and sits on the ledge, her body still facing the door.

"I would have appreciated anyone talking to me about it," She doesn't turn to Jinx, instead she keeps her eyes trained on the door in front of her, "even you."

There is so much silence. Vivienne can't stand it, every time she says anything, Jinx will wait. Like she is now. In fact, it doesn't even sound like Jinx is breathing, or moving. Vivienne can't hear her. She can't feel her either, like she could before. There is an emptiness beside her, an eerie emptiness. And with the emptiness, return the thoughts. Even on the roof, she doesn't feel safe. She doesn't feel as if she can escape them. Especially after what she just said, what *Jinx* had just said. Vivienne needs to talk; she needs to distract herself. Slowly, she brings her hand to her mouth, biting nervously on her nails.

"Stop that," Jinx says, turning around and swinging her legs over the ledge so she is sat closer to Vivienne. Not listening, Vivienne lowers her head, still frantically chipping away at her nails. "Come on, Carter." Jinx looks at her and pulls Vivienne's hands away, slowly separating them from the tight ball they'd been locked in. "Look at me," Vivienne does as she's told and turns around, finding Jinx looking at her. "You're crying? What's wrong?" She looks…worried?

"I-I am?" She didn't noticed, or she hadn't cared. It probably started when she was zoning out, when she was thinking about her Mum. Frantically wiping her cheeks, she shakes her head and inhales sharply.

"Stop that too." Jinx says, shuffling closer.

"Stop what?" Vivienne asks, snuffling and wiping her eyes with the palms of her hands.

"Hiding your emotions." Jinx takes Vivienne's hands and holds them in hers. "You're allowed to cry, if I were in your situation, I would be sitting in a dark corner somewhere crying until I couldn't breathe. Well, on the condition I had a Mum like yours, with mine it's a whole different story." Jinx breathes an airy laugh and wraps her arm around Vivienne's shoulder, pulling her closer.

Vivienne knows she should pull away, question why Jinx is doing this, but it feels nice. It feels nice *talking* about this, feeling *comforted* by someone. She doesn't care if it's Jinx, it's better than no one.

"Why did you come here if it makes you this stressed?" Jinx asks, squeezing Vivienne's shoulders. Resting her head on Jinx's shoulder, Vivienne sighs.

"Julian n-needed m-me," she whispers, silent tears falling down her cheeks. She can't remember the last time she cried like this in front of someone. Not even at her Mothers funeral. Even then she was keeping it together, standing strong and holding Ollie as he cried, watching her Dad take quiet moments away from everyone and coming back with red eyes. Vivienne had never seen her Dad cry, but when her mother died, it was all he seemed to do. Vivienne knew she couldn't, she knew that if they all cried, they'd fall apart, and she couldn't lose them too. So she put on a brave face and pushed through it, crying quietly in her room whenever she needed to, then rinsing her face and moving on.

When she felt overwhelmed and sick of hiding it, she'd walk to her mother's grave. It wasn't far, she was buried in the local church, and whenever Vivienne needed to say things, she couldn't tell anyone else, she told her Mum. Her Mum never interrupted her, never questioned her, she just listened, and Vivienne was grateful for that much.

Jinx is silent whilst Vivienne cries, her face pressed against Jinx's jumper. It's soft, like the one Vivienne has borrowed, and she can feel where her tears are beginning to soak it. Jinx doesn't have a bold sense of style, not in the typical way anyway, she wears very classical clothes, and no matter what she is wearing, no matter where she is, Jinx was always wearing a jumper, or a knit vest, sometimes even cardigans. It's something Vivienne has noticed, and she likes it.

"Thank you." Vivienne whispers through her tears, she isn't a loud crier, but it always takes her breath away. She doesn't think Jinx hears, it was very quiet, directed at her chest, and when she responds, Vivienne is surprised.

"I'm always here, no matter how much you hate me, I'll *always* be here."

Vivienne wants to tell her that she doesn't hate her, she wants to say she only acts the way she does because she thinks Jinx hates her, but she doesn't. Instead, she cosies further into Jinx's jumper, closing her eyes, the world falling away as she wraps her arms around Jinx's waist, letting her feelings embrace her.

Friends (ish)

Chapter 16 – Jinx
— . ˳˚ ☆: *.☽ .* :☆˚ . —

This is bad. Jinx knows this is bad, she knows she isn't supposed to be doing this, but for some reason, she is doing it anyway.

"Kit, if I get fired, I'm taking you down with me." Jinx says, nervously eyeing the door to the store whilst blindly making a coffee.

"Come on, what harm will it do, it's only four coffees'. Plus, it's helping a good cause." Turning round, Jinx raises her eyebrows at them.

"A good cause?" she asks, looking at three coffees' already in the cardboard takeaway cups. There are names written on them, each illegible and smudged. The first reads Julian, the second, Lilly, and the third, Jinx.

"Yes, it's helping you make friends, something you're seriously lacking." They say, smirking and looking at the cup in Jinx's hand. They're so preoccupied with that; they don't notice Jinx's hand sliding up behind them and flicking them on the back of the head.

"Hey!" They shout, jumping away and frowning.

"That is where sarcasm gets you." Jinx states, putting the lid on the cup and putting it in the holder with the rest.

"You're sarcastic all the time!" Kit protests, crossing their arms angrily over their chest.

"Yes, but I'm too pretty for people to care, so…" she shrugs, grabbing the holder and narrowly dodging the plastic lid that Kit promptly throws at her. Smirking, Jinx shoves her apron in her bag and pushes through the small door attached to the counter, now out of range. "Your aim is getting better." She laughs, beginning towards the door. Kit lets out a defeated sigh behind her as she opens the door and slips through, nearly dropping the holder as she does so.

*

"I'm here, do not panic, and as a bonus, I brought coffee." Jinx states, strolling into their spot in the library, where the others are gathered around a small table, discussing their arguments for the debate.
"I don't drink coffee." Julian sighs, looking enviously at the cup with his name on it.
"I know, and while I see it as odd, I have pitied your sad little habit and brought you herbal tea, instead."
He smiles and jumps up, his eagerness reminding Jinx of a puppy that's been told he's a good boy. He takes Lilly's drink along with his own, leaving Jinx with hers and Vivienne's. Vivienne doesn't look up from her work, she doesn't seem to notice that Jinx is there, which Jinx doesn't take personally, she never notices anyone when she's working.
"Carter, I've brought you sustenance, pay attention to me." Jinx taps her on the shoulder, which earns her a startled look and then a prompt glare. "Is that really how you look at the person bringing you coffee?" She waves the coffee in her face and Vivienne blindly reaches for it, but Jinx pulls it just out of her reach.
"Nope. You don't get it now, you were mean." Walking away, both coffees' still in hand, Jinx is partially surprised when she feels Vivienne jump up behind her and reach over her shoulder, trying desperately to grab the coffee.

"Nope." Jinx says, spinning around and stepping backwards. "Rude people don't get coffee, it's the rules."

"Jinx, come on, I've been up since five."

"Fine, but only because I admire your energy considering you're running on very little sleep." Jinx hands her the coffee and takes a seat at the table. "Up since five doing what exactly?" she asks Vivienne once she is also sat down, sipping her coffee gently.

"Studying." Vivienne states, returning to her work and tuning out everyone again.

"*Studying?* Why were you studying a six in the morning?" Vivienne doesn't answer and Jinx shrugs, laughing and dropping her head to her chest. Glancing at the others, she sees Julian staring with his mouth gaping open, and Lilly has her hand dramatically clutched to her chest. "What?" she asks, pulling out her notepad and pens, along with her copy of *Romeo and Juliet,* which is fully annotated and graffitied with multiple different colours of sticky notes.

"What happened? Has there been some form of cosmic anomaly?" Lilly gapes, turning to Julian. "Are you seeing this? I'm not just imagining it?"

"Yes, I am seeing it, but I don't think it's real…" Julian's eyes widen, and he turns to Lilly, "Maybe we're having a shared hallucination."

Jinx, extremely confused, looks to Vivienne for some kind of explanation, but her attention is still pinned on her work. Whatever she's doing must be important, because she is impressively tuning out the overwhelming oddness of the current conversation.

Meanwhile, in front of her, Julian and Lilly have bent their heads together in a conspirative manner, looking genuinely concerned.

"Will one of you tell me what's going on before I take the drinks, which I so kindly gave to you, away."

Lilly giggles and smiles, taking a large swig of her coffee and placing it on the table. Julian does the same, but with a calmer manner, and they both quickly return to their conversation. Giving up, Jinx opens her notepad and carries on her debate notes, occasionally opening her copy of *Romeo and Juliet* for reference.

Jinx truly hates this play, it's pathetic and boring, yet somehow annoyingly infuriating at the same time. Shakespeare is a great writer, and an even greater poet, but this play is a swing and a miss for Jinx. It's obvious that most of the literary community disagree with her, but it doesn't stop her from having her own views on the themes. Considering the assignment they were given is to construct their debates on whether women had a positive portrayal or not, Vivienne and Lilly have chosen the tricky side. It's easy to find weaknesses in Juliet's character, she defines her self worth based off of a man, she risks everything for someone who could leave her in an instant, *and* she kills herself over a *man* she's *just met*. The positives though, they are limited, in fact the only thing Jinx can think of is that she 'disobeys' her father and decides who she is going to marry, although it is a stupid decision.

"They're laughing because I'm talking to you without rolling my eyes," Vivienne sighs, looking up from her work and sipping her drink again, "although it is getting rather tempting."

"Why are you two being so nice, anyway? Last time I saw you, you looked about ready to stab one another." Lilly asks, closing her notepad and propping her head on her hand.

"We decided to put aside our petty grievances for the good of the debate, we do have to work together after all." Jinx smirks, eyeing Vivienne's notes. From the way she says it, it sounds sarcastic, but she is being genuine. After the hospital, Jinx used

Instagram to ask Vivienne how she was feeling, and after a short while, and a lot of awkward conversation, Vivienne asked about what they were now. She'd said something about how Jinx had behaved wasn't very 'rival like' and that it confused her, so Jinx proposed the idea of a friendship-like thing. It took Vivienne a whole hour to decide, and when Jinx finally got the message, it was a short, simple, 'Fine.'. She found it funny, Vivienne's utter aversion to a friendship with Jinx.

"*Really?* You got Vivienne to agree to *that?* Impressive." Julian says, leaning backwards in his chair and crossing his arms over his chest. "How much persuasion did that take?"

"Not as much as you'd think, actually, whilst you were getting treated at the hospital-"

Vivienne kicks her shin under the table and Jinx turns to her, raising her eyebrows. She calmly shakes her head and Jinx looks back at her notes. Why doesn't she want her to tell them? She doesn't seem to want her to tell anyone, even Julian, and he is her closest friend, apparently.

"How are you feeling?" Vivienne asks, directing the question at Julian and changing the subject, her haste clear.

"Vi, I'm *fine*. The doctors said it was just a combination of stress and lack of sleep, remember? Stop pestering me."

"I'm not pestering," Vivienne mutters, biting the end of her pen and looking across the table, at Lilly's notes.

"Yes, you are. You reminded me *six* times this morning to have breakfast, I was half convinced you were going to force it down my throat. And, last night you came into my room at *nine o'clock* and forced me into bed, saying you'd come and make sure I was asleep in an hour."

"That's not pestering you." Vivienne states. "That's caring for you, because you recently passed out due to *lack of sleep*."

Julian rolls his eyes and shakes his head, glancing at Lilly. Or at least that's what it looks like, until Jinx looks closer. He isn't looking at Lilly, instead he is looking at the bookshelf behind her, where a boy is browsing. She has to refrain from laughing as she elbows Lilly and gestures to the boy, who is now crouching to closely examine books on the bottom shelf. It's cute, how obviously Julian is staring at him, and how completely oblivious he is to Lilly and Jinx now staring at him.

"Talk to him." Lilly says, nodding her head to the boy. His dark skin is perfectly accented by his charcoal hair, which is short cut curling at the ends, much like Julian's. He isn't dressed too elaborately, his plain ripped jeans are paired with a plain white t-shirt, and he has a black leather jacket draped over his arm.

"Talk to who?" Julian spins his head around, looking directly at Jinx as his cheeks flush.

"Oh, I don't know, maybe the boy you've been ogling since we got here." Vivienne joins the conversations, this time shutting her notebook and looking at the boy.

"How- I haven't- I don't know what you're on about." Finally deciding on an answer, Julian crosses his arms over his chest and pretends to be interested in his drink.

"Yes, you do. You've been glancing over there every time you think I've not been paying attention."

Jinx smirks at Vivienne, partially impressed with her observational abilities. Despite it being funny in this case, it makes Jinx a little uneasy, for all she knows, Vivienne could be doing that with her. Sitting in silence, observing her, watching her every movement. Looking for weaknesses she could use after this doomed friendship crashes and burns. Wiping the smirk from her face, Jinx turns back to Julian, who is now glaring at Lilly.

"Even if he's straight, you could get a new friend out of it, you hang out with girls far too often, go and get some of that good old fashioned manly companionship." Lilly ruffles his hair, something she does a lot, and turns him around so he's looking at the boy again.

Julian takes Lilly's hand out of his hair and drops it on the table, "You are annoying enough, thank you."

Lilly sighs and rolls her eyes, tilting her head backwards. "Fine. I'll do it for you." She says, dramatically dropping her head down and standing up abruptly.

"Wait, what? Lilly no-" Julian starts, but he is too late, she is already halfway across the space, her hands draped lazily in the pockets of her loose fit denim jeans, which are hanging around her bear waist. She taps the boy on his shoulder, and he turns around, looking partially startled at the girl in front of him. Lilly isn't as short as Vivienne, but she isn't tall either, and unfortunately for her, this boy is nearly as tall as Jinx and Julian. Thankfully, Lilly has more confidence than their entire group put together, and it doesn't faze her at all. None of them can hear the conversation, but Julian looks tense. He has one hand tightly gripping the back of his chair and the other is tapping nervously next to it, you'd think he's never asked out a boy before. In fact, he isn't even asking him out, Lilly is doing it for him.

They talk for a long while, Lilly warming up to him and even laughing, until eventually, she turns around and strides back to the table. She doesn't mutter a word to anyone as she leans over the table, takes Julian's things, and starts packing them into his bag. Realising what's happening, Jinx smirks and looks over at the boy, who is patiently waiting beside the bookshelf, his hands nervously clasped together.

"What are you doing?" Julian asks, looking confused and holding on too the notepad Lilly is shoving into the open bag.

"What does it look like, genius? I got you a date."

"What? Right now?"

"No, next week. Of course now!" Lilly quietly exclaims, glancing over her shoulder and smiling at the boy. "Considering you're the smartest of us, you really are stupid."

"She's got a point," Vivienne says, "I haven't been paying attention and even I can see what's going on."

Julian sighs and looks over his shoulder, giving the boy a meek smile and helping Lilly pack up his stuff. The boy waves and smiles back, making Julian blush and swing his head back to the table, where he whispers quietly, "Lilly, the minute I'm back, I'm going to kill you."

"Fair." She shrugs and lifts his now full bag in front of him, "Go get 'em, slugger."

Julian flips her off in return, then he turns around and walks towards the boy, smiling. They disappear around a corner and Lilly laughs, turning back to the table and sipping her coffee.

"Proud of yourself?" Jinx asks, watching as Lilly leans back in her chair and crosses her arms, glancing over to the bookshelf. She folds her feet in a pretzel-like shape underneath her and sips her drink again, slower this time, like she's an evil villain in a kids show.

"You have no idea…" she smirks and kicks her chair forwards, startling Vivienne, who is working once again.

"Carter, are you capable of going five minutes without returning to your work, or is that too much socialising for you?"

She sighs and glares at Jinx, although there isn't as much malice in it as Jinx expected. Maybe she is actually willing to give this friendship a shot. Still, Jinx is being careful. She doesn't need Vivienne knowing everything, even Lilly doesn't know everything, and Jinx intends for it to stay that way.

None of them talk after that, and Jinx proceeds with her work on her own, after all, Lilly has just sent *her* partner off on some stupid date. While it is cute seeing Julian like that, Jinx can't help but fear for him on that date. That boy looked nice, he looked shy and considerate, but looks are deceiving. It is far too easy for people to put up façades, making them look sweet and loving, but they are all lies. Love isn't real, it isn't something that just happens, either, and if it ever does, it *always* faded. People tire of repetition, they tire of waking up to the same face every day, and eventually, others become subject to their attention. Relationships always end with someone getting hurt, no matter who breaks it off, or if it's a mutual decision, it *always* hurts *someone*. Sometimes, it hurts those who didn't want to be a part of it, like family. Sometimes facades are held up long enough for 'love' to become something more, for it to create something more. And of course, when that love eventually fades, those who have grown accustomed to it are suddenly pulled away, dragged deep into pits where reality comes as a harsh blow. It doesn't matter who's in love with who, it *always* hurts someone, because it *always* ends. Jinx doesn't want to see that happen to Julian.

They work for hours, only exchanging small snippets of conversation when they need notes from one another, which means Jinx talks even less, as she doesn't need anyone's notes. She can't understand why they are doing this task as a debate; it would be much more efficient if it were in essay form, which would mean Jinx could work on her own, unbothered by distractions.

"I'm bored." Distractions like that.

"Tough, carry on working." Jinx states, not looking up from her work. Talking to Lilly when she is like this is like talking to a naughty child who doesn't want to do homework, you have to be stern and not cause any distractions they can use to their advantage.

"Come on, we've been studying for hoouurrsss," she whines, turning to Vivienne. "Aren't you bored? Come on, be the fun one."

"As much as it pains me to admit, I agree with Jinx, we've only been at this," She checks her watch, "an hour and a half. We have tons more to do."

"Neither of you are any fun." Lilly pouts, crossing her arms and sulking in her chair, her notebook open in front of her. Jinx drops her head into her hands and rubs them over the back of her neck.

"Fine. A *ten-minute* coffee break, happy?"

Lilly jumps up from her chair, her smile pulled up to both her eyes, her bag already slung over her shoulder. "Thank you!" she says, her voice squeaky and high pitched. She really is like a child, but Jinx likes it. Sometimes the child in Lilly brings out the small, fragile child in her, something no one has done before.

"Coming, Carter?" Jinx says, closing her notebook and packing it away. Vivienne looks up at her, then she looks at Lilly, who is practically jumping from excitement.

"You really don't like to study, do you?" Vivienne says, rolling her eyes.

"Nope. It's horrible, and boring, and pointless, and sad, and-"

"Okay, I get it." Vivienne stands, packing her stuff away. She will never admit it, but Jinx is glad Vivienne is coming, she tends to overwork herself, and after what happened at the hospital, Jinx is watching her even more. She doesn't know why, but what happened at the hospital scared her. It scared her because she's *never* seen Vivienne like that, even in high school. She's seen her cry before, but what happened in the elevator…

Vivienne had gone entirely white; her eyes were glazed over, and she wasn't responding. Then she'd stopped breathing, or at least it appeared that way, that was when Jinx *panicked*. She'd seen it all before, she'd felt it all before.

"Jinx? You coming?"

"Hm, what?" Jinx looks up from where she'd frozen over her bag, her things half packed away.

"You zoned out, you okay?" Lilly asks.

"Yeah, I-I'm fine." She shrugs, continuing to pack her stuff away. She didn't know she'd done that, zoned out, but she needs to stop. If she starts to zone out, people are bound to start noticing, and she can't have people noticing. If people notice, if *Lilly* notices, she will start asking questions. Jinx doesn't need Lilly asking questions, mainly because Jinx knows she will end up answering them. Lilly can be far too persuasive, she has a way of getting things out of people, no matter how hesitant they are.

"You sure?" Lilly pushes, beginning towards her, but Jinx walks away, swinging her bag onto her back.

"Yes. I'm fine, drop it, will you?" She knows she shouldn't have been so short, but Lilly is asking too many questions, and she hates it.

"Ok, fine, sorry." Lilly says, lifting her hand in surrender.

"No, it's just," Jinx looks around, realising Vivienne is walking behind them. "Nothing, it's nothing." Sighing, Lilly bounds ahead, pushing the doors to the library wide open and inhaling deeply, as if she is outside. She isn't, in fact she is still technically *in* the library, except this bit is more tables than shelves. Jinx strides down the stairs, taking them two at a time, a habit she picked up over the years. She isn't sure why, possibly because it's quicker, she doesn't know. What she does know is that Vivienne can't do it, and it is hilarious watching her try.

Vivienne is a good ten steps behind her and Lilly, and she isn't trying to catch up.

"Come on, Carter." Jinx says, stopping and leaning against the handrail behind her.

"Oh, shut up Jinx. Unlike you, I enjoy walking, so I take my time." She rolls her eyes as she walks past, and Jinx bounds past her, still taking the steps two at a time.

"I enjoy walking, but I prefer to get where I'm going quickly so I can do what I need to do efficiently."

"My god, could you be any nerdier?" Lilly chimes in, now at the bottom of the stairs, stood with her arms crossed and her eyebrows raised.

"I'm not being 'nerdy', simply time efficient." Jinx says, standing next to her.

"Being time efficient is nerdy." Lilly nudges Jinx with her elbow and smirks.

"No, it isn't." Jinx insists.

"Yes, it is."

"No, it isn't."

"It i-"

"Will you two stop, you're acting like my little brother and his friends." Vivienne cuts Lilly off and jumps the last two steps onto the ground, nearly slipping on the polished floor. Jinx sniggers and covers her mouth to hide her smile, Vivienne really will fall over anywhere. Glaring, Vivienne begins to walk through the lower floor of the study hall, towards the small café in the corner. It's the one they always use when they are studying, but if they are out, they go to where Jinx works. Sometimes they run into Kit, who will go quiet and mumble until they eventually shuffle away. Jinx gets the feeling that they aren't very confident.

Sometimes, Lilly will come and talk to Jinx during her shift, and a lot of the time, she will get scolded by Tony for coming behind the counter and 'distracting his staff'. Of course, Lilly being Lilly, doesn't listen and will make it her goal to annoy Tony as much as possible before she gets kicked out.

She sits on the counters, stacks the cups on top of one another, all stuff you usually catch children doing. Jinx expects Tony to have thrown her out a long while ago, but for some reason, he's taken a shine to Lilly. He's nicer and softer to her than he is with everybody else, even Jinx, it's weird, but she likes it because it means she isn't always alone at work. Because Kit is still in Highschool, their work schedule is very chaotic, mainly because they have exams all throughout the year, and they are very bad at scheduling. Jinx has tried to help them, but they are extremely stubborn and had no attention span.

"What do you want?" Jinx asks, turning to Lilly and taking out her phone.

"I'll get my own, don't worry." Lilly offers, reaching into her bag.

"As much as I appreciate the fact that you want to pay for your own drink, I don't think you have your phone."

"Oh come on, I'm not that predictable." Lilly says, opening her bag wider and craning her neck to get a proper view. After a good couple of minutes, she sighs and swings her open bag back against her side. "Fine. I am a little predictable." Jinx smirks and walks towards the counter.

"What do you want, Carter?"

Vivienne stops and looks at Jinx, partially astonished. "What?"

"What do you mean, 'what?' I didn't pin you as stupid, annoying, yes, but not stupid." Jinx smirks.

"Very funny. I mean I don't need you to buy my drink, I can get my own." Vivienne says, looking at the steadily growing queue.

"Yes, but since I'm buying Lilly's, I might as well buy yours, what do you want?" Jinx joins the queue and Lilly starts to look around for somewhere to sit. Vivienne follows Jinx, not dropping the fact that she can buy her own drink. Jinx knows that, but she can't understand why Vivienne can't just accept a drink from her. They are meant to be *trying* to be friends, and this is a very friend-like thing to do, so where is the harm?

"Jinx, really, it's-" she starts, but she is cut off when a large boy cuts directly in front of her, knocking her to the floor. While it may have looked purposeful, Jinx knows it isn't, Vivienne is unbelievably clumsy, and it doesn't help that her laces are untied. The boy carries on walking, ignorant to the girl he knocked on the floor, and Jinx has half a mind to go after him and tell him to apologise, but she doesn't. Instead, she mutters insults under her breath and reaches a hand out to help Vivienne, who's entire face has gone bright pink. She looks embarrassed, and panicked, which isn't good.

"What an asshole," Jinx says as Vivienne takes her hand, hoisting herself upwards.

"It wasn't him; I was the one in the way." Vivienne says, looking at the floor and clasping her hands together in front of her.

"It wasn't your fault at all! That guy cut right in front of you and didn't even notice, explain to me how that was your fault." Jinx's eyes wander through the people around them, glaring at the ones she sees snickering behind their hands.

"If I hadn't been following you…" Vivienne trails off, her gaze still pinned on the suddenly interesting tiles beneath them.

Jinx goes to reassure her again, but she is cut off when someone at the counter calls them forward. They are being served by a boy who looks the same age as Jinx, in fact, he might be in one of her classes, John or something. He smiles at her and asks for her order, and she tells him the orders, not returning the gesture. As they make their way towards the end of the counter to await their drinks, Jinx notices how Vivienne still isn't looking around, and how her cheeks are still a deep shade of red. Is she really that embarrassed about falling over? She does it all the time, this can't be a new occurrence.

"Carter, listen, it wasn't your fault, no one noticed, and no one *cares*. All you did was fall over, something I have done countless times in public, and it's not as if you look like the one in the wrong, that boy clearly knocked you over." She doesn't reply, but she does lift her head higher up, looking at the counter instead. "Oh for god's sake, you owe me for this," Jinx mutters, sticking her hand out onto the counter and pretending to fall, knocking anything that was resting there, onto the floor.

She isn't sure why she does it, but she has, and it makes her look like a complete idiot. There is sugar all over the floor, wooden sticks dotted throughout them, but the worst thing is the large metal jug of milk that was just near the edge. It makes a loud, clattering sound as it hits the floor, grasping everyone's attention. Thankfully, it has a lid, but that doesn't stop it from rolling a couple of feet before stopping in front of an astounded looking professor. She doesn't know who they are, but they don't look impressed. So what, she doesn't need their stupid approval anyway, and she doesn't care if everyone is muttering and laughing at her as she bends down to frantically wipe up the sugar, purposely making a show of it. She doesn't care because Vivienne isn't looking at the floor anymore, she isn't looking at the counter either, instead she is looking at Lilly across the room and covering her mouth, obviously trying to withhold laughter.

The boy from behind the counter appears with a brush and begins to help. When they are done, Jinx whispers her thanks and stands up again, wiping her hands on her coat as she does so. She can hear people around her muttering to themselves and one person is outright laughing, but it doesn't matter, because Vivienne is smiling at her, holding their drinks.

"Better?" Jinx says, taking the two drinks in her hands.

"Thank you." Vivienne smiles, glancing behind her at the people who were still looking at them. "You didn't have to do that, though."

"It's fine, what else are friends for if not to look like idiots and take the attention off of you." Vivienne laughs, weaving throughout the tables towards where Lilly is sitting, conveniently, at the back. "That is what they're there for, right? I'm new to this whole idea." Jinx smirks and slides into a seat next to Lilly, Vivienne sitting across from her.

"You're asking me like I know what I'm doing, I'm just as new to this as you are."

"Well, we'll just have to be new to this together, then." Jinx smiles slightly, her voice dropping low as she props her head up on her arm that is lying on the table.

"What are you two smirking about?" Lilly asks, taking her drink from the holder and taking a large sip. She looks suspiciously between them, and Jinx finds herself having to cover her reddening cheeks with her cup. Unfortunately, Lilly sees straight through her and raises her eyebrows. Glaring at her, Jinx turns to look around the café, pulling her attention away from the table.

There aren't many people there, it's quite late, and most people are studying on their own in their dorms. A girl and a boy are sitting on one of the tables across from them, the girl twisting her hair in her hand and staring at the boy, whose nose is buried in a book. Jinx doesn't know why they're here, but they don't have coffee, and the girl doesn't have anything with her. Maybe they are on a date, but that's unlikely, because if they are on a date, the boy would be paying more attention. While he is relatively good-looking, the girl he is with is miles out of his league, and if they are dating, he looks like the sort who would be falling over his own feet trying to impress her. Maybe they are siblings? She doesn't know, but she likes watching them, seeing what they will do, trying to build a story behind them.

She does this quite often, when she is writing in a café, or sitting on trains, she will sometimes just watch the people around her. There isn't anything significant going on in her life, ever, not in a good way, and as much as she hates it, the phrase 'write what you know' tends to creep into the back of her mind. So, when she is completely drained of ideas and inspiration on what to write, she observes, watches, sees how different people live, how they hold themselves. She doesn't do it in a creepy way, she never wonders anything about their real lives, she doubts they'd be interesting, she just builds stories, she gives them lives. Sometimes she will find herself staring at the wrong people, boys who think she's interested in them, and she sometimes is, but she never acts on that. Her life hasn't been much, but it's all the evidence she needs to prove that romance is a fantasy. Fantasy's are good when they're in books, when they are a way to escape reality and leave behind a world that never much feels like her own, but when fantasy and reality mixed, it never ends well, never.

"Something interesting?" Lilly interrupts her thoughts and Jinx turns back to the table.

"No, not much, just marvelling at the ignorance of teenagers." She sighs, rolling her eyes at the couple as they stand and the boy wraps his arm around the girl's waist, putting the book in his bag. That, she has to admit, is surprising, but she really doesn't care. Like she said, she isn't interested in the people, it's the stories that she cares about.

"Two things, one, *you're* a teenager, and two, how are they being ignorant? They're just on a date." Lilly asks, her gaze following them out.

Vivienne laughs beside her and looks at Lilly. "You've clearly not been around Jinx long enough; she finds anything even remotely related to romance abysmal and the people involved ignorant."

"I know that much, when we have movie nights she won't even consider anything remotely related to romance, she always suggests Historical films."

Vivienne rolls her eyes and laughs, "That's not surprising."

"Maybe if you brought your own laptop instead of insisting on using mine, you would get more of a say in what we watched." Jinx says, sipping her drink and raising her eyebrows at Lilly, who is looking pleadingly at Vivienne.

"Why don't you come to the next one, that way we can vote on a film and watch something interesting for once." She says, stretching her arms across the table and taking Vivienne's hands in hers. "Please, I can't watch another historical film. If I do, I might end up dying of boredom."

Jinx sighs at Lilly's theatrics and looks at Vivienne, who is smiling in amusement at Lilly.

"While I'm not begging you, like an idiot," Jinx says, and Lilly scoffs at her remark sitting back up and taking another large swig of her drink. "It would be fun, if you wanted to, plus, I could do with a break from 'What's that?' Who's that?', and all the other absurd questions Lilly likes to constantly ask."

"I only ask questions because you pick complicated films!" Lilly says, crossing her arms and slouching back.

"It sounds fun." Vivienne nods and sips her drink, "But I am *not* watching a historical film." She clarifies, eyeing Jinx and raising her eyebrows.

"Fine, but I'm not watching a stupid rom-com either." There is no way she's going to let these two talk her into watching one of those mind-numbly predictable films, no matter how hard they try.

"Deal." Lilly states, "How about next week then?"

Jinx and Vivienne nod, but Jinx can't help but feel an uncertainty within her. This is good, she's sure, this is what friends do, right? This is a friend thing. Nothing else.

Chapter 17 – Vivienne

°•. ✿ .•°°•. ✿ .•°°•. ✿ .•°

"Vi, hurry up! Jinx said the food is already there, it's going to go cold!" Lilly shouts from outside Vivienne's door, knocking on it persistently.

"Unless you want me to come out there in a bra, you'll have to wait." Vivienne shouts in return, pulling her shirt over her head. As annoying as it is, Lilly does have a right to be impatient, they were supposed to be at Jinx's dorm half an hour ago. They would've been, too, if Vivienne hadn't let her phone die earlier, meaning her alarm didn't go off, which led to her losing track of time whilst reading.

"Why do you have to change, what you were wearing before was practically pyjamas anyway."

"I was in jeans and a sweatshirt, how is that pyjamas?" Lilly had insisted on them all wearing pyjamas whilst they watched the film, which is incredibly annoying considering it means they have to walk across campus looking like idiots.

Pulling her jumper over her head and shoving her feet into some slippers, Vivienne opens the door. She rushes past Lilly, who is sitting against her wall, and grabs her coat, making to leave the dorm altogether.

"Hey, wait!" Lilly says, jumping up and running across the room.

"You were just telling me to hurry up, make up your mind will you."

"Very funny." She says, opening the door and walking through it. Vivienne follows her, locking the door behind her, and they begin towards the exit. This is a stupid idea, going in pyjamas, watching a movie, watching a movie *with* Jinx. They had agreed to be friends, but Vivienne hadn't realised she meant this kind of friends, friends who watch films together and see each other in pyjamas.

She hasn't spoken to Jinx properly since the hospital incident, and she hadn't intended to for a long while. What happened at the hospital was something she is desperate to forget, and she hopes Jinx feels the same way. Thankfully, Lilly is coming. If Lilly wasn't with her, Vivienne wouldn't be going, she will never hang out with Jinx alone. Not by choice, anyway.

Lilly breaks into a run as they approach the main doors, and Vivienne follows suit, wrapping her jumper tight around her as she braces herself for the cold. When they are through the door, Vivienne's winces at the temperature and quickens her pace, taking over Lilly entirely. Weaving her way past benches and around puddles in the path, Vivienne laughs to herself as she realises what she is doing. She is running through campus, in her pyjamas, in the dark. Her Dad would be so proud of her. She's being a proper college idiot, and if she's being brutally honest, she is loving it.

So involved in her amusement, she doesn't take note of her surroundings, including the person who is walking slowly towards her, their attention on their phone. When she collides with them, they both topple to the floor, Vivienne landing on top of them.

"Shit, I'm sorry, I wasn't looking, I'm so sorry-" She begins to apologise, sitting up and brushing herself off, but she stops when she sees who she hit. In front of her is Jinx. Vivienne panics, but it quickly subsides when Jinx laughs and stands up, picking up her phone as she does so. The screen looks cracked, and Vivienne is worried she caused that.

"Jesus Carter, I don't think I've ever met someone as clumsy as you." She sighs, putting her phone in the pocket of her coat and taking out one of her headphones. Vivienne is still on the floor, looking up at Jinx in shock. "What? Did you expect me to shout at you or something? How much of a bitch do you think I am?" Her smile fades when Vivienne doesn't respond again, instead looking at her hand. She must've caught it when she fell, because there was a long slice down her forearm, which is slowly leaking blood. "Shit." She hears Jinx murmur, before she crouches down in front of her and takes Vivienne's arm.

Vivienne doesn't know where she gets it from, but Jinx places a tissue over her arm and mops up the blood. Then she pulls Vivienne's jumper down over her arm again and hoists her up onto her feet.

"You ok?" She asks, stepping back and surveying Vivienne.

Vivienne nods and smiles, "You're getting pretty good at this friend thing." She mocks, but she means it. Maybe this isn't going to be as bad as she thought.

"Aren't I just?" She smirks, putting her hands in her pockets and dawdling past Vivienne. Turning around, Vivienne wonders where she is going, but realises that she's travelling with Lilly when she sees her panting behind them.

"My god, Vi, you can run." She says, keeling over and putting her hands on her knees.

"Running? That's new, I didn't know you *could* run. I thought you just speedwalked everywhere." Jinx says, raising her eyebrows.

"Oh, I can run, I just never felt like it in Gym, so I made up excuses."

"As much as I would love to believe you, I think I might need proof." Jinx smirks and takes off her coat, handing it to Lilly. "Want to race?"

Vivienne looks at Jinx, who must be freezing. She's just wearing long, flowing pyjama bottoms and a bed bra, how is she not cold?

"Why would I want to race you?" Vivienne teases, walking closer to her and crossing her arms.

"I don't know, maybe to prove that you're faster than me, which you're not." Jinx teases back, running a hand through her hair. Vivienne walks ahead of her but stops once there is about a metre in front of them.

"You want to race? Come on then," Vivienne says, before bolting off down the path. She runs at full force, her breath hot in her throat and blood rushing in her ears. Moments later, she hears Jinx's ragged breath behind her as she catches up. Vivienne pushes herself further and accelerates a little bit more, but Jinx quickly catches up.

Daring a glance to her side, Vivienne expects to find Jinx glaring at her, or staring straight ahead, but she doesn't. Instead, Jinx is smiling at her. Her smile pulls all the way up to her eyes, showing her teeth, and she is looking right at Vivienne. Despite her best instinct, Vivienne smiles back, and she doesn't miss the pink creeping up Jinx's neck before she speeds up, taking over Vivienne.

They race through the campus, past the odd student, and all the way to Jinx's building, where Vivienne keels over with her hands on her knees. Her chest burns and her breaths are shallow, but she can't help but smile. Jinx sits against the wall, putting a hand to her chest and breathing deeply. She is still smiling, smiling in a way Vivienne has never seen before, and she can't help but enjoy it. She enjoys seeing Jinx smile, she enjoys seeing her laugh and be completely out of breath, it's nice.

They don't speak for a while, both equally out of breath, but Vivienne can hear Jinx laughing to herself in between fractured breaths. "Wow, you really c-can run." She pants, standing up and walking towards Vivienne, who is now stood up.

"So can you," Vivienne smiles, beginning towards the doors. Jinx's building looks different than Vivienne's, it's more modern, with glass doors and white walls. Vivienne's is darker, and the doors are those chunky metal ones that look like fire escapes.

"S-shouldn't we wait for L-lilly?" Vivienne begins towards the doors, craning her neck around to see where Lilly had gone.

"She'll take a while to catch up, and I am *freezing*. We can wait inside."

Vivienne forgot about Jinx's inappropriate clothing. Considering how cold she is, in both a jumper and a pyjama top, Vivienne could only imagine how cold Jinx is.

"Fair enough." Vivienne shrugs and walks through the door Jinx is holding open, gladly embracing the warmth of being inside once again. When both her and Jinx are inside, Vivienne turns and sits against a wall, wrapping her jumper tightly around her. "What were you doing outside? Aren't you supposed to be setting up the movie in your room?"

"It takes five minutes to click on Netflix, and I am very impatient, so I figured I would come and see what was taking so long."

Vivienne laughs subtly and rolls her eyes, "Why am I not surprised. You didn't strike me as patient."

Jinx smirks and sits on the floor beside her, lifting her legs so her feet are planted on the floor and draping her arms on her knees. "Why were you running?" she asks, setting her head back on the wall and exposing the columns of her throat. It is only now that Vivienne realises how close they are, how she can feel Jinx's bare arm brushing against her own ice-cold arm. She can see the soft rise and fall of her chest, how her hair has fallen around her face, and when Jinx goes to run her hand through her hair, she feels her leg bend, their shoes touching slightly.

"I was cold." Vivienne states, her breath catching slightly as Jinx breathes out deeply and tilts her head back again, further this time.

"And yet *you* were the one who collided with me, 'why am I not surprised'." Jinx mocks, shivering. Is she really *that* cold, maybe they should go up to her room, she must have warmer clothes up there.

"Are you really cold, because if you are then-" Vivienne is cut off by a frustrated scream from behind them. Jinx raises her eyebrows, intrigued, and stands up, craning her neck around the corner. Following her gaze, Vivienne rounds the corner and finds a tall boy frustratedly kicking the wall that is attached to the stairs. He doesn't seem to notice them as he proceeds to frustratingly curse and sit on the stairs, his head in his hands. Jinx recedes back behind the corner and looks at Vivienne, seemingly searching for guidance on what to do.

"Why are you looking at me, he's in your building, do you not know him?"

Jinx raises her eyebrows, "You think I know anyone here? Do I look like a social butterfly to you?" she whispers, and peers around the corner again.

"Good point. What do we do?" Vivienne asks.

"I don't know, I've never wished for Lilly more than now. We are both *far* too awkward for this." Jinx puts a hand to her forehead and sighs, "Well, you're too awkward, I'm too much of a bitch." She shrugs and Vivienne stifles a laugh.

"I can hear both of you, you're shit whisperers." He shouts from around the corner and Vivienne freezes. Jinx sighs and rounds the corner, grabbing Vivienne's sleeve and pulling her along. The boy is now standing, one hand on the railing of the stairs and the other in his jean pocket. Vivienne has a good, full view of him. His jeans are baggy, but not so big that it makes him look stupid, and his black jumper has a painting printed onto it. It isn't a painting Vivienne is familiar with, but it looks nice, and there is a name written above it in what looks like Japanese.

He steps aside to let them up the stairs, but Jinx stops beside him. "Do you live here?" she asks, leaning against the wall and crossing her arms. Not sure what to do, Vivienne tries to do the same, but instead of looking cool like Jinx, she slides down the wall and ends up falling down a step. The boy chuckles and Jinx glares at him, standing up straighter.

"Sorry," he mutters, looking at Vivienne, then to Jinx, "Yes, I live here, third floor."

"Same." Jinx says, colder than before. Had him laughing at Vivienne really annoyed her that much? Jinx nods up the stairs. "Are you in that room full of those loud wannabe frat boys?"

He sighs and looks up the stairs, "Don't remind me, I've had to buy noise cancelling headphones they're getting that loud."

Jinx smirks, relaxing a little bit. "Jinx," she says, then she turns to Vivienne, "That's Vivienne."

"I can introduce myself, you know." Vivienne protests, but neither seem to listen. They look at one another for a while, seemingly surveying each other. It's odd, they seem to have completely tuned Vivienne out.

"Dean." He finally says, crossing his arms as Jinx is.

"Nice to meet you, Dean." Jinx smirks, then looks behind him, to the door he must've come out of.

"Why were you shouting?" Vivienne asks, taking another step towards them.

"Your friend here knows, and I'll leave it to her to decide whether or not to tell you."

This is extremely confusing; how does Jinx know? Does she know who he is? But she said she didn't, maybe she was lying, or maybe she didn't know him from that far away. But why had she asked for his name? Maybe-

"What were you two doing down there?" Dean asks, smirking slightly and watching Vivienne's post-running breathes slowly settle down to normal.

"Racing each other, why?" Jinx states, the defensive tone temporarily returning to her voice.

"Wait, seriously? I thought you were-"

"We weren't, believe me." Jinx cuts him off and rests her hand on the handrail. What is Dean implying? What is the smirk for, what is Jinx denying?

"Do not fret, I have arrived." Lilly bounds up the steps but stops when she sees Dean. "Hi. I'm Lilly." She says, smiling at him. Still a little confused from the last reaction, Vivienne turns to Lilly, smiling.

"Dean." He says back, smiling, though not as broadly.

"What are you doing here?" Lilly asks, looking up and down the stairs, "Are you waiting for someone?"

Dean sighs and shakes his head, "No, I just needed to clear my head."

"And you thought a stairwell would be the best place to do so?" Lilly steps closer to him and raises an eyebrow. At first, it looks like Dean is going to tell her to piss off or step away, but he doesn't. Instead, he smirks and replies.

"Yes." He is blunt, but it makes Lilly smile. Lilly turns to Vivienne and Jinx, and before she can speak, they both understand what she is about to do. Unfortunately, neither of them speak up in time to stop her.

"We're having a movie night. Want to come?" Lilly doesn't hesitate as she invites this practical stranger, and part of Vivienne admires her for that. Although most of her finds it extremely annoying. Dean is quiet for a long while, then he looks at Vivienne.

"I don't want to impose; besides, I should be getting back to my dorm." As much as he tries to hide it, dread creeps across his face at the thought of having to return to his dorm, and Vivienne feels something pull at her to invite him again.

"Come on, it'll be fun. What's waiting for you in your room anyway?" Vivienne says, standing up straighter and walking three steps ahead of them all. "Trust me, we are brilliant company." She smirks, then turns to Jinx. "Well, most of us."

"Carter, do you want me to chase you up those stairs, because I can, and I will."

Vivienne laughs at the possibility but shakes her head. She is far too tired to have another race against Jinx, and she doesn't want to leave Dean alone with Lilly. As nice as she is, she tends to ask a lot of questions, and some people find that imposing. Dean doesn't seem like one of those people, but she doesn't want to risk it.

"Are you sure I won't be imposing?" Dean says, this time looking at Jinx and Lilly who are now walking towards Vivienne.

"No, trust me. If anything, you're doing me a favour. Maybe you can entertain this one," Jinx points at Lilly, "long enough for us to actually watch a movie."

"I let you watch movies." Lilly insists, grabbing the handrail and hanging off it on the balls of her feet.

"No, you don't. All you do is ask questions." Jinx sighs, beginning to walk away, Dean now in tow.

"That's because you pick confusing films." Lilly runs up two stairs and waves her finger in Jinx's face. Jinx breathes an airy laugh and pushes her hand away with ease,

"You do realise that the fact that you have to run up stairs to get to my height doesn't help you state your point."

Lilly crosses her arms and looks at Vivienne, "We need to find shorter friends." She states, then jumps up the last three stairs and into the third floor hallway.

Before she follows them, Vivienne stops and pulls Jinx back with her, only so they are a few feet behind the others. Jinx looks confused, but doesn't try and walk ahead, instead she stands and watches Vivienne, waiting for her to say something.

"What, Carter?" she says, glancing to the others. She doesn't sound annoyed, not even slightly, but Vivienne still feels she has to be quiet.

"Two things," Vivienne starts, shuffling closer so she can lower her voice, "What was Dean talking about? About you knowing something about why he wasn't in his dorm?"

Jinx sighs and looks back towards the stairs, checking no one is behind them. After seemingly convincing herself no one is in earshot, she looks back to Vivienne, "Dean is trans," she whispers, bending down slightly, "and when his roommates found out, well, they were very open about their opinions. They kicked him out for a few nights," She shakes her head and looks behind her again, "so I let him crash in mine for a bit. When he left he didn't want to talk about it, and I figured if I acted like I didn't know him, he'd feel better."

Vivienne is slightly taken aback, Jinx doesn't seem like the type to let a random stranger sleep in her room, even if they have nowhere else to go.

"What?" Vivienne asks, stopping and starting, "When? Why?"

"Should I expect a Who, Where, and How soon?" Jinx leans against the wall near them and crosses her arms over her chest. "And to answer you, last month, and I did it because I know what its like to get kicked out with nothing." Jinx freezes slightly, panic striking her face, but she shakes it off, regaining her careless demeanour.

"Oh," there is nothing else Vivienne can think to say, nothing she can think of that sounds right, so instead, she moves on, it was what Jinx seems to want to do. "Also, what did Dean think we were doing, when we were running in here? You seemed to get it, I didn't."

Jinx breathes an airy laugh and shakes her head, pushing up from against the wall and beginning towards the corridor. "Oh Carter, I admire your innocence." She mutters, and Vivienne walks beside her.

"What did he think we were doing, Jinx?" she asks again, tugging her sleeve and standing in front of her.

"Jeez," Jinx bends down again, whispering to Vivienne as if what she's saying is some big secret, "He thought we were making out, Carter."

Vivienne blushes, her entire face flushing, and steps back quickly. Jinx laughs again and begins towards the door, leaving Vivienne slightly shaken for a while before she follows her. Her and Jinx making out? Is Dean insane? They weren't, they wouldn't, and even if they did, it wouldn't be in the middle of the lobby. It would be somewhere private, not where everyone could see them, like in Vivienne's dorm, or Jinx's, not in the *lobby*. Not that they would, of course.

Chapter 18 – Jinx

── · ₀° ☆: *.☽ .* :☆° . ──

Lilly screeches and laughs, gripping onto Dean's arm as she buries her face in her jumper, "Why did we let the new guy pick the film! This is terrifying!" she exclaims, casting a cautionary glance to the laptop. Jinx laughs and surveys Dean, he seems to feel right at home around the three of them. Especially Lilly. When they'd gotten back to the room, Lilly had commandeered him and insisted that she didn't get a chance to fully meet him like Jinx and Vivienne had. Vivienne hasn't had much of a chance to meet him either, Jinx did most of the talking, and she's seen him before. It was a few weeks ago, and they didn't talk, but she'd seen him outside the frat boy room, along with two other boys. They were shouting something at him, a name that wasn't Dean, and saying all kinds of things to him. That's when it became apparent why they were doing it, and without thinking or stopping to consider what she was about to do, she stood in between the boys and him. One of them asked what she was doing, and when she didn't reply, he asked if she was a freak like him. That made her want to scream, but she didn't, instead she told them that she was close to multiple professors on campus, which is a lie if you exclude Miss Halloway, and that she could easily remember perfect descriptions of their faces if they didn't leave Dean alone. Then Dean explained that they had kicked him out for a while, but that he was sure they would let it blow over after a while, and Jinx had insisted he stay in her dorm. She knows the feeling of being kicked out way too well.

When she'd come out to her Mum, she'd been too drunk to understand, but her current boyfriend got the message. He was, unsurprisingly, a homophobic asshole who forced her out and locked the door. It was only for the night, and she'd stayed in the room above the coffee store with her boss, but it still sucked, mainly because her Mum didn't remember any of it. When she'd snuck in in the morning, her Mum airily asked her where she'd been, and Jinx hadn't hesitated to lie. She knew the guy would be gone in a week, so it wouldn't matter.

After a few nights, Dean thanked her and asked her to forget it happened, he didn't want everyone on campus knowing. Jinx had agreed and then he left, she hadn't seen him since then. She didn't want to interfere any further if he didn't want her too. If he needs help, he will ask for it, or somehow indicate he needs it. Unlike Lilly and Vivienne, Jinx doesn't see the point in pushing people's problems out of them. Sometimes private stuff is better being private, or only being told to close friends, not people you see in the hallway. That is why she'd pretended not to know him on the stairwell, he didn't seem to want to recount what happened and she didn't push, so they started again, on a fresh slate. Now, he is under around four blankets with Lilly, watching a thriller that makes him jump and laugh every ten minutes. He seems happy, and Jinx doesn't mind him being here if he is.

"Come on, Lilly, it isn't that scary. It's all extremely predictable, listen to the music, it builds up. That's the point." Jinx states, stretching a leg out in front of her and letting it rest in the empty space where Vivienne was just sitting. As if she knows what Jinx is doing, Vivienne comes out of the bathroom immediately afterwards.

"What have I missed?" She asks, looking at the laptop screen. Jinx is surprised Vivienne agreed to watch this, it's a thriller, and is particularly gory. Turns out, all she does is look away when there are excesses of blood, a little doesn't seem to do too much on a screen.

"The blonde one died." Jinx says, rolling her eyes at the predictability, "She was so stupid about it as well. There's a masked killer on the loose, and she's standing in a garage taunting him, *on her own*. People in horror films need to get more common sense. '*Please Mr Ghostface, I want to be in the sequel.*'" Jinx mocks the girls voice and shakes her head.

Vivienne rolls her eyes and goes to sit down, then she spots Jinx's legs sticking out from the end of the blanket. Jinx smirks as stretches them out further, sticking her arms out for comical effect.

"You sound like my brother." Lilly says as Vivienne forces Jinx's legs off the couch. It doesn't work, but Vivienne tries again, pushing harder this time.

"You could just ask if I can move my legs, Carter. That is the polite thing to do."

Vivienne scoffs and crosses her arms over her chest, "Can you move your legs?"

"No."

"That's it." Vivienne says, before using both her hands and what Jinx can only assume to be all the strength she can muster to yank Jinx's legs away from the couch. Jinx falls off the couch entirely and lands in a heap on the floor, blankets still covering below her waist. Lilly bursts into laughter and Dean joins her, while Vivienne sits on the couch, putting her legs where Jinx's had just been.

"Oh no you don't." Jinx says, smirking and sitting up. She grabs Vivienne by the waist and pulls her off the couch as well. Vivienne squeals in laughter and falls onto the floor next to Jinx, but before she can catch on, Jinx bolts up and jumps into her place on the couch. Vivienne goes bright red and mocks anger as she stands up, and Jinx can't help but genuinely smile at her reaction. This is fun, she didn't realise hanging out with Vivienne could be

257

this fun. At first she thought it would be awkward and that Vivienne would never trust her, but she can't have been more wrong.

"You think you're so clever?" Vivienne says, hands on her hips.

"Very much so." Jinx smirks back, but it is quickly wiped from her face when Vivienne jumps onto the couch. It isn't a big couch, in fact, when Jinx does stick her legs out fully, they go over the side, so when Vivienne jumps, Jinx doesn't know where she thinks she's going. She lands in the middle, feet sliding behind Jinx's legs and her hands resting on Jinx's waist to balance. Jinx smirks and pulls her cardigan around her neck to cover the stark pink creeping up it as Vivienne proceeds to sit on Jinx's legs, crossing her own in a pretzel shape. She doesn't say anything as she grabs a blanket to cover herself up, but when the chaos subsides and the film continues, she leans across and whispers,

"I win, Keller."

*

"That. Was. Horrifying." Lilly states, wrapping her blanket tightly around her and shivering. "I don't think I'm going to sleep tonight, you know."

"Seriously? Lilly it's a thriller from the eighties, the scariest things in it were the haircuts." Dean says, shaking his head and checking his phone.

"That's what you say, but maybe that's because *you're* Ghostface. Hm, what do we think?" Lilly looks around and at Vivienne and Jinx. Jinx smirks at Dean who frantically shakes his head. She can tell he's joking, as Lilly is, so she goes along with it.

"I agree, he gives off masked killer vibes."

"Well, it's not my fault you invited a random stranger from a stairwell into your dorm at night." Dean says, and Lilly raises her eyebrows at him, casting a glance to Jinx, then Vivienne, who is now looking at her phone.

"Vi, what do you think? Masked killer or normal boy?"

"Do I actually have to answer that?" She says, without looking up from her phone. There's a long pause and Jinx begins to think whether or not she means that as a joke, or if she really thinks it's stupid. Lilly frowns, but Vivienne isn't finished, "He's obviously a normal boy, what are the chances of there being two killers in one room?" She smiles and Lilly mocks a gasp.

"It's her! She's the masked murderer!" She exclaims and throws a pillow in Vivienne's direction, but it hits Jinx instead.

"Oh, that was a *big* mistake." Jinx says, sitting up on her knees and grabbing a pillow from behind her.

"You don't start a pillow fight with me and come out alive, Keller. I think you're forgetting I grew up with an older brother." Lilly picks up a pillow and Dean follows suit. Soon all four of them are stood up, pillows in hand.

"This is going to be absolute chaos." Dean says, before Lilly swings her pillow at Jinx and Vivienne goes for Dean.

Before long, they have teamed up and commandeered sections of the room. Dean and Lilly are near the door, a wall of small pillows protecting them, and Jinx and Vivienne sit up against the back of the couch. Vivienne pants beside her after going head-to-head with Dean, and Jinx pushes the hair, which had fallen out of her claw-clip whilst she was battling Lilly, out of her eyes.

"This is insane." Vivienne laughs, dropping her head into her chest and laughing.

"Yeah, well," Jinx pants and looks around the corner, "both me and Lilly are unbelievably competitive, so this could go on for a while."

"Wow, a match made in heaven." Vivienne smirks and Jinx panics, the unwelcome pink once again crawling up her neck.

"Oh, no, it's not like that." She stutters and glances around the couch again, willing her blushing to subside.

"Oh, I didn't mean it like that, I didn't think Lilly liked anyone like that anyway."

Jinx relaxes again, and lies against the couch, her legs up against her chest. "Yeah, exactly, that's why I was-"

"Yeah." Vivienne sighs.

"Yeah."

"Okay."

"Right, I'm sick of this, come on. We're getting them." Jinx says, standing on the back of her legs and crouching down. Vivienne nods enthusiastically and Jinx smirks. "We were literally the smartest in our year whilst we were in high school, we can win this."

"We do lack quite a bit of physical skill though, I'm clumsy and uncoordinated, and you have no spatial awareness." Vivienne returns, smiling slightly.

"Yes, but we don't need physical skill to win this battle. We just need a plan." Jinx sticks her head up one more time and see's Dean and Lilly looking at the couch. "You go left, around past the laptop and bookshelves, and I'll go right, past my bedroom door." Vivienne enthusiastically nods again, "And remember Carter," Jinx puts a hand on Vivienne's shoulder and mocks seriousness, "If it all goes south, I want you to know," she pauses for dramatic effect, "that I beat you for Valedictorian."

"Very mature." Vivienne says, her tone cold, but Jinx can see her lips slowly pulling up at the sides.

"I know." She says, before shuffling away and towards Lilly and Dean's mock-base.

Within minutes, they have completely destroyed Lilly's base and beaten both Dean and her, which leaves the whole group breathless. Dean tilts his head back against the wall where he is lying, a pillow propped up on his lap, and laughs,

"Months. I have been here for months and never had that much fun."

"Glad we could help," Jinx says from her spot on the couch. Vivienne is now sitting beside her, her legs stuck up and over the back of the couch and her arms hanging at her sides. She stretches, and Jinx tries to focus on Lilly, not the fact that Vivienne's top lifts slightly when she moves, exposing some of her waist.

"I like you. You need to hangout with us more often." Vivienne says, shifting completely upside down, her hair falling at the sides of her face. "I think Julian would love you, as well. Plus, I don't think he'd mind adding a boy to the group, he is currently extremely outnumbered."

"There's more of you?" Dean asks, putting his hand over his chest and mocking shock.

"Yes, can you believe it!" Lilly copies him. "I think we should invite that boy Julian's going out with into our group, too, he seems fun."

"Julian's been going out and coming back late loads recently, but I've never actually got to meet this mystery boy." Vivienne pipes up.

"Who, Damion?" Jinx asks, looking down at Vivienne, who is now turning a bit red. "I've met him." Lilly gasps and Vivienne sits upright. This is odd, seeing Vivienne like this, Jinx is used to seeing her reserved, serious self, or at the most the part of her that laughs, but not all this. It's nice, nice to see Vivienne come out of her shell, especially around her.

The Vivienne Jinx had known in high school would never have had pillow fights with anyone apart from her brother, and she would never have sat upside down on a couch in front of people. If Jinx is being honest, she prefers this part of her, she prefers the human part of her that isn't college centred. She likes the part of her that is able to relax, the part that doesn't have panic attacks from stress, and if she is being honest, she doesn't want to lose it when the project ends.

"*You* met Damion?" Vivienne asks, raising her eyebrows and looking a little hurt.

"Relax, Carter, Julian didn't let me. He was walking out of the main building, and I ran into him, so I struck up a conversation. It's not as if he knew who I was."

"You actively started a conversation with *another human?*" Lilly and Vivienne both look shocked, and Dean looks confused but amused.

"I know, impressive, right?"

"Who is Damion? I know he's seeing Julian, but I don't know who Julian is, either." Dean laughs and looks around the room, shrugging.

"Basically," Lilly explains what happened with Damion and Julian in the library, about how Julian had later confessed to having a huge crush on him, and how they are now seeing each other. She doesn't forget to highlight her annoyance at the fact that Jinx got to meet him first, either.

"Wait, what do Julian and Damion look like?" Dean sounds intrigued, and Jinx quickly takes out her phone and shows Dean Julian's Instagram, then Damion's. He smirks as Jinx pulls away her phone and takes her spot on the couch, where Vivienne is now sitting on the back of the chair, her feet on the bottom cushions. Is she capable of sitting normally? Jinx doesn't think so, but she doesn't mind, it's kind of cute.

"Why are you smirking so menacingly?" Vivienne presses, propping her head up on her arm that is resting on her leg.

"I saw something…" Dean trails off and smiles, mainly at Lilly.

"Tell. Us." She demands, sitting up and beaming at Dean. It's funny how they had literally found him on some stairs hours ago, and now they're all this close. Sharing secrets about dating and having pillow fights. Sometimes it surprises Jinx just how quickly people get comfortable around each other, even if they are complete strangers. Dean doesn't feel like a stranger though, not anymore.

"Well, when I was going out for coffee in town, I saw those two…" He attempts to trail off, but the effect is quickly ruined when Lilly squeals like a child and claps her hands together.

"No way," Vivienne exclaims, leaning forwards.

"I can't wait to make fun of him for this, it's going to be hilarious." Jinx smirks and Vivienne looks at her, nodding.

"I might join you in doing so." She smirks, "As payback for not telling me."

"Look at our little group growing, how many of us will it be?" She counts the names on her fingers, and when she's done, sticks them out excitedly, "Six! There will be six of us! And to think, we started off as two separate pairs."

"I don't like the number six, it's an annoying number if I'm honest." Dean sighs, rolling his eyes and smirking.

"We could very easily narrow it to five, don't go offending six." Lilly smirks and throws a pillow at him. Jinx likes this, she likes having a big group, despite the dread that burrows within her. Despite the worry that they might leave. For now, though, she decides to ignore it, let it sit at the back of her mind where she doesn't care what it does, because she wants to enjoy this, even if it doesn't last long, she wants to enjoy having friends. She's never had friends before, and only now is she realising all the fun she's been missing.

Chapter 19 – Vivienne

°•. ✿ .•°°•. ✿ .•°°•. ✿ .•°

Julian crosses his arms across his chest and sighs, looking at Vivienne with envy from across the room. She laughs and closes her book, raising one eyebrow at him. "You can come and join me, you know?"

"I can't, I have stuff to do." He whines, dropping his head into his chest and beginning across the room. "You're so lucky you took an essay subject, most of your work for the semester is done already." Julian drops his textbook on the table and the sheer size of it makes a sound that echoes throughout the room. Vivienne jumps at the noise and glares up at him,

"That's only because during the first month I worked religiously. Now all I have to do is turn in my assignments on time."

He rolls his eyes and sighs, "Unfortunately, I have tests, *constantly*. That isn't an exaggeration, either, I haven't gotten the results for the last one and I'm already preparing for another one that's in just over a week."

Vivienne's heart drops in her chest and she tries to hide the frown creeping across her face, her birthday is next week. She knows Julian has to study for his tests, they are really important for him and his career, but she also really wants him at her party. She's saying 'party', but it's really just her and her friends messing around in her dorm. Everyone in their group is invited, including Jinx, and she is also thinking of inviting Damion. Jinx says she's met him, and she offered to invite him on Vivienne's behalf. She really wants to meet him in person, partially because he seems nice, but also to assess whether or not he is actually worth Julian's time. If he does even the tiniest little thing suspicious, she has the full intent of telling Julian and making sure he doesn't get hurt too badly. Julian is her first real friend, and that makes her naturally very protective of him, especially considering how protective he is of her in return.

"I can see your thoughts spiralling, relax, I'll be at the 'party'," he makes air quotes with his hands and smirks, but Vivienne doesn't return it.

"You don't have too, I know you're busy and have tons of exams, if it's too much-"

"Vi," he cuts her off and smiles at her, his eyes lighting up with the familiar kindness that always plays with his features, "why do you think I'm working like a maniac now? There's no way I'm missing your birthday, it's far too important, and it won't inconvenience me, or get in my way, or make me mad, or any other stupid thing you think it's going to do. Stop worrying."

Vivienne can't help but smile at him as he picks up his textbook again, dramatically lugging it towards his room. "Want some help?" Vivienne asks.

"Nah, I'm good." He smirks, faking an exhausted glance over his shoulder.

"Good," Vivienne says, smirking and stretching her legs out onto the entire couch. "Because I am far too comfortable and this book is getting very good." She opens the book, but peers over the top at Julian, who is now holding the book normally and standing in the doorway to his room.

"Do you have any idea how much you just sounded like Jinx?" He smirks, "She's rubbing off on you."

"Very funny." Vivienne turns her attention back to her book and pulls it closer to her face.

"That isn't hiding the blush, by the way." Julian says, walking into his room and closing the door until only his face is visible. Vivienne sits up and throws a pillow at him, but the door shuts quickly, meaning the pillow ends up in a sad heap on the floor instead. She isn't blushing, not intentionally anyway. Why would she intentionally blush at the thought of Jinx, she's just a friend, in fact until not long ago she hadn't even been that. She doesn't know what Julian is thinking, but whatever it is, he's wrong. The looks he keeps giving her are pointless and pointing out her reddening cheeks means nothing. Nothing.

Vivienne's phone vibrates in her pocket, and she slowly closes her book to check. Now that her friendship circle is steadily expanding, it could have been any one of her friends, but the name on the screen catches her off guard, Jinx. What does she want? They never text privately, in fact the last message that appears in the chat thread, aside from the hospital messages she is trying to ignore, is one from months ago, when Jinx had teased Vivienne about her jumper. A jumper she still hasn't returned. It isn't as if Jinx has asked for it back, she never brings it up, so Vivienne keeps it, if only to avoid how awkward it would be to give it back, of course.

Jinx: 5:37pm
Carter, I have a favour to ask.

Vivienne smiles and begins to type her reply, eager to know what this favour could be. Jinx never asks her for anything, not politely anyway, despite the truce they made. Jinx never asks anyone for help, actually.

Vivienne: 5:38pm
A fabour, intriguing…

Vivienne: 5:38pm
favour

Jinx: 5:39pm
It really takes away from the mocking tone of the message when you make spelling mistakes.

Vivienne laughs to herself and drops her head into her chest. Of course Jinx would pick up on that, it makes sense, but now, for some reason, Vivienne doesn't mind. She doesn't mind when Jinx points out her flaws, at least it means she's paying enough attention to notice.

Vivienne: 5:40pm
What's the favour?

Jinx: 5:40pm
Well, there's this kid I work with at the coffee shop, they go to the local high school. They don't have many friends, in fact I don't think they have any, they won't tell me, but can they come to the party? I know you don't know them, but they're really nice, I mean they have to be, they put up with me for hours a day. They're not like a kid-kid, they're a senior. It is your party, and I haven't told them anything so you wouldn't be disappointing them, but I was just wondering.

Vivienne: 5:41pm
I don't believe it, this can't be happening, are you being nice? Jinx Keller, you really are full of surprises.

Jinx: 5:41pm
Aren't I just. And, to make it even better, I don't get anything out of it. Can you believe that?!

Vivienne laughs outright, then nervously looks at Julian's door, she doesn't need him knowing what she is laughing at, not when it will just lead to further teasing. There aren't many people who can be sarcastic through text and have it not come across rude, but Jinx is one of them. Either that or Vivienne just knows her well enough to know that she isn't being genuine. To anyone who doesn't know her, that might have come across rude and self centred, but Vivienne knows better.

Vivienne: 5:42pm
This is some real character development, I'm impressed.

Jinx: 5:42pm
I'm glad. Now, back to the matter at hand, can Kit come?

Vivienne: 5:43pm
Of course they can. I think we both know what it's like not having any friends in high school.

Jinx: 5:43pm
Yeah, although I didn't mind it much, most of the people at our school were jerks anyway.

Vivienne: 5:44pm
Fair point, but I would have taken jerks over eating lunch alone in the library.

Jinx: 5:44pm
Technically, you weren't alone. I was there.

Vivienne: 5:45pm
Yes, but you hated me, and I yob.

Vivienne: 5:45pm
*you

Jinx: 5:46pm
Well, while we were both alone, we weren't lonely. We were alone together.

Vivienne reads the text at least four times over, this time fully aware of the heat flooding her cheeks. She can't control it this time, but it doesn't matter, no one is around to see it. Why does Jinx have to be so damn poetic? It isn't fair, she teases her in a way that borders flirting, and it makes Vivienne question everything. It makes Vivienne question her feelings towards Jinx, and it brings unwelcome ideas into the back of her mind. Unwelcome feelings.

It feels like forever while Vivienne tries to script a message to reply with. Everything she writes feels wrong, she thinks about every letter, every piece of punctuation. She has never thought about a text this much before, never, and she can't understand why she is doing it now. She is texting Jinx, just Jinx, it doesn't matter what she says, Jinx probably won't care anyway, so why does she?

Vivienne: 5:49pm
Do you have any idea how poetic that sounds?

Nerves rack at her whilst she waits for a response. Maybe she waited too long to reply, left it too late, maybe she annoyed her. When her phone finally lights up with a response, Vivienne is dangerously eager as she swipes up her screen.

Jinx: 5:51pm
Yes, I am fully aware. I've made a habit of reading poetry, it's fun.

Vivienne: 5:52pm
You read poetry?! No way. I don't believe you.

Jinx: 5:52pm
You seem shocked, does my ability to read surprise you that much?

Vivienne laughs and shakes her head at Jinx's remark. Despite her faults, Jinx is pretty funny when she tries. Although she never does seem to try too much, she's just naturally funny.

They text a little longer, until Jinx finally says her boss is coming and that he doesn't allow phones whilst working. That also makes Vivienne laugh, causing Julian to finally storm out of his room, demanding what is making her laugh so much. She smirks at him and shakes her head, but he doesn't drop it and makes towards her phone.

"Who is it?" he says, raising his eyebrows and reaching his hand across the back of the couch. He drops his head into his chest and sighs, "Please Vi, I am far too tired, and this is way too much effort."

"I guess you won't know then, you have to put in the effort for knowledge."

Julian looks at her, his face straight, "Vivienne Carter, I am currently doing a medical degree, I do at least three hours of revision *every night*, I think, of *all* people, *I* would know that you need to put in effort for knowledge."

Julian flops onto the couch, his legs hanging off the edge and his back resting on Vivienne's legs. She smiles at him and pats his head like a dog, to which he just sighs.

"Please just tell me who you were texting. I'm tired, overworked, sad, and I need entertainment." He drags out his words and rubs his nose into Vivienne's blanket.

"Fine, but you can't make fun, or be mean, or say other dumb stuff, okay?" this is probably a bad idea, she shouldn't tell him. But why does it matter anyway? It's not as if it's anything, she was just texting Jinx. Jinx. That's all it is, nothing else, and she doesn't know why she is so worried about telling Julian. It's only the same as her texting Lilly, or Dean, or anyone she knows. It's just Jinx, just Jinx.

"Jinx. I was texting Jinx."

Julian's head instantly sticks up and he props himself up on his elbows, "I'm *sorry?*" he raises his eyebrows and smirks at her, "What are you texting *her* about?"

"The party, that's all." Vivienne tries her hardest not to blush, but despite her effort, Julian catches her anyway. He sits up and swings his legs around, crossing them. Vivienne moves her legs from under him and pulls them up to her chest, resting her chin on her knees.

"'That's all'," He mimics, waving his arms about and hiding behind his hands. Vivienne smacks his arm away from his face and glares at him, but he only laughs, "She was right, back at the start of term, you do look like a baby rabbit when you glare."

Blushing once again, Vivienne picks up her phone, scrolling through her feed.

"Oh no, you can't ignore me." Julian takes her phone from her hands, standing on the couch and dramatically jumping off. "Maybe I should text Jinx." He holds her phone out in front of him and begins to mockingly text on the blank screen. Vivienne quickly stands from her spot on the couch and runs at him, but he swerves and steps around the couch, simply striding out of her reach.

"Give it back!" she yells, smiling at him and standing on the couch. Even with the advantage of the cushions beneath her, she is still only just matching his height. Jumping over the backboard, she crashes into him and reaches over his shoulder to where he is now holding the phone alone.

"'Oh Jinx, you're so sweet, I love it when you text me'," he mocks, leaning backwards as Vivienne makes a desperate grab for the phone. "'I pretend to hate you, but I really don't'," he raises his voice to a higher pitch and pretends to be faint. "'Jinx, I'm so glad you're coming to my party, it just wouldn't be the same without you',"

Using his lower height to her advantage, Vivienne jumps onto Julian's back and holds onto his shoulders, something she instantly regrets. He stands up once again, Vivienne now desperately trying not to fall off, and lifts his hands in the air in declaration.

"Oh Jinx, please text me again, my life is a void without you!'" he exclaims, and Vivienne curses at him.

"What the hell am I witnessing?"

They both freeze where they are as Lilly's voice cuts through their commotion. Julian looks at her, a smirk spreading across his face, while Vivienne slowly slides off his back and onto the floor, blush creeping up her neck and clouding her cheeks. Why does she have to blush so easily and obviously, it's as if she has no control over her own facial expressions.

"Why is Julian loudly expressing what sounds like love for Jinx?" Lilly raises one eyebrow at them, crossing her arms over one another. Neither of the two speak, until Vivienne sighs and says,

"Julian thinks I like Jinx, or at least that's what I'm assuming, considering his excessive amount of mocking."

Lilly smiles at her, then at Julian, her eyes lighting up with a familiar ecstatic spark, "You like Jinx?!" she shouts, not seeming to care that the dorm door is wide open.

"No." Vivienne states, walking back to the couch and sitting on top of her blankets, "Julian just thinks I do because-"

"Because Vivienne always blushes around her, she's been giggling for the last hour because she's been texting her, and she *still* has her jumper, despite her usual politeness when it comes to other people's things."

Lilly gapes at them both, her eyes wide. Vivienne doesn't personally see it as that shocking, considering she *doesn't* like Jinx. Julian is being delusional, she only blushes because Jinx teases her, she only laughs because Jinx is funny, and she only kept the jumper because...well she doesn't really have a reason for keeping the jumper, but it definitely isn't because she likes her.

"I *don't* like her." Vivienne assures them both, shaking her head at their bewilderment. "And I can't see why you're so determined to think so." She glances at Julian, who is now shutting the door and scolding Lilly about letting the warm air out. Their building is known throughout campus for being absolutely freezing, none of the windows are effectively lined and the walls are thin, so Julian's brother had brought over a heater a while ago to keep their dorm warm. It has been working for a while, but when people like Lilly leave the door open, the heat leaks out into the corridor and leaves them shivering.

"You totally do, Lilly, agree with me here?" Julian says, sitting on the arm of the couch and casting a pleading glance to Lilly, who is still standing in the centre of the room, her expression full of shock. Lilly has a habit of doing this, whatever she feels, she is clear about it, when she is happy, it radiates around her, and when she is mad, the whole campus sees it wise to keep well away.

"You definitely like her. I've read enough romance books to know the signs, you're just in denial, that's all." Lilly smirks and sits on the table in front of them, one leg lifted beside her and the other on the floor.

"Kindly get off our table, I have only just gotten the last footprints you left on there off. What was on your shoes that stained that much?" Julian mutters, waving his hand at Lilly's feet.

"I don't know, but if it annoyed you, it had to be something good. I don't think medical labs are as clean as this place, it's the definition of spotless."

Lilly has a point; Julian keeps their dorm clean to the point Vivienne sometimes messes it up just to feel normal. Whenever her Dad does happen to appear in the dorm, he always asks how it's kept so clean, as he knows how naturally messy Vivienne is. Her room is a state, books scattered everywhere, her laptop hiding under a pile of jumpers, and half her assignments are piled on the bed, the other half spread over her desk. While she likes to call it organised chaos, her Dad and Julian both see it as just chaos.

"I'm not in denial, I can't be, there's nothing to be in denial about." Nothing, there is absolutely nothing. Jinx is a friend, that's all Vivienne sees her as, nothing more, nothing less. It isn't as if she can see her as anything more anyway, not without being let down.

"You are totally in denial, or you're lying and have acknowledged your feelings for Jinx already and won't tell us." Lilly teases, taking her feet off the table and standing up straighter. She walks towards Vivienne and places her hands on her shoulders, her hair falling out of the clip holding it back. Confused, Vivienne looks past Lilly and towards Julian, but he just shrugs and smirks.

"Vivienne Carter," Lilly says, and Vivienne's attention is immediately back on her. Her grip tightens on her shoulders, "Do you or do you not have feelings for Jinx Carter?" She asks. Even more confused, Vivienne just looks at her and replies,

"I don't have feelings for Jinx." She keeps her tone hard and looks Lilly in the eyes, but she doesn't seem to believe her.

"Liar." She states, smirking and pulling back.

"What? How can you tell?" Vivienne asks, sitting up and following Lilly with her gaze as she proceeds to sit back on the table.

"You bite your lip when you lie." Lilly states, looking at Julian. "Do you ever see it?"

"I do, actually. Like when we ran into your Dad in town, and you said I was your *study partner*. You bit your lip so hard it started bleeding."

"I don't." Vivienne insists, her cheeks flushing red. She picks up her book and chucks it at Lilly, who catches it and looks astonished.

"I know you're annoyed, but don't take it out on the books. What have they ever done to you?"

She hadn't realised how observant Lilly is. She knows that she bites her lip when she lies, she'd known for years, it's her own little tell, but she didn't know those two had picked up on it. Like her blush, she can't seem to control it, and now it has given her away, both to her friends, and herself.

Lilly cackles in front of her as she observes Vivienne, her eyes still wide. Julian joins in with her laughing and they both smile at each other.

"That's it," Vivienne states, standing and grabbing her coat, "If you two are just going to be annoying, then I'm going for a walk."

Julian ceases his laughing and smirks at her, "Going to see Jinx?" he asks, raising his eyebrows and grabbing the attention of Lilly.

"No." she states, turning around quick enough to stop them noticing the small mark where she'd bitten her lip.

Chapter 20 – Jinx
— · ₀° ☆: *.☽ .* :☆° . —

    The store door rings behind her as Jinx waves through the glass, where Kit and Tony are still standing cleaning the surfaces and smiling. Kit waves back, and Tony nods his head, which is about as much affection she ever gets from him. Despite his generally happy demeanour, he is quite cold sometimes. Thankfully, Jinx knows him enough to see that he isn't being rude or dismissive, he's just being himself, and he can't help that. Somehow, she and Tony have some kind of connection, not an obvious one, but one that speaks not in their words, but their actions. One moment that always sticks in Jinx's mind, something she'll never forget, was last month. Her Mum, as usual, was badgering her about money, asking why she never called, all the usual stuff she does to try and guilt Jinx into feeling bad, and this time, it nearly worked. She was tired and nearing the end of her shift, and whenever her phone went off, she felt a weight in her chest get gradually heavier. After about an hour of constant ringing and notifications, Tony finally picked up the phone, ready to scold Jinx for what she assumed he thought was her friends. Jinx didn't have the energy to argue with him or try and take the phone, in fact she hadn't even registered that he had it until he was already looking at the countless messages on her home screen.
    He was silent for a long, long while, and Jinx just looked at him. She must've looked as tired and sick as she felt, because Tony gave her a pitying glance and said, "You know the rules, Jinx. I'll have to confiscate this until the end of your shift." She didn't protest as he slid the phone into his apron pocket, still

looking at her with something more than pity in his eyes. She didn't once ask him for it back, and he didn't offer. He'd never taken anyone's phone away from them before, and she didn't think he ever meant too, but he had done it for her, and not because she was texting too much, but because she couldn't text any longer. She needed someone to take the phone away, to relieve her of her Mum, because if Tony hadn't, she didn't think she would've been able to leave it alone. Over the years she's gotten good at ignoring her Mum, she normally just let the texts ring out long into the night, or responds and just tells her no, but sometimes, sometimes she is too tired to fight it, to fight her. Thankfully, Tony had been there when she was. This time, anyway.

Slowly walking away from the window and beginning down the street, Jinx pulls out her headphones and phone, plugging one into the other. She hits play on her music and places her phone back in her pocket, letting it hang there. While she does want to go straight home and sit in her dorm, the only light coming from the screen of her laptop, she has an errand to run. That's why she left the coffee store early, normally she helps Kit lock up and leaves the keys with Tony, but today he let her go ahead, she needs to get to the theatre before it closes. Checking her watch, Jinx quickens her pace as she realises it's later than she thought, and the theatre is going to start closing any second. She isn't one for stage plays, she doesn't really enjoy them and finds them quite dull, but she isn't going there for her. She is picking up some tickets she ordered a while ago, to a live production of the traditional *Romeo and Juliet*. The tickets are usually quite expensive, however Tony knows someone at the theatre, someone high up she presumes, who gets him, and therefore her, a discount. She also bought them quite early, before the rarity of seats made the prices rise. This isn't her first time buying something out of her usual budget.

Speeding up her pace further, she is practically jogging as she pulls out her phone again and opens her emails, where the receipt for the tickets is. She could've just had them emailed to her, like every other normal person in the world, but that would ruin the effect of them being a gift, and she has no doubt that who she is getting them for will appreciate the solidity of the gesture.

Rounding the corner of the street, she sees the theatre still open, people slowly filing out, laughter following them. Relaxing a little, she regains her steady walking pace and places her hands in her pockets, her phone still open on the email. She is nearly at the doors when she hears someone shout her name from behind her,

"Jinx!"

Taking out one of her headphones, she turns to the voice. With the music blaring in her ears, she couldn't recognise the voice the first time, but now she can see quite clearly who it is. Vivienne. Taking the second headphone out and placing them in her pocket, Jinx waves and glances behind her, where the stragglers from the last play are now stumbling through the doors. Vivienne is walking down the street in front of her, her coat wrapped tightly around her and a hat on her head, waving. When she catches up with Jinx, she smiles and sighs.

"Do you have any idea how fast you walk?" she sighs, breathing deeply and looking behind Jinx. "What are you doing at the theatre? Watching some depressing artsy play where all the characters die in some melancholily realistic way at the end?"

Jinx scoffs at the remark and turns towards the theatre, Vivienne closely on her tale. Opening the door, she steps aside to let Vivienne in, and before she realises what she is doing, follows her in. Vivienne can't be here; it ruins the point of this whole endeavour. The whole point of this is so the tickets surprise her on her birthday, hence the avoidance of the email, but if Vivienne sees her withdraw them here, it won't take a genius to assume who they are for.

"I'm picking up some tickets." Jinx mutters, turning to find Vivienne far behind her. She had stopped to take her hat off and place it in her bag, but she'd clearly gotten the zip stuck. "Jesus, Carter, it's like babysitting a toddler being around you sometimes." Jinx says, walking back to her and taking a hold of the bag. She zips it up with ease and begins to smirk at Vivienne, only to stare blankly instead. Strands of her hair have fallen around her face, waves of coppery red shaping her cornflower eyes. The cold wind has made the tops of her ears turn pink, and her face is pale with the exception of her cheeks, which are a vibrant red and frostbitten. The freckles that dance across her nose are slowly fading, but still visible, and she has snow on the ends of her eyelashes. She looks-

"Tickets for what?" Vivienne's voice cuts through her thoughts, and Jinx steps back quick enough that she nearly trips over her own feet.

"A play, what else would I be buying tickets for in a theatre, a theme park?" Jinx says, an unintentional bite in her voice. Immediately aware of her tone, she turns to Vivienne again, who looks unfazed by Jinx's harsh words, which is a relief. Well, sort of. It could just mean that she is that rude so much that Vivienne has grown used to it, which isn't good.

"I know that, genius, but what play?" She pushes, following Jinx up to the counter, where a drained man is standing, his eyes glazed over and his expression blank. Jinx would've said he's being rude, but she knows what it's like when your shift is about to end and someone comes in, daring to drag it out longer.

"I'm collecting tickets, under the name Keller." Jinx says, sliding her phone under the glass screen and watching as the man reads the email. He scans her phone screen and looks up at his computer,

"*Romeo and Juliet*, is that correct?" He drawls, looking at her with every bit of energy he can seem to muster, which isn't a lot. Vivienne bursts into laughter behind her, shaking her head at the poor man,

"That can't be right, Sir. This girl isn't the type to buy tickets to a romance play, *especially Romeo and Juliet*." She carries on her laughter as Jinx sighs and looks at the man, who is so obviously confused.

"Ignore her, those are the correct tickets." She assures him, and Vivienne goes silent behind her. The man nods and shuffles away, into the backroom where he no doubt has to print the tickets. The longer she is here, the worse of an idea this is beginning to seem, especially with Vivienne here. Why had she even come looking for her anyway? This all makes no sense.

"Why are you buying tickets to-"

"Why are you here?" Jinx cuts her off and leans against the service counter, looking behind her and towards the tall door the man had disappeared through. The quicker he is, the quicker she can get out of here and hide the tickets in one of her notebooks, along with the card she'd intended to put it in.

Vivienne raises her eyebrows and follows Jinx's gaze, "I could ask you the same question." She smirks, but it ends up looking like a genuine smile. She really is bad at mocking people, and if Jinx didn't know better, she'd say it's cute.

"I asked you first." Jinx states, crossing her arms and raising her eyebrows. It's times like this when she wished she could raise just one, like Vivienne.

"Fine. Lilly and Julian were being particularly annoying, and I was bored, so I figured I'd come find you at the coffee shop and get a drink. Only when I'd gotten to town did I realise it would be shut, but I saw you crossing the street and tried to catch up to you."

"Why didn't you just shout after me?"

"I did. Multiple times. You, however, have a very bad habit of constantly having headphones in. Then you checked your watch and practically started running, which was extremely intriguing, so I carried on following you."

"That's creepy." Jinx butts in, smirking.

Vivienne ignores her and carries on with what is now a lengthy story, "Now I'm here, watching you buy tickets for a play you once said was the 'equivalent of torture'."

Jinx sighs and checks her watch, technically the theatre was supposed to shut ten minutes ago, but one of the plays must've run over, because people are still walking down the stairs. This isn't a big theatre; it only has two halls. One is a small, cramped, dusty room reserved for up-and-coming playwrights and artists who don't have enough funding to perform anywhere else, the other, however, is the opposite. Jinx has never been in it, but it's supposed to be beautiful. A large, spacious theatre with red cloth chairs and an amazing front stage. That is the one she's bought the tickets for, where a well-known troupe of actors are performing a world-renowned play.

"Now you go. Why are you buying tickets for *Romeo and Juliet*?" When Jinx doesn't respond, Vivienne smiles at her, narrowing her eyes at the door. "Are they a gift?" Still, Jinx doesn't say anything, instead pretending to be invested in the price range for the snacks. Vivienne laughs and shakes her head, "Are they for a *date*? You would never come to a play like this alone, in fact I'm surprised you're even coming with someone.

Damn, they must be special." Vivienne is now beaming, a wide smile spread across her face. Now Jinx really needs to get out of here, she needs to wipe this entire interaction from her memory and just get the tickets and go. In fact, she might just leave the tickets and bolt now.

"It's not for a date." Jinx mutters, glancing at her watch again. How long does it take to print tickets?

"Oh really, then what's it for, hm? Go on, tell me. If you don't, I'm just going to assume it's for a date." Vivienne stands beside her and leans against the counter, copying Jinx's stance and crossing her arms. How can she be so annoying and yet so amusing, it doesn't make sense, and what makes even less sense was why Jinx puts up with it. She never used to let people mock her, or make fun of her, even Vivienne, but now? Now it's all she seems to let Vivienne do.

"It's not for a date." Jinx repeats herself, but Vivienne doesn't seem impressed.

"I don't believe you. These tickets can't have been cheap, considering *Romeo and Juliet* is showing in the fancy hall, and you wouldn't get something like this for Lilly because we both know she doesn't have the patience for plays, she can barely sit through a film. I can't think of anyone else you would be getting them for, there isn't anything too important coming up for any of us, and this is an extremely romantic gesture, so it can't be for Julian, I'm still convinced you hold a little disdain for him. You may not read romance, but as someone who does, I know for a fact that theatre dates are the most romantic ones, so, in conclusion, this is inevitably a date. Who for, I don't know, *yet*, but it must be someone special." Vivienne inhales deeply, not seeming to have breathed at any point in her analysis, then stands in front of Jinx. "Does that sound about right?" she says, putting her hands on her hips and tilting her head.

For someone who is so smart, she really can be simple, well, either that or she just can't seem to acknowledge herself. Jinx has noticed that through the years of knowing her, whether it's through hate or friendship. Vivienne has a habit of being very self-sacrificing, and while most see it as a nice, unselfish trait, Jinx can't help but see something darker and deeper behind it. It has always made her wonder why she can't see her own needs, and why she insists on putting others in front of herself.

"Carter, you really can be quite simple sometimes." Jinx mutters, turning to see the man walking back out, two old-style tickets in his hands. "Thanks." Jinx says, taking them and beginning towards the door, not bothering to check if Vivienne is behind her.

When she pushes through the door and out into the cold, she hears Vivienne behind her, but still doesn't look. She doesn't know if Vivienne had heard what she'd said, but it doesn't matter, she needs to get out of here. Everything Vivienne had said about the gift is getting to her head. She hadn't intended for it to be romantic; she hadn't intended for it to be anything, she'd just gotten Vivienne what she thought she'd like. She'd been banging on about this play for the last month, it is all she talks about, but she said she can't find any tickets for a reasonable price. She seemed gutted that she couldn't go, so Jinx thought she'd get the tickets for her as a surprise. How is that romantic?

Chapter 21 – Vivienne

°•. ✿ .•°°•. ✿ .•°°•. ✿ .•°

Everything is ready, or at least that's what Vivienne had been told by Julian when he ordered her to sit in her room. She 'isn't allowed to leave unless it's a matter of life or death', apparently. How there can ever be a matter of life or death when she is merely sitting in her dorm makes no sense, but she isn't about to question Julian, he seemed stressed to the point of near explosion last time she'd seen him. That was about an hour ago, when she'd made the mistake of coming back 'too early' and was quickly blindfolded by his hands, ushered in an odd pattern to her door, and told to sit patiently.

Now she is sitting on her own, a quiet record playing in the corner of her room and the book she has attempted to read lying open beside her. She knows she should be grateful, for the effort they are putting in, for the lengths they've gone to in order to surprise her, but she can't help being nervous. No matter the manner of them, she hates surprises. Whether they come from her father's good nature, or her friends' attempts to plan a party, she hates them. They are too unpredictable, too uncertain. Vivienne needs a schedule, something she can follow in a linear pattern so nothing catastrophic happens, if not, she spirals. She *hates* spiralling because she *hates* losing control. While she can't control much, the very little she can, she holds onto with an iron grip. Far too much had been out of her control when she was younger, some of which should have been, so she'd vowed to make sure everything around her was ordered, controlled, scheduled when she was older. Everything except her room. For some reason, her room is always in a state. She's terrible at tidying, cleaning, anything like that.

When she was little, her Dad used to joke and say it was because she was too busy organising her life to stop and organise her room, but soon, both had become hopelessly disorganised.

The only time her room was ever clean back home was every Friday afternoon, right after school. That was when her Mum used to clean it for her. She'd spend the whole week kindly reminding her and asking how she could live in it, then every Friday, like clockwork, she would cave. Sometimes it made Vivienne feel bad, knowing that her Mum was the one who cleaned up after her mess, so she tried tidying too. She tried to organise her drawers, make her bed, put her clothes away all neat and folded, but every Friday, no matter her effort, she found it completely redone. All her books ended up on her bookshelf, not just frantically piled on her desk, her clothes and drawers were completely re-arranged, and her bed was done properly, pillows and all. That was just how her Mum was, 'Everything has a place, where it belongs' her Mum used to say. The only thing is, now she's gone, Vivienne can't seem to be able to find a place for anything, everything feels wrong everywhere.

"Damn Carter, what bomb exploded in here? You didn't strike me as the messy type." Jinx's voice cuts through her thoughts and startles Vivienne, she hadn't heard her come in. Pushing away her thoughts again and glancing around her room, she forces a smile as she looks at Jinx.

"Oh, and you expect me to believe your room is any better?" she says, watching as Jinx wanders around, one of her hands resting easily by her side, tucked away in the pocket of her pants. She isn't dressed as usual, in her almost cosy-looking shirts and checked pants, now she's wearing long, loose black pants that look like they've been pressed, and a long sleeved, white turtleneck top that tightens around her chest. Her other hand is hidden beneath a black leather jacket that is slung over her back.

"You're staring." Jinx smirks, turning to face Vivienne and sitting on the end of her desk, one foot on the chair in front of her. She has large, black boots on, with yellow linings at the bottom and a band logo stitched onto the side of it.

"Did you do that yourself?" Vivienne says, changing the subject and pointing at the stitching. Now she is looking closer, it looks more like a cloth badge that has been stitched on.

"No, one of my Mum's boyfriends did before he-" Jinx seems to catch herself and shakes her head, looking at the boots again. "Do you even know who these are?" she asks, raising her eyebrows at Vivienne.

"Yeah, definitely…" Vivienne trails off and looks at the boots, leaning in closer. She squints at the logo and searches her memory, but absolutely nothing comes to mind. "The…Wavy lines?" Vivienne guesses and sits back. Jinx sighs and brings her hand to her head.

"You really are musically uneducated, aren't you? It's *The Arctic Monkeys*." Jinx says their name like it's supposed to jog her memory, but it doesn't, Vivienne has never heard of the band. After a long moment of silence, Jinx laughs and leans back on the desk, pulling out her phone. "Sometimes I forget all you're capable of listening to is *Taylor Swift* and *Lorde*." She eyes the record player, which has been peacefully playing *Folklore*. "Although your record player is pretty cool, I'll give you that."

Vivienne tries to hide the smile playing on her lips, but hopelessly fails, so changes the topic of conversation again. "Why are you in here?" she asks, moving along her bed and taking the book from beside her. She gestures for Jinx to sit on the bed, and she does, lying back on it and stretching her arms behind her head. Vivienne is momentarily stunned by Jinx's actions before she shifts her focus to her shoes again. She hasn't looked at Jinx properly since she came in, all she's really looked at are her clothes.

"You're really finding my shoes interesting tonight," Jinx says. Vivienne feels the bed shift as Jinx sits up, her jacket left behind her. "Am I really that off-putting in appearance tonight?" She teases, but Vivienne can't help but hear a small amount of hurt in her words. She never meant to give that impression; she just doesn't know how to look anymore. It's either too long of a look, or too short, she can't get the lengths right anymore, and when she tries, she just looks stupid. This is all stupid, she knows Jinx doesn't care, or notice if she looks too much, and it isn't as if it's the same the other way around. Jinx barely even looks at Vivienne, she doesn't seem to care unless she's teasing her.

"I'm sorry, am I not giving you enough attention?" Vivienne smirks and turns to face Jinx, trying to steal the slight pink crawling up her neck. She stops when she finds Jinx is already staring at her, a look of triumph painted across her face. Vivienne, however, is too concerned with what she is seeing to care whether or not Jinx thinks she's won. Jinx is wearing *makeup*. Not an absurd amount, in fact it might not have been noticeable if they weren't as close as they were, but Vivienne can see it. She wasn't aware Jinx even owned makeup, but apparently, she does. Her lips are darkened by a smooth, wine-coloured lipstick, her eyelashes are lengthened by mascara, and her hair had been curled, no doubt by Lilly. Half of it is held back with a golden pin, revealing earrings shaped like musical notes. She looks beautiful. She looks different, but in a way that makes her almost look the same, and it's truly beautiful.

"See, now you're just staring at my lips, Carter." Jinx mutters, smirking slightly, her eyes on Vivienne.

"What?" Vivienne lifts her gaze up slightly, meeting Jinx's.

"Never mind," Jinx says, her voice nearly a whisper.

They are closer now, Vivienne could feel Jinx's leg brushing hers, the smooth material of her pants pushing Vivienne's own pastel-blue dress against her bare legs underneath. A small piece of Jinx's hair falls out of her clip and Vivienne finds herself having to resist the urge to fix it, to bring her hand up that close to Jinx's face, which is close enough that she could see the small dimple as she smiles slightly, drawing closer.

"Vi, we're ready-" Julian begins in, opening the door widely, and both her and Jinx shoot backwards, Jinx standing up and grabbing her jacket off the bed. Julian stands in the doorway for a second, smirking at Vivienne, then moves and gestures for her to follow him. "What took you so long, all you had to do was tell her we were ready." He asks Jinx, smiling slightly and lifting his eyebrows.

"I know, but I had to do it with the appropriate amount of teasing, thus drawing out the process." Jinx replies, easily twisting her words and smirking at Julian as she leaves.

Leaving the room, Vivienne smiles at the fully decorated room. 'Happy Birthday' is printed on a banner that is hung from the bookshelves, and Vivienne can see where someone has written 'Vi!' next to it with a marker. Balloons are scattered on the floor, all of them pastel blue or green, and a small cake with a sparkler in the middle is being held by Dean, who is standing in the middle of the room, smiling.

"This is amazing-" Vivienne starts, but she is interrupted by a loud, tone-deaf voice singing happy birthday from the top of her lungs. Lilly has never been one for subtlety.

Julian joins in, along with Dean who is now holding a phone in one hand, balancing the cake in the other. Jinx walks off to meet him and Vivienne is left to stand alone, listening to her friends wish her a happy birthday. She smiles at them all, watching as Lilly bounds up to her and wraps her arms around her shoulders. Parties have never been her thing, even if they are just between friends, but this is nice, sort of. Julian ushers her in the centre of the room, where their coffee table has been laden with a cloth that has 'Happy Birthday' written on it in every colour imaginable. Lilly sits beside her, Julian still standing behind them, and Dean joins them, sitting across from Lilly. Perching on the arm of the couch is a boy she assumes is Damion, smiling very obviously at Julian.

"What do you think?" Julian says, sitting beside Damion and putting his arm around the now blushing boy, the cake having been left on the counter. Damion, she notices, is wearing Julian's hockey jacket, along with some jeans and a white buttoned shirt. Lilly is wearing a flowy lilac dress that is wholly inappropriate for the weather, and Julian has his nicest shirt on, which is half deep green and half white, split down the middle. Dean is wearing his usual navy, turtlenecked jumper, but instead of ripped jeans, he is wearing beige pants with a brown belt. They've all dressed up in their own way, and the thought of it makes Vivienne smile again. Somewhere in the room, someone's phone is quietly playing *Million Dollar Bills* by *Lorde*, and Vivienne wonders who's choice it was, because personally, she loves it.

"Go on, open your first gift." Damion urges, smiling at her. She's not met him before, but he already seems nice, she likes him. Julian smiles at him and he relaxes back into his arms. Damion seems pretty comfortable considering he is around a bunch of strangers, but that just seems to be the way he is, which is nice. Of all the things she loves about having friends, there is one thing she hates, the awkward period where you don't know what to say around each other, but thankfully, Damion doesn't seem like that type.

Vivienne laughs as she picks up the one in the centre of the table, the largest yet somehow lightest. She eyes Julian as she looks at the card, where he has scrawled 'Vivienne' in handwriting fit for a doctor. He smirks at her as she unwraps it, already sure of what it is. The wrapping tears away to reveal a large, checked blanket with a note in the middle.

For Vi, so you can stop stealing mine!

Vivienne laughs and opens the blanket, wrapping it around herself. When she does so, something falls out of it and lands on the floor, a small box that looks like it holds jewellery. Guilt pulls at her as she lifts it up, she really doesn't want Julian to do too much, she doesn't want him to waste too much money. She hates it when people get her gifts, mainly because she feels guilty that they use their own money to buy something for her. Normally, when people get her anything, she will get them something in return, even if it is something small, but according to her father, that is 'rude' on your own birthday.

When she opens the box, her smile somehow widens as she looks at the small picture inside it. Encased in metal and glass is a picture of her and Julian from months ago, at one of his hockey matches she'd gone to watch. She is standing on the side, wrapped in a scarf, looking absolutely freezing, and he is balancing next to her on the ice, his helmet resting on his forehead, stick in hand. He'd won that match, one of the first of the season, and she'd been there. She smiles at Julian and thanks him, beaming from her seat on the floor.

Next is Lilly's gift, or so she assumes, from the fluorescent bag it's in.

"That's from me!" Lilly says, watching as Vivienne opens the top and peers inside. She can't see much through the large amount of tissue paper, so she starts to take it out.

"Damn Lilly, how much tissue paper did you use?" Jinx smirks, and Vivienne turns to see her standing behind her, leaning against the wall with her arms crossed.

"Far too much."

"I think we've established that." Julian laughs, leaning in, "My god, it's never ending."

Vivienne gives up and turns the bag upside down, its contents spilling over the floor. A small, wrapped square sits in front of her, along with a packet of chocolate and some fancy tea.

"Did you cut down an entire forest to wrap this?" Dean asks, glancing at Lilly and raising his eyebrows.

"I don't think what's in the wrapping is going to help my case." She sighs but smiles, watching as Vivienne tears away the paper. When it's all gone, it reveals a book in her hands, but not just any book, a special edition of one of her favourites.

"Holy shit Lilly, this is amazing." Vivienne's smile widens as she hugs Lilly. When they pull apart, Vivienne surveys the book again, taking in all of it.

"Look inside." Lilly urges, and Vivienne does as she's told. On the very inside cover, Vivienne finds a note, along with a signature. The author's signature.

"Holy… Lilly, this is amazing!" She hugs her again, longer this time. "You have no idea how amazing this is!" Vivienne looks at the signature again, "How did you even get this?"

"My brother's friend works at the publishing company, and he sent it off. I was worried it wouldn't get back in time, but it arrived yesterday."

Lilly has no idea how much this means to her, this is amazing. These books had meant everything to her for so long, they were all she had, and now she has this, a signed, special edition.

"Lilly, you have no idea how much this means to me, I can't…" Vivienne trails off and looks at Lilly.

"I knew it would." Lilly smiles at her, then looks at the table, "Now, come on, open the others. I am incredibly nosy, and impatient, this is torture."

Vivienne laughs and shakes her head, reaching for another one of the gifts. Before she can open it, a knock sounds from the door and everyone's attention shifts.

"It's open." Julian shouts, none of them moving to open it for the ominous guest.

"That's probably Kit, they're not the most punctual of people." Jinx says, pushing off the wall and making her way to the door. She sighs as she opens it, shaking her head at whoever is standing just out of sight, "Why are you just standing at the door? You have to actually come in to socialise."

Jinx strides back to her spot at the wall, Kit now in tow. They look nervous, with their hands twisting in front of them. Vivienne wasn't aware her group was so scary, although she imagined she would be terrified too. If high school her had been put in a room full of college students, she might have spontaneously combusted just to get out of it.

"Hi," they mutter, standing next to Jinx like a scared puppy who won't leave its owner.

"Jesus, they're not going to kill you, not that I'm aware of, anyway." Jinx says, raising her eyebrows at the kid, "Last time

I spoke to you, you were ecstatic about this party, now you look ready to bolt."

Julian laughs from his seat on the couch, making Damion jump a little. Lilly stands up from the floor and walks towards Kit, smiling,

"Come on, you can't have fun if you're standing in a corner." She says, glancing at Jinx, "Unless you're like this brooding alternative-wannabe who's 'too cool for fun'."

Kit laughs and looks at Jinx, "She's even worse at work, you should see the faces she pulls when the customers aren't looking."

Jinx tilts her head and strides past them both, taking Lilly's seat on the floor beside Vivienne. "As much as I'm glad you're talking, I don't think it's fair for you to be slamming me, especially considering I'm the reason you're here and not sitting at home doodling."

"They are not doodles." Kit states, following Lilly to the spare seat on the couch, next to Julian. Kit sits down, but stays up straight, like they aren't ready to be too comfortable, meanwhile Lilly sits behind them, on the back of the couch itself.

"You draw, Kit?" Lilly asks.

"Yes, I'm thinking of taking art in college, although I don't know what I'll do with it." They mumble, their hands clasped together again.

"I do art!" Lilly says, excitement riddled in her voice. Kit looks up at her, tilting their head back to try and look at her face. "It's a really nice subject to take, although it had more research in it then I intended."

"Yes, we all know that Lilly, because you never shut up about it." Julian says, shaking his head. "I'm surprised Jinx doesn't do half of it for you, you get on her nerves that much." They all laugh and slowly the party gets back on track. Vivienne opens everyone else gifts, thanking each of them as she does, and occasionally the entire focus of the room shifts, like when Julian says he can do a press-up with Lilly on his back. None of them believed him and have to test the theory, but to everyone's surprise, he can. The seating arrangement changes multiple times, until eventually Jinx is back at her place at the wall, Lilly is sitting on Dean, and Julian and Damion are on the floor in fits of laughter. Kit hasn't moved, but she doesn't expect them too, they still don't seem entirely comfortable.

When the group settle back into the comfortable rhythm they were in before, talking about anything that comes to mind, someone once again knocks on the door. Vivienne looks around and sees the surprise on everyone else's faces too. Lilly counts their heads as if they're in a comedy, a quizzical look on her face.

"Do we know anyone else?" she asks, looking at Julian. He shakes his head and laughs, looking at the door again. "Hello?" Lilly shouts, and Vivienne finds it funny that not one of them is actually moving to open the door. Sighing, Vivienne stands up and makes her way towards it, puzzled at who it could be. Their food came ages ago, most of it is gone by now, and as Lilly had observed, everyone they already know is here.

Opening the door, her questions are quickly answered when her brother practically tackles her onto the floor, squeezing her legs tightly. "Vivi! Happy birthday!" he shouts, pulling away and smiling at her. Only then does he see the rest of the room and hides behind Vivienne's legs, childlike shyness taking over him.

"I'm presuming this is your brother?" Dean says, looking at Ollie with his eyes narrowed, "Either that or you've befriended a random eight-year-old."

"Ten." Ollie demands, stepping out from behind Vivienne and crossing his arms.

"No, I think you're eight, you're far too scared to be ten. Ten-year-olds are tough and brave, they don't hide behind their sisters." Jinx smirks from across the room and Ollie beams at her.

"Jinx!" he says, running across the room and jumping up at her. She catches him and places him back on the floor, smiling as she does so.

"Jinx, how do you know Vivienne's brother so well?" Lilly asks, glancing at Vivienne and smirking.

"Jinx is Vivi's-" Ollie starts and a sudden panic takes hold of Vivienne. She keeps forgetting what her brother and Dad think her and Jinx are, she still hasn't told them it's a lie.

"Ollie, where's Dad?" Vivienne says, shutting the door behind her and rushing to her little brother. She ushers him to the couch, where he jumps up and looks at Lilly. He tilts his head to the side and scrunches his face up, like he's considering something. After a short, awkward silence, he sticks his hand out to her, something he's never done before. Julian laughs and Vivienne raises her eyebrows, shaking her head at him.

"I'm Ollie, who are you?" He asks. Lilly shakes his small hand and smiles at him,

"Lilly." She seems to find his odd introduction cute, as does everyone else when he proceeds to go around the room. Vivienne has *never* seen him do this before, and if she is being frank, it's funny. The change of character must've happened in the last few weeks, because when she'd last seen him, he was still introducing himself like a child, not a middle-aged man from 19th Century England.

"Oliver Carter, how many times have I told you not to run off-" Vivienne's Dad opens the door, calling after her brother, but stops when he sees the little group surrounding her. He looks at every one of them, analysing and taking every detail in, before turning to Vivienne.

"You don't happen to have seen your brother?" He asks, looking around the room, his gaze lingering on Dean, Julian, and Damion.

"Yes, he's-"

"Boo!" Ollie jumps out from where he had hidden behind the couch and runs up to her father. He sighs and shakes his head, looking only at Ollie.

"What have I told you about running off, especially in new places?" Her Dad looks at her, then to the group again. "Are you having a *party?*" he says, both shock and amusement written across his face.

Smiling, Vivienne looks at her friends, who are now smiling at her Dad. Lilly jumps up from her seat and walks towards her Dad, beaming at him.

"I'm Lilly." She says, looking at Vivienne, then back to her Dad. "You two don't look anything alike." Her Dad smiles at Lilly, seemingly pleased that one of her friends has actively introduced themselves. He waits in silence and Vivienne begins to introduce them, pointing as she does.

"Dad, meet Julian, Damion, Dean, Kit, and Jinx." She smiles, proud to have something to show to her Dad and prove she isn't too lonely.

"Wow," her Dad says, looking at the decorations scattered throughout the room and the presents piled on the table, "You've gone from having no friends to having six, that's impressive Pumpkin."

Jinx stifles a laugh in the corner, covering her mouth with her hand, and Vivienne nudges her Dad with her elbow. She doesn't mind the nickname, in fact sometimes she finds it cute, but not in front of her friends, *especially* Jinx. She's already heard it, of course, at the coffee shop, but that doesn't stop it from being embarrassing. As far as Vivienne is aware, Jinx had forgotten about it, but that was a nice, fresh reminder.

Vivienne takes her Dad to the side as her friends carry on their conversations, Ollie sitting in her spot, a smile growing across his face from the attention. All his friends have older siblings, and they have friends that come around all the time, so when Vivienne didn't bring any back from high school, he'd been very disappointed. He wanted to 'show off' all of 'his' older friends, why, Vivienne never understood, she was the oldest despite her Dad, and he wasn't much to show off to a younger audience. Only she finds him funny, only she laughs at the terrible jokes he makes a habit of telling with no prompting, and only she finds him 'cool' in a sense, although what that sense is is still a mystery.

"What are you doing?" She whispers once they are out of earshot, which is hard but just about manageable. "We went out for dinner yesterday, I thought that was it?" Looking over her shoulder, she smiles at Julian, who waves at her and smirks to her Dad, miming something she can't understand.

"This is brilliant," her Dad says, waving at Julian and smiling, "Of all the things I thought you would be doing tonight, this is not one of them. Ushering away your poor Dad to hang out with your friends, I must admit, I'm impressed." He smiles at her, and his eyes scrunch up, showing the faint lines in his face. He looks genuinely happy, he looks so proud of her.

She'd gotten into one of the best colleges in the country, she'd passed all her exams with top marks, she'd accomplished so much, and he is proud of her for having friends. *Friends*, that's all it takes, that's all he'd ever wanted from her, and she knows that. She knows he didn't care if she went to college, or passed her exams, or even got out of Highschool. She knows that deep down, he doesn't need her to be clever and witty, he needs her to be kind and lovable, he needs her to find her people at college so she won't be on her own, and she had. Julian, Lilly, Jinx, Dean, everyone that is here tonight, they are her people, they are her college family, and she knows that they will always be there for her, some more than others, but they will all still be there.

"Well, if you're that impressed, you wouldn't mind standing quietly in the background?" She knows it's a futile attempt to get rid of him. She loves him, there is no doubting that, but no teenager wants her Dad hanging around with her friends. Unfortunately, her Dad doesn't seem to grasp that concept and begins towards the group, who are now laughing at something Ollie has said, him still beaming in the middle.

"Dad," Vivienne grabs him by the arm before he is out of her reach, "don't be embarrassing, ok? No old pictures, no stupid stories, just be *normal*." While she may appear to be being dramatic, she knows it's necessary. If her Dad isn't kept under her eye, there is no limit to the amount of embarrassment he can bring. He never clears his phone, which means the kid photos are endless, and he's recorded stuff for as long as she can remember, so videos aren't rare either. If he shows any of this to the group, or to someone like Jinx, the teasing will never stop. It would actually be endless.

"I'll be as normal as possible, *Pumpkin*." He smiles and pulls away, properly introducing himself to the group. Everyone else does the same and the party begins to follow its rhythm again, Vivienne's Dad staying quiet for the most part, silently observing everything. Ollie is the opposite, he asks all kinds of questions, tells long, pointless stories, and always seems to be laughing at something with either Lilly or Dean. For some reason, those are the two he's taken a liking too, Lilly is understandable, she's practically a ten-year-old boy herself, but Dean is usually quite cold and standoffish before you get to know him, although she doubts he's like that with Ollie. Either that or Ollie is too young to take his coldness into account and bothers him anyway.

They play some of the more typical party games, truth or dare and never have I ever, then somehow the topic of their shared class comes up. They haven't spoken about *Introduction to Classical Literature* for a while, they haven't even studied it much. Technically, they are still a 'study group' of sorts, but the basic line up for their debates is set up, they've all done the reading and know what they are doing, so the studying slowly became just going out for coffee or going to Julian's hockey games.

When they need to, they will meet up and discuss strategies, or have minor discussions about the themes and representations, but they only occur maybe once fortnight. They are prepared and ready, they don't need much more until the weeks before the exams approach them.

"I still don't know how you can work on the Con side of this masterpiece." Lilly says, looking at Julian and Jinx, who are smirking at her.

"And I don't know how you can work on the Pro side of this boring, typical, play. That's all it is, a play, and you treat it like it's something that changed the world." Jinx sighs, sitting on the arm of the chair. Her phone buzzes in her pocket but she ignores it, still focused on the debate. Laughing, Vivienne moves to sit next to Lilly, actively joining the debates sides.

"It's a masterpiece, a dramatic love story between two forbidden lovers, it's a classic, how can you hate it?" Lilly asks, putting her hand to her heart and faking shock.

"It's pathetic," Julian says, "They have an entire city of people to choose from and they *have* to choose each other, they met *once, once* and they are completely infatuated with each other. They get married after, what, a week? And have you even looked at their ages, Juliette is about fourteen and she's running off with this boy she met a week ago."

"Not to mention the fact that Romeo *kills himself*, and so does she, just because her 'true love' is dead." Jinx scoffs and shakes her head, standing from her seat on the couch, "'Oh no, the love of my life is dead, well, there's no point living anymore. Fetch me my dagger, good Sir!'"

Julian stands from his seat and bows to her, "'Here you are, my good Lady, and I wish you a happy death, although I'm afraid your *entire family* will miss you dearly.'"

"'My family, oh well. My boyfriend's dead, so I must die too.'" With those words, she plunges an imaginary dagger into her chest and keels over. Vivienne bursts into hysterical laughter, and the rest follow as Julian and Jinx bow, nodding their heads to the group.

"Ladies and gentlemen, Jinx Keller and Julian Patterson." Lilly shouts, holding her hand out in demonstration to the two, who are now sitting down.

"Honestly, you two are made for the stage." Dean laughs, quietly clapping.

"Aren't we just?" Julian says, turning back to Lilly, "Now, back to the debate." Lilly laughs at him and shakes her head, but doesn't resist, starting the conversation again. This time, Vivienne joins in more with her views on it, and so do Dean and Damion. Much to everyone's surprise, Damion likes *Romeo and Juliet*, and takes the opposing side to Julian, and not to any surprise, Dean joins Julian's side. Kit sits quietly, watching the group as the antics unfold, until everyone turns to them. They will be the deciding vote, whatever side they pick will decide who has the most people. Considering this started as a mock debate, no one is taking it seriously, but they seem to.

"I'm more of a *Macbeth* person, really." They smirk, looking at Julian. He cheers and high fives Dean, who goes to do the same to Jinx, except she isn't there. She isn't anywhere.

"Where did Jinx go?" Lilly asks, looking around the room and craning her neck towards the bathroom.

"I don't know, probably outside or something." Dean says, pulling a small, battered book from his bag. This instantly grabs the attention of Lilly, who demands to see what he's reading, and everyone settles down, the attention on Jinx gone. Well, almost gone, Vivienne is still wondering where she is.

Jinx isn't the most sociable of people, but she doesn't seem like the type to just disappear from a party, she hasn't even given Vivienne her gift yet, which she's been assured she has by Lilly earlier.

"I'm going to go get a drink," Vivienne says to no one in particular, before standing to leave. Thankfully, no one seems to know that the vending machine down the hall hasn't worked since September, so no one questions when she grabs her bag and leaves. Her Dad stops her at the door and asks if she is okay, which she assures him she is, and lets her go, stopping her little brother in his tracks as he tries to follow her.

Closing the door behind her, Vivienne begins down the corridor, the opposite way of the broken machine. While no one else seems bothered by Jinx's disappearance, Vivienne is. Despite her actions during the party, she'd seemed a little off put by their interaction beforehand. She didn't really speak much unless she was prompted to by the group, *Romeo and Juliet* theatrics excluded, obviously.

Walking down the corridor and wrapping her arms around herself against the cold, Vivienne isn't prepared to find Jinx at the end of the corridor, a phone pressed to her ear.

"Yes, Officer," She mutters, pacing up and down, one hand still in her pocket. "Of course, I totally understand." Her voice is calm, but her features are twisted into a sad anger. When she pulls the phone away from her ear, she stands in silence for a long while before letting loose a frustrated scream and kicking the wall. "Fuck!" she shouts, looking at the phone again before she turns to walk back to the party. When she sees Vivienne she stops dead, her hands limp at her side and her face pale.

"Carter," she mumbles before shaking her head and walking straight past Vivienne.

"Jinx, wait," Vivienne says, turning to follow her. She's walking fast enough that Vivienne has to jog to catch up to her, "Jinx, please." Still, she doesn't stop, she doesn't even respond. Quickening her pace, Vivienne tries to catch her up, until, when they are nearly back at the dorm, Vivienne grabs Jinx's arm and pulls her to a stop. "Jinx what's going on?" she demands, not letting go of her arm. They stand like that for a long while and a small part of Vivienne tells her that she should let go, but she doesn't. She's worried, whatever that phone call was, it wasn't good. Jinx doesn't lose her temper, she doesn't scream and kick things, she's calm, collected, and she keeps her emotions in check, so whatever has made her act like that, it can't be good. She was talking to an Officer, or at least that's what it sounded like, like she was talking to someone important, like a police officer. But why would she be talking to a police officer? That doesn't make any sense, Jinx also isn't the sort to break the law, not that Vivienne is aware, anyway.

"Please, tell me." Vivienne says, her voice calmer and her face softening. She still doesn't let go of Jinx's arm. Again, there is a silence, and Vivienne's thoughts spiral, descending down into the depths of her mind, until Jinx appears to snap.

"Fine, you want to know? Turns out my deadbeat mother has gotten that drunk she's been arrested and locked in an *actual* holding cell. Now I, as the only family she has anywhere near her, need to find a bus that will take me home at eleven o'clock at night, then spend two hours signing paperwork and paying bail, before finding a bus that will take me home. That won't be until around one in the morning, and I don't know if you can think of any buses that run through our tiny ass town at one in the morning, but I can tell you I can't, so I then have no way of getting back to school, and I am not eager to spend the night watching my mother run to the bathroom every ten minutes. Happy?"

Vivienne doesn't know what to say, she doesn't say anything for a long while and watches as horror takes over Jinx's face at the realisation of what she'd just said.

"I need to go," she mutters, turning back to the corridor, not bothering to get her coat from the room.

"Wait," Vivienne says, holding out her hand to stop her again. She sees Jinx hesitate before nodding slightly, her face still stricken and pale. Vivienne offers her a weak smile and turns back to the room, walking in again and slowly shutting the door behind her.

Chapter 22 – Jinx
── · ₀° ☆: *.☽ . * :☆° . ──

This isn't happening, this can't be happening, she can't have *let* this happen. She can't have let someone get this far, told them this much. Except she has, and of all the people, it was Vivienne that she'd told, Vivienne that she'd shouted at in the corridor, Vivienne that she'd watched go into the dorm and come out with her Dad, who quietly began towards the door. It was Vivienne who explained she'd only told him, and that he'd told everyone else that he was doing something special with her, so it didn't look suspicious. It had been Vivienne who had guided her to the car and gotten in beside her, in the back, the seat at the front, next to her Dad, empty. And it was Vivienne who is now sitting beside her, silently watching out of the window and occasionally looking at Jinx, worry now painted across her features.

They don't talk, not for a long while. Jinx sits in silence, shame taking over her and stopping any words she hopes to form. Shame about her mother, shame about needing help, shame about everything. Not only that, but guilt is making her feel sick. Pulling at every thought, ruining anything she tries to use to distract herself. This is her fault. They are driving because of her, Vivienne's Dad is doing this because of her, Vivienne is missing her own birthday because of *her*. Because *she* can't deal with her own problems, because *she* had to tell someone, because *she* had to be selfish and rope someone else into her problems. This is *all* her. It *always* is.

Guilt, shame, that's all she is. That's all she will ever be, that's all she's ever been. No one has seen her as more, or less. Her family hates her, her Mum doesn't care about her, her Dad hadn't even wanted to know her, everyone who is supposed to love her either hates or doesn't know her. Some do both. Like her grandparents, and her aunts. They don't talk to her, they talk to her mother, they give her money and pity her, but Jinx? They *hate* Jinx and have made it very clear. According to her Grandparents, she is the reason her mother didn't get into college, why she didn't graduate or get a mathematics degree like she was supposed to, and according to her aunts, she is the reason for her mothers drinking.

Apparently if she had been an 'easier child' her Mum might've been able to cope. It isn't as if they know how easy of a child she had tried to be, how she burned herself countless times when she was eight trying to use the oven to cook her own dinner, how she'd nearly poisoned herself with laundry detergent when she was six because she'd used it wrong in her own washing, or how she'd had to learn how to use a medical bandage at seven when she'd slit her arm on a knife whilst doing the dishes. They didn't know about any of it, they didn't see any of it. All they saw was a worthless, unwanted child who'd ruined the life of their most promising sister, their most promising daughter.

The last time they'd come round was when she was twelve, during the month her Mum had tried her hardest to become clean. They'd come around during one of her good days, of course they had, god forbid they come around when she was actually struggling, when she actually needed them. After being given a two-day notice, Jinx had completely scrubbed down and cleaned the house. Everywhere was spotless, everything was put away, their apartment looked like a normal, functional family lived there. Her Mum was nice to them, made them tea with the last sugar they had, gave them the last of their biscuits, she'd even used some of the electricity to dare and put the TV on when they wanted to watch the news. Then they'd asked about Jinx. She'd been in the room the whole time, but when she went to the toilet, they started pressing her Mum. Jinx stood at the door and listened to their whispered words, they asked if she was causing trouble, how her Mum was coping, if she was being a good student and obeying her teachers. Her Mum, of course, didn't know how to answer any of the questions, because she knew nothing about Jinx. Twelve years of being Mother and Daughter, but all she could remember was her name. She forgot that sometimes, too. When she was silent for a long, long while, they'd assumed that it was because Jinx was being bad and started the same conversation they had every time they were there. Most times Jinx just sat there, at the door, listening to every bit of it and taking it all in, vowing to be better, but not this time. This time she was old enough to know that whatever she did, no matter what she achieved, no matter how many times she tried to impress them, to be good, they wouldn't care. They never would care, they would only ever see her as a disappointment, someone they wouldn't associate with, *something* they didn't care about. So she stopped caring. She stopped trying to impress them, when they came round, she was herself. When they made comments, she challenged them, when they picked fights, she fought. And she won, every damn time. Except once. Once.

"Jinx," Vivienne whispers, looking at her Dad. He had put headphones on at some point, apparently. When, Jinx didn't care to notice, but now it's all she can see. "Are you okay?" Vivienne asks, looking at her, her eyes soft.

"I'm fine." Jinx says, leaning back in her seat and tapping one of her legs on the floor. "I'm just pissed."

"At your Mum?" Vivienne asks, uncrossing her arms from across her chest.

"At my Mum, at myself, at everyone, really." Jinx says, but instantly realises what she's said and sits up straighter, holding her hand up at Vivienne. "Not at you, though, or your Dad."

Vivienne sighs and shakes her head, "I didn't think you meant me, if I'm honest." Something is wrong. Jinx can tell by the way Vivienne speaks, the way her voice wavers and how her hand hands are tightening in each other. This time it's Jinx asking the question, "Carter, are you alright?"

She doesn't answer, until after a long while she sighs, "Why didn't you tell me?" She says, looking at the floor. "Why didn't you tell *anyone*?" Her voice cracks and she looks at Jinx again, this time her eyes shining with water.

"I don't know." Jinx mutters looking at the floor.

"Shit, I didn't mean to make you feel bad," Vivienne says, reaching out to Jinx and taking her hand. "Sorry." She squeezes her hand and Jinx looks out the window, dropping her head into her chest and hiding the pink crawling up her neck. She can't let Vivienne see, not when she knows she'd make the connection. She's hidden it so well, for so long, but this is making it so much harder. Being at college together, being in the same friendship circle, working on the same project, and now this. Jinx doesn't know how much longer she will be able to hide it, but she can't risk telling her. She can't risk telling anyone. She hasn't told anyone, ever, no one knows. No one in high school, no one in college, and she doesn't intend on changing that. She barely admits it to herself, partly because she doesn't want to but also because she knows she can't. Because the problems she causes as a friend are nothing compared to what she imagines she'd cause as something more, Vivienne is her friend right now and she is currently missing out on her own birthday to drive Jinx halfway across the state to pick up her drunk Mother from a jail cell. She can't ruin Vivienne, not when she's already ruined herself enough.

"Jinx?" Vivienne has moved along a seat, her seatbelt now undone and her legs brushing against Jinx's. The details. She *has* to stop seeing the details. She has to stop noticing her perfume, or knowing when she has makeup on. She has to stop thinking about every small movement, every brush of hands, every bump and tease. She has to stop thinking about all of it. Except she can't. For some stupid reason she can't.

Jinx's phone rings in her pocket and Vivienne sits up straighter as she answers it, grateful for the distraction. She puts the phone on loudspeaker and a muffled, digitalised female voice comes through the speakers,

"Is this Miss Jinx Keller?" she asks, and Jinx hears the sound of paperwork in the back, except it sounds different to her last call.

"Yes." Jinx says, trying to listen into the background of the call by bringing the phone closer to her. A siren sounds in the background and speakers ring with the words 'Code Blue' repeating over and over. Code Blue, where had she heard that before? She doesn't know where she is getting the call from, but she knows for a fact that it isn't a police station, not anymore.

"Jinx, Code Blue, that means…" Vivienne mutters as the woman's voice comes through the phone again.

"Okay, good, this is the Hospital, we're calling about your Mother, Beatrice Keller?"

What. Her Mother. A hospital. There must've been a mistake. Her Mum is at a police station. Her Mum isn't at a hospital, her Mum *can't* be at a hospital.

"What?" She says, but when the nurse responds Jinx isn't listening. Her Mum is at the Hospital.

Code Blue. She remembers what it means. She's heard it before.

An Emergency.

*

This doesn't make any sense, why can't she see her, the police said she had only gotten into a minor accident. The nurse had assured her that what she'd heard was for another patient, but there was a small part of Jinx that doesn't take that as reassuring. Her leg starts to shake again, bouncing in its painfully stationary position while the seconds pass by on the clock. Her Mum had gotten drunk, that isn't out of the ordinary, but this, this is new. She's never gotten hurt before, *ever*. Everything Jinx holds against her Mum, all the anger, the fear, everything that makes her pull away, stay out of touch, it all subsided when Vivienne's Dad altered his route and took her to the hospital. She had come here with the intent of calling her mother a taxi and barely speaking to her, but that had changed, that had all changed when the doctors said she wasn't in a fit state to see anyone. What could make her unable to see anyone? Jinx doesn't know much about the medical field, but she doesn't think they say anything like that unless it's serious, and it scares her. Her Mother may be an alcoholic, someone who can barely take care of herself never mind her daughter, Jinx may have spent years building up for resentment for her, avoiding her, staying far from her self-destructive nature, but in the end, no matter what she's done or not done, there are moments she remembers her trying. Trying to be a mother, trying to overcome her own problems to deal with Jinx's, trying to stop Jinx taking the path she had. In the end, in moments like this, Jinx can only see her Mother as one thing, her

Mum. *Her Mum* who is currently behind doors she can't cross, having god knows what done to her for an injury Jinx can only hope is minor.

But she doesn't know. She can't know because no one is telling her anything. They expect her to sit here patiently when they haven't clarified what is going on with her Mum, whether she is safe, stable, *alive*. Jinx knows nothing, and she hates it.

"Jinx," Vivienne's calm, steady voice cuts through her thoughts, taking her attention from everything. "You're bleeding." She murmurs, sliding her hands in between Jinx's, where they had been steadily picking away at her nail beds. She hadn't noticed she'd gone that deep, she hadn't noticed her own blood on the tips of her fingers, although she isn't noticing much anymore, only the steady clapping of the ER door opening and closing, hope pulling at her every time a doctor comes through.

"Sorry," she mutters, putting her hands in fists at her sides.

Vivienne looks at her and takes one of her hands in hers, "Don't apologise, you idiot," she squeezes Jinx's hand and looks at the door, "You're allowed to be worried."

Vivienne's Dad sighs from beside Vivienne, looking at his watch, "What are they doing that's taking this long, I'm going to ask again." He says, standing from his seat and shaking his head. "Does anyone want anything, a hot drink or something? I'm going to run down to the café."

Jinx wants a drink, she wants something that will calm her nerves, settle her down and back into her calm rhythm, but she can't ask. She doesn't know why; her mouth can't form the words and a small panic began to pull at her again as she looks at the door.

"Two teas, please, Dad." Vivienne says, smiling at him. He returns the smile, although his isn't as strong as he glances at Jinx, who's leg hadn't stopped bouncing.

She doesn't know much about Vivienne's Dad, only that he's a tutor and lecturer at the college near their town. She also knows that he lost his wife years ago, and that he hasn't remarried, dated, or so much as flirted with a woman since. Vivienne told her that, why, she doesn't know, but she's glad she had. This can't be easy for them, being back in the hospital after spending so long in it in the past, and it makes Jinx feel guilty.

Guilty at the fact that she's roped Vivienne into this, that her Dad has to drive her up here, that they are both in a place that brings them so much pain, because of her. They are here because of *her*. This is *her* fault. In fact, everything is, this whole incident is probably somehow related to her. She is probably the reason for the accident, after all, it has been implied that she is the reason for her Mothers drinking many times.

Her Aunt had said so before she left for England, her grandparents are constantly saying about how her Mother had had such a bright future before her, her entire family see her as the problem, and they are probably right. Wherever she goes, she seems to attract pain, ruin, they seem to follow her. She is destructive, that's all she is, and she's now managed to destroy her Mum.

"I'm looking for Beatrice Keller." A deep, male voice says from the desk. He is facing the nurses, looking at the screen behind them, but Jinx can see who he is. She can't forget, not after everything he's done, to both her and her Mum. After he's drained their bank accounts and left, only to show up when he is broke again. He supplies her Mum with the drink that destroys her. He leaves and comes back again, then tell her Mum she is lucky he does.

And she'd believes it. She believes every word of his bullshit and laps it up like a dying plant does water. The sight of him makes every part of her seethe with anger. If he's here, it means her Mum is in more danger than she could ever be in any hospital room. If he is here, she won't go out by herself, which means she won't get home. Jinx needs to make sure he isn't here when she comes out, she needs him gone. Her Mum can't protect herself, so Jinx has to do it for her.

Standing and letting go of Vivienne's hand, she doesn't think as she storms across the floor, straight towards Kyle. By the time she reaches him, he is leant against the wall opposite the desk, scrolling through his phone and smirking. Anger clouds her features as she takes his phone from his grip and stands in front of him, her hands clenched tight enough into fists beside her that the knuckles are beginning to whiten. Kyle smirks at her and looks her up and down,

"Well, well, haven't you grown." His eyes linger over her chest, but she doesn't break her gaze.

"What are you doing here?" she spits the question at him and doesn't miss the amusement play across his face when she does.

"What does it look like, beautiful, I'm picking up your Mum. She is my girlfriend, after all." He looks over her shoulder and Jinx turns to find Vivienne standing behind her, her gaze also fixed on the poor excuse for a man in front of her.

"Jinx, who is this?" She asks, stepping closer, so she is beside Jinx. Kyle laughs and looks at Jinx, smiling,

"Who's this, your little guard dog?" he asks, laughing at Vivienne.

"Leave her out of this." Jinx says, stepping in front of Vivienne, letting one of her fists go. "Vivienne, go and check where your *Dad* is." She says, and watches as Vivienne doesn't move. "Go, Vivienne." Jinx demands and nods to the corridor her father had walked down. She doesn't move for a long while, until finally, after more prompting, she begins away, glaring at Kyle.

Before Jinx can react, Kyle reaches out and grabs her arm, pulling her away from the desk in a skilled way that doesn't attract attention. Jinx knows she should pull free, smack away his hand, tell him to let go. She should do *something*. But she can't. The moment he touches her, the minute she feels his grip on her arm, she freezes.

She feels the colour drain from her face, her arms go limp, and her legs go weak beneath her. All she can see, all she can feel, is him. Him *everywhere*. Her skin crawls and burns, sending sickening shivers down her spine as he pulls her down the corridor and pushes her against the wall by her stomach. No one is around, the hall is practically empty, no one can see her, no one can see *him*. She is *alone*.

"I've never gotten this far," he whispers, pushing down on her stomach again, "No matter how much you pretend to fight, you'll never win." He smirks and looks over his shoulder. Jinx follows his gaze but finds no one, *no one*. Vivienne is gone, the corridor is empty. The corridor is empty. No one is there. She starts to shake as he puts his hand on her shoulder and slides it up her neck, pushing her hair away from her ears. Her breath comes sharply in her chest, and she falls against the wall, her legs collapsing.

"Oh no you don't." Kyle grabs under one of her arms and forces her up. She can't move. She's frozen, his grip tightening on her arm and sparking pain through her shoulder. Her vision clouds and her entire body trembles, all she can think about is his hands running down her side, her memories clouding her thoughts. He'd given up last time, but he'd done enough damage beforehand.

Her breathing becomes sharper and higher, the air leaving her lungs and refusing to return. A small, panicked whimper escapes her mouth, and he laughs. *He laughs*. He has reduced her to a cowering child, and he is laughing. It makes her feel physically sick.

"Jinx!" Someone shouts from down the corridor, and she feels herself drop as Kyle lets go. She hits the floor, but the pain doesn't register in her mind, all she can see is him. All she can feel are his hands again. Painful memories she forced down, hidden away, all out in the open, taunting her and forcing her down. Down into the pit of her past she'd tried so desperately to avoid, to push away and keep far from her life. It was going so well; she was doing *so well*. With her friends, Lilly, Vivienne, everyone. She had almost left it behind, almost succeeded at a new, fresh life away from it all. *Almost.*

Vivienne drops onto the floor beside her, and another type of fear strikes Jinx, not one coming from her own experiences, but one from the present. Why is Vivienne on the floor? *What has he done?* Looking around, Jinx finds that Vivienne hasn't been struck down, instead she finds that she is kneeling beside her, watching her and saying something. All Jinx can see is her lips moving, her ears ringing, draining out all noise except the piercing screech. Vivienne's Dad is standing beside them, Kyle in his grip while Doctors run down the corridor. What is going on, why is Vivienne's Dad here? Why is Vivienne on the floor? Why is Vivienne's Dad holding Kyle by the shoulders? Why are there Doctors everywhere? Questions push forwards in Jinx's mind and her head begins to spin, her heart racing in her chest.

"Jinx?" Vivienne's voice echoes through her mind as the world fades away, darkness taking over, drowning out the chaos until all she can see is black. Peaceful, welcoming black.

Chapter 23 – Vivienne

°•. ✿ .•°°•. ✿ .•°°•. ✿ .•°

Jinx is in the hospital. She is in the hospital. She collapsed. *That man* had caused her to collapse. She knew she shouldn't have left her, something seemed off when she'd told Vivienne to go, to get her Dad, but she'd left anyway. She'd left her alone, and that man had taken advantage. He'd pushed her up against the wall and he talked to her. Whatever he said, whatever he was doing, it had shaken Jinx, and it made Vivienne want to scream.

If Vivienne hadn't had run ahead of her Dad, if she hadn't sped up and not stopped to talk to the doctors, if she had tripped up once, slowed down for *anything*, she didn't think she would've gotten there in time, not before whatever was happening escalated.

Vivienne should've seen what was going on, she should've noticed what she had previously ignored, what she'd seen that was so obvious now she knew. But she hadn't. She hadn't noticed, she didn't see, and Jinx had ended up collapsing with that man pushing her against the wall, shaking with panic. He had made Jinx *shake*. She was stuttering, barely breathing, she couldn't speak, she couldn't seem to hear what Vivienne was saying. That man had brought out such fear in Jinx. Every idea she'd ever had about Jinx, everything she remembers, all the cocky, cool arrogance, how she seems so disconnected and careless, how she is always so quick and witty, all that was gone. When Vivienne had seen her in that corridor, with that man, she hadn't seen any of that. All she had seen was Jinx, a young, broken girl stuck in a situation she couldn't get out of, trapped by a man she couldn't fight. In fact, that was the scariest part of it all. Vivienne had seen Jinx defend herself against men twice his size, like the man at the stationary store months ago, but she couldn't get away from him. He had trapped her in more ways than one, and Vivienne hates what she thinks is the reason, what she *knows* is the reason, but has been to blind to see before.

She'd been too blind to notice when Jinx flinched away from male teachers in high school, when she'd taken detailed notes in the class no one else cared about, how she'd gotten defensive when the guys started mimicking instructions. Vivienne hadn't noticed any of it, she hadn't paid enough attention to notice.

"Mr Carter?" A nurse calls out from the desk. Vivienne's gaze shoots up from where it had been pinned on the floor and she glances at the nurse, who is scanning the room, waiting for someone to respond to the call. Her Dad isn't here, he had followed some of the Doctors that were dealing with the man, as he is the only conscious legal guardian remotely connected to Jinx. If her Mum had been awake, she imagined they would've gone to her, but Vivienne is glad she isn't. From what Jinx has let slip about her Mum, she doesn't seem very strong willed or responsible, and if that man really is her boyfriend, Vivienne doesn't think she will be much help defending Jinx.

Vivienne wants to follow her Dad, to see what they will do with him, but she doesn't. She doesn't know how long it will take, and she doesn't want to leave Jinx on her own when she wakes up.

She had *passed out;* she'd lost consciousness because of what that man had done. Vivienne hadn't taken in much of what happened before, but now she can't help but see it. She can see Jinx looking at her, fear and panic stricken across her face while Vivienne tries to talk to her. Then she sees Jinx collapse, sees her fall against the wall, her eyes falling closed and her face fading into an eerie, relaxed calm.

"Mr Carter?" The nurse repeats, now getting the attention of a few people around her. Vivienne stands from her seat quickly and makes her way to the desk, wringing her hands in front of her until they turn white.

"I'm n-not Mr Carter, I'm his daughter, Vivienne." She mutters, watching as the nurse looks behind her, then back to the computer.

"Do you know where your father is, dear?" She asks, offering her a weak smile as she looks at the screen, seemingly reading something. She's an older woman, with greying hair and deep wrinkles around her eyes. She looks nice, she smiles a lot, but Vivienne doesn't care to notice. She needs to see Jinx.

"N-no, he went to speak with some Doctors." Vivienne stutters over her words and looks at the door behind the nurse, no doubt the one visitors use. The woman sighs and clicks something on the computer, shaking her head.

"Do you know when he'll be back?" She asks, her full attention on Vivienne now.

"N-no. They d-didn't say anything." Panic begins to pull at Vivienne, why are they asking all these questions, what is going on? Can she see Jinx, is she okay? Why isn't the nurse telling her anything?

"Okay. Do you know this girl, a," She pauses again and starts to click through the computer.

"Jinx Keller. I'm here to see Jinx Keller." Vivienne says, putting one of her hands on the desk. "She was admitted an hour ago, she passed out, can I see her?" Vivienne stares at the woman, no doubt looking as panicked as she felt. She needs to see Jinx, she needs to make sure she is okay.

"Well, normally, no," The nurse mutters and Vivienne feels her heart drop into her stomach. "But we don't have any family listed here, apart from the mother, and she's…" she trails off and looks at Vivienne. "Can you prove that you know her? It's just a safety procedure, sweetie."

"I can, I can." Vivienne reassures her and pulls out her phone so frantically that she drops it on the floor. Quickly grabbing it, she opens her phone and shows the nurse her messages to Jinx, pointing at the number and name to try and clarify it. She then opens the photos Julian had sent her from the party, where her and Jinx can be seen very obviously talking to one another. She's never been so thankful of Damion's love for photography, and the fact that he sends Julian all his photos.

A long moment of silence passes before the nurse nods and points to the door beside the desk, "Go down that corridor, then turn left, she's in room 304."

"Thank you." Vivienne sighs, smiling at the nurse before practically running to the door.

Pushing through it, she nearly trips up on the lace of her shoes but doesn't bother stopping to tie them, she doesn't have time. She doesn't have time to stop and look out the windows, or dawdle and tie her laces, she needs to make sure Jinx is okay. She needs to.

The corridor is practically empty, the walls are a dull, sterile white, and the floors are polished beige tiles. Every door looks the same, a painted blue stripe across it and dull grey numbers printed onto them.

300
301
302
303

Vivienne turns sharply round the corner and stops at the first door she sees, *304*. It looks the same as all the others, and yet one number's difference makes it mean so much more. Behind that door is Jinx. Not the cocky, confident Jinx who doesn't need anyone and mocks Vivienne, but a different, fragile one. A Jinx she that needs someone more than ever. A Jinx who has kept quiet for so long, suffered through so much, and has still carried on. She forced herself through high school, pushed herself for the top grades, and got into a top college, all the while dealing with the weight she carries on her shoulders like a permanent burden. This Jinx needs someone more than Vivienne has thought she had, someone to talk to, to find comfort in, to feel *safe* with, and Vivienne will gladly be that person. She will always be that person, she will always be there, and Jinx can always count on her.

Her hand hovers over the handle for a long moment as she tries to think of what to say, what to do, there has to be something. There has to be something she can do, but what? She doesn't know. She doesn't know and it scares her. It scares her because not knowing how to help means that if she tries, she could make it worse, and if she makes it worse…

She can see Jinx standing on the ledge the last time they were at the hospital, how she seemed so distant, so far away. How she'd looked down at the fall below her and looked as if she wanted to draw nearer to it, so close that her toes were hanging off the ledge. She couldn't let Jinx get that close to the ledge again, she wouldn't. She would be the reason she stayed on the roof, the reason she enjoyed the view from a distance, the reason she kept her feet on the ground and not falling through the air.

Opening the door slightly, Vivienne breathes deeply and unclenches her fist that had unknowingly clenched by her side.

"Are you coming in, Carter, or are you going to stand outside until I have to come and get you myself?"

She's awake. She's talking. But something sounds different. When she speaks, no matter her words, her voice shakes. It's quieter, harsher, like she's been screaming.

Pushing the door fully open, Vivienne stands in the doorway, taking in every detail of the room, every detail of Jinx. Sitting up on the back of the hospital bed, she is still in her clothes from the party, but her boots have been cast aside, and one of the sleeves of her jacket has been rolled up, revealing a cast that covers the palm of her hand and wraps around her wrist. It isn't thick enough to assume that she's broken it, but it's still enough damage to require a cast. She's hurt, actually *hurt*. Vivienne is suddenly glad she hasn't gone with her Dad; she doesn't know what she would do to that man if she saw him now.

"Y-your arm…" She trails off and stares at the bandages.

"Yeah…. Second time in as many months," Jinx shrugs, but Vivienne doesn't notice. Instead, she is looking at her face, how all the colour has drained from it, and how her eyes are red around the rims, like she's been crying. She wants to scream, she wants to find that man and make him see what he's done, make him pay, she wants to make him feel the pain he inflicted on Jinx, she *hates* him.

"You look ready to kill someone, Carter."

She is. She is ready to kill him, she *wants* to kill him. How can Jinx be so calm? How is she not bursting with rage?

"Rage gets you nowhere, trust me, it never helps." Her voice shakes again, and Vivienne looks at her, at how she is sat a little straighter, her eyes a little darker.

Walking towards her, Vivienne takes off her coat and puts it on the chair beside Jinx's bed. This is all familiar. She's been in this position too many times before, but this time it's different.

This time she will be present, she will be there, she won't let her fears rule her. Jinx needs her, and nothing can stop that. Sitting on top of the coat, Vivienne doesn't speak, she doesn't know what to say, how to say it, but after a long silence, Vivienne puts her hands behind her neck and mutters,

"I want to kill him."

Jinx sighs beside her, "Killing him will do nothing, it won't reverse what happened, well, what nearly happened. Nothing will." She sounds so scattered, like she isn't really there, as if she is off somewhere else. Her words drift into one another, and she isn't looking anywhere in particular, instead her gaze just floats around the room, like she is following something Vivienne can't see.

"I know, but – I just – what he was doing –" Vivienne drops her head further into her hand. "Why didn't you tell me, why didn't you tell *anyone*." Her voice stutters and she feels her eyes well with tears. Why hadn't Jinx told her, why hadn't she told anyone she knows. She has suffered for so long, and she's done it on her own, completely on her own.

"I don't know." Jinx says, her voice breaking and cracking. Vivienne looks up and sees her fighting tears that are brimming in her eyes, looking at the door, then the wall, then the chair. "I don't know, Vivienne." She drops her head into her chest and brings her hand to her mouth. The tears steadily start to fall from her eyes, rolling down her cheeks and the bridge of her nose before dropping onto her trousers, stifled, shattered sobs escaping her.

Vivienne moves from the chair and sits on the side of the bed, carefully putting her arm around Jinx's shoulder. She doesn't know if she wants to be touched or not, but when Jinx tilts her head into the dip of Vivienne's shoulder, she knows she's made the right decision. Sometimes talking doesn't work, sometimes things are too painful to talk about, too hard to word.

"I don't know why I didn't tell anyone; I didn't think they'd listen-" She says, quiet sobs taking her voice until all she can do is cry silently, Vivienne's whole arm now wrapped around her shoulder, squeezing her arm and holding her against her chest.

Neither of them speak, Jinx can't, and Vivienne knows she doesn't need to. Right now, Jinx needs this, just this. Silent comfort. Words never do as much as they need to. There is nothing Vivienne can say that will make Jinx feel better, nothing she can do to erase her experiences from her mind, but she can do this. She can be here; she can make her feel safe in this moment. In this moment nothing else matters, nothing can distract her from this, nothing can stop her from making sure Jinx is okay, making sure she feels safe. Nothing.

*

Her Dad comes in a short while after. By then, Jinx has stopped crying, but her head is still bent into Vivienne's chest. Vivienne's legs are stretched to the length of the bed, or as far as they will allow, and Jinx's are bent up, so her knees hide her face. Vivienne doesn't think much of it, how close they are, how can she when all her thoughts lie elsewhere, when her entire mind is focused on what is happening.

When her Dad comes in, Vivienne sits up to talk to him, and Jinx follows her, wiping her eyes as she does so.

"What's going on?" Vivienne asks, bringing her knees to her chest and looking at her father expectantly.

"I don't know yet, not properly anyway, but they said you two can go back." He looks at Jinx, his expression solemn. "Your Mum is alright; she just needs to be kept the rest of the night so they can monitor her. She hit her head quite hard, so they want to make sure she's okay before sending her home."

Jinx nods and tries to smile at him, but it looks painful and worried.

"And don't worry about picking her up, they said they'll send someone home with her to make sure she gets there. And they're going to look into someone to help her, too. Someone who isn't you, you're too young for this."

This time Jinx's smile looks a little less forced, but it still isn't the same. At least she has the worry about her Mum lifted off her shoulders, but everything else still hangs in the air, causing an uncomfortable silence to settle around them.

"Kyle is being dealt with by hospital security, and they are going to speak to your Mum about it when she's in a better state. Aside from that, I don't know what else they are going to do, and unless you want to come forward and say something, I don't think much else can be done."

Jinx nods slowly, then looks at her hands. She seems so small, so little, like a child, and it makes Vivienne want to hug her again, to tell her she'll be okay, but she doesn't. She lets her speak,

"You said we could go, what about you?" She asks, looking at Vivienne's Dad, guilt painted over her face.

"They said I could as well, but I want to stay a little longer. I'm going to speak to your Mum myself, I want to tell her what happened, so she understands what's going on."

"No, you don't have to. You need to go. I'll stay with my Mum." She offers, her hands shaking in her lap.

"No. You need to go home, both of you. If you stay here, you're in more danger of running into him again. Go home, keep Ollie with you, and I will be back in the morning." He smiles at Jinx and softens his gaze, placing his hands on hers. "Trust me." He mutters, and Jinx looks at him again, not flinching away from his touch like Vivienne had expected. She nods slightly and her

Dad's gaze moves to Vivienne, "Take the car, drive safely, and I will come get it tomorrow." Vivienne wants to protest, to insist on keeping it here, but she doesn't. There are certain times she knows when to not question her Dad, certain faces he pulls, the way he says things, and this is one of them. Vivienne knows there is no point in fighting him on this, so she doesn't.

"C'mon, I'll walk you to the car." He says, and Vivienne stands up, Jinx following her.

Chapter 24 – Jinx

──· ₒ° ☆:*.☽.*:☆°.──

Vivienne's Dad waves them off as Jinx begins driving, her hands gripped tightly on the steering wheel and her eyes dead set on the road in front of them. That is all she needs to concentrate on, that is all it feels safe to concentrate on. The road. She is thankful Vivienne doesn't know how to drive, it gives her an excuse to focus on something other than what happened, what had nearly happened.

She's driven before, she's had to, she has been the designated driver since she turned 16 and legally could be. Of all the things her Mum has made her do, or that she has had to do because of her Mum, this is one of the things she hates less, purely because if her Mum drives herself home, she will cause accidents. Like she had tonight.

As it turns out, her Mum had gotten drunk to the point where she could barely stand at a bar earlier and had gotten into a fight with some other woman. The police don't know why, but they'd arrested her, brought her in, then called Jinx. Then, at some point whilst she was driving up, her Mum had been released, or gotten out, or something, and taken her car, which she then drove into a tree. Then the hospital called. Then the hospital called, and Jinx answered. Jinx answered and went to the hospital. The hospital where Kyle was waiting, patiently awaiting her Mum. But Jinx had gotten to him first.

He saw Jinx first, he grabbed Jinx first, and she couldn't fight him. She didn't fight him, she didn't scream for help or keep Vivienne with her, she'd let him take her. She'd let him take her, she did nothing while he pushed her up against the wall and taunted her. She couldn't, but thankfully Vivienne could. Thankfully Vivienne had read the signals, she'd seen something wrong, and she'd gotten her Dad. She'd ran and gotten Doctors, Security, people who could help her, and Jinx had never felt so grateful before. Vivienne had saved her, and for that, she is permanently indebted to her, and she knows it.

"Thank you." Jinx mutters, easing her pressure on the accelerator as she begins down a one-way road. This is what she needs to focus on, driving. Driving is simple, linear, it follows rules. Driving is predictable, or at least more so than her thoughts, and even when it isn't, the faults are predictable. Predictability is stability, it keeps order and prevents chaos. It's the reason Jinx reads the same books over and over again, why she sticks to the same shows and movies, and why she likes writing. When she is writing, she is in control, she controls predictability, life, choices, everything. Nothing happens in her book that she doesn't know about, and it feels nice. It feels nice to know she can control something, even if it means nothing.

"You don't have to thank me." Vivienne says, bringing one of her feet onto her seat and propping her head on her knee. "I did what I should've done a while ago, if anything I should be apologising." She says, looking out the window and sighing.

"Jesus, Carter, none of this is your fault, and if you start apologising, I will drive this car off the next bridge I see." Jinx says and relaxes a little when she hears Vivienne laugh. Laughing is good, laughing is safe. If they are laughing, it means not much has changed, not too much anyway.

"You know you can talk to me, right?" Vivienne says, looking at Jinx this time. Moving her hand to change gears, Jinx freezes when she feels Vivienne take her hand and squeeze it. When did all this suddenly become okay? When did this stop being weird? It made sense that Vivienne had hugged her when she broke down, but why is she doing this?

Despite all the confusion, Jinx doesn't pull away when she answers, "I do, now." She mutters, glancing at Vivienne before returning her eyes to the road.

"Good. I need you to know that. I know you won't talk to anyone, but I need you to talk to me. You have nothing to hide around me, and besides, if it's a secret thing, who am I going to tell?"

Jinx smiles and breathes a laugh, shaking her head, "You do realise you have friends now, right? You have at least five other people you can tell this too." A pit forms in Jinx's stomach when she realises what she's said, because she is right. Vivienne can tell anyone about this, she can tell everyone about this.

"I won't tell anyone, and even if I did, what do you think our friends would do, spread it around campus? We aren't in high school anymore, people don't enjoy watching others suffer, they don't spread pain with gossip. If anyone found out, they would be worried for you, just like I am." Vivienne says, sliding her fingers in between Jinx's and tightening her grip. "You have to promise me you'll talk to me if you need to, whether you want to or not, you have to, okay?"

"What are you going to do if I don't?" Jinx teases, trying not to think about what Vivienne has said, how she is worried.

"I'll never talk to you again." Vivienne threatens, pulling her hand away and crossing her arms in a mock pout, "And we both know how much you'd hate that."

Jinx laughs and shakes her head, "Fine, I promise to tell you anything and everything,"

"Good-"

"Including every possible thought I have on a daily basis, every tiny thing that happens to me, all the boring stuff I do every day that I wouldn't bother telling anyone else because it's really, truly boring." Jinx says, raising her eyebrows at Vivienne.

"And I would find it fascinating." Vivienne smirks back, leaning against the car door and raising one eyebrow. Jinx turns back to the road and tries to hide the red creeping up her neck by dipping her chin.

"Oh yeah, and why would that be?" She says, trying to smirk but smiling instead. This is nice, she isn't thinking anymore. Vivienne wanting to talk about this is natural, and Jinx knows she should, but right now, right now it is too much to talk about. Right now she doesn't want to think, she doesn't want to focus on everything, she wants to ignore it, even if it is only for the temporary drive home.

"Because it's you." Vivienne says, and Jinx doesn't miss the blush that crawls over her cheeks, making her freckles stand out on the bridge of her nose. Vivienne always blushes when she is trying to be cocky, and if she didn't know better, Jinx would say it is cute. Except it isn't cute, because it is Vivienne, and Jinx can't find Vivienne cute, she just can't.

They sit in silence for a while, before they both burst into laughter, Jinx dropping her head onto the steering wheel. This feels good, this distraction is nice, being around Vivienne is nice. Of all the people she could've chosen to be here with for what had happened, she would have chosen Vivienne, every single time. Because Vivienne somehow knows what to say, she somehow knows what to do, and she makes it better. She makes the situation bearable without even talking, just her being here is enough. She just sit's there and for a moment, everything is good, everything feels safe. She is perfect, and even if she'll never say it to her face, Jinx is unbelievably grateful that she's been offered the chance to be her friend, that she was thrown into that group and they'd accepted it, that Vivienne had put up with her teasing and cockiness and tolerated her. She is grateful Vivienne let her feel safe around her, safer than she's ever felt around anyone else before.

"Thank you, again, for everything." Jinx says, her cheeks red from laughing but her expression serious. Vivienne looks at her and her gaze softens, the light of a passing lamp bouncing off her eyes and illuminating her features.

"I will always be here. Always." Her voice is soft, and Jinx's entire focus is on her, the curve of her neck, the light slanted across her lips, the way her eyelashes flutter. There is a long moment of silence before Vivienne mutters, "You might want to pay attention to the road." And Jinx shoots backwards, sitting up against her seat and staring at the road in front of her, her gaze set.

She hears Vivienne snigger before she gasps, grabbing Jinx's attention again. When she looks to her, she sees Vivienne's eyes alight, holding Jinx's coat. What is so interesting about her coat, and why had she gasped like she'd seen a ghost?

"What's so interesting?" Jinx says, watching as Vivienne slowly pulls her hand out of one of the pockets, a small envelope in her hand. Jinx slows as she realises what it is, the cursive font on the front giving it away. Vivienne's birthday gift. The birthday gift she'd intended on giving her when she was leaving, so she didn't have to watch her open it, so she didn't have to see her reaction.

"What's this?" Vivienne teases, beaming at the envelope before her. "'For Vivienne.'" She reads, tilting it on its side. "You have beautiful handwriting." Vivienne says, looking at the front again. "It's nice and cursive."

Jinx smiles and turns her head to the window, hiding the red in her cheeks.

Vivienne carefully opens the envelope, stopping whenever an edge starts to tear, then tips the contents onto her lap. Jinx watches her expression when she sees two tickets separate onto her lap, and smiles when Vivienne gapes at them, her eyes wide. She smiles so widely her eyes squint as she picks up the tickets and examines them. "Jinx, are these-"

"Tickets for the *Romeo and Juliet* performance at the theatre, yes, they are." Jinx smiles at her as Vivienne stares at the ticket, her expression pure, delightful, shock.

"These are so expensive, Jinx I can't," Her expression fades as she looks at Jinx, but she just shrugs.

"Normally they would be, however when your boss's brother runs the company performing it, you tend to get some pretty nice deals, required you promise to stop using your phone during shifts." Jinx laughs, smiling at Vivienne again, "Relax, Carter, they probably cost the same as that signed book Lilly got you."

Vivienne sighs, but smiles once again, "Thank you so much, if you weren't driving, I'd hug you." She holds the tickets out in front of her one final time before slipping them into one of her coat pockets, the envelope still on her lap. "Oh y'know what…" Vivienne quickly lunges across the gap between them when Jinx slows and wraps her arms around her neck, pulling her closer. Jinx blushes furiously, hesitatingly putting a hand on Vivienne's back and holding it there, that is fine, right? Nothing major, just a hug, a normal, friendly hug.

"You have to come!" she says, and Jinx jumps at her sudden enthusiasm, she hadn't realised the tickets would make her this happy, but she is glad they did.

"While I appreciate the offer, sitting through that play is a perfect definition of torture for me." Jinx sighs, turning another corner and stopping slowly when the lights in front of her turn red.

"Come on, it'll be fun! I know you hate it, but I'd be there, and we both know how much you love being around me." Vivienne smirks at her before putting her hands together in front of her, "Please. Julian hates plays, Lilly doesn't have the patience to sit through one, and Dean will just sit there and read, I'm out of options." She pleads, smiling at her.

"Why don't you take Damion, or Kit?" Jinx says, tilting her head to the side to see what's causing the delay in traffic. The lights had turned green, but no one is moving. Vivienne sits back in her seat like a petulant child and crosses her arms.

"Are you really going to make me say it?" She asks, raising an eyebrow at Jinx, who just smirks.

"Say what?"

"I swear to god if this were anyone else, I would've given up by now," Vivienne sighs, shifting in her seat to look past the dashboard and onto the frozen traffic.

"Glad I'm worth your time." Jinx smiles, uncrossing her arms and letting her legs fall apart, knees hitting either side of her chair; this traffic isn't moving, and she is getting tired.

"You are stubborn sometimes," Vivienne murmurs, sitting up and looking at Jinx, "Jinx, I would *like* you to come to the play with me. I don't want to go with Damion or Kit, I'd like to go with *you*." She says, annoyance painted across her face. "Happy?"

"Very." Jinx says, uncrossing her arms and taking the wheel again, the traffic has started to move. "And yes, I will go with you."

Chapter 25 – Vivienne

"Vivi, get up! Get up!" Oliver jumps in the air and lands on the foot of Vivienne's bed, jumping up and down until she is forced to sit up, her eyes blurry from sleep. She runs a hand through her hair and takes out the light tie holding in the lazy plait she'd tied last night before bed, letting her hair fall over her left shoulder. Oliver jumps towards her and sits on top of her legs, beaming at her and holding the bed covers by the front. "Come on, get up!" He pulls her covers back and jumps off the bed, bouncing up and down on the spot.

"I've not missed this while I've been away," Vivienne sighs, rubbing her eyes and sitting up slowly, her vest-top rolling up around her hips. "What is so important, Ollie?" She asks, swinging her legs over the side of the bed and standing, her head spinning slightly. She shoves her feet into fluffy white slippers, which have little bunny ears on them, and holds herself up with her hands.

"Julian bought waffles!" Ollie exclaims, jumping a final frantic time before bolting back into the other room, laughing to himself.

Vivienne begins to reluctantly follow him, running her hand through her hair and brushing it over to one side so it's out of her face again, it really is a mess this morning.

She will never understand why Ollie always gets so excited about things, how waffles excited him to the point where he is jumping in the air, although from the smell, they do seem like pretty good waffles.

The light in the dorm room is much brighter than hers, and when she walks in, she squints against the light, holding her hand up to the window. What time is it for it to be this bright already, she can't have slept in that much, can she?

"Vi, you're up, finally." Julian murmurs, the crinkle of a paper bag following his words.

"Coffee." Vivienne groans, sitting down on the couch and dropping her head into her hands. Ollie squeals, sitting eagerly beside her and staring at the bag, "And some earplugs."

Julian laughs and shakes his head, emptying what is in the bags onto some plates, then handing one to Vivienne. "Eat, I'll get you some coffee."

Grabbing the plastic cutlery from in front of her, Vivienne cuts into the waffles and shoves an obscene amount into her mouth, hunger racking at her for no particular reason. Sitting down again and pulling his own plate towards him, Julian sighs as he places the proper cutlery on the table, casting annoyed glances to both Ollie and Vivienne, who's mouths are full of food.

"Did no one teach you manners as children?" he asks, taking his cutlery and cutting a small piece of his waffle.

"Nope." Ollie declares through a mouth of waffle. Vivienne laughs and shakes her head, swallowing the last of the food in her mouth and sipping the coffee Julian has made for her.

"He's right, we have no manners." She smiles at him and takes another lump of waffle. He laughs and does the same but doesn't take nearly as much. Before Vivienne has finished, someone knocks at the door and Julian bursts into laughter, clearly remembering something he'd forgotten. He stands up and makes his way to the door, smugness dripping from him as he does so. Confused, Vivienne looks at her brother, but he merely shrugs and looks at the door, his brow furrowed in a childish attempt at concern. Julian smirks as he opens the door to its full extent and reveals Jinx leaning against the door, both her hands gripped on the top of the door frame.

Vivienne chokes on her food and frantically swallows what is left in her mouth before sitting up properly, her cheeks turning a frantic red.

Jinx smirks and looks at Vivienne, then her little brother, who are both still in their pyjamas at whatever time it is on a Thursday. "You do realise it's," Jinx makes a show of checking her watch, then raises her eyebrows at Vivienne, "10:00 in the morning. Don't you have classes?" She walks in and Julian closes the door, laughing to himself quietly, no doubt about how much of a fool Vivienne has just made herself in front of Jinx.

"Why are you here?" Vivienne asks, drinking her coffee and slouching back in her chair again, watching as Jinx sits across from her, propping one of her feet up on the couch. Jinx doesn't seem fazed by what she'd said, in fact, she doesn't seem different at all. Their conversation last night plays through her head, her expression when Vivienne had mentioned the others, is she really that scared of them knowing? Vivienne wonders why, but she doesn't ask, if Jinx wants to act fine in front of their friends, then so will Vivienne.

"I need some of Julian's notes for the debate, I've lost some of mine in the sea of notebooks in my room and I really can't be bothered to tear apart my room to find them." Jinx smirks at Julian as he disappears into his room and comes out again with a notebook. "Thanks, I will give them back to you at some point."

"Anytime, but if you lose these ones, we're both screwed." Julian sits next to Vivienne and reaches across the table, taking his waffles and pouring syrup on them. Vivienne sits up and reaches for the syrup, but he pulls it away and smiles at her, pouring more on his. Sighing, Vivienne sits back again and cuts another piece from her waffle, reaching across and dipping it in Julians growing pool of syrup.

"Hey!" he shouts, standing up and moving next to Jinx, where she is sitting, just smiling at them. Vivienne's brother laughs at Julian, then looks at Jinx,

"Do you not want any waffles?" he asks, shovelling more into his mouth and smiling at her. Jinx shakes her head, looking at the food.

"No, I only came here for the notes, and I doubt there's enough for me anyway." Vivienne doesn't miss the way she looks at the food in front of her, or how she keeps smiling at Ollie when he eats so carelessly.

"C'mon, there is enough." Vivienne says, standing and getting another plate for Jinx.

"No, Carter, it's fine, really." Jinx protests, standing up to follow her. Vivienne grabs the plate, but Jinx stops her midway, "Really, I'm fine." She assures Vivienne, but she doesn't listen, as pushes past her. When they sit down again, Vivienne pushes one of her waffles onto the empty plate and passes it to Jinx, who reluctantly accepts it. For a while she just sits there with the waffle on her lap, but after some time, she begins to pick at it, and after half an hour, the entire thing is gone.

Julian clears away the plates, then checks his watch. He's already been to two classes today, meanwhile Vivienne hasn't gone to any. This is one of the annoying days where all of his classes are in the early and mid morning, while hers are rammed into the afternoon, so they don't see each other for a while. His next class is in half an hour, so he grabs his textbooks and study notebooks ready for it. He is calm as he does so, despite the fact that his first two classes appear to have drained him, but when he gets his coat, he freezes for a second. When he does, Jinx and Vivienne sit there, both equally confused, until he pulls something out of Vivienne's coat pocket, something that must've been hanging out.

The tickets.

"What are these?" he asks, holding them in the air and examining them triumphantly, like he's found some hidden trophy. "Who got you these?" He looks at Vivienne, who is staring at the floor with intensity, then to Jinx, who seems completely unbothered.

"Just a gift, put them back Julian." Vivienne says, walking up to him and reaching for the tickets. She tries to grab them, but Julian merely lifts them out of her reach and waves them aloft.

"Yes, but this isn't any old gift, this is a fancy, romantic gift. It's literally tickets to *Romeo and Juliet*. Whoever got you these was clearly looking for an excuse to ask you out." Julian raises his eyebrows at Jinx, who merely shrugs,

"Don't look at me, I hate that play with a passion, you wouldn't catch me dead watching it."

Unconvinced, Julian looks back to Vivienne, "Who got you these, because it wasn't me or Lilly."

"I have other friends," Vivienne lies, biting her lip as she does so.

"Liar, mainly because I know you don't, but also because you're biting your lip." Julian laughs as he brings the tickets closer and looks down his glasses at them. "Come on, tell me." He waves them in front of Vivienne's face, and she tries to grab them again, missing terribly. "If you don't, you don't get the tickets back."

Vivienne sighs and shakes her head, trying to think of a way of telling him without lying. He knows when she lies, and she will face an enormous amount of teasing if he knows who she is really going with, not to mention the fact that Jinx is *right there*.

"A girl in one of my classes got them for me." she says, grabbing them from his hand and sitting down again, crossing her arms over her chest as she does so. Jinx smirks, crossing her legs on the chair, her boots now cast across the floor. Ollie giggles beside her, the arms of his jumper pulled over his hands, and jumps off the couch, running at Vivienne.

"You have a date!" He says, beaming at her, excitement riddled in his voice. He'd clearly forgotten about her and Jinx whilst swept up in the moment, and Vivienne isn't about to remind him.

"It isn't a date." She assures him, then looks over his shoulder and at Julian. "It *isn't* a date."

Julian raises his eyebrows, then looks at Jinx, smirking to her. She laughs and he turns to leave, laughing to himself as he does so.

When the door shuts behind him, Jinx bursts into laughter and bends over in her seat. Vivienne blushes and looks at the floor, focusing on a spot on the floor instead of looking at her. Ollie squeals and runs into her room, but Vivienne doesn't bother to follow him, she doesn't think to. She just sits on the couch, leaning back slowly and uncrossing her arms. Jinx smirks at her, but Vivienne doesn't miss the slight pink in her cheeks, the heat crawling up her neck.

Vivienne laughs and shakes her head, slowly standing up and making towards her room. She has to change; her class is in an hour and she wants to get a coffee before she gets there. Julian would have a field day if he knew, after all, she's already had one this morning. Normally, she wouldn't be having this coffee, especially considering she had an amazing night's sleep when she got back last night, however she has one of her most boring lectures today, for two straight hours, and she needs all the energy she can get to stop her falling asleep in that class.

When she walks into her room, she finds her brother spinning on her chair, his legs crossed and his hands gripping the edge of the seat. Sighing, she stops it with her foot and takes off her shirt, revealing the bed bra she wears every night. Her brother jumps off the seat and runs out of the room, not making a sound, and Vivienne shrugs to herself. Whatever was in those waffles has given him a sugar rush, something she does not need this morning, and she doubts Jinx does either. Despite getting back late last night, or early in the morning anyway, Vivienne has somehow slept more than usual, Jinx however, well Vivienne is sure she hasn't slept nearly enough, considering the fact that she is already up.

Vivienne gets fully changed, at the exception of her shirt, which she can't find anywhere. It's the only one that goes with her pants, and all her others are in the laundry basket anyway, so she is running out of options.

"Hey, Carter, I think your Dad's-" Vivienne turns to Jinx, who has moved into the doorway, completely forgetting how she is dressed. She only notices when Jinx's neck goes bright red, and she is suddenly very interested in the floor. Vivienne grabs the closest thing to her, which happens to be the cardigan she wears far too often, and quickly wraps it around herself before sitting on the bed.

"Jinx, what are you-" she starts, but Jinx cuts her off.

"Your Dad's here." Jinx says, coughing awkwardly and not looking away from the floor. Vivienne almost laughs at her reaction and has to withhold the laughter as she stands up and walks past Jinx, peering out of the room through the crack in the door.

"Correction, my Dad *was* here, he's not anymore." Vivienne laughs, closing the door again. "And my brother isn't either."

"Wait what?" Jinx says, looking up from the floor and beginning towards the door. She opens it, looks out, then walks out of the room, coming back moments later, visibly confused. "Why did he just leave?" She asks, looking out the door again, then the window. Vivienne laughs, Jinx is cute when she's clueless, maybe because it's so rare, she doesn't know exactly why, but it just is. Jinx looks at her, her brow furrowed, "What is it? What's the joke?"

Vivienne's phone vibrates on her desk and Vivienne picks it up, clicking on the message from her Dad. This time there is nothing stopping her from bursting into laughter.

"Carter?" Jinx says, taking her phone and reading the message. Vivienne doesn't stop her, she wants her to see the message. She doesn't know how she hasn't made the connection yet, she is normally so quick, but apparently not in situations like this. Her eyes scan the screen, and Vivienne watches as her eyebrows shoot to the top of her forehead, a smirk growing across her face. Vivienne laughs again, bending over.

"Had you forgotten?" She says through bursts of laughter. How can she forget, she is the one who orchestrated it. She is the reason her Dad thinks they are dating, which means she is the reason he had assumed something and stayed well away from her room.

"Yeah, I had." Jinx says, looking at the phone a little longer before bursting into laughter as well, sitting on the bed and dropping her elbows onto her knees. Vivienne stops laughing first, catching her breath frantically, but Jinx doesn't stop, and Vivienne realises this is the first time she's seen her fully laugh, on her own. She isn't a loud laugher, it is more of a quiet chuckle, something Vivienne hadn't expected, but likes nonetheless. While Jinx laughs, Vivienne finds herself just watching her, enjoying watching her be at complete peace where she is, being completely comfortable right here, with her.

When she finally stops, she looks up at Vivienne, who quickly changes her focus and grabs her phone. Thankfully, at some point in their hysterics, her phone had gone off and she had multiple notifications from the group chat. Opening her phone, she sees Jinx do the same in the corner of her eye but tries not to pay too much attention to it as she clicks on the Instagram logo.

Julian: 10:44am
Has anyone got plans on Saturday?

Lilly: 10:45am
No, why?

Vivienne does not like where this is going, but it is already too late, her fate is sealed as she reads the rest of the messages.

Julian: 10:45am
Vivienne has a date at that fancy theatre on Sunday. I want to ambush her and force her to go shopping for a dress but I'm not convincing enough to do it on my own.

Dean: 10:46am
You do realise she's on this chain, right?

Julian: 10:47am
Yes, I know, but she's terrible at answering her texts so I reckon we have at least another two minutes before she finds out, and by then I'm hoping to have you all on my side.

Lilly: 10:47am
HOLD IT. VI HAS A DATE???

Lilly: 10:48am
How am I only just hearing about this??

Julian: 10:48am
Relax, I only found out this morning. Now, who's in on my plan?

Damion: 10:49am
I'm in, sounds fun :)

Kit: 10:50am
Same.

Julian: 10:50am
Dean, Lils?

Dean: 10:51am
Sure, I need some new books anyway.

Julian: 10:51am
Lilly?

Lilly: 10:52am
OF COURSE I AM!!

Julian: 10:52am
Good, now she has no choice

Jinx laughs beside her and Vivienne sighs, "I swear to god, Julian is going to pay for this." Jinx stands up and throws something at her from the bed. Catching it, Vivienne looks at her shirt in her hand. It must've been on her bed, and she'd just missed it.

"Maybe he can pay for the dress instead," Jinx smirks, walking towards the door. "Now hurry up, I want a coffee before my next class, and I don't want to go on my own."

Vivienne smirks at her as she leaves, but once she is out of sight it grows into a wide smile. If she wasn't in such a good mood, she would be annoyed at Julian for pulling a stunt like that, but she doesn't care. All she can think about now is getting a coffee with Jinx, whatever is next can wait, because she likes where she is now.

*

"I swear to god, if you pick up another pink dress, I am going to make you sit outside." Julian says, his face red and lips pursed. Lilly smirks at him and turns to Vivienne, holding it up to her. The dress isn't any different to the others she's seen, it's ankle length, with straps and a slit down the leg, the only thing that has changed is the colour. Shaking her head, Vivienne watches as Lilly puts the dress back on the rack and turns to Julian, who is now standing with his arms crossed over his chest. They've been here for at least an hour, picking out dresses and shoes, all of which Vivienne doesn't like. Lilly has a habit of finding pink dresses for her to try on, but she keeps saying no. Pink isn't her colour, it flushes her out and doesn't go with her hair, but Lilly keeps insisting she try them, which infuriates Julian to the point where Damion has to stop him from snatching the dresses from Lilly.

"I don't know why it annoys you so much," Dean smiles from his seat on the plush chair beside them, "But it is hilarious to watch."

Julian sighs and sits beside him, dropping his head into his hands, "It's the fact that she has been purposely rotating the same three dresses for an hour, and won't stop despite Vivienne saying no."

"But why does that annoy you?" Kit asks, coming out from behind a rack and leaning against it. Vivienne still doesn't know much about them, but she likes that they are here. Jinx mentioned how they don't have many friends at high school, and Vivienne relates to that far too much, so whenever she goes out with the group, she makes sure they are included.

"I don't know, it just does, and she knows it." Julian says, glancing at Lilly, who is routing through another rack, smirking to herself. She knows what she is doing, and despite it annoying Julian, Vivienne finds it pretty funny.

"How about this one?" Damion shouts from behind three racks of dresses. Vivienne peers above them, but can't find him anywhere, and gestures to Julian.

"Can you see him anywhere?" She asks as Julian stands beside her, hands on his hips. They'd lost both Damion and Kit multiple times before, whether it's because they wandered off or just got lost, and it takes them a while to find them each time.

"Wave please." Julian says, leaning over one of the racks and peering over it. Damion's hand shoots up from behind one of the far racks and they begin towards him. After the last time they lost him, they created a system where they had to wave whenever they couldn't find him each other, something that worked, but is a tad humiliating if there are people around. When they reach Damion, he is holding a dress behind his back, beaming at them. Dean moves to look at it, but Damion steps away, keeping it hidden.

"What are you doing?" he asks, trying to look again.

"Let Vivienne try it on, *then* make your judgements." Damion says, smiling at her. "It looks stupid when it's hung up, but trust me."

Vivienne smiles back at him and nods, following Damion to the dressing room and smirking at the others. When they reach the curtain, he hands her the dress, and she tries to force her smile. It really does look stupid when it is hung up, it looks more like pieces of tulle tied together than something she can wear. Noticing her expression, Damion laughs, "Trust me, I know it looks horrendous, but it really does look nice. My sister loves stuff like this and they always look this bad on the hanger."

"Okay." Vivienne smiles at him and walks into the box, closing the curtain behind her. Today has turned out better than she thought, and although she will never admit it to Julian, she is loving it. She's never been out with all her friends before, she's never had enough to, and now they are all here. None of them have made up excuses to leave, or done anything stupid, or made fun of her, it really is amazing, and she is glad Julian had organised it.

Sliding her arms into the sleeves of the dress, which aren't long and hang off the sides of her shoulder, she reaches behind her to do up the ties that tie it all together. As it turns out, Damion isn't wrong about this dress, it looks better on, in fact, it looks amazing.

Turning to look in the small mirror beside her, Vivienne finds herself smiling at her own reflection, something she hasn't done for a while, as she twirls around, the dresses hem flowing around her ankles. The sage green skirt and bodice are embroidered with careful white flowers, their stems reaching out slowly, and a corset top pulls lightly against her chest when the ties are done up fully. Delicate strings matching the material of the skirt tied together the top of the bodice, creating a small bow that hangs at her chest, and next to her clothes on the floor is a small ribbon, matching the dress, that she uses to tie half of her hair up, completing the look. This is perfect, she loves it, everything feels perfect, even the corset, which is something she doesn't usually wear. All she needs now is the others' opinions, well that, and some shoes.

Sticking her head around the curtain, she blushes when she sees only Jinx sitting on the chair in front of it, sipping a coffee. She smirks at her and tilts her head, "Have you picked something out?" She asks, looking at the curtain, then out into the store.

"Where is everyone, Damion was just here." Vivienne says, not coming out from behind the curtain, she doesn't want to show Jinx yet, that's why she'd asked her to go get coffee for everyone.

"Damion went to find the others, so he's probably a good ten minutes in the wrong direction by now." She laughs and takes another sip of her coffee, "Are you coming out or do you intend to hide behind there forever."

Vivienne blushes and shifts further behind the curtain, "I don't want you to see it, why do you think I sent you to go get me a coffee?" Speaking of, where is her coffee? That was the point of Jinx's little outing, and yet she's only holding one. "Where *is* my coffee?"

Jinx shifts in her seat and reaches to the table beside her, taking a large cardboard cup from behind it. Standing to give it to her, she stops a few feet from the curtain, still holding both drinks.

"Please don't," Vivienne starts, but Jinx is already smirking and waving the coffee slightly in front of her. Resisting a smile, Vivienne sighs and reaches for it, careful not to move the curtain.

"Ah, no sleeves, interesting." Jinx smirks, taking a sip of her coffee. Damn it, she'd fallen for Jinx's trick, like Jinx knew she would.

"Come on," she sighs, reaching again. Jinx takes a step backwards and shakes her head, smiling.

"Show me the dress." She insists, leaning against the wall opposite Vivienne and dragging her eyes over the curtain. Vivienne doesn't want to ruin the impression her dress has tomorrow, but then again, why would Jinx care either way. They are just going to watch a play, that's all, and Jinx won't care if she sees the dress now or then anyway. Plus, she really needs someone's opinion and the others don't seem like they re going to be back any time soon, the store is massive, confusing, and Julian had looked ready to fight Lilly when she'd left.

"Fine. But don't make fun, and you *have* to give me the coffee." Vivienne sighs, and Jinx sits down again triumphantly, but also a little shocked. Vivienne doesn't think Jinx thought she'd give in that easily, but she wants to buy this dress soon, they have plans to go to the food court after and she is getting hungry.

"Deal." Jinx smirks, and Vivienne pulls the curtain back, a blush creeping up her neck and clouding her cheeks.

The dress twirls around her ankles again as she turns to give her a full view, but when Jinx says nothing, a panic spreads through her. Maybe it really does look bad, and Jinx is trying to figure out a way to tell her that it does. Maybe her hair looks a mess, and she's tied it up wrong, or she hasn't put it on properly and it is all bunched up at the back. Facing Jinx again, Vivienne shrugs and looks at her, but her expression isn't of disgust or discomfort, she looks shocked more than anything.

"Is it really that bad?" Vivienne winces as she says it and looks in the mirror again, smoothing invisible creases with her hands. Maybe the flowers are too much, or the material is wrong. Maybe it looks too old, or isn't modern enough, maybe she just needs to pick another dress.

"No, it isn't..." Jinx mutters, looking at the dress, her eyes drifting up and down slowly. "It's beautiful." Beautiful. She thinks it's beautiful. Jinx thinks the dress is beautiful. That can't be right, she must've misheard her, she can't have said that. Jinx never says anything like that.

"What?" Vivienne says, the blush furiously spreading across her face.

"You're beautiful." She mutters, staring at the dress, then Vivienne herself. *What.* She didn't say that, she doesn't mean that, how can she? Jinx has said she is beautiful, she never says anything like that to *anyone,* never mind her of all people.

"What..." Vivienne repeats herself, looking at Jinx, who is merely sitting on the chair, taking in the girl before her. This can't be right, she can't have said that, surely, she's misspoke. "Did you..." Her voice drifts off as she takes another step towards her, her head spinning. Jinx shifts in her seat, now looking at the floor, at Vivienne's shoes. "Jinx, I-" Vivienne starts, but is cut off when Jinx stands up, taking a step towards her.

Vivienne's heart stops in her chest and her breath catches in her throat. She can't think, she can't breathe, all she can see is Jinx. Her hair, her lips, her eyes. She isn't looking at the floor anymore, now she is looking straight at Vivienne. Something tightens in her chest as she takes another step closer, the blush that has furiously taken over her face fading slightly. This isn't happening, this can't be happening, Jinx can't be doing this, getting this close. Surely Vivienne is misreading this, there must be another reason she is doing this, there is definitely another reason she is getting this close-

Jinx's hand wraps around Vivienne's waist and she pulls her closer, closing the distance between them. Without thinking, Vivienne puts her hand on Jinx's cheek and brushes the side of her face with her thumb.

"Jinx-" Vivienne begins again, but her words freeze in her throat as Jinx bends towards her, kissing her. Vivienne's hand moves down Jinx's cheek, sliding down her face and resting on the nape of her neck. She pulls her closer and Vivienne feels Jinx's other hand move to meet the other, resting on her hip. The room falls away as Vivienne runs her hand through Jinx's hair, knocking the clip she uses to hold it up onto the floor.

This can't be happening; she is kissing Jinx. Jinx, who teases her at every opportunity, who hates romance with a burning passion, who shot down every signal Vivienne thought she'd misconstrued. Except she isn't kissing that Jinx, not anymore. Now, now, it's the Jinx who'd waited with Vivienne at the hospital, who'd found her brother and stopped him from running away, who'd helped Vivienne when she'd been hit with a football, now she is kissing the Jinx who, without any prompting, without knowing how it would benefit her, had caught Vivienne on the stairs. Who, ever since the start of the year, had been picking Vivienne up, even in the smallest ways. This Jinx is different, she has changed, or maybe she hasn't. Maybe she hasn't changed at all, and it's just that Vivienne is seeing her differently, looking past what she put up as disguises and walls, and seeing what she truly is, and what she is, is beautiful.

Jinx smiles against her lips, and slowly, carefully, pulls away, blushing and smiling broader than Vivienne has ever seen before. She doesn't speak, and neither does Jinx, they just stand there for a while, Vivienne's hands still on Jinx's neck, and Jinx's hands still on Vivienne's hips. It's like they've both forgotten how to speak, how to act around each other, but that doesn't seem to matter. They don't feel uncomfortable, they are happy here, standing here with each other and no one else. After all, they aren't lonely, they never were. They had always been alone, but they were alone together.

Vivienne smiles and starts to laugh, dropping her head into her chest, and she's not surprised when she hears Jinx do the same, her chest rising and settling slowly.

"Well," Vivienne smiles, looking up at her again.

"Well indeed, Carter." Jinx smirks, dropping her head low again and quirking it forwards, taunting her. Vivienne smiles and brushes some of the hair out of her face, tucking it behind her ear.

"Beautiful," Jinx murmurs, and she kisses her again, knocking her off her feet.

Chapter 26 – Jinx

── · ｡˚☆:*.☽.*:☆˚. ──

"What do you want?" Lilly's questions pass through Jinx's mind, but she doesn't pay enough attention to notice, her thoughts are somewhere else entirely. The temptation to trace the spot on her lips where Vivienne had kissed her is far too prevalent, but she forces herself to ignore it, and instead thinks about the moment itself. Vivienne's hand on her neck, her hands running through her hair and pushing out her clip, the feel of her fingers tracing her cheekbones. It had all felt so real before, but now, now Jinx finds herself having to herself assure that it happened. Telling herself that it is real, that Vivienne actually kissed her, and liked it. She hadn't pulled away or pushed her back, she'd pulled her closer, she'd pushed towards her, so much so that Jinx's neck ached, a fact that made her laugh to herself.

"What's so funny?" Lilly asks, raising an eyebrow to her and crossing her arms.

"Nothing." Jinx denies, panicking and turning her attention to the board in front of her. There are all kinds of foods lit up in fancy writing, each sounding miles different to the other, so she just gestures to the cheapest one, which Lilly's orders for her without hesitation. She really is impatient sometimes; Jinx hasn't really noticed that before. Maybe she'd only noticing now because everyone seems impatient compared to Vivienne, who is one of the most patient people she knows.

"Come on, tell me." Lilly pesters her, sitting at a table, a small slip of paper with their order on it in hand.

"It's nothing." Jinx repeats, craning her neck to search the rest of the food court for the others. "Where did everyone go? It's not a very big food court." She asks, bringing one of her feet onto her chair and resting her chin on her knee. Lilly starts to explain where they went, but Jinx isn't listening again. She is back in the changing rooms, Vivienne's hands wrapped around the nape of her neck, her lips soft on her own. If she could've, she would've stayed there forever, with Vivienne and her at peace, but Damion had started calling for them, and they'd panicked. Jinx had grabbed her clip from the floor and by the time she'd turned back around, Vivienne had disappeared back into the cubicle, where she'd changed out of the dress and declared to Damion, who found Jinx standing holding her own coffee, that she was going to buy it. While he tried to insist on seeing it, she wouldn't let him and practically ran out of the room before he could ask her again, her eyes trained on the floor. Damion followed her and for a short time, it was just Jinx again, stood in the room on her own, still with both coffees.

"What do you think then?" Lilly says, nudging Jinx with her foot and grabbing her attention again.

"What?" Jinx says, still looking around the room, scanning the crowds for any sight of Julian. She knows she should be looking for Vivienne, but that is rather pointless, as she is too small to be able to pick out, however Julian, he towers over most people, making him much more spottable.

"I was saying, what do you think about going to the bookstore after this?" Lilly sighs, shaking her head.

"Uh, yeah, sure…" Jinx murmurs, checking her phone this time.

"Jeez, what is up with you? You're hardly listening to me, and I know you rarely do that anyway, but you normally respond with more than just 'yeah' and 'sure'."

This time Jinx moves to look at her, trying her best to focus on the conversation going on, and not on her thoughts of Vivienne's hands running down the back of her neck. "Sorry," she says, sighing at Lilly, who is looking at her with a quizzical expression.

"What are you thinking about?" She asks, beginning to tie her hair up, then changing her mind and dropping it back down, around her chest. She's dyed it again recently, not to anything different, she's just had the roots of her coral touched up, meaning the top looks a little more vibrant than the rest. Sometimes Jinx wonders why she chose pink, of all the colours she could've picked from, she chose a vibrant, noticeable pink, but then again, she is Lilly, subtle isn't exactly her thing.

"Nothing, okay." Jinx sighs, eyeing the ordering counter and desperately wishing for their order to be called to distract Lilly.

"That's the third time you've said nothing, which means it's definitely something." Lilly smirks, tilting her head to the side. "Don't tell me you're seeing someone too." She sighs as if she envies her, but they both know that is far from true. Lilly loves romance, she loves reading about it, watching it in films, and she'd told Jinx before that she wishes she could experience it, but she's also said that she has come to terms with the fact that she won't, and that it doesn't bother her that much.

Unfortunately, Jinx doesn't entirely believe her, and wishes she could be happy, but she knows it isn't her place to say that. No matter how many prolonged stares she catches at happy couples, how many frustrated sighs she hears when people in her books are being picky, Jinx knows she isn't the one who needs to talk to her. Thankfully, Lilly does know people she can talk to. She has this little group chat online full of people like her, and

Jinx knows it makes her feel better, makes her feel more welcome towards herself, and she's glad.

"It's not that…" Jinx trails off again, then sits up when she spots Julian in the crowds of people, cardboard boxes of food in his hands. She waves him down and he makes his way towards them, Damion and Vivienne in tow, each holding cups and boxes. How much food have they gotten? Do they realise there are only seven of them, because it looks like they've bought enough for twenty.

"How much have they bought?" Lilly says, standing and making her way towards them. She takes some boxes out of Julians hands and places them on the table before sitting down again, leaving the seat next to Jinx empty this time. Julian drops his stuff on the table and sits next to Lilly, running his hand through his hair before smiling as Damion sits next to him. They seem so happy, it's sweet, although she'll never admit it, of course. Vivienne stands awkwardly for a second, trying to put stuff on the table without dropping it, and Jinx moves to help her, taking some of it and smirking. She sighs as she hands it over, but Jinx can see the smile that tugs at her lips, and the blush that runs up her neck when their hands brush under the box. Thankfully, Jinx doesn't do the same, she is slightly better at hiding her feelings compared to Vivienne, and sits down calmly, still smirking.

Sitting next to her, Vivienne sits in her chair, her back unusually straighter than normal. Laughing, Jinx slouches and worsens her posture instead, taking one of the drinks they bought. No sooner has she taken a sip when someone from the nearby counter calls her and Lilly's food. She begins to stand, and Lilly does too, but Julian stops her.

"Stay here, it's easier if me and Damion go." That's true, she's been cornered into her seat by the others, and getting out would mean having to manoeuvre through multiple oddly placed wooden chairs, but she still feels like she needs to go.

"Are you sure, I don't mind." She says, resting her hand on the table and standing up a little more.

"No, really, it's fine." Julian smiles, watching as Damion stands with him. They follow Lilly up to the counter and join the queue of people waiting to collect their food, leaving just Jinx and Vivienne alone at the table. Sitting again slowly, Jinx brings her foot onto her chair again, resting her chin on it. Vivienne laughs beside her, but quickly quietens herself.

"What?" Jinx asks, smirking at her and eyeing the others, who don't seem to have moved at all.

"Nothing," Vivienne smiles, looking at Jinx, her cheeks red.

"No, go on, what is it?" She asks again, leaning forwards and tilting her head at Vivienne.

"It's just the way you sit," Vivienne laughs, shaking her head, "It's just…" she smiles and looks at the table, seemingly heavily interested in the stain in the wood.

"It's just?" Jinx teases, leaning closer and taking her foot off her chair. Vivienne looks at her again and laughs quietly, her eyes wandering to the group. Following her gaze, Jinx finds that they are standing behind a couple of people from the counter, but nothing seems to be moving. Surely when they call out your order it means they are ready for you, but apparently not.

"It's just funny, that's all," Vivienne mutters, playing with the ends of her hair and twisting it around her finger. "And cute." She smirks as Jinx blushes and sits back again, leaning against the barrier behind her.

"Funny and cute? Such high compliments, Carter." She smirks, crossing her arms. She knows Vivienne has said that to tease her, and she wants to tease her back, but she doesn't know how.

"Well don't get too excited, it's annoying too." Vivienne smiles at her and raises one eyebrow. It's so cute when she tries to tease her, especially when it's supposed to look mean.

"You think this is annoying?" Jinx says, smirking at her. "What about this?" She picks her feet up off the floor and stretches them out, so her legs rest on Vivienne's, "Is this better?" she teases, moving her feet side to side and relaxing into her seat.

"No." She tries to sound annoyed, but Jinx can see the smiles growing on her face and the light in her eyes. She tries to push her feet off her lap but fails as Jinx merely puts them back on her.

"You don't like it?" She asks, smiling, "I'm finding it quite comfortable." She smirks as Vivienne sighs.

"Yes, well you're not the one with big, chunky boots on your lap." Vivienne says, looking over to the group again. Jinx looks too and finds that they are now the first in the cue and are collecting their food. Without thinking, Jinx pulls her feet back and sits how she had before, barely composing herself before they round the table. Vivienne isn't as quick.

"Jinx what have you been doing; Vivienne looks all flustered." Lilly sighs, shaking her head, "Honestly, I thought you were friends." She sits across from Jinx, placing the food they'd ordered amongst the rest. Why do they have so much food? The table is nearly full, and Dean and Kit aren't even back yet, there is no way they are going to be able to finish all of this.

"Just because we're friends doesn't mean I don't get to tease her. I do it to you all the time." She lies back against the barrier, balancing one foot on top of her legs and smirking at Lilly.

"Yes, but when you do it to me, I don't really care. Vivienne, on the other hand, gets all awkward and flustered." Lilly sighs, smiling at Vivienne, who is laughing and shaking her head.

"That's why I do it." Jinx says, sitting up at the sight of Dean and Kit, who's food will complete the little feast they've acquired.

"Why do we have so much food?" Kit asks, shifting into the seat across from Dean. They survey the large amounts of boxes covering the table and sigh, "There is no way we can eat all of this."

"That's what I've been saying," Jinx agrees, pulling one of the boxes closer to her. Dean sits next to Vivienne, grabbing one of the drinks from the centre of the table as he does so. They haven't assigned food or drinks; they've all just chipped in on different stuff and it's an organised free for all. They have food from all over the court, sushi and noodles from the sushi bar in the corner, burgers from the 90's style dinner in the centre, all kinds of food from all kinds of nationalities. Jinx picks out some of the sushi and reaches across the table for the chopsticks that have been cast down to the end. She's always loved sushi, it has been her favourite food since she was a kid, and when she taught herself how to use chopsticks, it was all she ate for a good while. They all reach across to different points in the table and take the food they want, and the table is mildly chaotic for a bit until they've all taken what they want and brought it closer to them.

Jinx doesn't talk whilst she eats, and neither do Dean or Vivienne, and they leave the conversations to Kit, Damion, Lilly, and Julian. They have quite literally put the talkative people on one side of the table, and everyone else on the other. The irony of it makes Jinx laugh to herself, and Vivienne glances at her as if there is something wrong. When Jinx doesn't do anything,

Vivienne returns to her food, joining in the conversation little by little.

"Have any of you watched *Gilmore Girls*?" She asks, looking around expectantly at the group. When no one answers her, and some start to shake their heads, Vivienne sighs. "Come on, out of seven people I can't be the only one who's watched it."

When they all start shaking their heads again, Lilly jumps in, "If it helps, I've heard of it."

Vivienne laughs and shakes her head, "I was going to make a reference to it, but it won't make any sense if none of you have watched it." She sighs again and returns to her food, letting the conversation drift on without her. Jinx glances at her, then back to the group, she can't believe no one has watched it, out of all of them, and it makes her feel a little bad. Before she could forget, while no one is paying particular attention to her, she pulls out her phone and types in the name,

Gilmore Girls.

Surely if Vivienne likes it, it can't be that bad.

Chapter 27 – Vivienne

°•. ✿ .•°°•. ✿ .•°°•. ✿ .•°

This doesn't look right, nothing looks right, why doesn't any of it look right? The dress she'd loved a day ago now looks wrong, it falls too low at the shoulders and the hem sways differently, why? Why does it all look so stupid now, why does her hair feel different, and her shoes suddenly feel too high, this doesn't make any sense.

Pushing out an invisible wrinkle in the fabric, Vivienne sighs as she looks in the mirror, surveying herself again, taking in the too-tight corset and the badly tied bow, she looks so stupid. How could she have let Damion talk her into getting this dress, she wants to look nice, but she doesn't feel like she does, not anymore, now she just feels… she doesn't know what she feels, but it isn't pretty.

"Will you stop doing that, you look amazing." Lilly sighs, lying on Vivienne's bed, her back propped up on the pillows. She came over a while ago and said she wanted to help Vivienne get ready, but they both knew she was lying, she just wants to press her for more details. "I'm sure whoever it is will find you beautiful." She stands up and walks behind Vivienne, standing next to her and glaring up. "But I'm not really a fan of the heels, I'm now the shortest of us."

"Aww, poor kid." Vivienne mocks, petting her on the head like a child, something she can do with her new heels on. They don't add too much to her height, but considering Lilly is barely the same height as her, it means she now towers over her. "I imagine this is how Julian and Jinx feel." She mutters, looking back in the mirror and flattening the dress again, fully aware that there are no creases in it.

"Will you stop that," Lilly says, smacking her hands away from the dress and shaking her head. "You loved this dress yesterday, what's changed?"

Vivienne doesn't want to admit why things have changed, she doesn't think 'well the girl I'm supposed to be going out with tonight kissed me yesterday and I'm now overly aware of how I look and act around her' will go down well, especially considering it won't take long for her to connect the dots on who it is. There are many things Vivienne isn't sure of involving this whole situation with Jinx, but what she definitely knows is that they aren't telling anyone, they'd agreed on that during a hurried conversation yesterday, before they left the mall.

"Is she messing with the dress again?" Julian asks, walking into the dorm and sitting on the end of the bed, "How many times do we have to tell you that it looks amazing, and I'm sure this girl will love it too." He sighs, shaking his head and laughing to himself, "Although it would help us draw more conclusions if you would tell us who it is."

Vivienne blushes and suddenly becomes very interested in her own reflection again, playing with her hair and checking if the ribbon looks okay. Lilly curled her already wavy hair with curlers earlier, and now it's nicely settled in beautiful rings, some of which are tied back with the bow. Julian laughs and pulls out his phone, scrolling through it for a short while before placing it in his pocket.

"C'mon, Vi, I need to know, it's romantic and you know how much I love romance." Lilly begs, standing in front of her, her hands on her hips.

"No." Vivienne states, turning away from Lilly and routing through her desk for her lip gloss. She doesn't have much makeup, she doesn't like wearing it, and the rare things she does have sit unused in the back of her drawers, meaning they are harder to find when she actually needs them. "If you want to hear about romance so badly, why don't you talk to Julian, he actually has a boyfriend."

"Yes, but his relationship is old news now, it's boring." She sighs and is promptly met with a pillow to the face by Julian. She glares at him, but he doesn't seem to care, and checks his phone again.

"Vi, what time are you supposed to be meeting this mystery girl." He asks, his eyes wandering to the window. She doesn't know what he thinks he's going to see out there, Jinx isn't stupid enough to wait out in the open, she knows how nosey their friends are.

"Nine, why?" Vivienne looks for her phone under her jumpers and other clothes, and when she finds it, she panics. The screen is already lit up with multiple notifications, and above all that is the time, 9:17pm. Shit.

"I've got to go." She mumbles, grabbing her phone and swiping up on it as she walks out the room. She has three different messages from Jinx, all of which seem more worried than annoyed, and a sudden guilt grows in her. How long has Jinx been waiting for her, she didn't realise she'd left it this late.

"Yes, we gathered." Julian says, following her out of the room as she runs to grab her coat. Pulling it over her arms and frantically tying it together at her waist, she hits the call icon at the top and brings the phone to her ear. Lilly and Julian raise their eyebrows at her and Lilly attempts to peer past her hair, at the name glowing on the screen, but thankfully, she can't see.

The phone begins to ring out as Vivienne pulls open her dorm door and practically runs out into the corridor, tripping on her heels as she does so and ramming elbow into the wall.

Cursing, she forgets all about the phone held to her ear until she hears Jinx's voice coming through it.

"Carter, are you okay?" she asks, and Vivienne sighs, laughing quietly as she begins down the corridor and towards the stairs.

"Yes, yes, I'm fine, I just hit my elbow on the wall." She says, still adjusting her coat as she begins down the stairs. She's so preoccupied by her coat, that she doesn't pay too much attention to when the stairs start and finish, so when she finally reaches them, the first drop catches her off guard and she trips, dropping her phone. Helpless, she watches as it bounces down most of the stairs and lands, cracked, on the carpet of the next level. Cursing again, she makes her way down the stairs, careful to hold onto the handrail as she does so, god knows what would happen if she didn't.

Halfway down the stairs, Vivienne hears someone else coming in the opposite direction, the soft click of their shoes on the stairs drawing her attention away from the phone. She is partially unsurprised to see Jinx rounding the corner of the stairs, a stupid smirk on her face as she bends down to pick up the phone, which doesn't look in too bad of a state despite its journey down the stairs.

"Do I want to know?" Jinx asks, smiling at Vivienne and coming up the stairs to stand next to her, where she has stopped and is simply looking at Jinx. Her black pants are paired with a matching blazer that hangs off her shoulders instead of being actually on, and underneath is a long-sleeved cuffed shirt that is unbuttoned at the top, revealing a small necklace that hangs around her neck. The shoes she'd heard clicking on the stairs are slim, black boots that shine in the light, and the slight heel on them makes Jinx even taller.

"Like what you see?" she teases, leaning against the wall and placing both hands either side of her on the handrail. Silver rings decorate her fingers, matching the style of her necklace, and Vivienne notices how she's put a clear coat on her nails, something she's sure she's never done before.

"I- Well, it's-" Vivienne stutters, her eyes darting away and looking at her shoes. She's making such an idiot of herself, why is she being so awkward? This doesn't make any sense, it isn't as if she is meeting someone new, it's Jinx, just Jinx.

A door shuts at the top of the stairs and Vivienne becomes suddenly aware of where they are, Julian or Lilly could come down these stairs at any moment and catch them, what is Jinx doing here? "Wait, why are you here?" she asks, then becomes quickly aware of the vagueness of her question.

"We're going to the play, remember?" Jinx teases, but Vivienne isn't finding it funny, not openly, anyway.

"I mean what are you doing *here.*" She says, grabbing her by the wrist and pulling her down the stairs, tripping multiple times as she does so. "I thought we were meeting off campus, so no one would see us?" She asks, suddenly tightening her grip on Jinx's wrist as she trips again. Maybe heels weren't the best idea, she can barely get down the stairs in them.

"As much as I'd like to answer your question," Jinx says, wincing as Vivienne loses her balance again, "At least let me hold your hand, because you're about to break my wrist, *again.*" She winces again and Vivienne quickly drops her hand, letting it fall to her side. Thankfully, she'd grabbed the wrist that is free of a cast, if she hadn't, she doubts Jinx would be being as polite.

"Sorry," she mumbles, staring at the floor intently and watching every step. Jinx steps closer to her and intertwines her hands in Vivienne's, sighing and shaking her head. Her hands are warm, and when her fingers wrapped around Vivienne's, she feels her chest tighten, her hands were always so cold, this is a nice change.

"I didn't say to stop, I just asked to hold my hand instead of my wrist." She smiles, and a furious blush spreads across Vivienne's face. Damn it, Jinx always makes her blush, and whenever she does, Vivienne feels a little bit stupider around her. She knows she shouldn't, that isn't why Jinx does it, not anymore anyway, but she still does.

"Jinx Keller, are you being nice to me?" She asks, raising one eyebrow at her as she takes the last steps onto the corridor floor. She tries to smirk but ends up just smiling entirely. How is Jinx so good at it, how do her smirks not grow into smiles like Vivienne's do? It's hardly fair.

"So what if I am?" Jinx smirks, red creeping up her neck, but getting no further. Vivienne's smile softens as Jinx carries on walking, pulling Vivienne with her by their linked hands, "C'mon, we're going to be late." She says, dropping her hand to her side again and pushing open the door, gesturing for Vivienne to walk through. Her hands feel cold again, now that the warmth of Jinx's have been torn away, but she doesn't mention it, how can she? As much as she's enjoying this, which is more than she'd thought she would, she has to admit it's a little confusing. How are they suddenly so comfortable around each other, how is Jinx suddenly this relaxed. Surely they should be stuck in some awkward stage where they have no idea what they are doing, but they aren't. Maybe it's because they've known each other for so long, hate or not, they've still been in each other's lives the longest, since they were fourteen.

"Such manners," Vivienne mocks, walking through and watching as Jinx follows her, her hands now hanging in her pockets.

"I am a true gentleman." Jinx returns, sticking her arm out in an old fashioned way. "M'lady," she teases, and Vivienne laughs, knocking her arm down and watching as it slides back into her pocket.

"Ready for 'your definition of hell'" she smiles, beginning down the path and towards the campus exit onto the street.

"Only if you're coming with me." Jinx smirks, striding alongside her and laughing.

*

The theatre isn't too crowded when they arrive, and the few people who are there are bargaining with the people in the ticket booths to try and get cheap tickets to various different shows, so Vivienne and Jinx cut through and make their way towards the large double doors that lead to the theatre. The girl on the door smiles at them and Vivienne routes through her bag, pulling out the tickets and handing them to her.

"You're pretty early." She says, handing the tickets back to Vivienne, then shifting her gaze to Jinx. Her eyes linger a little longer on Jinx, who is obliviously looking around the theatre, unaware of the eyes travelling up and down her. Without thinking, Vivienne slips her arm around Jinx's waist, and smiles at the girl again.

"We're pretty punctual." She says, her voice unusually snide. She doesn't know what she's doing, but the girl looks a little taken aback, and Vivienne's smile grows. Jinx, who had been clearly paying no attention, looks a little taken aback at Vivienne, but smirks at her anyway, her arm wrapping around Vivienne's waist too. The girl quickly composes herself and opens the door for them. "Have a nice evening." This time there is a clear bite in her voice, that both Jinx and Vivienne seem to notice, and the minute the door shuts behind them, Jinx bursts into laughter. She shakes her head and brings her free hand to her chest, her breath shortening, and Vivienne is extremely confused.

"What's so funny?" she asks, releasing her hand from around Jinx's waist and crossing her arms over her chest. Jinx doesn't answer for a while, before straightening up and walking towards Vivienne.

"Nothing, it's just that you didn't strike me as the jealous type, Carter." She smirks, wrapping one of her arms around Vivienne's waist again and pulling her closer. Vivienne's voice catches in her throat and her chest tightens, her own heartbeat loud in her ears.

"I-I'm not." Vivienne mutters, increasingly aware of the small space between them. "It's just that she was..." she trails off as Jinx steps closer, closing the gap between them.

"You're cute when you're jealous." She mutters, dropping her head down again and bringing it closer.

"Oh really?" Vivienne mutters, smiling as their lips brush one another's. No matter how close they get, Vivienne still finds that she has to reassure herself this is real. It doesn't seem very real, none of it does, nothing about this seems possible. They've gone from hating each other, to being awkward friends, to this? The jump between the three has been so sudden, this one especially, and Vivienne thought she'd need time to adjust, but she doesn't. For some reason, this all feels right, it all feels easy.

"Yeah..." Jinx mutters, kissing her slowly and sliding one of her hands to the nape of Vivienne's neck, dipping her head. Vivienne steps closer, but no matter how close she gets, it still doesn't feel close enough.

When they finally pull apart, both her and Jinx are blushing, and Vivienne knows she's smiling like an idiot. "Maybe I should be jealous more often then." She mumbles, leaning towards her again. Their lips graze lightly, but the door behind them opens and they pull apart quickly. Vivienne doesn't bother to look at who has come through, and quickly begins down the corridor, Jinx following just behind her, laughing to herself.

They find their seats, and while Jinx checks something on her phone, Vivienne takes in every detail of the beautiful room they are sitting in. This is by far one of the fanciest theatres she's ever been in. The deep crimson ceiling is rimmed with gold edgings that spread out into all types of swirling patterns, and above the large red curtain in front of them are intricate pieces of artwork, painted on in the same gold as the trimmings, a ship with sails busting out in front of it and spindly flags that are blowing in the wind, bordered by birds flying around it. From the dome ceiling above them hangs a large chandelier-like light, that reflects the golden glow of the theatre, and below them, the seats look so small from the height they are at. The railing is mere inches from them, blending in with the whole room. She can't believe she's here, sitting on the balcony of a theatre, something she never thought she would do, not while she was in college anyway.

"Have I told you how much this means to me?" Vivienne says, not taking her eyes off the ceiling.

"Yes, you have." Jinx smirks, following her gaze. "It really is beautiful, isn't it."

"It really is," Vivienne mutters, completely taken in by the sheer beauty of the place surrounding her. She is finding this so hard to believe, and yet it all feels so real, everything, including Jinx's hand sliding into hers, the warmth once again sweeping over her. Her attention shifts from the theatre and back to Jinx, who is merely looking at her, her expression soft and happy.

"What?" Vivienne asks, looking at her. Jinx shakes her head and smiles, making Vivienne even more confused.

"Nothing." She mutters, still smiling brightly, "You just look so mesmerised by this place."

"It's truly beautiful, do you not think so?" Vivienne asks, maybe she is overreacting. Maybe she shouldn't be so openly interested in the room, maybe she looks weird. Her doubt must clearly show on her face, because Jinx's smile drops, and she squeezes Vivienne's hand.

"I didn't mean that like it was a bad thing, shit, sorry." She looks suddenly worried, and Vivienne smiles at her, looking back around the room. They are pretty early, despite Jinx saying they were going to be late, there aren't many people in their area of the theatre. In fact, there is practically no one there.

"Didn't you say we were going to be late?" Vivienne asks, raising one eyebrow at Jinx and smirking.

"Well, in my defence, the last time I read the tickets was a week ago, I could've easily mixed up the times in that short period." She does have a point, Vivienne really should've checked the times before she left, just to make sure they weren't going to be late.

"Fair enough," Vivienne mutters, looking at her phone. "Oh for the love of god." She says, showing Jinx all the messages from Julian and Lilly, asking her who she is with, how is it going, have they kissed yet, and all the other annoying things they could think of asking.

"I have an idea," Jinx says, holding out her hand for the phone. Vivienne reluctantly gives it to her, careful of what she was going to do.

"What are you doing?" She asks, watching as Jinx holds up the phone like she is going to take a picture.

"Pose for the camera," Jinx teases, and Vivienne does as she's told, smiling and tilting her head to the side. Jinx smiles and brings the phone so Vivienne can see what she's doing, and

Vivienne smirks. Jinx had loaded the picture up into the message box of her messages to Lilly, and is clearly waiting for Vivienne to click send, which she does, still very confused.

"What was the point of that?" she asks, watching as the message goes unread for a little while.

"They keep asking who you're going out with, so I showed them." Jinx says, sitting back in her seat and reaching for her own phone.

"What do you mean?" Vivienne asks, checking her phone again.

"Well who are they going to think took that photo?"

"Yes, but it doesn't show them who-"

"But it will confuse them long enough to leave you alone," Jinx laughs, putting her phone in her pocket and sitting back into her chair, her legs naturally falling to either side, one of her knees knocking Vivienne's. She had long since disregarded her blazer, and the sleeves of her shirt pull at her arms, tightening around her chest. The unbuttoned top means the collar falls lazily to the sides; however, it is still refined, crisp around the edges despite the careless manner at which it's been cast aside. Vivienne tries to refrain from staring, concentrating on the slowly filling theatre around them, but still finds her gaze wandering back. She's done something with her hair, it sways more, but it's also gotten shorter, moving up at the sides and flicking at the ends.

"When did you cut your hair?" Vivienne asks, sitting up and craning her neck so she could see the front of Jinx's face. It looks different from there too, she's shortened her bangs, and they too flicked out, backwards, into her hair.

"Yesterday." Jinx says, running her hand through it and shaking her head. Is she offended? Maybe Vivienne should've noticed sooner, when she first saw her, although her mind had been on other things then, not falling down the stairs being one of them.

"It looks nice," Vivienne smiles, shifting further off her seat to get a better look from the front. "It suits you." She says, noticing a stray strand of hair that had fallen loose and found its way across her face. She must know it's there, Jinx doesn't miss much, and it's very obvious, but Vivienne points it out anyway. "Wait, I'll do it." She mutters, when Jinx brushes it to the side, only for it to fall forwards again.

Sitting back in her chair again, Vivienne tilts Jinx's head so it's facing her. She doesn't enjoy sitting on the edge of her chair, it puts too much weight on her heels, and she doesn't trust them at the moment. Jinx follows her movement and stays still while Vivienne moves the strand from her face, tucking it behind her ear and making sure it stays there. The feel of her hair between her fingers is new, she isn't sure if she's ever felt anyone's hair before, but now she is. Now she has strands of Jinx's hair tucked in between her fingers, the smooth softness of it making it hard for her to keep her grip.

"I think it's sorted, Carter." Jinx smirks, and Vivienne pulls her hand away quickly, how long had she held it there? Was it obvious what she was thinking? Jinx laughs at Vivienne's furious blushing, and she sits further into her seat, shaking her head. "You blush so easily," she mutters, squeezing her hand and running her thumb over Vivienne's wrist.

"I don't." Vivienne states, the feeling of Jinx fingers making her heart race once again.

"Yes, you do." Jinx turns to face her and quickly pulls her hand away, not loosening her grip. Vivienne is pulled forward by their interlinked hands and finds herself leaning against the armrest of her seat, her body hanging over onto Jinx's chair. Jinx quirks her head again so they're inches from each other, and despite her best efforts, Vivienne finds herself blushing, again. "See." Jinx mutters, not moving away, the smirk on her face slowly growing.

"I'm only blushing because you're making me." Vivienne says, pulling away and crossing her arms over her chest, letting go of Jinx's hand. She mocks a pout and watches as Jinx sighs, not moving her hand from Vivienne's armrest, her palm facing upwards. Vivienne pout lasts a great few seconds before she finds herself sliding her hand into Jinx's again, intertwining their fingers.

"Why is it so hard to stay mad at you all of a sudden?" Vivienne sighs as Jinx's thumb starts running up and down her wrist again, its warmth contrasting with Vivienne's icy skin. "I managed it for years, years I held a grudge against you and hated you, and now I can't stay mad for more than a few seconds." She shakes her head slowly and tuts to herself.

"Maybe it's because you've finally realised you have no real reason to hate me?" Jinx suggests, tilting her head to the side and raising her eyebrows. Vivienne used to hate it when she did that, but now she loves it. She used to find it annoying and cocky, but now it's cute, flirty almost.

"No, that's not it." Vivienne says, the smile spreading across her face making her attempt at sarcasm look worse.

"Really?" Jinx laughs, bringing her free hand to her chin, like detectives in old films. All she needs is a silly hat and a cigar and she'd be ready to audition for Sherlock Holmes. "What could it be then…" she trails off and looks around the room, seemingly pondering some important issue.

"You look like Sherlock Holmes." Vivienne laughs, watching Jinx as she pulls a stern expression.

"Well, that would make you Doctor Watson," She says, lifting her chin and squinting. "What be your theory, Watson?" She says, somehow managing to keep a straight face.

"Hmmm, it is a very difficult question." Vivienne joins in, pointing her chin into the air and playing with an imaginary beard. They look at each other for a long while, holding their serious faces, before Jinx bursts into laughter, bending over in her chair, one hand going to her stomach. Vivienne follows suit, but uses her hand to cover up her mouth, muffling her laughter slightly. Their laughter lasts a long while, the both of them unable to hold it together, and it only subsides when the lights around them darken, and the rest of the theatre slowly goes silent.

As the curtain slowly begins to lift, revealing a stage set with the props to imitate a town, Vivienne relaxes into her chair, her attention solely on the unfolding play in front of her.

The reality hits her one final time before the dialogue starts, she is sitting in a theatre, an actual theatre, watching her favourite play unfold right before her eyes. She is watching *Romeo and Juliet,* and she isn't watching it on her own. is was sitting, in a theatre, with the girl she's spent the last four years of her life hating. She is sitting in a theatre with Jinx, and she is watching *Romeo and Juliet,* a play they've taken such extreme sides on before. But that isn't true anymore, whether Jinx hates the play or not, she's here. She's sacrificed hours of her life to watch a play she hates with Vivienne, and she isn't complaining, she is putting her own interests aside and is making sure Vivienne isn't alone. She bought the tickets, she'd agreed to come, and she hasn't once complained, in fact she seems to be having fun, it's all so perfect. Julian was right, this had been a romantic gesture, and it's a beautiful one.

It feels just like the classics, in every single way.

Two Months Later

Epilogue - Jinx

── · ｡° ☆ : *.🌙 .* :☆° . ──

"I can't believe you're actually doing this." Vivienne smiles, sitting on the couch, her legs crossed underneath her.

"Well, it makes you happy," Jinx sits next to her, wrapping the cardigan she grabbed from the table around her tightly. Vivienne rolls her eyes at her and watches as she sits back, sticking her legs out and shifting to the side.

"When did it swap from me stealing your clothes to you stealing mine?" she mutters, typing her password into her laptop and clicking open *Netflix*.

"Since you started wearing oversized cardigans." Jinx smiles and Vivienne shifts to lie beside her, grabbing the blanket she'd gotten from Julian as she does so. He'd given that to Vivienne on her birthday, nearly two months ago, and even that feels like ages ago. She can't believe they've been doing this for nearly two months, that she spent Christmas at Vivienne's, that she spends more time at Vivienne's dorm than she does her own, that they are just them. *Them*. If someone had told her this at any point in the four years they spent together in high school, she wouldn't've believed them, in fact, she probably would've thought it was some sick joke.

"Yes, but-" Vivienne begins, placing her head in the dip of Jinx's neck and wrapping her arm around her waist.

"Tell you what, you give me my jumper back and I'll stop wearing your cardigans?" Jinx interrupts, smiling and watching

375

as Vivienne sighs, looking at the jumper lying on the floor beside them, covered in cold water.

"Fine, you can wear the cardigans." She says begrudgingly, but Jinx can feel her smiling against the soft material of the cardigan.

"Now, what are you forcing me to watch?" Jinx carries on, watching as the company names start to fill the screen, like at the start of every movie. "Because I like you, but I don't think I like you enough to watch *another* insufferable romcom."

Vivienne shakes her head, her hair falling over her face slightly and covering one of her eyes. She pushes it back, but it falls to the front again, and Jinx brushes it back this time, the hand that had been hidden around Vivienne's waist now holding the piece in place in her hair.

"It's not necessarily a romcom…" She murmurs, slipping her leg around Jinx's under the blanket. Jinx knows she's lying, whenever she picks a film it's a romcom, but she doesn't fight it. Instead, she lies back further, making herself comfortable on the couch, and watches as a fancy suburban house appears on the screen and *10 Things I Hate About You* is written on the screen in scrawly writing.

*

Jinx startles awake to the door of Vivienne's dorm slamming shut, and as she sits up, she realises Vivienne is still asleep on her chest, her hair falling around her face.

"Is your sole purpose in life to make me feel as single as humanly possible?" Dean says, sitting on the table across from them and taking off his shoes without thinking twice. "Because doing this," he gestures to the asleep Vivienne, "is definitely helping."

Jinx laughs and sits up, shaking Vivienne awake as she does so. Dean laughs and shakes his head, watching Vivienne rub her hand over her face, then ball her hands up into fists and rub her eyes. Jinx has noticed she wakes up in a very movie-like way, and she always looks flustered but cute when she does. Her cheeks are flushed, her hair always a little bit messy, and her eyes are still partially closed for a while afterwards.

"Hey," she says, her voice quiet and high pitched, eyes still slightly closed.

"Hey," Jinx repeats, kissing her on the cheek before looking back to Dean. "Remind me why you're here?"

He puts his feet up on the couch, next to Jinx's legs, and crosses his arms, eyebrows raised. "I'm your friend, do I need an excuse to be here?"

"Normally, no, but when I'm asleep, yes." Jinx runs a hand through her hair and tries to sort her bangs out, which have gone completely askew whilst she was asleep.

"Fine, my excuse is I'm bored, Julian is out with Damion, and Lilly has done her little disappearing thing-"

"No I haven't." Lilly's voice cuts Dean off and Jinx resists a sigh. More people, great. "I was getting a coffee." She says, holding said coffee in the air and waving it in front of Dean.

She sits next to him on the table, also taking her shoes off and placing them next to Deans. Lilly has gotten into an odd habit of just completely disappearing lately, and while no one can figure out why, everyone has taken guesses. Damion thinks she is studying, which everyone has safely assured him isn't it, Julian thinks she's just walking around campus, getting inspiration for her art and Vivienne agreed. Personally, Jinx doesn't have a clue where she keeps going, but she doesn't feel like asking either. If anyone knows the importance of secrets, it's her, and she knows being interrogated for them sucks.

"Yeah, sure you were..." Dean says, turning to face her and taking his feet off the side of the couch. Whilst he is talking, Vivienne takes the blanket off her and Jinx, folding it and putting it on the arm of the couch. Jinx takes the laptop and closes it, putting it on the table next to Lilly, and after a quick readjustment, Vivienne is sitting with her legs sprawled across Jinx's lap, listening intently to Dean's conversation. Jinx puts her hand on Vivienne's ankle and sits up a bit more, her hair still not entirely fixed.

"What do you mean 'sure you were', I have a coffee in my hand!" Lilly says, thrusting the cup towards Dean again. He clearly isn't happy with this and raises one eyebrow at her.

"How come it takes you an hour to get a coffee then? Because you left Julian an hour ago, I asked, and no one has seen you since."

"I was, well, I-" Lilly starts and stops, then after deciding she can't explain, pulls out her phone. She swipes up and down for a while, then, after a short silence, holds the phone screen to her chest. "Promise you won't overreact, or get really excited, or, just, anything like that? It's not a massive thing, it's just one piece."

"Lilly, you want *us* to not overreact?" Jinx laughs, shaking her head, "You do realise that's *your* distinguishable trait, right?"

Lilly smiles slightly, then holds out her phone, displaying an Instagram post from an art exhibition. It's covered in water colour and pride flags for all kinds of identities and sexualities, but right in the middle is Lilly's full name in block capitals. Above it, in slightly smaller writing, it says "Featuring a piece by..." and Jinx's smile broadens. Vivienne jumps towards Lilly, taking the phone and looking at it again. She smiles and squeals slightly, climbing over Jinx entirely and hugging Lilly tighter than she has ever seen.

"This is amazing!" she says, pulling away and smiling broadly at her, "How are you not ecstatic about this?"

Lilly shrugs, but Jinx can see the smile pulling at her lips.

"Come on, Lilly, this is huge." Jinx says, and Vivienne sits back down, but this time she perches on the arm next to Jinx, her feet in her lap once again. She has the little fluffy socks she always wears when she's watching a movie, they are pink with little bunnies on them. "This is an *actual exhibition*."

"Yeah," Lilly sighs, looking at her phone again, "I guess it is." What she is saying sounds good, but her tone sounds miserable, and she is looking at the phone with despair written across her face.

"Lilly, what's up?" Dean asks, shifting closer to her and putting his hand on her shoulder.

"What if people don't like it?" Her voice is barely a whisper, and she is looking at the floor. Dean goes to answer, but Jinx cuts him off, leaning forwards so Lilly can see her.

"Are you insane? What could possibly make you think that? Lilly, you are one of the most talented artists I know. I don't pretend to know much about art, I hardly pretend to like it, but what you draw, what you paint, I *love* it. It is true beauty, and I can guarantee this piece is too, and if people can't see that and don't like it, they are absolute idiots. If a critic writes about it in a negative way, or someone makes a comment, just remind yourself how many art pieces *they* have at an exhibition, how many pieces *they* have had chosen." Lilly is looking at her now, but she isn't finished, "Trust me, if you've put half the heart you put into your normal pieces into this, then it will be absolutely beautiful, and I know it."

"Really?" Lilly mutters, a small smile growing across her face.

"Lilly, I don't think I've ever heard her talk about *anything* like that before," Vivienne says, putting a hand on Jinx's shoulder and squeezing it.

"I mean when she came back from that theatre date you guys went on-"

"Dean," Jinx cuts him off, "We're talking about *Lilly.*"

He laughs and watches as a blush creeps up Jinx's neck when she sits back.

"What were you saying about me?" Vivienne smiles, looking down at her from her perch on the couch.

"I want to know this too, actually," Lilly smirks, watching Jinx cross her arms across her chest and stare at the window.

"Something very similar to that, just not about art…" she mutters, not looking at any of them. Lilly laughs, any fear having left her mind, and Jinx blushes furiously, not looking at Vivienne.

"Seriously?" Vivienne says, sliding off her perch on the arm and landing in Jinx's lap, a smile plastered across her face.

"Well, I knew Dean wouldn't tell anyone, and I just-" She starts, very quietly, but Dean cuts her off.

"Rapidly expressed how much she loved it at a speed barely audible and with an excitement I have never seen her show."

"Anyway," Jinx says, louder than she needs to, "Lilly is in an Art Show, someone tell Julian and Damion!" and with that she stands up and tries to leave, but Vivienne grabs her wrist when she reaches the door.

"Did you really say all that?" She mutters, and the other two submerse themselves in conversation.

"Maybe," Jinx mutters, watching as Vivienne steps closer, her face lighting up. Vivienne stands on her tiptoes and kisses her, her hand sliding around Jinx's neck, and Jinx wraps her arm around her waist. After a short while, Jinx pulls away slowly, but Vivienne drops her forehead against Jinx's.

"Don't go." She mutters, looking Jinx in the eyes and smiling.

"I have to," Jinx mutters, kissing her again before pulling away completely, "I have that meeting with the publisher." She whispers, making sure the others don't hear. Vivienne smiles and grasps her hands.

"Good luck." She whispers, watching the others cautiously. Jinx hasn't told any of them that she is meeting with a publisher, or that said publisher has read her manuscript and wants to discuss publishing options. She's told Vivienne, of course she's told Vivienne, but apart from that, it's their little secret. Something that's theirs, and only theirs.

Printed in Great Britain
by Amazon